*Smyrna, Asia Minor, 1865*
Reluctantly, the fortune teller turned a
so close, Dimitra involuntarily recoiled
    'My dear woman,' she said gravely, ... ... ..... woman,
may Allah preserve you from the evil eye. Death surrounds you like a shroud.
You must kill a sacrificial lamb with black eyes and spill its blood around
the house. Beware of trickery. Beware of the child with the flaming red
hair; she has been kissed by the devil. Heed my words at your peril, for this
child will bring about unhappiness for your family far beyond your wildest
imagination.'

*Athens, Greece 1941*
As Greece faces the brutality of the Nazi Occupation, Sophia Laskaris recalls
the prophecy told to her by her beloved grandmother years earlier. Faced
with the terrifying realization that the girl with the flaming hair could be
a member of her own family, Sophia's life spirals out of control with devastating
consequences.
    'Kismet,' Dimitra had said. 'We cannot escape our destiny.'

# KATHRYN GAUCI

*For Charles*

This edition published in 2017 by Ebony Publishing
ISBN: 978-0-6481235-1-4

This narrative has been prepared for an international readership
so American spellings have been used throughout.

"And thus their crime has yielded them no fruits.
Revenge is barren. Of itself it makes
The dreadful food it feeds on; its delight
Is murder – its satiety despair."
*William Tell (1804) by Friedrich Schiller*

# CONTENTS

# HISTORICAL NOTE

As the storm clouds of nationalism gather over Europe, on March 25, 1821 the Greek War of Independence breaks out in the Peloponnese and Danubian provinces of the Ottoman Empire. The Orthodox Christians declare war on the Ottoman Turks. A month later, the islands of Spetsai, Hydra, and Psara declare independence. The island of Chios, lying just six miles off the Turkish mainland, hesitates.

The jewel in the crown of the empire, Chios is the richest island in the Mediterranean, enjoying unparalleled freedoms that have allowed its merchants and ship owners to prosper for hundreds of years. Throughout autumn and winter, a stalemate exists, until a Samian revolutionary, Logothetis, lands troops on the island. Watching the events unfold from the saray in Constantinople, the Grand Seignior Sultan Mahmud II is outraged. The tyrant's anger knows no bounds and he seeks vengeance.

In April 1822, the Sublime Porte issues a jihad against the infidel Christians. The Sultan dispatches the Ottoman Armada under Admiral Kapitan-Pasha Kara Ali, along with four thousand troops. Another seven thousand set sail from Smyrna on the Turkish mainland. The orders are to kill all males over twelve, all women over forty, and all children under two years old. The rest are to be sold in the slave markets of Istanbul, Cairo, and Tripoli.

Chios trembles.

# MAP OF THE BALKANS

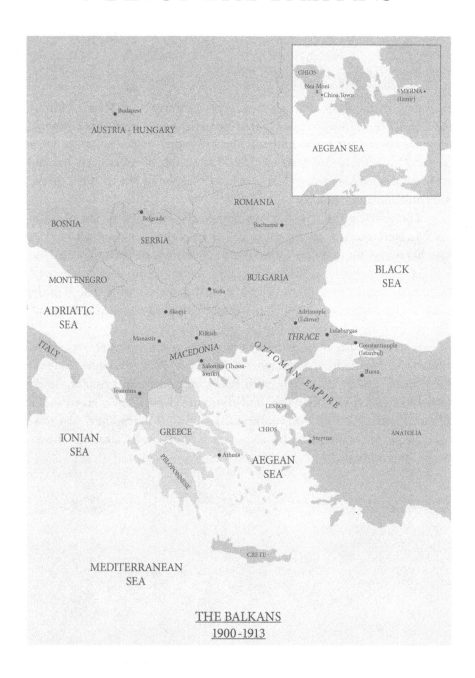

CHIOS
Nea Moni
Chios Town
SMYRNA
(Izmir)

AEGEAN SEA

Budapest

AUSTRIA - HUNGARY

ROMANIA

BOSNIA          Belgrade          Bucharest

SERBIA

MONTENEGRO                    BULGARIA          BLACK
                                                SEA
                    Sofia

ADRIATIC          Skopje          Adrianople
SEA                               (Edirne)
                                             Lulaburgas
        Monastir    Kilkish          THRACE
                              Constantinople
          MACEDONIA    OTTOMAN    (Istanbul)
            Salonika (Thessa-
            loniki)                    Bursa
      Ioannina                EMPIRE

ITALY                          LESBOS

          GREECE     CHIOS          ANATOLIA
IONIAN                    Smyrna
SEA                  Athens
          PELOPONNESE    AEGEAN
                          SEA

MEDITERRANEAN          CRETE
SEA

THE BALKANS
1900-1913

# PROLOGUE

*Chios, April 12, 1822*

Darkness falls and an eerie silence descends over the landscape, broken only by the sound of cicadas and the occasional hoot of an owl. The night sky is a canopy filled with millions of twinkling stars: diamonds on black velvet.

In a race against time, the two women make their way up into the hills following ancient donkey tracks that meander through scrubland of myrtle thickets, oleander, and broom. In an agonizing journey fraught with danger, their only hope of salvation is to find sanctuary in the Monastery of Nea Moni.

Swaying and clutching her swollen belly, the young woman collapses onto the soft, warm earth moaning in pain. Euphrosyne kneels over her, coaxing her to make one last effort. Their lives hang in the balance. She cannot give birth here, not now; they are alone and within reach of the Turk. Untying her sash, Euphrosyne takes out a silver flask and pours the last drop of precious water onto the woman's dry crimson lips. Even in such distress, Artemis is still the most beautiful creature she has ever known. With her perfect almond-shaped face and flawless alabaster complexion, in the moonlight she resembles a goddess. Uttering a prayer to the Virgin to protect the mother's milk, Euphrosyne reaches out and tears away the water-logged leaves of a succulent plant, opens the delicate silk bodice, and tenderly massages Artemis's supple breasts, bursting with milk, until the leaves have released all of their medicinal properties. The child kicks violently in her belly.

'Not now, my child, not now,' Euphrosyne whispers, gently running her withered, bony fingers through the falling tresses of Artemis's thick, raven-black hair and wiping away the tiny pearls of perspiration from her brow.

A glorious silver moon hangs over the Straits of Chios and the sea shines like a silver mirror. The Turkish fleet lies in the harbor and beyond on the horizon is the dark shadow of the Turkish mainland. Flashes of red light tinged with yellow illuminate the sky over Chios town, and a thin column of smoke ascends into the heavens. A screech owl swoops overhead, flapping his wings, disappearing into the shadows.

'Look, Artemis,' cries Euphrosyne. 'The messenger of the Goddess Athena; it is a good omen.'

Artemis forces a smile. The light in her amethyst eyes intensifies.

'It is not the destiny of this child to be born here,' Euphrosyne adds. 'Remember that the miraculous icon of the Virgin was found hanging from a myrtle bush nearby. It is she who will guide us to safety.'

The two women struggle in silence until finally, from the brow of the hill they see the monastery nestling amongst the cypress trees, protecting itself from the outside world. As they approach, they hear a soft humming noise. Gradually the noise becomes louder and they recognize the pitiful sound of wailing. The great wooden doors open to reveal a scene of abject human misery. Women, half-crazed with terror, shriek and cry; desperate children clutch their mother's skirts, trembling in fear. A monk helps Artemis across the cobblestones, pushing his way through the desperate throng. Two thousand souls awaiting salvation are crammed inside the walls of this great Byzantine monastery.

'Pray for us,' they cry. 'Pray to the Virgin.'

Finding a place in the church, Euphrosyne spreads out her woolen cloak on the ancient marble floor in preparation for the birth. Artemis sinks to her knees as the monk lays her down, blessing her forehead with the sign of the cross. With not a moment to spare, under the splendor of the eleventh-century domes ablaze with gold mosaics, the child is born. The Christ Pantocrator and holy saints of the spiritual world gaze down on mother and child. Artemis looks up at the Virgin dressed in her shimmering blue robe, as Euphrosyne wraps the child in her warm shawl and hands it to her.

'You see, Artemis,' Euphrosyne says. 'It was not her destiny to be born on a hillside. Look above you. In such pitiful conditions, to be born with all the saints of Christendom looking down on you for protection is something miraculous. God will watch over this child.'

The church door flies open. 'They are here, the Turks are here,' a woman screams.

Panic and fear grip everyone. A mother of two small children who are cowering against the wall faints, leaving her little ones crying helplessly. The monks reach for their guns.

'Courage, my children, courage,' they cry, as they run towards the gate.

Artemis clasps Euphrosyne's hand. 'You must take the child and escape while there is still a chance.'

Euphrosyne looks at Artemis in horror. How can she leave her here alone, and to such a terrible fate? She had watched this woman grow from a child and blossom into the most beautiful woman in Chios. She owed her life to this family. Rescued from the slave market by Artemis's father, that family was all she had in the world. Her own family had perished at the hands of the Turks in reprisals for Greek freedom fighters attacking a Turkish village. It was unthinkable to leave.

'Euphrosyne,' Artemis pleads. 'I am begging you. I am too weak to move. My end is near but the child must live. You said that she is the child of destiny. Her life is in your hands.'

Artemis unties the embroidered silk sash from around her hair and secures it around the tiny bundle. Taking the precious locket from around her neck, she kisses it and places it over the child's head, securing it between the folds of silk.

'Go. Run as fast as you can; don't look back. God be with you.'

Euphrosyne gathers the child in her arms and in a sea of tears runs to the door. Against Artemis's wishes, she turns and takes one final look. Artemis seems to be searching for something in her clothing. She catches Euphrosyne's eye.

'Run,' Artemis urges, 'while there is time.'

Euphrosyne runs as fast as her weary bones can carry her. With blind determination, she makes her way to the far side of the monastery. Behind the monks' houses stands a narrow stone stairway leading to the top of the outer wall. Behind her is Dante's inferno. The screams of slaughter ring in her ears and the sounds of gunshots grow nearer. Reaching the upper ledge, Euphrosyne makes a rope from her sash and ties it to the small bundle. Carefully lowering it over the outer wall onto a soft patch of wild thyme, partially obscured from view by the bough of a wild fig tree, she lets the sash go. Turning around, she freezes. At the bottom of the stairs stands a Turk, yataghan in one hand and scimitar in the other. Euphrosyne runs along the ledge until she can run no more. Leaning against the wall, she turns her head. The Turk, his face and clothes smeared with blood, laughs at her. In defiance, she spits in his face.

'The devil take you,' she curses.

Angrily, he raises his bloodied scimitar to strike but defiant to the end, Euphrosyne throws herself over the monastery wall. She falls to her death on the rocks.

The remaining souls barricade themselves inside the church. Finally, the doors break open and the Turks, showing no mercy, slaughter all except for the young women destined for the slave markets. In the center of the church, under the Christ Pantocrator, lies Artemis, as if asleep, a cover pulled over her body. A Turkish officer stands over her and in the midst of so much devastation he pauses, catching his breath at such beauty.

'*Korkma kadin. Sen benimsin!* Fear not! You are mine,' he leers, tearing away the cover only to reveal her blood-soaked clothing. Like Euphrosyne, Artemis has cheated them out of killing her. She has plunged the jade dagger once given to her for protection by Yasim-Ali into her heart.

As the sun rises the next day, the sound of hoof beats galloping through the scrub becomes louder and louder. A blood-bay stallion approaches the thicket of wild fig. The horseman is agile. In an instant, he lifts the tiny bundle onto his saddle and gallops away through the trees. A Painted Lady butterfly flutters over the ground where the infant had lain. Nearby, the bright red wild tulips unfurl their petals to the morning sun and a quiet peace descends over the monastery.

# PART I

# A DANGEROUS
# GAME

# CHAPTER 1

*London, September 1972*

Ever since it opened ten years earlier, the Knightsbridge Gallery had held a string of successful exhibitions. Judging from the interest shown by the public, this latest one on rare fourteenth-century Byzantine icons promised to be the best to date. With so many last-minute details to attend to, the past few weeks had been exceptionally hectic for Eleni and she was exhausted. She looked at her watch. It was almost ten-thirty. Making sure that everything was in order for the following day's media release, she said goodnight to her colleagues and went home.

Earlier in the evening there had been a huge downpour. Instead of catching her usual bus she decided to walk the rain-soaked pavements from Knightsbridge to Bayswater in an attempt to clear her head. Just lately she found it hard to stop thinking about her work; it had become too consuming. The walk took her past the Greek Orthodox Church of St Sophia. She knew the church well, having visited it on several occasions with her father – usually at Christmas or Easter. Since his death, she had rarely ventured inside. For some strange reason, that night she felt a strong compulsion to enter.

Enveloped in the thick air of incense and the glitter of burnished metal, women who were oblivious to those around them knelt in front of icons, touching and kissing them, chanting and crossing themselves. These were not the priceless icons that would be unveiled to the public tomorrow, yet they served the same purpose: offering comfort, hope, and forgiveness to the believers, just as they had done through the centuries.

Eleni took a thin white candle from a gold stand, lit it and placed it in the sand alongside others. Immersed in a feeling of tranquility, she crossed herself and thought of her mother.

No sooner had she arrived home when the telephone rang. Thinking it was the gallery, she picked up the receiver wondering what sort of problem necessitated a call at this late hour. In broken English, and clearly distressed, the woman at the other end of the telephone introduced herself as Chrysoula, the long-time maid and close companion of Eleni's Aunt Maria.

'I'm sorry to call you so late, Eleni, but I have bad news. Your Aunt Maria is seriously ill. The doctor has given her only a few days to live and she's desperate to see you. Can you come to Athens as soon as possible?'

'That might be difficult,' Eleni answered. 'I've got something very important…'

'Eleni, please, I'm begging you. She calls for you.' There was a sense of urgency in Chrysoula's voice and she began to weep. 'Only your presence can console her and allow her to die in peace.'

Eleni felt a tingle run down her spine—she knew so little about her mother's sister. It had been years since she came to visit them in London, and even then she only stayed a few days. After that, they never heard from her again. Why, after all this time, would she need to see her? Whatever it was, Eleni felt a growing anxiety that refused to settle and she found herself answering: 'Yes, Chrysoula, tell Aunt Maria I will be there as soon as possible.'

Pouring a strong drink to steady her nerves, she picked up the black and white photograph that stood on the mantelpiece. She had never known her mother, yet this beautiful woman sitting on the steps of the Parthenon, running her hand through her shiny black hair and smiling at the camera, wasn't a stranger. In fact, she had an unbearable affection for the woman whom she liked to think had kept watch over her all these years from her vantage point on the mantelpiece; the woman she often talked to as easily as if she were beside her. For years, Eleni had longed to go to Greece and get to know her mother's homeland. Something deep within her stirred. The timing was bad but the gallery could carry on without her for a while. She felt an inexplicable urge to find out more.

*Athens, September 1972*

31 Thessaly Street in the leafy suburb of Kypseli in Athens had once been an elegant townhouse but years of neglect had reduced it to a sad state of disrepair. The warm pale-ochre stonework had long faded into a blotched gray that exposed large areas of crumbling plasterwork, and dark-green paint peeled from the wooden shutters. A narrow balcony protruded over the imposing front door, precariously held together by a blue filigree wrought-iron balustrade. Surrounded by modern apartment blocks with spacious wide balconies filled with an array of potted plants, the house now looked out of place—a relic from another era.

Eleni rang the doorbell and waited for what seemed like an eternity. It was, at three-thirty in the afternoon, siesta time; the hot Athenian sun beat down mercilessly onto the quiet empty street. She took shade under a Syrian hibiscus tree next to the front door, admiring its delicate purple flowers drenched in sunlight. Across the road, a woman emerged from a bakery carrying a large baking tray of hot food, a loaf of bread tucked under her arm, and disappeared into one of the nearby apartment blocks, leaving the lingering aroma of baked lamb infused with cinnamon. Eleni heard the sound of footsteps clattering through the hallway towards the door.

'*Irthe, irthe,*' cried a shrill voice. 'I'm coming, I'm coming.'

The door opened to reveal a bird-like woman clad in black. Her face, with its large dark eyes, partially clouded by cataracts, wore a sad aspect. It was made sadder by her mistress's dying. Chrysoula greeted Eleni warmly, wiped away her tears, and ushered her inside.

'She has been waiting for you. Another day and it would have been too late,' she whispered, crossing herself. 'But now she sleeps and I don't want to wake her. Come. I have prepared food for you. You must be hungry after such a long journey.'

Stirring the contents of an enormous black pot, she scooped large spoonfuls of steaming lemon-scented chicken and rice soup into a bowl and placed it in front of Eleni. Wiping her hands on her apron, she pulled out a chair at the other end of the table, sat down, and fixed her eyes on the young woman seated in front of her.

Eleni was a little unnerved. She cast a glance around the kitchen. It was much larger than she had expected, with a high ceiling decorated with raised square panels filled with rosettes, and walls covered with glass-fronted cupboards and open dressers displaying an assortment of glassware and hand-painted ceramics. Pots of sweet-smelling basil, mint, and oregano stood on the nearby windowsill next to an old marble sink, and a pair of French windows opened into a garden courtyard filled with a profusion of flowers. Sunlight streamed through the doors, warming the stone floor.

Eleni's father had often spoken about this house, about how it was always filled with love and gaiety. He and her mother had spent wonderful times here when the family entertained close friends on name-days or during the Greek Orthodox celebrations. On those occasions he described the table, the very one that Eleni was sitting at, as groaning under the weight of mouthwatering delicacies. He remembered the clay amphorae brimming with ripe black olives, which Eleni observed still stood there, and the bottles wrapped in basket-work filled with *kokkinelli*, the local red wine, and the resin-scented retsina which always reminded him of Athens. And he told her how he and her mother would laugh and chatter in the garden during the hot siestas when the rest of the family was asleep.

Theirs was a vanishing life, and yet as old and as run down as the house was, Eleni felt at home here. It dawned on her that she never did feel at home growing up alone with her father in London. It had been a lonely childhood and the house of her youth had not been blessed with the same love as this house had.

Chrysoula cleared away the empty soup bowl and replaced it with a plate of plump purple figs, their flesh bursting with fragrance in the warmth of the afternoon. She resumed her seat and crossed herself again.

'You are just like her,' she murmured. 'You are the image of your mother.'

Eleni felt her chest tighten. Nobody had ever said that to her before, not even her father.

Eleni's parents met on the eve of the Second World War. Her father had been sent to Athens as the British Diplomatic Envoy to the Balkans. It was to be the last, long, hot summer of freedom for many years. During one of the many social evenings thrown by dignitaries at the British Embassy, he met her mother Nina. This was a story he often repeated, especially in later years when all he had left were his memories.

'It was love at first sight,' he recalled. 'There were many pretty girls at the party that evening, but when she walked into the room my heart missed a beat. Dressed in a strapless evening gown of steel-gray silk taffeta, she wore a striking flamingo-pink sash around her waist, embroidered with an unusual design of stylized rose-pink tulips. Her black shoulder-length hair framed her delicate pale-olive features, highlighting her glittering dark eyes bordered with long silky lashes. There was something exotic about her. She was captivating. I was not her only admirer that night; almost every unattached man wanted to dance with her. At some point during the evening, she joined our table. Champagne flowed yet we were all preoccupied with the events taking place in Europe. With Hitler's conquest of Central Europe in 1938 by means of the Anschluss and the Munich Agreement, many were of the opinion that war in Europe was inevitable. What would happen in the Balkans? Would Greece stay neutral? Most worrying was a possible invasion of Greece by Mussolini; he was already walking into Albania. Listening attentively to our conversation, Nina looked into the eyes of those who spoke, and after a while everyone seemed to be talking only to her.

'Our host spared no expense that night and had hired one of the best bands in Athens. Out of the corner of my eye, I glimpsed Nina write something on a serviette, fold it over, and hand it to a waiter. She whispered something in his ear. He walked straight over to the band and gave it to the singer. A few minutes later, the band started to play one of the most popular songs of the day: *J'attendrai*. With the first few bars, she rose to her feet. We all stopped talking. All eyes were on her yet she looked directly at me. "I adore this song," she smiled, holding her hand towards me. "Come, dance with me."

'She was bewitching and I was bewitched. From that moment I lost my heart to her.'

Eleni's parents married soon after, the specter of war already on their doorstep. On October 28, 1940, Mussolini issued an ultimatum to the Greek government. The uncompromising stand was firm: 'No.' By the end of the winter of 1940 to 1941, despite the Greek army's successes against the Italians, it was obvious that the German army would invade. It was too dangerous for her father to stay in Athens and he was posted to Cairo. By then, Nina was pregnant and Eleni's grandmother urged her to join him. As Hitler attacked Greece, she gave birth to Eleni in Cairo. The only news of her mother's family came from letters smuggled out by servicemen escaping behind enemy lines. Sometime in late 1942 her mother told her father that she wanted to return to Athens. They argued. She implored. Her mother needed her, she argued, and despite the obvious danger she assured him she would be safe. 'It's only for a few months,' she pleaded. 'And then I will be back, safe and sound and your worry will have been for nothing.'

Her father was distraught. Eleni was only a baby. He gave in on the condition that Eleni would remain in Cairo. He knew that this would make her return quickly. She agreed. Within a few weeks Nina was back in Athens, leaving behind a despondent husband with her child cared for by an Egyptian nanny.

At first, letters would reach him via the covert smuggling routes through Turkey or any of the numerous smaller Greek islands. He never knew how they arrived, he just knew that the occasional letter addressed in her handwriting and pushed under the door signified that all was well.

'Soon she will be back to us, Eleni,' he said, rocking his daughter on his knee and singing her a lullaby. But it was not to be. The letters stopped and after a few months he received word that her mother and grandmother had been taken prisoner and executed by the Germans. After the war, her father returned to London with his daughter and they settled in the Greek area of Bayswater. His only link with Athens was an infrequent letter sent to Aunt Maria, but for years there was never a reply. Then one day, quite out of the blue, she visited them. Eleni was about fifteen at the time. A somewhat larger than life figure, Aunt Maria arrived, looking stylish in a sweeping calf-length mink coat with matching leather shoes, handbag, and gloves. Her perfume filled the house, and at once Eleni felt that her aunt added the fun and liveliness that they had been missing. It was not to last. After a few days her father and aunt began to argue. The atmosphere became heavy and when Eleni was in her room at night, she could hear their raised voices downstairs. Soon after, Aunt Maria announced that she was going back to Athens.

Eleni's last recollection was of standing on the doorstep, waving her aunt off as the taxi rounded the corner. Her father was already inside. That night, Eleni was woken by her father going downstairs into the lounge room. She listened and heard the chink of a glass as he poured himself a drink. Moments later she heard the gramophone playing and the sound of Rina Ketty's voice singing 'J'attendrai.' Once again, her father was lost in his wartime memories. For days after, Aunt Maria's perfume lingered in the house. She faded from their lives—until now.

The Aunt Maria Eleni saw that day was not the one she knew in London. Gone was the vibrant woman whose smart looks and fancy attire had left a mark on Eleni's imagination. In her place was a living corpse supported by pillows. Her once lustrous copper hair was now white and thinning. The odor of death lingered in the air and Chrysoula opened the shutters to let in some fresh air. She fussed around the bed, plumping up the pillows once more.

'Hello, Eleni,' said Aunt Maria, weakly. 'Doxa sto Theo: thank God you have come.'

Eleni leaned over the bed and with affection kissed her aunt's forehead. With a flick of her wrist, Maria gestured to Chrysoula to leave them a while.

Eleni sat in the chair next to the bed and her aunt feebly held out her frail hand. She wore a ring set with a magnificent sapphire. Eleni remembered her wearing it when she came to visit. Extravagant to the end, she thought to herself, recalling her aunt peeling off her long black gloves to light a cigarette with the sapphire ring sparkling on her formerly immaculate manicured hands.

The bedroom was claustrophobic; it was full of heavy, dated furniture. An immense ornate wardrobe with a full-length mirror in which Eleni could see herself stood opposite the bed. Nearby was an old-fashioned dressing table with winged mirrors, its shiny surface covered in an array of trinkets, perfume bottles, jars of creams, a silver hairbrush with matching comb, and a few framed photographs. Somehow, Chrysoula had found a space to place a vase of freshly cut roses and sprays of jasmine there. Eleni was grateful for their perfume in the oppressive atmosphere. Oriental carpets now slightly threadbare through decades of use covered the floor, and on the bed was a faded damask coverlet which was once a rich red but now just a blue-tinged rose. The starched linen sheets had a homespun feel to them, and the matching pillowcases were monogrammed M L—Maria Laskaris. A pair of Venetian crystal lamps stood on the bedside tables, their soft light highlighting Aunt Maria's overly rouged cheeks.

'What did your father tell you about me?' her aunt asked softly.

Eleni had to think. He had told her very little, but she was aware that the family had once lived in Turkey and later settled in Greece when her mother was seven years old. She knew that her grandmother Sophia raised the two girls on her own in very difficult circumstances. When Eleni had asked about the Turkish connection, her father said that her mother had never talked about it, probably because the departure had been so traumatic for them all. Apart from that he had said little else. The whole episode was far too painful for him and as he suffered from increasing bouts of depression in later years, they just tried to put it behind them. In fact, he never really talked about Eleni's aunt at all. It was as if Aunt Maria didn't exist.

Maria gripped Eleni's hand tighter and looked into her eyes.

'I have to tell you something, something you need to know,' she whispered, gasping slightly for breath. 'I have carried the burden of guilt for too long. It is an unbearable torment—it's too immense and overwhelming.'

'What is it?' Eleni asked, almost afraid of what her aunt was about to say.

'God makes us suffer sometimes. How cruel he can be. He throws us challenges and if we fail him…' Her voice tapered off and her eyes filled with tears. 'For my sins he made me barren. I am an old woman now, without beauty, without allure.'

At first it occurred to Eleni that her aunt was delusional.

'When you walked into the room, I thought you were her—my dear, beautiful sister. How you have grown into a fine young woman. She lives in you, *koritsi mou*.'

Maria wiped her eyes with her perfumed lace handkerchief.

'What I am going to tell you, I have never told anyone else. God will not let me die without telling you, but I must begin at the beginning.'

That afternoon, she told Eleni her story. Woven together like a fine piece of cloth, the story was also that of her mother and her grandmother—a story of happiness yet tragedy.

# CHAPTER 2

*Constantinople, Spring 1909*

The three women sat under the shade of a spreading magnolia tree sipping chilled lemonade and eating sweetmeats. On such a perfect summer day when a gentle breeze from the shimmering waters of the Bosphorus cooled the air, it seemed that their lives were blessed. Beyond the lawn Selim the gardener tended the rose garden, occasionally clipping delicate pink rosebuds into a glass bowl to be used later that evening to decorate and flavor one of Sevkiye's famous pilavs. Thanks to him, the garden looked particularly lovely this year. The fruit trees had blossomed early, and the almond trees in particular had been extraordinarily showy—soft pink clouds floating against a backdrop of blue sea. And the new pavilion, carefully positioned to frame the spectacular view of the Golden Horn with its domes and minarets was a mass of fragrant honeysuckle interspersed with vivid blue clematis. Nearby, water splashed from the fountain given to Sophia by the Italian Ambassador. Fashioned from the finest Carrara marble, the rumor throughout Constantinople was that it was she who had posed for the water nymph who knelt so sensuously over her reflection in the running water. A maid replenished the lemonade.

Amidst such a tranquil setting, the women sought respite from the tumultuous events taking place around them. For how long, no one knew. The mighty Ottoman Empire that once spanned the area from the gates of Vienna to the Arabian Peninsula was now 'The Sick Man of Europe,' and on the brink of disintegration. Just one year earlier the Young Turks, plotting from their base in Salonika, surrounded Constantinople, forced Sultan Abdulhamid into exile and restored the constitution. 'This is kismet,' the Sultan was reported to have said on learning of his fate.

The revolutionary movement that spawned the Young Turks was only one of many. Macedonia in particular was a hotbed of conspiracy, and further afield Russia and Austria hovered like vultures waiting to devour the pickings. Foreigner was pitted against foreigner, Muslim against Christian, and secret agents from every dominion filled the capital. La Belle Epoch was drawing to a close.

Dimitra's hands blazed with jewels in the sun. In her left hand she held a small crystal saucer under which was placed a fine muslin napkin, its tip embroidered in crimson silk. She sipped chilled lemonade from an exquisite tiny glass and dabbed her lips with the napkin.

'Today is an important day in the history of our empire,' she said to her daughter. 'The old saray at the Topkapi is being closed. The women of the palace are being sent home and they will emerge from a closed and protected world into one much different to the one they have known.'

Photeini agreed. 'I have seen the advertisements placed in newspapers asking for relatives to come and collect them.' Looking over the water towards the domes of the Topkapi Palace in the distance, she sighed at the thought of their fate. 'It must be bewildering. Many of them have no relatives at all, and others have relatives so far away that they will never see the newspapers, even if they can read. What will become of them? Will we see foreigners offering a pittance for their stories, telling the world about the mysteries of the harem?'

Since the fall of Constantinople to Mehmet the Conqueror in 1453, the Palace of the Sultans had been a place of mystery and intrigue to the outside world. In all that time very few outsiders ever ventured past the State rooms into the heart of the saray, the Imperial harem, the women's quarters. At one time the harem was said to number well over one thousand women from the lowliest servant to the Valide Sultan herself. For centuries, the mother of every reigning Sultan had ruled with an iron fist, unflinchingly protecting her son until his death, when she would be stripped of her power to make way for the new Sultan and his mother. With the proclamation of the Second Constitution in July 1909, harems were now outlawed: the secret world of the gilded cage was no more.

Dimitra, her daughter Photeini, and her granddaughter Sophia were among the privileged few to visit the inner sanctum of the harem. Dimitra had been the first, being sent for by the Sultan's mother many decades earlier. At that time she was becoming known for her fine embroidery skills, creating works of art which far surpassed those of the court embroiderers. More recently it was Sophia who took over this role, establishing her clientele in the palace, especially during the last few years as the Ottoman Empire underwent major social changes in a new and more modern cosmopolitan world.

Photeini helped herself to a slice of pistachio-studded halva. 'Are we doing everything we can do for these women?' she asked Sophia.

'Some of the women are excellent embroiderers and seamstresses. I have taken on several and I'm sure they'll be a great asset to the business.'

For years the family had given work to women from all walks of life, especially to those who were the most vulnerable: orphaned girls, destitute mothers forced into prostitution in order to feed their children and, more recently, refugees fleeing from all parts of the empire. All were given a chance to prove themselves in the family business and begin a new life. They were one of the most charitable families in the Greek community and, as Father Yannakos was fond of pointing out, God would look favorably on them in the next life.

The sound of approaching footsteps caught their attention. Ali Agha arrived with Dimitra's narghile, stationed himself beside her, and began the ritual of lighting the coals and preparing the right amount of tobacco and molasses to ensure the correct sweetness. He was an expert at this, having done it since he was a small child—well before the days when he came to work for the family. Sophia watched him, recalling the day he first came to them. Her mother and grandmother were returning from a visit to Sultanhamet when they spotted Ali's master beating him mercilessly. Appalled, they offered the man money just to make him stop. The old scoundrel greedily snatched the money, counted it, and pushed the boy towards them.

'Take him!' he cried, running away into the alley. 'Ungrateful wretch of a boy, child of a black whore.'

It was thought that Ali was about nine years old then. Nobody ever knew his real age, or for that matter where he came from. The women also discovered that he had only recently been castrated, with the procedure performed in such a barbaric manner that for weeks afterwards he lay writhing in agony, clutching his lower parts. The family nursed him back to health but the infection, which had spread to his groin, left him with a permanent limp. Forever indebted to them, Ali never wanted to leave, and when Sophia married he became her manservant and trusted family friend.

Sophia checked her watch. 'Please excuse me, Mama, Grandmamma,' she said, rising. 'I have an important appointment. Fatme Hanim, wife of Ismail Pasha, is coming for a fitting. Stay awhile and enjoy the garden. Zubeyde will bring you more refreshments.'

Dimitra watched her granddaughter walk down the garden path towards the house. 'I'm proud of what she has achieved,' she said to Photeini when they were alone. 'She has taken our business to new heights. Constantinople is a vibrant city with much to offer, especially if you are young like her, but...' She paused, a worried expression crossing her face. 'But there's something about this city which makes me uneasy. I'm always happy to be here, yet I'm even happier to return to Smyrna.'

'I couldn't agree more,' replied Photeini. 'But Sophia has made Constantinople her home. She belongs here and it's here where our business flourishes now. Nevertheless, there are too many changes taking place for my liking. The political situation is volatile. Who knows where it will all end?'

Zubeyde returned to the garden carrying a tray of coffee and a bowl of fresh fruit from the orchard. Photeini smiled as she watched her mother lazily draw back the smoke through the long pipe. Fashions had changed greatly over the years, but still Dimitra preferred her oriental dress and pipe to any of the latest Paris fashions. Sitting 'a la Turk' on a large silk cushion with golden tassels, the matriarch closed her eyes, inhaling the pungent tobacco infused with the sweetness of garden flowers.

Sophia's family was one of the wealthiest in the country. Their wealth had been built on textiles. The Ottoman Turks had such a passion for decoration that the greatest of craftsmen were held in the highest esteem—often venerated in the works of great poets. Textile art, in particular embroidery, was one of the finest of all Ottoman decorative arts and in a traditional society where art was elevated to a divine status, it was one of the few areas in which a woman was encouraged to excel.

It was said that Dimitra was born with a needle and thread in her fingers. As a child she could dazzle her elders with her fine hand. Yet unlike Photeini and Sophia, Dimitra had not always known great wealth. Her early years were obscured. For some reason she never wanted to speak about that period of her life. All that the family knew was that in 1847 she arrived in Smyrna as a young bride with her husband, the French painter Jean-Paul Lamartine. They arrived with very little, intent on seeking their fortune in the empire's most vibrant and cosmopolitan city. Smyrna was a city dominated by Greeks who built up flourishing businesses over generations, as had the Armenians and Jews. It was home to a thriving European population too. At any time of the day it was possible to walk along the crescent-shaped harbor front into the heart of the city and hear a multitude of languages. Smyrna was the gateway to the east: to Aleppo, Damascus, Baghdad, and the fabled cities of the Silk Road. This was something that appealed to the adventurous Jean-Paul.

At first, the couple rented rooms in a less than modest area of town. Shortly after, their money ran out and they were forced to live on their wits for a while. Jean-Paul took commissions from the city's elite and Dimitra sold her embroidery. Navigating her way through the winding alleyways of the bazaar to source the finest of materials, she developed an eye for rare and unusual silks. A keen negotiator, she soon built friendships with merchants who often put work her way.

After a while the couple scraped enough money together and moved to a larger home on the outskirts of the Turkish quarter. Finally, after all the hardships, their fortunes improved and it wasn't long before Dimitra's talents were talked about in Constantinople. One day a messenger arrived from the saray. Her presence was requested by none other than the Valide Sultan herself.

Working well into the night, Dimitra embroidered a sash to present as a gift to the Sultan's mother. Worked in gold, silver, and silk thread on a fine silk ground, a row of three identical floral sprays bordered each end of the sash. Each complicated spray was held together by a stylized ribbon, and among the foliage nestled a pair of songbirds sewn with such fineness that their very wings appeared to be in flight. It was the most exquisite piece she had ever produced. The Valide Sultan and her ladies were captivated.

'Hanim Efendi,' exclaimed the Valide Sultan. 'Your fine hands create images that only Allah can express. Like a work of art, you dye your colors and spin your silks until they blossom in the spring. As we see each flower unfurl, before us lies a meadow.'

She ran her fingers over the embroidery.

'Light and shade enhance the beauty of such composition that never before have all my senses become so aroused as when I touch your silken threads. I smell the fragrance of your roses and I hear the melodious song of the nightingale.'

The Valide Sultan called for the Treasurer of the Privy Purse. As a token of her gratitude, Dimitra was presented with a magnificent ring in raised gold set with a brilliant Burmese sapphire, surrounded by a single row of sparkling diamonds.

'Wear it when you embroider, Hanim Efendi, and may Allah watch over you. It will remind you that you have a friend in Constantinople.'

From that moment, Dimitra was never seen without the ring. As her work became recognized she acquired the patronage of other women in the Imperial Harem, and of the wives and concubines of great pashas throughout the empire.

With the business expanding, Jean-Paul and Dimitra still found time to raise a family. In all there were seven children, the last being Photeini, who worked alongside her mother. Much to Dimitra's distress, none of the others survived past childhood.

Although the business now employed several hundred workers, from dyers and spinners to embroiderers, it was always known as Dimitra of Smyrna's Embroidery Atelier. Commissions would be carefully wrapped in a woven fabric known as a bohça, and sent out to the far reaches of the empire. The wrappings themselves would be embroidered. Bohças that left

Dimitra's atelier always carried her signature 'leitmotif' which was a blood-red tulip embroidered discreetly somewhere within the design. The tulip was a favorite in Ottoman decoration, not only because of its recognizable and occasionally rare shape, but because its name in Turkish—*lale*—when spelt in the Arabic script, resembles the Muslim protestation of faith, which starts with the words *la Allah*.

For Dimitra, the tulip held a much deeper meaning.

It was the custom of itinerant vendors to walk through the streets peddling their wares. Selling everything from water, fried food, sweets, sherbets and nuts to old clothes, threads, and lengths of ribbons, the special call of each vendor added a pleasant and lively atmosphere to daily life. A great favorite of children and adults alike was the storyteller. Whenever Ali the Hunchback was in town, Dimitra and Jean-Paul took the children to the square or the courtyard of the Great Mosque where under the shade of a plane tree, Ali rested his broken body on a rush-bottomed stool. For a small price he would transport his audience into the fabled realm of the *Forty Viziers*—a world of wonder haunted by mysterious *djinns* and playful *peris*. It was a world where legends spoke of wise kings and graceful princesses flying through the air on magic carpets.

But for many women, especially those whose life was confined to the home, boredom was relieved by a multitude of fortunetellers and soothsayers. One day, the *simitdji,* the peddler selling freshly baked sesame-covered bread rings, stopped outside Dimitra's house.

'Dimitra Hanim Efendi,' he said, bowing before her. 'I have been told there is a stranger in town who has been granted great powers by Allah. She can see into the future. People are whispering that she only has to look into their eyes and she sees their kismet.'

Dimitra thought for a moment. Jean-Paul had little time for these charlatans, as he called them, but she was not so sure. All her life she had lived among women whose mysterious powers were able to cure the sick or destroy a life with their potions and incantations, and never would she be without the blue glass bead which was her protection against the evil eye. But Jean-Paul was far away in the ruins of Palmyra on a painting expedition. What harm could it do to offer a little hospitality to the woman? Dimitra gave him a silver coin and sent her manservant Mehmet into the alleyways in search of the stranger with the seeing eyes.

After a while Mehmet returned with the stranger, followed by a gathering crowd of onlookers. Dressed in brightly striped pantaloons with an embroidered waistcoat, she wore a large, round, silver buckled belt fastened tightly around her expansive waist; her waist-length hair was plaited with a narrow ribbon onto which were threaded an assortment of brightly colored glass beads. Ornate silver jewelry studded with coral and turquoise covered her ample breasts and adorned her arms and ankles, and silver coins jangled playfully when she walked. Dimitra welcomed her, observing her purposely blackened teeth, which were a fashion for women of certain tribes. Her skin was dark and leathery and her eyes were as black as a moonless night.

Dimitra sat on a cushion and motioned to the woman to begin. The seer prepared to invoke the spirits, throwing incense onto the mangal until the room filled with smoke. She sat on the floor, emptied her small bag of colored stones onto the carpet and concentrated on them. After a few minutes, her facial muscles jerked and her eyes rolled until all that could be seen was a milky whiteness. Beating her chest wildly in what could only be described as black fits, she let out a devastating cry and gasping for breath, rocked to and fro as if in severe pain. Dimitra looked on in bewilderment.

Eventually she stopped, and after wiping the sweat from her brow, concentrated once more, gathering the stones and throwing them down again and again until finally she scooped them up and threw them back in the bag. Her actions alarmed the other women of the household; they backed away in terror.

Mehmet threw her a scornful glance. 'Speak to my lady,' he demanded. 'Tell her what you see before Allah strikes you down and you see no more.'

'Sshhh!' Dimitra cautioned. 'Be calm.'

The seer tucked the bag of stones into her pocket and hurriedly made for the door.

'Please, kind lady, won't you tell me what you see?' asked Dimitra.

Reluctantly, she turned and gazed into Dimitra's eyes, her face so close Dimitra involuntarily recoiled from the stench of her putrid breath. 'My dear woman,' she said gravely, 'you are a saintly and noble woman, but may Allah preserve you from the evil eye. Death surrounds you like a shroud. You must kill a sacrificial lamb with black eyes and spill its blood around the house. Beware of trickery. Beware of the child with the flaming red hair; she has been kissed by the devil. Heed my words at your peril, for this child will bring about unhappiness for your family far beyond your wildest imagination.'

She held out her hand expectantly. Mehmet lifted his hand to strike her. 'Wretched woman; you have insulted my mistress with your ill-omened words.'

Dimitra moved a hand to stop him and gave the woman a silver coin. Greedily, she pocketed it and hurried away. The onlookers who had gathered outside the house fell silent when they saw the look on her face. Christians and Muslims alike said a little prayer and walked away quietly. That very night Dimitra had a dream from which she woke in a cold sweat. Jean-Paul was calling to her.

A few weeks passed and everyone in the household seemed to have forgotten the incident—all that is except Mehmet, who could be heard each night saying a little prayer to appease the evil spirits.

'Allah adina gitmek,' he cried solemnly. 'Go away, in the name of Allah.'

One evening, there was a knock at the door. It was a friend of Jean-Paul's, a fellow French painter. His cheeks were white and he trembled violently.

'Madame, I bring you terrible news. Jean-Paul is dead. Our caravan train was attacked by bandits on the way back from Aleppo and he was killed with a single gunshot to the back of the head. We buried him not far from where he died.'

Dimitra froze. She now began to understand the significance of the fortuneteller's prophecy. Distraught, she thought her heart would break. No chanting, no slaying of the sheep with the black eyes could have prevented this, she told herself. Nothing afflicts mankind more harshly than the force of destiny. I have lost my husband, my lover, and my confidante. It is kismet. Together they had been invincible. Now she was alone. She must learn to survive for her family's sake in a man's world. That night, Mehmet left. He could no longer stay in the house with the bad luck. They never saw him again.

The years passed. Business prospered. Photeini fell in love with a Greek schoolteacher from Salonika and they married soon after. Soterios was a studious man with a gentle yet resolute disposition that complemented Photeini's sweet nature, and he encouraged her in the family business with her mother.

These were turbulent times. In 1878, the year of their marriage, Serbia declared independence. Just two years before that the first Ottoman constitution was proclaimed. For the first few years of their marriage, the couple eagerly followed the news that leaked back from the far provinces of the empire. Over a quarter of a million Christians were massacred. Soterios was outraged. Under cover of darkness and out of respect for his mother-in-law, he would leave the family home and meet with like-minded friends—all of them devoutly Greek Orthodox. They would discuss their longing for the day when the Christians would be freed from the Turkish yoke. Dimitra noted his actions with dismay.

In 1885 Photeini gave birth to Sophia. Blessed with extraordinary beauty, she was adored by all; by none more so than Dimitra, who saw something of herself in her grandchild.

# CHAPTER 3

*Constantinople, Spring 1912*

Every Thursday afternoon, the Palm Court Café at the Pera Palas Hotel reserved a table by the window for Sophia and a small circle of friends. There they would sit on white wicker chairs at a marble-topped table and take afternoon tea. Exchanging their oriental sherbets and sweetmeats for a variety of delicate confectionary prepared in the European style, they watched the comings and goings of people making their way to the Grande Rue de Pera nearby. The waiter brought over a pot of fine china tea and the ladies chose a selection of tempting morsels from the sweet trolley: snowy meringue swirls, chocolate éclairs, and tiny sponge cakes swathed in pastel fondant.

The Grande Rue de Pera was *the* place to be seen in Constantinople. Revered for its prestigious stores and luxury goods, it was here that society's wealthiest, most stylish, and most influential shopped, buying the finest of European goods in the newly opened department stores, all of which displayed their signs in a multitude of languages.

Sophia looked out of the window. Across the road, the sign writer added last-minute touches to his work and tradesmen cleared away the last basket loads of rubbish from the pavement. La Maison du l'Orient—the sign over the entrance to the grand new building was executed in the latest style: gold lettering on a shiny background, bordered with a simple flourish of sinewy art nouveau swirls. Finally, Sophia had achieved her dream, her very own designer house. She could hardly believe it. For years she had dreamt of this day and now it was a reality. With the encouragement of her mother and grandmother, she now headed a fashion house to rival the great houses of Paris. The move from Smyrna to Constantinople had certainly been a fortuitous one and what could be better than premises directly opposite one of Constantinople's finest hotels—the Pera Palas—near the much sought-after Grande Rue de Pera.

Sophia sipped her tea and watched. The imposing dark wooden doors with their gilded details on the panels opened and Andreas stepped out onto the pavement with the architect. They looked up at the sign approvingly. The dream had been his as much as Sophia's. Like her grandfather, Andreas was a fine painter and had made a name for himself at the Academy of Fine Arts, where he lectured. It was he who had overseen the whole project for her, hiring the best craftsmen in the country, and consulting with her on the interior design. Of particular pride to them both were the wall frescos in the Grand Salon. He had labored on painting these for months. Now they were finished—masterpieces in their own right.

The sign writer attached a small brass plaque to the wall at the side of the door. In finely engraved script, it read:

LA MAISON DU L'ORIENT

MADAME SOPHIA LASKARIS

HAUTE COUTURE

He gave the plaque a final polish until it gleamed in the afternoon sun. No sooner had he finished when she saw her grandmother's phaeton arrive in front of her premises. Out of it stepped Iskender, Dimitra's longstanding bodyguard and manservant. A tall, dark, and altogether formidable figure, he was always dressed in an embroidered waistcoat made especially for him by Dimitra, baggy black trousers and a crimson fez that matched the crimson sash around his waist in which he kept his pistol and a dagger.

Under Iskender's watchful eye, several porters uncovered two enormous carpets and carried them through the door. Sophia recognized them. They were a matching pair of richly colored carpets from Kashan. These rare and beautiful carpets were a gift from one of the ruling Qajar princes to Sophia's grandmother in appreciation for his young bride's wedding dress. When Sophia informed her family of her intentions to open the new salon, Dimitra declared they were to be given to her as a gift for her hard work. Woven in silk, the designs were of stylized hunting scenes depicting huntsmen on horseback pursuing lions, leopards, and other animals in a field of floral arabesques. Richly colored, they were among the most luxurious carpets she had ever seen. She recalled her grandmother teaching her, as a child, the intricacies of dyeing and of her astonishment on learning that such rich and diverse colors came from plants and berries: the remarkable range of reds, from pink through to brilliant scarlet and a deep brown-purple from madder root; extremely light-fast yellows from the Resida lutoeola plant; and for blue nothing surpassed indigo, a root first cultivated in the Indian subcontinent. 'Observe nature,' Dimitra used to say. 'It gives us our richest gifts.'

The day after the completion of the salon, the family gathered for the blessing of the new premises, an age-old ritual that insured against menacing evil spirits and bad luck. Father Yannakos, the Greek Orthodox priest in the Phanar district who was a longstanding family friend, was the first to arrive. Wearing his distinctive ankle-length black cassock and chimney-pot hat like all priests, he wore his graying locks in a little roll tied neatly above the nape of his neck. His untrimmed beard was long and lustrous, the result of so many years of stroking it whenever he spoke. He was a tall and slightly overweight man with a kind-hearted and jovial nature. When not serving his flock, more often than not he could be found in the local café enjoying a drink and a game of backgammon or cards.

'No harm in a little raki,' he would say with a twinkle in his eye when tempted by the offer of a charitable drink from the owner.

Father Yannakos placed a brass burner on a marble console in the entrance hall and dropped small round discs of incense onto the hot coals. A thin line of gray smoke curled up between the sweeping staircase, slowly rising towards the gilded ceiling with the magnificent Baccarat crystal chandelier. Opening his bible, he began to chant prayers of good tidings in his deep mellifluous voice. In his other hand he held his pectoral cross, slowly moving through the house and ritually pointing it at all parts of the rooms. The family silently followed him, occasionally making the sign of the cross for good measure.

Soon after, it was the turn of Abdul Hodja to bless the building. It had been Dimitra's suggestion that the premises should also be blessed in the Islamic tradition.

Abdul Hodja arrived wearing his white turban and flowing green cloak, followed by a boy leading a sacrificial ram with its gold painted ears and ornate decoration around its neck. Behind him walked the butcher, carrying a silver bowl inscribed with a verse from the Koran. In contrast to the long shiny beard of Father Yannakos, Abdul Hodja wore a short and tidy salt and pepper beard, and his neat moustache had been recently blackened. He smelt of musk and sandalwood.

At the entrance to the building, the Hodja summoned the boy to bring forth the ram. He proceeded to read from the Koran while the butcher firmly held it by the horns, took a sharp knife from his sash and deftly slit its throat. As the last gasps of air left the creature, the boy caught the warm crimson blood in the silver bowl.

'*Bismillahirahmanirrahim, bu bina sizin icin sansli olalim,*' the Hodja proclaimed, holding up the bowl of foaming dark red liquid. 'In the name of Allah, let this house be lucky for you.'

*

34

The small boy sat opposite Sophia, quietly swinging his legs. He was a delicate, fragile child and the red high-backed damask chair in which he sat seemed to dwarf him. He hummed a little nonsensical tune to himself as he played with his wooden toy, running the painted black and red wheels up and down his legs. Occasionally he looked up, watching his mother as she sat working behind her desk. When she had finished, she moved a mound of fabric samples from a stool and sat down beside him. Taking his little ankles in her hands, she drew his feet onto her knees, took one of his hands, and gently kissed it. She wished she could spend more time with him but the collection was taking all of her spare time.

'When the next few weeks are over we'll all go away for a holiday—perhaps to Grandmamma's home in Smyrna. Would you like that?'

His eyes lit up. Her face glowed with pride as she held his small hand. He was her first-born and a great joy to both parents. It was easy to love Leonidas. With his soft black curls framing his round face and with flushed rosy cheeks he was a sweet and adorable child. Long dark eyelashes accentuated his dark brown eyes; these were sensitive eyes that melted his mother's heart. How different he was to his sister. Sophia recalled how easily she had given birth to Leonidas. Even her pregnancy had been a joy. Deeply in love with Andreas, Sophia blossomed as the child grew inside her. People commented on her complexion and the ease with which she went about her daily work, and she hardly ever experienced morning sickness or felt the need for long rests, working until the final pangs told her that she was about to give birth. And when the child was delivered, his parents thought him the most perfect baby in the whole world.

Dimitra and Photeini cautioned Sophia and Andreas: 'Avoid excessive compliments. Too much talk about this boy's beauty and good health will attract the evil spirits.'

Whenever they came near the cradle, they would feign a spitting sound towards the child and check that the blue bead and clove of garlic still hung securely under the silk canopy. Throughout his first few weeks a never-ending procession of visitors came to the house to bless the child and his mother. They brought with them gifts of gold coins and were served coffee, tea, and special sherbets made of red dyed sugar and cloves. Sipping these, the women called on God to bless the mother's milk. And encouraged by Dimitra, they attempted to drive away the evil spirits by making a din and puffing clouds of smoke into the air from their narghiles.

Within a year Sophia became pregnant again, but this time it was a difficult pregnancy and a painful birth. The doctor was constantly at her bedside and both Abdul Hodja and Father Yannakos paid regular visits to the house. She became morose and lost interest in everything. For a while it seemed she would never be herself again. When the time came for the birth the delivery was long and arduous. Everyone became concerned as Sophia slipped in and out of consciousness. After a grueling ten hours she delivered a baby girl. The women threw up their hands uttering prayers of thanks. The midwife wrapped the child in linen and handed her to her weak mother. Propped up by a lace pillow, Sophia stared listlessly at her daughter: the birth had robbed her of all feeling.

Dimitra entered the room, walked over to her granddaughter and pulled back the cloth wrapped around the baby's head. Taking one quick glance at the infant, her face turned white. Emitting a little cry, she drew back in horror. Everyone looked at her. A sense of foreboding filled the room.

'This child has flaming hair,' she cried, and walked out of the room.

For Dimitra, this was the moment she hoped would never come. Remembering the prophecy of the fortuneteller all those years ago in Smyrna, every time there had been a birth in the family she waited silently and fearfully until she was sure that the infant did not have red hair. Each time she saw black or brown hair she uttered a small prayer. There had been so many births during those years, yet she was never moved to forget the prophecy. Walking into the garden to be alone, she collapsed on her knees, put her head into her hands, and for the first time since Jean-Paul's death, she sobbed uncontrollably.

'Kismet,' she said, crossing herself. 'We cannot escape our destiny.'

Sophia's thoughts were interrupted by a knock on the office door. Munire entered carrying a ledger. Sophia moved her son's legs away and walked over to her.

'Kyria Sophia,' said Munire, opening the ledger at a page with a long list of names. 'All the dresses are ready. We finished sewing the last one a few hours ago.'

Each dress had been allocated a name and a number and a neat tick denoted its completion.

'I've sent the girls home in preparation for tomorrow. Everything is ready for you.'

'Thank you,' Sophia replied, checking the list. She closed the book and looked at Munire. The woman was exhausted. 'Tomorrow is a big day; you should also go home and get some rest. You've worked so hard and I can't thank you enough.'

She heard the entrance door softly close and the sound of Munire's footsteps on the cobblestones as she walked down the street. Munire had been with her for over five years now, ever since the birth of Maria. It had been Photeini's idea to hire her, and having been trained by Photeini and Dimitra, her credentials were impeccable. With a refined countenance, pleasing looks, and possessing the utmost patience with clients, she soon progressed to Photeini's assistant. When she was offered the position of vendeuse at La Maison du l'Orient with Sophia, Munire was overjoyed and Sophia couldn't even begin to imagine how she would have survived without her.

In the quiet of the evening, Sophia thought about the launch of her collection, which was to take place the next day. For almost a year she had poured her heart and soul into this collection and in her view it was her best so far. Each year she labored on new ideas and each year her collections were well received, bringing a new clientele. This year she had taken a different approach. For the first time there would be two collections. The first she was sure would be well received but the other was a gamble, a show of artistic creativity that, if successful, would make La Maison du l'Orient one of the most influential and most sought-after design houses of the time.

The fashionable people of the Ottoman Empire adored anything Parisian. It had been this way for decades. Ever since Sultan Abdulaziz's visit to the World Exhibition in Paris in 1867 Turkish fashions had changed; at first this was with the ladies of the saray, and later with the wives and daughters of influential pashas and beys. In many ways it was seen as a means of looking forward—a transition phase as the empire tried to shake off its past in order to be accepted into the modern European world. In everything from politics through to the arts, fresh ideas were eagerly taken up by the influential elite of the empire's three greatest cities: Salonika, Smyrna, and Constantinople. By 1910, the ideology of Ottomanism had more or less collapsed and to hold onto the old values was considered by many as a backwards step.

In fashion, petticoats had long taken the place of baggy salvars and waistcoats. Where once a décolleté would have been scandalous, it was now acceptable and as the décolleté plunged, the Turkish fashion of covering the flesh with a transparent, filmy fabric added extra mystique, shrouding the sensuous curve of the bosom in a mist.

Every year, accompanied by Andreas, Sophia traveled to Europe. Taking the Orient Express, they stopped off in Vienna for a few days and then continued to Paris. Twenty-three years earlier in 1889, when the Paris–Constantinople line was finally finished, Dimitra had made the same trip. Paris was an exciting city and both Andreas and Sophia reveled in the art scene, eagerly soaking up each controversial movement. While there, Sophia visited cloth merchants and embroidery workshops. The turn of the century had seen a huge resurgence in embroidery in Europe and by 1912 there were at least three thousand embroidery workshops in Paris alone.

The last two years in particular had been of even greater interest to her. For a while, Sophia had admired the work of the great couturier Charles Worth. However, there was another name on the lips of every Parisian: Paul Poiret. It was his controversial theme of orientalism in particular which interested her. In 1910, the Ballets Russe performed *Scheherazade*. The opening night was a great sensation and orientalism, which prior to then had been the domain of a select few, notably artists and the aristocracy, was expanding to the wider populace. The following year, Paul Poiret threw a lavish party and named it 'The Thousand and Second Night.' All his guests were required to dress in oriental costumes. Sophia, Photeini, and Dimitra were asked to create costumes for four of their French clients, and by all accounts guests had remarked favorably on such exquisite creations, with their luxurious fabrics and attention to detail. As reports of the party filtered back to Constantinople, the three women smiled. Orientalism was something they had known all their lives but had never put a name to, and Dimitra in particular was the embodiment of everything Poiret's women aspired to be. Her graceful body had never been restricted by corsets and tight-fitting bodices. For her, loose-fitting salvars—now known as harem pants in Europe— flowing tunics, and velvet slippers were nothing new. She wore them daily and she wore them with panache.

Now Sophia was reversing the situation. She was ready to bring home the oriental spirit, back to the home that had nurtured it for almost five centuries, but she was unsure of just how it would be received in Constantinople.

'Mama, can I look at Papa's paintings again before we go?' Leonidas asked, knowing Sophia would never refuse him.

Sophia loved the interest her son showed in her work and secretly hoped that one day he would grow up to work by her side—the first male in the family to carry forward the name. But as much as Leonidas loved to see what his mother was doing, he really showed more interest in his father's painting, and Sophia knew that he was destined to follow in his father and great-grandfather's footsteps. He was at his happiest when sitting next to his father, drawing pictures with his crayons and charcoal.

At the end of each visit to the atelier, Leonidas always wanted to look at his father's wall murals and it became something of a ritual that either she or Andreas would take him by the hand and lead him up the grand marble staircase and into the Grand Salon. Here he would immerse himself in his father's work. The mural covered all the walls and was a never-ending view of Constantinople. From the domes and minarets of Sultanhamet, to Pera and Galata with its Genoese Watchtower, and across the waters to the hills and valleys of the Asian shore, a plethora of konaks and waterside mansions graced this bucolic setting. Flowing through all of this, the calm blue waters of the Bosphorus lay dotted with boats and ships under a gentle sky of soft delicate clouds. The Salon was grand but the ambiance was serene.

Leonidas liked to begin in the middle of the room where he would twirl around like a whirling dervish. 'Look, Mama. I am an eagle and I can see Constantinople from the sky.'

It was true; Andreas had given the observer a bird's eye view of one of the most majestic capitals of the world—the meeting point of East and West, the city of the Roman Emperor, Constantine—Constantinople. There was no beginning, no center, and no end.

Sophia followed her son as he pointed out the places he knew. 'Here is the Padishah's home,' he cried, pointing to the Dolmabahçe, the ornate, partly European and partly oriental palace of the Sultan. 'And there is the Topkapi, his old home, and this is ours.'

Peeking out of a clump of trees was the red-tiled roof of the house that Sophia and Andreas had built together. Its wide sweeping views over the water had given Andreas the inspiration for the mural. Sophia watched her son run around the room pointing out other places of interest. There was great excitement in his eyes and she knew he had transported himself into another world.

A full moon in a cloudless night sky looked down on Pera that evening, as eminent guests began to fill the reception hall at La Maison du l'Orient. To the music of Puccini, Offenbach, and Tchaikovsky, an army of well-trained waiters offered aperitifs to the guests. This was an evening in the social calendar that the fashionable set of Constantinople looked forward to all year. They knew they would not be disappointed. The guest list was impressive: princesses and pashas' wives accompanied by their distinguished husbands; Greek shipping magnates; Jewish and Greek bankers; German steel industrialists; Turkish and American tobacco entrepreneurs; English carpet traders; and Azerbaijani oil tycoons. All mixed with foreign dignitaries and painters, writers, and poets of the art world.

Carrying themselves with poise and dignity, the women arrived in beautiful shimmering gowns of satin and silk. Brilliant jewels set in necklaces, pendants, and earrings glinted under chandeliers. Boucheron, Fabergé, Lalique, Cartier, and Fontenay. The finest creations from these master jewelers graced the necks of beautiful women. For once, the guest list outshone that of the prestigious Hotel d'Angleterre and the Pera Palas.

As guests moved into the Grand Salon, the magnificence of the occasion became apparent. The air was filled with the fragrance of sweet-smelling tuber roses and elegant consoles were covered with crystal glasses, fine French wines, and champagne bottles in enormous silver bowls filled with ice. And for those for whom alcohol was forbidden, there were goblets of delicately flavored sherbets and chilled fruit juices of every description.

To rapturous applause, Sophia released her first collection. Daring, off-the-shoulder gowns with deep décolletés edged with ribbons of velvet and silk in a palette of watercolor pastels; creamy ivory, mother of pearl; the soft tones of wet pebbles and seashells; the translucent blues of the Aegean; the soft silvery greens of olive leaves as they shimmer in the hot sun. It was an elegant collection, romantic and overwhelmingly feminine.

Anticipation filled the air as the next collection was about to be released. The lights dimmed and a hush descended over the room. The orchestra began to play Rimsky-Korsakov and guests were immediately transported to the fabled palaces and deserts of the world of *Scheherazade*. One by one a mirage of Eastern beauties stepped into the Grand Salon. There were gasps of delight as these sensuous creatures, looking as if they had stepped out of a Persian miniature, moved gracefully through the room. Gone were the contrived silhouettes, and in their place were flowing silken salvars, fragile gossamer robes, and luxurious gold and silver embroidered kaftans held in place with finely woven sashes and lavishly worked silver belts. But it was the fabrics that gave these clothes their splendor. Extravagantly embroidered silks were layered with floating silk-chiffon and cobweb-thin metallic lace. The opulence was spellbinding. Here were the colors of the spice markets and of rich natural dyes. Perfumed in oils of sandalwood, musk, and Damask rose, their hair tumbling freely down their backs, occasionally twisted with strings of pearls or narrow colored sashes, the women exuded mystery combined with a touch of wild gypsy spirit.

Sophia received a standing ovation that swept over her and she breathed a sigh of relief. Resplendently dressed, her curvaceous figure was wrapped in a finely pleated pale turquoise silk dress, over which she wore a long robe in shades of lapis edged in silver. On her feet, she wore a pair of turquoise velvet slippers made by her grandmother; discreetly embroidered at the back was a tiny crimson silk tulip. In her long black hair, she had carefully positioned a Damask rose. At least one male guest was heard to say, 'A more beautiful spectacle was never presented to my eyes.' Thanking everyone present, Sophia conceded that this collection would not have been possible without the high-quality bespoke embroidery produced by Dimitra, Photeini, and their artistic and highly skilled team of embroiderers in Smyrna.

Champagne flowed into the early hours of the morning and Munire's appointment book overflowed. Sophia could not have been happier; she had reached the pinnacle of her career.

Nobody there that evening could possibly have foreseen that this was to be the last great collection ever shown at La Maison du l'Orient. The Ottoman Empire, already on its knees, was about to collapse, and as the tragedy unfolded millions of people would see their world torn apart with such devastating consequences that it would take generations to heal the pain and suffering.

After the last guests had departed, Sophia noticed Andreas and her father quietly disappear through the door behind the brocade curtains into the Petit Salon. Moments later they were joined by several other men, all members of a tightly knit circle of friends. The door was firmly locked behind them. Just lately Sophia had become accustomed to the clandestine meetings of the Philiki Etairia and yet they still gave her a deep sense of unease.

Something else happened that evening. Munire handed Sophia a calling card. 'You were busy when the gentleman left and he asked that you be given his card.'

*Grand Duke Nikolai Orlovsky*
*Prinkipo*

'I can't recall him, yet the name is familiar,' Sophia said, turning the card over for more clues about the man.

'His wife came to the atelier a few weeks ago for a fitting but never returned.'

She thought for a moment. 'Ah, yes, now I remember the name; the Grand Duchess Anastasia Orlovsky.'

Munire moved closer to her. 'His eyes were on you all evening, and he was adamant that I would give this to you personally.' She tapped the side of her nose to denote that this would remain their secret. Sophia put the card in her bag. She would go home alone again that night. The closed door was a sign that Andreas would be here until the early hours of the morning.

Later that night, undressed and ready for bed, Sophia sat at her dressing table brushing her hair. She looked at herself in the mirror and then at the empty bed. How long would these late-night meetings continue? She reached for her bag and took out the calling card. Looking at it again she smelt the faint scent of ambergris.

# CHAPTER 4

*Constantinople, 1912, the next day*

The exquisite scent of gardenias filled the early morning air on the terrace, as the family ate breakfast in silence. Despite the fact that the previous evening had been an overwhelming success, the atmosphere was tense. A maid cleared away the plates. Their breakfast of soft white cheese, boiled eggs, bread and butter, and conserves had hardly been touched. Sevkiye brought out a pot of freshly brewed tea. Sophia poured Andreas a cup, added a thin slice of lemon, and handed it to him.

She turned to her father. 'It's good to have you with us for a while, Papa. Will you stay, or will you return to Smyrna with mother?'

'I intend to stay for a while,' he answered, his eyes still fixed on his newspaper. 'I have business to manage. Your mother will return without me.'

'Well, Andreas and I are only too happy to have you with us. The children will be pleased too.'

It was not often that Soterios visited Constantinople. He was always too busy with his teaching in Smyrna, and Photeini usually made her visits without him, complaining that she could not tear her husband away from his books.

Andreas rose to leave. He approached his wife and put his hand gently on her shoulder. His look was one of seriousness and she became concerned.

'Come, Sophia,' he said softly. 'It's a beautiful morning. Let's take a walk in the garden.'

Aware that he wanted to talk out of earshot of the servants, she followed him down the pathway until they heard the splashing water from the fountain of the nymph. He turned and clasped her hands firmly.

'Sophia, I know you were worried last night, but there are things you should know. Last night we received news from Macedonia. Things are very bad; it's even worse than we thought, and the situation cannot be contained. You are already aware of the rumors but now we know for sure that they are true. It's only a matter of time before war breaks out and we believe it will be soon.'

Sophia listened intently. All morning her thoughts had drifted to the calling card but now Andreas had her full attention.

'Is that why Papa is staying on?'

'Yes. Nobody knows what's happening there better than your father.'

She knew her father still had relatives in Salonika and over the past couple of years he had returned, always, as he put it, 'on business.' During his youth, her father had attended the very first teacher-training college in Salonika and still kept in contact with some of his colleagues. Now he was a teacher at one of Smyrna's finest Greek schools and was considered by many within the Greek population to be a learned and distinguished man.

'There will be many more late nights and I want you to be strong. We must brace ourselves for the inevitable. The family must stay close, and remember...' He paused. 'Not a word to anyone outside the family. The Ottomans are nervous and will use any excuse to take it out on us.'

He reached out and plucked a pink rose, kissed it and gave it to her, planting a kiss tenderly on her lips. He was such a gentle, kind person and a wonderful husband, and Sophia felt ashamed that her thoughts had strayed to the mysterious man and his calling card.

The weeks passed and both Photeini and Dimitra returned to Smyrna. Her father stayed on and the nightly meetings continued to take place in the Petit Salon until the early hours of the morning. Sophia was busy with orders from her collection. Every day she and Munire juggled appointments, rushing to and from the workshops where the seamstresses worked until late in the evening.

As the scorching heat of summer turned into the mild days of autumn, Sophia used her work to distract herself from the political situation unraveling in the empire. Italy had demanded that Tripoli—the Ottoman Empire's last possession in Africa—be handed over to her, and on top of that, the Young Turks had granted Monastir, Scutari, Kosovo, and Ioannina to Albania. It was this last move in particular that had angered the secretly formed Balkan League. She saw less and less of Andreas, and her father was still with them. In late September, Soterios prepared for another short trip to Salonika, this time taking Andreas with him. Sophia begged him not to go but he told her he wanted to see for himself how things were. He assured her that he would be away for no longer than a few weeks. Nothing she could say would persuade him to stay.

For weeks after Andreas left, Sophia found it hard to shake off the idea that something bad would befall them. She had been raised in a family where politics played an important role in their lives. As a child, she often recalled her father telling her of the Philiki Etairia—the secret society established in Odessa in 1814 which was partly responsible for the uprisings which led to the Greek War of Independence. 'And now, we Greeks of Asia Minor also share that dream,' he had told her. 'One day in the foreseeable future, in our lifetime, we will once again join the Kingdom of Greece to form a Greater Greece, just as it was in the glorious days before the Byzantine world of Constantine collapsed under the might of the Ottomans.' In this ideal world, the Greeks would be free of the Turks, and be rulers in their own right once more. And just like Andreas, he had warned her never to voice these thoughts outside the family. 'It's far too dangerous,' he told her. 'The Turks' vengeance knows no bounds.'

It had been a while since the launch of her collection. Sophia had managed to push any thoughts about the Grand Duke to the back of her mind until one day she arrived at work later than usual and found Munire quite agitated. She handed her another calling card. 'He had urgent business to attend to and couldn't wait. But he did say he will return again tomorrow afternoon.'

Sophia looked at Munire. All of a sudden, tomorrow couldn't come quickly enough.

By two-thirty the following day, Sophia was unable to concentrate and she busied herself in the workshop with the seamstresses and embroiderers, checking hand-worked buttons and finely embroidered lengths of fabric. Munire watched her from a distance, aware that she was on edge. After a while she returned to the office, where from time to time she found herself at the window, waiting, watching. She was just about to take afternoon tea in her office when she heard the sound of a carriage draw up outside the building. Several minutes later, he was standing in front of her.

Munire introduced him. 'Grand Duke Nikolai Orlovsky.'

After all these weeks, she was suddenly face to face with him. He stepped forward confidently, taking her hand and kissing it politely.

'Madame, I kiss your hand and have great respect for you.'

He bowed and she smelt the sweet, earthy scent of ambergris again. Sophia felt the flush of her cheeks—something to which she was not accustomed. He apologized for not being able to converse in Greek or Turkish, assuring her that he was trying to learn both languages.

'Well, I speak no Russian,' she smiled, 'so French is fine.'

Sophia offered him a seat and instructed Munire to bring another tray of tea and cakes.

'It is most kind of you to see me at such short notice. I am here on business and will leave Constantinople tomorrow.'

'I see that you live in Prinkipo,' Sophia replied. 'I've been there on several occasions and I'm surprised we've never met.'

'Until recently, most of my time has been spent in Paris. On the other hand, my wife prefers to stay here.'

At the mention of his wife, Sophia wanted to know more.

'Ah, yes, I am told that the Grand Duchess Anastasia came for a fitting a few months ago and did not return. I do hope that she was not displeased with us in any way,' she remarked, quite concerned.

'That is why I am here. I'm afraid that my wife is very ill. We were hoping that her illness could be cured, but she seems to be getting worse. This is one reason why I will travel to Paris less often from now on.'

Sophia suddenly felt embarrassed. This man had a wife he obviously cared for. How could she possibly have thought there was another reason for his call? Over the years she had dealt with the occasional flirtations from a few of her clients' husbands. Why should this man be any different? Why should someone she barely knew have such an effect on her? She struggled to understand what had got into her.

'I'm sorry to hear that. Is there no treatment for her at all? We have fine doctors here and I'm sure that in Paris you would find the best.'

She couldn't quite bring herself to ask what the illness was. It seemed too impolite, yet she longed to know. Munire returned and placed the tray beside him. She was as intrigued as Sophia to know more about him.

Sophia studied him carefully. He was quite unlike anyone she had ever met. Tall and solidly built with an olive complexion—due more to the sun, she thought, than to birth. He wore his slightly oiled dark hair short and combed back, accentuating his face, which was as striking as his stature. His lips were well defined and his eyes penetrating—thoughtful one minute, playful the next—and he was exceptionally well groomed with a confident and aristocratic manner. Sophia was struck by the beauty of his voice. Deeply resonant, it took her breath away. There was no doubting that he was handsome, but she had met many charming and handsome men before yet there was something intensely charismatic about him.

'How can I help you?' she enquired.

'My wife would still like the gown she chose when she was last here. Is it possible that you could still make it for her?'

'Of course, we still have the details. When do you require it?'

'I would like you to make it a priority,' he answered. 'And I would like you to deliver it personally.'

It seemed that his eyes penetrated to the very depths of her soul. He held her gaze.

'It would be a pleasure. I shall look forward to it.'

He rose to leave. 'Madame Sophia, I am indebted to you. It has been wonderful to meet you.'

His eyes never left hers as he took her hand, raised it to his lips and kissed it again. Was it just her imagination that told her his lips seemed to linger on her flesh longer than propriety dictated? Whatever it was, Sophia was captivated. She hardly had time to compose herself when the children arrived with their governess from their Greek lessons.

'Mama…' Leonidas rushed over to his mother and she bent down to kiss him.

'How were your lessons today, *kriso mou*? And you, Maria, did you enjoy your lessons?'

She held out her hand to her daughter, but instead of taking it Maria brushed by her and sat in the chair, arms folded and legs swinging in a defiant gesture. Sophia was saddened that she didn't have the same closeness with her daughter as she had with Leonidas. The girl seemed to be in a world of her own. How could it be, she thought to herself, that someone as warm and passionate as she was could have given birth to such a cold child.

Sophia drew Leonidas to her and hugged him. He loved the way she always smelt of Damask rose. Today it seemed that the scent was more powerful.

# CHAPTER 5

Andreas and Soterios had still not returned when news started to filter through to Constantinople that Muslim farmers throughout the countryside of Macedonia and Thrace were being attacked, their crops burned, and their homes destroyed. At first these seemed to be sporadic outbursts that would most likely be contained. Sophia worried about them and tried to busy herself with her work and the children. Leonidas, in particular, kept asking when his father would be home.

The gown for the Grand Duchess was ready and Sophia made preparations to take it to Prinkipo. She was looking forward to the break. In her warm velvet coat edged with an enormous ermine collar, cuffs, and matching muff and hat, she found herself a seat on the upper deck of the ferry and watched the skyline of the Golden Horn slowly disappear from view as the ferry headed south, towards the Sea of Marmara.

Prinkipo, known as 'the large island,' was one of nine islands in the archipelago known as the Princes' Islands. It was here that some of Constantinople's wealthiest families built their summer homes. The ferry hugged the coastline of the Asian shore and a fresh autumn wind lifted the sea spray onto the deck. Sophia pulled her coat tighter. Two hours later, Prinkipo came into view and she felt a slight tingle run down her spine. It wasn't the cool weather. She realized that she had never really stopped thinking about the Grand Duke. In fact, he had become an obsession and she couldn't understand herself for feeling this way.

When she reached the island, the Grand Duke was pacing the portico of his mansion in anticipation of her arrival. Helping her down from the carriage, he kissed her hand once again—the same lingering kiss as before. Her senses already heightened, she noticed every small detail about him. Sophia had never met a man quite like him before. Intensely sensual, he oozed magnetism and she felt powerless to extricate herself from the spell he cast over her; it was as if the sun peeped through the dark clouds once more.

A radiant pale-apricot glow filled the room as the morning sun filtered through the lace curtains. The warmth of the sun on Sophia's cheeks woke her from a blissful sleep. She indulged herself by lying in bed for a while, thinking of the previous evening and how much she had enjoyed it.

Outside, two dogs began to bark. She heard a man's voice call and the barking stopped. Throwing on her robe and pinning up her tousled hair, she walked out onto the balcony just in time to see the Grand Duke disappear down the garden path with the dogs. Like a lazy cat she stretched her body to the sun and leaned on the balustrade, admiring the view.

The garden extended down towards the water where she could just make out small boats going about their daily business. The house was a blend of Italianate rococo and oriental, in shades of pale rose with white louvered shutters and recessed balconies; it was surrounded by a pretty garden. Pathways meandered through clumps of white daisies and a multitude of roses. Here and there massive palms dotted the landscape, adding an exotic feel. Birdsong filled the early morning air. It was a world away from the hustle and bustle of Constantinople and, as she discovered last night, a world away from the turmoil of the backgrounds of the Grand Duke and his wife.

Throughout the previous evening—over a fine Russian dinner supervised by the Grand Duchess herself—Sophia had learned much about the couple and she began to feel as if she'd known them for ages.

'Nikolai loves his vodka,' said the Grand Duchess. 'Chilled so that, as he puts it, the bottle "sheds a tear" on being brought to the table.'

He poured Sophia a glass and passed her a platter of Blinis and caviar.

'Do you know,' said Nikolai, 'in some fishing villages along the Volga, excess caviar is slapped onto the roofs of cottages, and I am told that it makes excellent waterproofing.'

'What a waste of good caviar,' she replied, laughing at the thought of it.

Sophia found the Grand Duchess to be a delightful person. She was a gentle woman with a kind and sweet disposition, yet Sophia detected a hint of sadness in her deep blue eyes. Both of them were active in the exiled Russian community, attending charitable evenings and helping other émigrés less fortunate than themselves.

'A place changes you,' said Nikolai sadly. 'We appreciate the kindness that has been shown to us here, and gradually we have learnt to reinvent ourselves.'

This was something Sophia found hard to imagine and she wanted to know more.

'Many people left Russia with nothing,' said Anastasia. 'We lived in fear of our lives after the 1905 revolution, and it's only a matter of time before the people rise up again.' She hesitated. 'And when they do, the country will be plunged into terror on a far greater scale than before.'

Sophia was familiar with Russian politics. It was not unusual for the educated classes to take an interest in countries that bordered the Ottoman Empire, and there had been many occasions when Soterios would discuss with her 'the Russian situation,' as he called it. The conflicts between the two empires were a recurring problem, and any hint of trouble in Russia could spill over and create another war.

'At one time, there was a chance that the empire might save itself,' said Nikolai.

He was referring to the momentous reforms of Tsar Alexander II when he freed the serfs, and was in the process of instigating more reforms until his untimely assassination almost twenty years later. 'Then his despotic son came to the throne and the country took a backwards step. After Tsar Alexander III died, Russia had the misfortune to see his son Tsar Nikolas II on the throne. He is a misguided man, someone who is guided more by God than by the wisdom of a good government,' he continued passionately. 'And now, the fool believes more and more in miracles. Russia needs a miracle to rid her of such an influence.'

'Nikolai,' his wife said softly. 'Perhaps Sophia doesn't want to hear all this.'

'No, please go on,' Sophia replied. 'I'm very interested. In some ways, your husband reminds me of my father. He is a quiet man, but becomes extremely passionate when politics are discussed. Please, Nikolai, do continue. I want to hear more about your country.'

'My country,' he continued, pouring himself another drink, 'despite a war which killed thousands, is one of the richest in the world, but the peasant on the land sees none of this wealth. His life is one of deep poverty, misery, and despair. When the revolution took place, I felt a great sympathy for those people. But rather than fix the situation, the Tsar and his advisors dreamed up the Russo-Japanese War, a bloody and needless disaster for us all. The Russian frontier was a sea of blood and the overwhelming defeat destroyed the soul of the Russian people. Afterwards, the struggle intensified. Left-wing terrorism put down by Tsarist oppression and years of religious and racial hatred knew no bounds.'

Sophia thought of the changes in her own country; of the violence and terror meted out to Christian minorities. She had witnessed the hatred, especially against the Greeks and Armenians, and she knew that there was still an undercurrent of dissent—something that her father said was ready to explode on their doorstep.

Anastasia listened in silence, occasionally looking at her husband and nodding in agreement.

'Yes,' he said, sadly. 'I supported the peasants and their need for reform, but they still killed my parents.'

Sophia felt a sense of unease but Nikolai wanted to continue.

'We were a prosperous family and could trace our ancestors back to the time of Peter the Great. We owned large estates of farming land near the Urals. One year, my father went to Baku in Azerbaijan and purchased an oil well. A short while after, he bought more and amassed a fortune, as many others did in that oil-rich country. My mother preferred to spend her time in St Petersburg, but my father eventually managed to persuade her to join him for a few months in Baku. On the way there she was kidnapped by bandits. My father paid the ransom—a huge amount at that time—and she was released, unharmed. The trauma was too great for her and they decided to return to St Petersburg. A few months later, they were taking a stroll along the Nevsky Prospekt when a bomb went off. My mother was killed instantly and my father died of severe wounds a few days later. The family leased out the oil wells, as Baku became too dangerous a place to live. It had become a microcosm of intrigue and everyone was viewed with suspicion. Wealth and privilege were no guarantee of safety. In fact it was the opposite. Then news reached us that the peasants on our land had murdered some of the overseers. Nowhere seemed safe.'

In a moment of tenderness, Nikolai took his wife's hand.

'And my dear Anastasia had the misfortune to witness the murder of her mother and two brothers.'

'Yes,' Anastasia responded sadly. 'It's true. We were driving out of the gates to our home when a stranger stopped our carriage. My mother saw that he had a gun and screamed at us to get down on the floor, just as he shot the driver. I managed to get down and I pulled a fur rug over myself. Then I heard my mother plead for our lives. A second later, he shot her through the head. My two brothers were hysterical and tried desperately to scramble out of the other side, but it was no use...he felt no pity for them. I lay on the floor, frozen with terror until a footman rushed to the carriage. I will never forget the weight of my mother's body as she slumped over me, with the blood on the carriage floor seeping into my hair and clothes. The murderer got away; we never knew who it was. My beloved mother was so beautiful. My brothers were so young. Dmitri was eleven, and Sergei only five. The nightmares are still with me. I miss them so much.'

It seemed that the family had been deliberately targeted. After that terrible event, Anastasia never went anywhere without her small-caliber pistol. She carried it in her muff or in her bag, but it was in her home that she would come to use it. The maid, a girl who Anastasia had known for years, brought in her breakfast tray. As she turned to leave the room, Anastasia saw her in the mirror, trying to take a gun out of a pocket underneath her apron. In an instant she reached under her pillow, pulled out her pistol and fired two shots, point blank, killing the maid instantly. The year after, she met Nikolai and agreed to marry him on the proviso that they begin a new life in another country. That country was to have been France, but Anastasia fell in love with Constantinople. Looking at this delicate, slender woman, Sophia could not imagine her killing someone, or even being a witness to such horrors.

'I know what you are thinking,' said Anastasia, reading her mind. 'You cannot possibly understand what comes over you—survival, yes, and a deep instinct to live that numbs the emotions. I pray, Sophia, that you never have to kill someone. War contaminates everyone and we are transformed into people we never thought we could become.'

Sophia found it hard to sleep that night. Their story disturbed her. But what preyed on her mind more than anything was Nikolai himself. It was there in their first glance, an instant arousal…and it frightened her. She had found herself hanging onto his every word, yet listening to their story consumed her with a deep sense of guilt.

Anastasia and Sophia were finishing breakfast when Nikolai joined them after his walk. The dogs were tall, lean, aristocratic wolfhounds that sat at his feet. Anastasia was subdued, her complexion pallid and her eyes swollen.

'I want to thank you again for the beautiful gown,' she said after a while. 'It fits me like a glove. God willing, you may create more wonderful dresses for me.'

She tried to stifle a cough, willing it to go away until she could hold out no longer. Covering her mouth with her handkerchief, she turned away from Sophia but it was too late. Sophia recognized the bright red stains on the fine white cotton. There was no way of concealing it any longer. Anastasia was dying of consumption.

Nikolai looked at her and said nothing. He pushed the chair away and walked out of the room, the dogs following him.

Sophia felt helpless. She knew that Anastasia needed her husband more than ever now. As hard as it was going to be, she resolved to avoid seeing him again.

# CHAPTER 6

*Constantinople, October 1912*

It was nine-thirty in the evening when Sophia and Munire heard loud banging on the atelier door.

'Who on earth can that be?' asked Munire, running to the door. 'The entire street will hear them.'

She had hardly unlocked the door when two of Andreas's close associates rushed inside. Sophia's first thoughts were of Andreas.

'What is it, Markos?' cried Sophia. 'What's happened?'

Markos and Lefteris ushered her into her office, closing the door behind them. In hushed tones, they gave her the news.

'Sophia, brace yourself; war has broken out. The group needs to meet. Please allow us to use the salon.'

Sophia felt her blood drain. There was still no news of Andreas and Soterios, and she had no idea where they were.

'It's bad. The Porte has failed to implement reforms in Macedonia and the time for peaceful negotiations is over.'

'But who exactly has declared war?' Sophia asked.

'The Balkan League: Montenegro, Serbia, Bulgaria, and Greece,' replied Markos.

They heard a soft click as the entrance door to the atelier closed. The men looked at each other.

'It's alright,' Sophia reassured them. 'It's only Munire. She's gone home.'

It was hard for Sophia to keep certain things away from Munire. They had been friends for too long, but Sophia realized the less Munire knew of the group's activities, the better it was for all of them. For her part, Munire never pried.

She slumped onto the chair, her heart pounding. 'What about Andreas and my father? Have you heard anything?'

'Only that they left Salonika almost a week ago. They'll be safe. There are people who will look after them.'

Somehow their words failed to calm her. Lefteris reached inside his jacket and pulled out a map of the Balkans. He brushed aside the samples on Sophia's desk and spread it out, smoothing its tattered edges. The map was covered in scribbles, circles, and coffee and raki stains. The three of them huddled over it as Lefteris pointed to strategic areas.

'Yesterday, the Bulgarian army marched into Thrace. Three units of the Third Army were deployed to form a triangle by the Tùndzha and Marica rivers. The Bulgarian High Command has deployed the Second Army westward to contain Adrianople. The Third Army is advancing southwards towards Kirk Kilisse. Soon, the lines of communication will be severed in Thrace. The Bulgarians far outnumber the Ottoman Army. It won't be long before they're pushed back to Constantinople.'

'What about the rail lines in Macedonia? Surely the Ottomans will mobilize their troops quickly,' suggested Sophia.

'They are trying to break these lines,' replied Markos. 'The Serb High Command is to deploy armies under Crown Prince Alexander in the upper Morava Valley and advance towards the Ovce Polje region. General Bozidar Jankovic's Third Army is directed to march towards Pristina and then to Skopje, and there is to be another Serb division and one Bulgarian division which is to be directed west from Kyustendil.'

He circled an area on the map vigorously. 'And then all three armies are to unite at Ovce Polje where it is expected that the Ottoman army will be cut off from Monastir to Nis.'

'And Salonika…?' Sophia asked. 'If the Ottomans lose it, the consequences don't bear thinking about.'

Markos knitted his brows in a frown. 'We have to be strong. It's inevitable that the city will fall. The Hellenic army has made it their prime objective to capture it.'

'When the lion is weak,' Lefteris laughed, 'the wolf attacks. Isn't that an old Turkish saying? When the Ottomans retreat, it will be an unimaginable disaster for them.'

'And what will happen afterwards?' asked Sophia. 'The hatred between the Bulgarians and the Greeks is notorious. Even my father feels animosity towards them.'

'For the moment, we must stand united. We have a common enemy. This is a matter of life or death.'

Lefteris picked up the map, carefully folded it, and put it back inside his jacket.

'So, Sophia, will you allow us to meet in the Hellenic room?'

The small adjoining room to the Grand Salon was known by all in the atelier as the Petit Salon, but to members of the family and the Etairia it was known as the Hellenic room. It was agreed that the group could meet after Munire and the seamstresses and embroiderers left in the evening. Sophia would signal the all-clear for them to enter by leaving a pink tea hat on a hatstand in her window. As an extra precaution, she suggested that if for any reason there was a risk of danger—however small—there would be no hat at all. She gave them a set of keys and made them agree that they would be out of the building by four o'clock in the morning so as not to arouse suspicion from guests or staff at the Pera Palas.

The following morning, Sophia went upstairs to the Grand Salon. She pulled back the red brocade curtains, unlocked the door to the adjoining Hellenic room and surveyed it. There was nothing to suggest a meeting had taken place there the night before. This was Andreas's most treasured room—even more so than the Grand Salon. Sophia liked to call the murals covering these walls his folly. Here, in all its glory, the mythology of ancient Greece unfolded. In an Arcadian scene of mountain peaks, steep valleys, and pale blue skies dwelt the pantheon of gods where Zeus reigned supreme. Ruins of the classical world depicted the Parthenon with the goddess Athena holding her emblem, the screech owl, and nestling in the firs below Mount Parnassus was the Oracle of Delphi with Apollo, the God of Light. Like a frieze from the Parthenon, lesser gods played the lyre and the flute. The scene might be of the classical world, but the decor was distinctly oriental. Dimitra's hunting carpets covered the floor and a divan surrounded the walls and was covered in opulent silk bolsters and cushions and, except for a few low tables and the occasional oil lamp, the room was sparsely furnished. Sophia ran the tips of her fingers gently over the figure of Pan, recalling the time Andreas painted it and how he made hundreds of sketches, and his excitement at seeing the images come alive. She could even smell the fresh paint again.

Locking the door behind her, she returned downstairs to the workroom where Munire was trying to calm a group of hysterical women.

'Kyria Sophia. What are we to do? The women have just heard that the Bulgarians have attacked Thrace. They're frightened. Some haven't even turned up.'

Sophia tried to reassure them that Constantinople would be un-harmed.

'My two brothers are in the army,' cried one tearfully. 'I have already lost another brother to the Bulgarians in a previous skirmish.'

'And my relatives live in Thrace. What will happen to them?' cried another.

Sophia was at a loss what to do but her assurances seemed to calm them and they returned to work.

'The Greek women have not arrived at all,' whispered Munire, when they were alone.

The women were under no illusion about what would transpire if the Ottomans lost. Sophia was too exhausted to think about it. She had hardly slept thinking about Andreas and her father. Their safety consumed her.

For the first time in years, Sophia found herself with time on her hands. Very few of her customers came to order new gowns and she saw even less of her foreign customers. Many stayed away from Constantinople altogether. Rail travel was unthinkable in a war zone and with the Greeks blockading ports in the Aegean, fashion was the last thing on their mind. As the days passed, the sewing room came to a standstill.

Almost a month into the war, Sophia received a letter from her father. It had been carefully concealed in a bolt of silk sent by Photeini. She went into her office and anxiously opened it. Her hands trembled as she read it.

My dearest daughter,

I arrived home safely after a long and exhausting journey. We left Salonika a few days before the Bulgarians attacked Thrace. We had just left Kavala when it became too dangerous to continue. In the countryside, the skirmishes had already begun. Bulgarian farmers attacked Turkish villages and in retaliation, the Turks killed Greeks and Bulgarians. I felt it was impossible to go on without risking our lives. Unlike Andreas, I speak little Turkish and my 'Greekness' would have put us in danger. We parted ways outside Kavala. I found a Greek fisherman willing to take me to the island of Thasos. From there, I hid for days until finally another boat took me to Lesvos.

My dear daughter, I am happy to have lived long enough to see my city finally liberated. Byzantium awakes once more.

I pray to God that Andreas returns safely home to you.

Your loving Papa

A feeling of nausea overcame her. She did not want to think the worst. Her mind was a whirlpool of thoughts. She told herself that Andreas was a cautious person and would never take risks.

Her thoughts strayed to Nikolai. How could she have thought of him when Andreas was risking his life? None of it made sense. Was her family going to suffer...as thousands of others had? In a state of despair, she grabbed her coat and walked out of the atelier towards the Grande Rue de Pera. She needed air and, more importantly, she needed to lose herself in the crowds.

By early December, the cold biting winds from the north added to the already despondent mood in the Laskaris household. Frequent snowstorms and blizzards kept people indoors, only venturing out for long enough to buy a simmit or a glass of warm nutritious salepi from the street vendors who were braving the weather.

Sophia spent more time at home with the children. They constantly asked when their father would return but they were nevertheless pleased to see more of her. She was constantly informed of the progress of the war by Markos and Lefteris, who still used the Hellenic room to meet during the night. Although the war had not gone well for the Ottomans, Sophia felt this was only the beginning of something even more disastrous. Of what she was not sure, but she felt it in her bones.

On December 4, an armistice was declared between the Balkan League, excluding Greece, but it was short-lived. Except for Adrianople, Thrace was now in the hands of the Bulgarians. The Ottomans had been pushed back to the outer defenses of Constantinople. Hassim Taxim Pasha, the Governor of Salonika, surrendered to the Greek army on November 7. The following day, the Greek Seventh Division marched into the city. One thousand officers and twenty-six thousand soldiers were taken prisoner. Salonika's Muslims kept off the streets as the Greek army was welcomed amid wild cheers of jubilation by the Greeks. Calm seemed to have been quickly restored, but still hundreds of Muslim families fled from the city, heading for Constantinople.

In November, Ottoman military resistance in Macedonia finally collapsed. By the time the armistice was signed, the Ottoman Empire— whose vast European lands once extended to the gates of Vienna—was now reduced to the garrison of Ioannina and Albania, where they still held Scutari.

As times grew harder, Sophia recognized that there might be a niche for simple, cost-effective clothes and with Munire she worked on a range of ready-to-wear clothes. Although she missed the fun and creativity of her earlier extravagant collections, she found her new work challenging and was immensely grateful to have any work at all. The week before Christmas, after the last person left the atelier in the evening, Sophia went into her office to prepare the pink tea hat for the window. Arranging it on its stand, she noticed a man standing in a narrow doorway next to the Pera Palas. It was then that she remembered seeing someone loitering there a few nights earlier, but she had never thought any more about it until now. In an attempt to have a better look, she took a while to arrange the hat into position, turning it this way and then the other. The light from the street lamp threw shadows across the road, but she could clearly see the man partially hidden in the doorway and was convinced that he was watching the building.

Moving away from the window, she turned out the light and standing in semi-darkness, she looked back across the road. He was now out of sight but she could see his shadow. Turning off all the other lights in the building, she lit a small oil lamp and made her way towards the Grand Salon. At this time of the evening, Ali Agha would be arriving to take her home. What would he think if he saw the building in darkness? Hurrying towards the Hellenic room, she unlocked the door, put down the lamp, and walked to a small window on the far side of the room. From this vantage point she could look down into the street. Across the road, the figure still remained partially huddled in the doorway. She quickly removed the hat. Minutes later, Ali Agha arrived and seeing the atelier in darkness, jumped down from the phaeton and hammered loudly on the door.

'Kyria Sophia, Hanim Efendi,' he called out. 'Are you there?'

Sophia quickly left the premises and found that the carriage blocked her view of the doorway. As the phaeton pulled away, she endeavored to take a better look but it was too late: the man had vanished. Until she could find out who he was, it was far too dangerous for the Etairia to meet there; and so, for the time being, the pink tea hat was not put back on display.

Lefteris and Markos remained deep in thought as Sophia recalled the incident of the man in the doorway.

'A quarter of an hour at least,' she told them. 'That's how long I watched him; goodness knows how long he was there before that.'

In the darkness, Markos looked out of the window of the Hellenic room. He was agitated.

'Do you think this has something to do with Andreas?' she asked.

'Have you told anyone at all?' asked Lefteris pointedly. 'Munire—what does she know?'

'Nothing at all, she doesn't know that meetings take place here. Nobody has a reason to be near this room. Only we have a key.'

Sophia felt a tinge of anger that they should doubt her integrity.

'Well, one thing is for certain. We've got to find out who he is and that means setting a trap,' said Markos gravely.

Sophia arranged for the two men to enter the atelier by the rear entrance. That meant scaling the wall of the adjoining garden at the rear of the premises, but being strong and athletic, this did not present them with a problem. They would then wait patiently until the man came again. The rest of the area was to be monitored by other members of the group.

More than two weeks passed before the man came again. Outside, the temperature had dropped below zero and soft snowflakes began to fall, covering the road in a ghostly white film under the lamp light. Casting his long dark shadow across the snow-white road, the man watched the premises for almost an hour. This time there was little doubt about it. He was clearly watching the place.

Keeping watch from the Hellenic room, Markos also saw him. Together they left the atelier and resisting the urge to look in the man's direction, they walked arm in arm down the street away from the busy thoroughfare of the Grande Rue de Pera until eventually they turned into a quiet side street. Taking the bait, the stranger followed them. In a nearby alleyway, Lefteris—accompanied by another member of the Etairia—lay in wait in the darkness. Within seconds, the stranger was overpowered. Not far away, Ali Agha waited with the phaeton. Leaving Sophia in safe hands, Markos ordered him to take her home as quickly as possible.

'Be careful,' she cautioned him nervously. 'I couldn't bear it if anything happened to you.'

In the shadows, the stranger trembled in fear for his life. Blood poured from a deep cut to his forehead and spots of blood splattered the fresh snow. Lefteris had the man's head pulled back and held his dagger at his throat while Panayiotis kicked him in the stomach for good measure, assuring him there was worse to come if he didn't talk. There was not a shred of doubt about what these men were capable of doing. The man spoke Greek but Markos detected a Turkish accent. Another severe beating in which he almost lost an eye made him confess that he worked for a branch of the secret police.

'They forced me to do this,' the man cried. 'But I am only one of many. If you kill me, there will be others to take my place. This war has shown us where the loyalty of the Greeks lies.'

Panayiotis kicked him again, this time in the mouth. His teeth shattered and blood trickled out of his mouth.

'How long have you been watching us?' asked Markos, calmly lighting a cigarette, as if he had all the time in the world.

The stranger began to choke on his own blood. Lefteris forced him to sit up and answer.

'Two months ago, your friend was caught in Thrace. He was taking shelter in a Bulgarian village. He would have met the same fate as the villagers if it had not been that he was recognized by an old acquaintance—an officer from Constantinople who allowed him to leave unharmed. As a Greek in a war zone, he should have perished along with the Bulgarian dogs. The unfortunate officer was condemned to death by his superior when he heard the story.'

'Where is this man now?' asked Markos, exhaling the cigarette smoke into the cold night air.

The man said nothing. He was fast losing consciousness.

Lefteris held his head tightly. In a flash, he sliced off his ear. The man writhed in agony.

'Piece by piece, I will cut you until you tell us,' Lefteris hissed in his other ear.

Markos knelt down. He looked into the man's face. His eyes were full of terror.

'I am asking you for the last time. Where is that man now?'

'After he left, no one saw him again. That's the truth. I'm begging you, please have mercy. That's why I was told to watch the building. We don't know where he is.'

Tears mixed with the blood and the sweat of panic on the man's face. Markos stood up, looked at Lefteris, and nodded. Seconds later, the man slumped onto the wet cobblestone, his throat cut with Lefteris's razor-sharp dagger.

# CHAPTER 7

*Constantinople, February 1913*

At any time of the day, Zaharoplasteion Olympia in the Grande Rue de Pera bustled with customers. This elegant cake shop and café with its decorative wall mirrors, marble tables and bentwood chairs was famous throughout the city for its vast array of syrup-drenched confectionary and paper-thin pastries. Sophia was a regular there, but on this particular day she had an important meeting with Markos. Welcoming her with his usual good cheer, the owner, Constantine, showed her to a table in a quiet corner of the café, well out of earshot of other customers. Markos was already waiting for her.

'Your usual, Kyria Sophia?' Constantine asked, pulling out a seat for her. Within minutes, a smartly clad waiter with slicked-back hair placed two *kafe metrios* and two slices of custard-filled *galatoboureko* in front of them.

'So, it is possible Andreas is still alive, isn't it?' Sophia asked Markos. 'There is still hope.'

Markos ignored her question.

'This is only going to get worse. Somehow, the Turks will find a way of making us pay for their losses. Of that I am sure.'

'How could it be,' she answered, thinking back to the time when the Young Turks had promised change in the empire, 'that we were promised something and the next moment the situation worsened? It only seems like yesterday that Enver Bey made his famous speech in the Place de la Liberte in Salonika promising us all equality.

'"Today, the arbitrary ruler is gone. Bad government no longer exists. We are all brothers. There are no longer Bulgarians, Greeks, Serbs, Romanians, and Jews. Under the same blue sky, we are all equals, we are all proud to be Ottomans." Do you remember that speech?'

'How could I forget? Everyone desired peace but it was too late. The bird had flown. We were deceived…once again.'

'Why are we unable to resolve our differences without all this bloodshed? Where will it end?'

'It's a fact, Sophia: men must die in order to win the freedom they deserve. Don't you want your son to grow up in a better world? Do you wish for Leonidas' subservience under the Turks?'

Sophia cautioned his outspokenness. He looked at her sternly.

'Your father often talks of the people who have influenced the Committee of Union and Progress. How are we to deal with such supremacist ideals? Ziya Gokalp himself, the ideologist of the Young Turks, has already said that coexistence, willing or not willing, is no longer possible. And Namik Kamal, another member of the party, preached that compromise with the Christians will only happen when we accept their position of dominance. The CUP listens when people like this talk. We cannot trust them.'

The groundswell of nationalism that had begun over a century earlier now permeated their lives; it was inescapable. Everywhere, people were aligning themselves with one ideology or another.

'Where are the Great Powers when we need them? Can't they exert more influence?'

'They're looking after their own interests,' scoffed Markos. 'This ceasefire has given everyone time to realize their grievances. Even the Turks have their pride. Do you think they will forgive us for their loss in Salonika—the home of the Young Turks—or in Adrianople, where they first set their dreams on conquering the Balkans and Constantinople hundreds of years ago? No. They will wait for an opportunity for revenge.'

Sophia listened as he spilled forth his prophecies of doom.

'Look at the faces of the thousands of refugees clogging the streets now. Will they forget?'

She knew he was right. For months now, a torrent of terror-stricken refugees fleeing the war-torn lands of their ancestors had been steadily streaming into the city. Societies sprang up everywhere trying to help them; she had donated to the various charities. Added to these long lines of human misery were the exhausted and wounded remnants of a once-proud army, their twisted faces and empty eyes displaying the sickening horror of the battlefield.

'They have been humiliated,' said Markos.

Sophia thought about her fortunate life. Her family had enjoyed the protection and patronage of sultans and pashas and she found it hard to conceive that these people could possibly turn on them. Markos read her thoughts.

'Not everyone has had your privileged life, Sophia, but don't take it for granted. This brings me to something else. For the moment, it's better for the Etairia to stay away from the atelier. It's far too dangerous for all of us. We have another room over the workshop of Georgos the watchmaker.'

Sophia knew him well. Georgos had been a master watchmaker until his eyesight deteriorated, and his wife of many years, Xanthe the Barren, was a beautiful woman in her youth. Many thought her barrenness the result of the evil eye and after years of slavish attention to traditional folk cures with their potions and charms, the couple finally accepted that they would be childless. Within walking distance from the Grande Rue de Pera, their house was situated in a shady courtyard next to the premises of Lame Niko the cobbler and Hagop the Armenian saddler.

'One of our group, Yianni Mandakis, looks after his father's coffee house there—O *Galazio Mati*, The Blue Eye. Being open all day and late into the evening, Yianni keeps an eye on everyone who enters the courtyard. I trust them like my brothers.'

Markos escorted Sophia back to the atelier. Nikolai's black carriage was waiting outside the entrance. Her heart pounded. What could have brought him back to La Maison du l'Orient? He was already waiting for her in the reception hall with Munire. She would have recognized his scent anywhere.

'What brings you to the city?' asked Sophia, overjoyed to see him once again. 'And how is the Grand Duchess? I do hope she is well.'

It had been a few months since Sophia sent Anastasia a new gown. The request came via another Russian acquaintance from Prinkipo and she had been somewhat relieved that she did not have to face Nikolai again. But now here he was, standing in front of her and she felt her body stir again just as it did before.

'That's why I'm here,' he answered solemnly. 'I have something to tell you.'

Sophia ushered him into her room.

'Is everything alright, Nikolai? You look weary.'

He walked over to the window and stared outside, his back to her.

'Nikolai, what is it? What has happened?'

She walked over to him and tenderly touched the back of his arm. He turned towards her. His eyes glistened as he fought back the tears.

'Anastasia is dead, Sophia. She died two weeks ago.'

'Dear Nikolai. I'm so sorry.'

On the verge of tears, he told her how only six weeks earlier he had sent her away to a sanatorium in Switzerland. 'There was nothing more that could have been done. I wanted the best for her, but we both knew that it was too late and she knew that I could not bear to see her suffer. I think that in the end she agreed to go to spare me her death.'

Sophia listened sympathetically as he poured his heart out.

'My poor Anastasia suffered so much after we left Russia. Her heart was broken. She did not only die of consumption, she died of a broken heart for her country. I felt helpless and to blame.'

Sophia had sensed the melancholy in Anastasia and knew that nothing could cure her tuberculosis. And she understood that her love for Nikolai was too great to let him see her suffer. His news also made her aware of just how fragile her own mind had become. She wanted to pour her heart out to him, to tell him about the months without Andreas, and the uncertainty of it all.

'Forgive me,' he continued, pulling himself together. 'I'm burdening you with my sorrow. Tell me, what is your news? How is Andreas? Has he produced more wonderful paintings?'

Sophia did not answer but her body language gave her away.

'It's alright, Sophia. I'm a friend.'

She choked back the tears until her throat threatened to burst. Nikolai reached for her hand and clasped it tightly. Any other man would have thought this gesture impolite, but he wasn't just any man and they both knew that. Sophia felt her body respond. She was vulnerable—and so very tired of putting on a brave face for the world. It had been a long time since a man had shown her such tenderness and compassion.

'I heard he went away. You don't have to say more if you don't want to; I just want to know if he has returned and if he's safe.'

She looked at him, unable to restrain herself any longer. Finally, after all the months of bottling up her sorrow, the tears rolled down her cheeks and her chest heaved with pain and anguish. He pulled her close to him, holding her tightly in his arms and stroking her hair to ease her pain. She cried for herself, for her children, for the burden of keeping her business going under the strain, for the sadness that now enveloped her once-charmed and happy life. Most of all she cried for the uncertainty of the future.

For a while, neither spoke. There was little to say. They were as one, their deep losses drawing them together. Sophia felt secure in his arms. His strength invigorated her. Believing that she could trust him completely, she unburdened herself, telling him everything—about the secret society, Andreas and her father's journey to Salonika, Andreas's subsequent disappearance, and of the atelier being watched. She knew she was breaking a great taboo by telling him all this. She felt that this man who had suffered so much in his life would understand. He listened sympathetically without uttering a word.

Munire left early that evening. She left without a word of goodbye to her mistress, sensing that she did not want to be disturbed. Knowing that they were alone, Sophia took Nikolai upstairs, pulled back the red brocade curtains, and unlocked the door to the inner sanctum that was the Hellenic room. Nikolai was taken aback. He had been an admirer of Andreas's work since seeing the walls of the Grand Salon, but when he saw the majestic murals in this room, he was speechless.

'Only a man with a passion for his subject could paint such a magnificent work of art,' he observed. 'It's truly a great pity that a masterpiece like this should be hidden away.'

She prepared him a light meal of olives and cheese accompanied by a fine bottle of wine, just as she had done so many times for Andreas. It seemed so long since she had enjoyed such pleasant company. Whether it was the wine that unleashed their inhibitions or the profound hunger in his eyes, Sophia was intoxicated in a way she never thought possible. Her heart pounding, her body burning with desire, she gave herself over to him completely. His lovemaking unleashed a passion in her she never knew existed. It all seemed so natural, as if they had known each other for a long time. When it was over they lay in each other's arms, neither one wanting to break the spell.

After a while Nikolai sat up. 'There is something I wish to say. Dear woman of my heart, from the moment I laid eyes on you, I knew I loved you. Since that time, I am ashamed to say that I thought only of you. I tried to put you out of my mind, but it was impossible. Often I have gone to bed tormented with a heavy heart, so heavy that I thought I could not carry on. And then when you came to see us, I saw that same look in your eyes and it gave me hope.' He paused for a moment to brush a lock of hair away from her forehead. 'I love you but I can never have you...'

Sophia sat up, and put her finger on his lips.

'Sshhh...Not another word. Let's just bathe in the joy we give each other. I can be content with that.'

He shook his head. 'There's something else. I'm going to sell the house in Prinkipo.'

She looked at him anxiously. 'But why? Where will you go? Surely you're not leaving Constantinople?'

'Since we're confiding in each other I will tell you—although I am greatly embarrassed. I cannot afford to keep the house. The money from our investments in Russia has gradually dried up and the treatments and sanatorium costs for Anastasia have left me impoverished. So you see, my dear Sophia, I am to join the ranks of other Russian émigrés that I have sought to help in the past. What use is a grand title without money?' He laughed loudly—the laugh of irony that she had heard in Prinkipo. 'Through my contacts I will try to get work with one of the European companies.'

Sophia ran her bare toes through the supple velvet pile of the hunting carpet and thought about what he had just told her. She couldn't bear the thought of him leaving.

'Do you mind if I ask you something?' she said, with her gaze fixed on a gold leopard entangled in a colorful field of arabesques. 'Why don't you consider helping me at La Maison du l'Orient? Work is building up again and with Andreas away, I really need someone to manage the business. With your skills and your superb command of languages you would be ideal, and we might even bring back our old European customers.'

He looked at her hard before answering.

'That's a very generous proposal, but I suggest you discuss it with your family in Smyrna first. It's a big step for them to have someone like me in the business—a foreigner and not a family member. If they agree, I will gladly accept your offer.'

'The crow does not take the eyes of another crow,' said Dimitra, in response to Photeini's concern at employing Nikolai. 'There are no other men in the family to fulfill this role, and Leonidas, God bless the child…in the absence of his father he needs a good role model. Yes, he is Russian, but he is one of us.'

'By that I presume you mean of the Orthodox faith,' Photeini replied.

'Albeit, the Russian Orthodoxy, yes. The Russians have long offered protection to the Christians of the empire. We have that much in common and I would have thought that you, of all people, would find that comforting. What has Soterios to say about all this?'

'I know he instructed Markos to check his background, and to date he can find no reason to doubt the man's sincere friendship with Sophia. He considers him to be a man of the utmost integrity.' She paused for a moment. 'But what about idle gossip, Mother?'

'An idle tongue always wags, my daughter. How many flourishing businesses do we know of in Smyrna who promote outsiders of the family to positions of importance? Many. We may still see camel trains walking through our streets, but modernization of commerce throughout our major cities is essential. There is much to manage and Sophia cannot possibly do all that by herself.'

'Well, I suppose a man of Nikolai's standing and intellect would be well suited to the challenge,' replied Photeini. 'And there is always the possibility that when Andreas returns, Sophia will have his help and guidance again.'

Dimitra studied her daughter carefully. '*If* he returns, in what sort of condition do you think he will be? After everything that has happened in Thrace, do you suppose he will be the same Andreas as the one who left? Wars are not for the soft-hearted.'

The women had made this special journey to Constantinople to meet Nikolai, and in the end they gave him their seal of approval. Sophia noticed that despite her mother's slight reservation, Dimitra delighted in his company. In fact she was quite charmed by him. She took this as a positive sign, as her grandmother was an astute judge of character.

Nikolai was formally invited to dinner with the family to cement his position with the company. After the meal they retired to the drawing room where Dimitra engaged Nikolai in conversations about Russia. At one point, Sophia heard her grandmother laughing loudly. She had not heard her laugh like that for a while now; the recent political troubles had weighed too heavily on her mind.

'My dear child,' Dimitra called to Sophia. 'Come here and listen to this.'

Sophia smoothed the folds of her dress and sat next to her.

'Do you know what Nikolai has proposed? He thinks that you should stop using the phaeton and buy a car...and he wants Ali Agha to learn to drive it, like a chauffeur!'

'Does he, Grandmother? And how does the Grand Duke propose to pay for this?'

Photeini noticed her daughter bristle with anger at not being consulted first.

'Sophia, forgive me if I offended you. It was an idea, a very good idea if I may be as bold as to suggest it. It is both fashionable and a necessity in today's world, and a sensible thing too. I am sure that if Andreas were here he would be the first to agree,' Nikolai replied.

'I agree,' her grandmother added, blowing a cloud of sweet-smelling tobacco smoke into the air.

At the mention of Andreas, Sophia bristled even more.

'I ask again, who is going to pay for this?'

'I am,' he replied, 'with the proceeds from the sale of the house in Prinkipo. I have taken the liberty of ordering it from Germany already. When it arrives, please consider it as my gift to you for your kindness. If you choose not to accept it, then I will sell it.'

'And what about Ali Agha? He has the old ways. You can't teach an old dog new tricks.'

'I will personally take care of that. He's an intelligent man. Don't underestimate him. You never know, he may be even happier.'

Sophia shrugged. For a brief moment, she wondered if she had made a big mistake. Then she looked at him and knew that was not so. Photeini looked at her daughter and then at Nikolai and knew that before long the car would be hers.

'I think it's an excellent idea, Nikolai,' Dimitra concluded. 'An excellent idea indeed. Bravo!'

Their bonhomie was suddenly interrupted by loud screams coming from upstairs. Over the past few weeks, Leonidas had begun to experience recurring nightmares which left him shaking and terrified. The governess had even moved her bed into his room for reassurance, but still the dreams persisted. They were always the same dreams. He would hear his father's voice calling his mother, who walked out of the house in search of his father, never to return. His dream always ended with him standing on the doorstep alone, just in time to see his mother vanish, leaving only a pair of her shoes. As he ran towards the shoes he would wake, screaming.

His sister, Maria, taunted him at every opportunity, calling him a crybaby. Since Andreas's disappearance, Leonidas clung to his mother even more and despite Sophia's constant affirmations of love towards her daughter, Maria began to despise her brother.

Dimitra feigned a spitting sound.

'Outside a doll, inside the plague,' she remarked, referring to Maria. 'See how she torments the boy. That child is a curse.'

# CHAPTER 8

*Constantinople, Spring 1913*

The dark, damp days of winter gradually gave way to the soft warm days of spring, as Sophia waited for news of Andreas. The First Balkan War ended in April 1913. The Greeks had finally taken Ioannina—once the home of the infamous Albanian Ali Pasha. And Adrianople was conquered by the Bulgarians, thus concluding the Thracian campaign. In another blow to the Ottomans, Chios—once the jewel in the crown of the Mediterranean Islands, together with its wealthy neighbor, the olive-rich Island of Lesvos— were ceded to the Greeks.

Amid cheers of 'Byzantium lives once more,' another tragedy struck Salonika. In March 1913, the sixty-eight-year-old King George of Greece was killed. Fearing reprisals, the Moslems of Salonika bolted themselves behind closed doors until calm was restored. It was soon discovered that the murder was not politically motivated but had been the random act of an insane man. All the same, the response showed just how precarious the political situation remained.

After breakfast, Sophia took her customary stroll through the garden. Sitting by the fountain of the nymph, she recalled the day that Andreas plucked a rose for her and told her he was going away. It all seemed so long ago. The fruit trees were bursting with sweet-smelling blossoms once again, and the air was redolent with the perfume of spring flowers. She saw Selim the gardener in the distance. He still tended her garden as if there had been no war. What did he think about it all? It dawned on her that she had never even bothered to ask him. There was a dull ache in her heart and she realized that had it not been for Nikolai, she would have drowned in a sea of melancholy.

'Liberty, equality, fraternity,' she said aloud to herself. 'Damn these false promises. Liberty? At what cost?'

Her thoughts were interrupted when Zubeyde came out to tell her Kyrios Markos was waiting for her in the drawing room.

'What is it?' she asked, surprised to see him so early in the day.

'Prepare yourself, Sophia. Andreas has returned. I'm here to take you to him. He's at Georgos and Xanthe's house.'

Her heart leapt with joy, but the look on his face told her all was not well and she began to panic.

'Why didn't he come home? Please tell me he's alright.'

'He's alive, but you must brace yourself...' He hesitated, realizing that she had to be told something. 'He's not the same man who left us.'

'Dear Lord,' she uttered, raising her hands to her mouth.

They entered the cobblestone courtyard just as Yianni Mandakis was opening the kafenion. The aroma of Turkish coffee wafted through the air as Yianni rearranged wooden tables and chairs under a gnarled centuries-old plane tree. He nodded a silent gesture of acknowledgement to her as she and Markos passed; out of the corner of his eye, he watched Xanthe unlock the door to let them in.

'*Doxa sto Theo,*' she whispered nervously. 'Thank the Lord you are here.'

She led them up a dark and narrow wooden staircase. On hearing their footsteps, Georgos came out of a room to greet them.

'Sshhh,' he gestured, his finger to his mouth. 'He's sleeping.'

Sophia's eyes fell on a frail and emaciated figure lying on a makeshift bed, partially covered by a thick cotton sheet. She looked at the figure and then at Georgos. She wanted to scream: 'This is not my husband, my husband does not have white hair!' but the words would not come out. There was no escaping, no waking up from a bad dream— the stranger was Andreas.

For a moment she stared outside the window into the courtyard below. Outside, the day continued as normal. Inside this small room was hell on earth—a nightmare from which she thought she would never waken. The tattered rags tied to the branches of the plane tree over the years by Xanthe in the superstitious belief that this would help her bear a child fluttered in the gentle morning breeze. Under the tree, Yianni served his first customer. He looked up at the window and then turned away.

She pulled herself together and kneeling over her husband took his limp hand and pressed it to her mouth. Markos and Georgos watched in silence. In the background, Xanthe wailed like a mother who had lost a son. Georgos walked out of the room towards her.

'Quiet wife; your tears are of no use. Go and bring us a drink to quench our dry throats.'

Sophia ran her soft, smooth hands over Andreas's once-handsome face, feeling his sunken cheekbones. His skin was a pale, blotched gray, and with the shock of unkempt white hair he looked like a living corpse. '*Agape mou,*' she whispered to him. '*Agape mou*; my darling, how you must have suffered.'

Bending over to kiss him, a tear rolled down her face and onto his lips. Markos bent down beside her.

'Tell me everything,' she implored.

Xanthe arrived with glasses of sweet tea. She laid the tray beside them and disappeared into another room.

'Before I tell you, there is something you must know. I don't want you to jump to conclusions but there's another woman here. Perhaps the word "woman" is not really correct—more of a child really. She's in the next room. Xanthe and Georgos are taking care of her.'

Sophia stared at them. Georgos looked at the floor. She began to shake.

'The girl is heavily pregnant,' he continued. 'And I would say that from the look of her, she must be almost ready to give birth.'

As Markos spoke, Andreas began to speak. At first the sounds were unintelligible, but gradually the words became clearer.

'Gulay,' he mumbled. 'Gulay, not much longer…take care…Gulay…'

He fell back into a deep sleep.

Sophia recognized the name 'Gulay.' It was a common Turkish name meaning 'rose mouth.'

'Show me the girl,' she said to Georgos.

He opened the door to the adjoining room. A slip of a girl, heavily pregnant, lay on the kilim, her head propped up by an old cushion. Xanthe was bathing the girl's forehead with a wet towel. The fragrance of rosewater filled the room. Like Andreas, the girl—who looked no more than ten years old—was skin and bones. Her swollen belly seemed abnormally huge on her emaciated body. With her black hair swept back into a long braid, her features told Sophia that she was a Turk.

'She's very ill,' said Xanthe. 'But *doxa sto Theo*, she will live.'

The girl's dark eyes looked at Sophia with fear.

'Who are you?' Sophia asked, in Turkish.

'She's from Thrace,' answered Georgos for her.

Xanthe started to rock backwards and forwards on her knees, her head in her hands. 'Have pity on the child,' she implored.

Markos pulled Sophia out of the room, closing the door behind them.

'She saved his life, Sophia, and he saved hers. The child is not his. Don't jump to conclusions and judge her harshly. Without her, Andreas would not be here. Sit down. I will tell you the little we know. Thanassos, one of our men, has a bakery on the outskirts of the city. It's along the main road and for months now he has watched the never-ending procession of refugees and war-weary soldiers head for the safety of Constantinople. Every day, the starved and half-crazed took to besieging his shop until he or his wife were forced to stand outside and offer loaves of bread to these poor unfortunate souls. In exchange they gave him news from the provinces. One day, he noticed what seemed to be a familiar face walking alongside one of the heavily laden oxcarts. At first he thought he must be mistaken, as the man he thought he recognized bore no resemblance to the man he once knew. His face was shrunken and pale and his emaciated body was clad in an ill-fitting Turkish uniform. Thanassos called out, but Andreas stared ahead, shuffling, as if in a trance. Even worse, his hair was no longer dark and his eyes bore the lifeless look of death, a look that had become all too familiar to Thanassos on this dusty stretch of road. Calling to a neighbor for help, they quickly pulled him away. Andreas tried to resist but he was no match against the two strong and healthy men. He began to sob and with his arms outstretched towards the cart, called out a girl's name. Thanassos looked back at the cart rolling along the road. Among the disheveled faces and bundles of possessions, a young girl listlessly stared back. Andreas begged Thanassos to save her. Without thinking, Thanassos ran after the cart and pulled the girl down. He and his wife cared for them both until they arrived here.'

'Do you know what happened when he was away?' asked Sophia impassively.

'We know little. And what we do know is from the girl. It seems that after the Turkish officer allowed him to escape, he made his way through the tobacco fields and into the Rhodope Mountains.'

'So that must have been the same Turkish soldier who was executed for his kindness,' said Sophia, 'the one that the man who worked for the secret police mentioned.'

'It's very likely. Anyway, sometime later he came to a Turkish village. There he was given food and shelter, when the village was suddenly attacked by Bulgarian troops. What happened next is unclear except that the girl, her brother, and Andreas were the only ones to survive.'

'What happened to her brother?' asked Sophia.

'He died shortly afterwards.'

Sophia asked about the pregnancy.

'The girl was raped by the soldiers,' said Markos, sighing heavily. 'And now she bears the result of it. Perhaps it would have been better to let her die.'

Sophia was speechless. She knew rape was a weapon all too often used in war, but until now she had never known anyone affected by such a barbaric act. The thought of it made her retch.

'What about the Turkish uniform?' she asked.

'It seems that he took it from the body of a dead Turk after the defeat of Lüleburgaz. The girl didn't know which battle, but by her accounts of the thousands fleeing the area it is where I presume he stole it.'

'But the Battle of Lüleburgaz was at the end of October. Why did it take so long for them to reach the safety of the Çatalca Line?'

'A cholera outbreak forced them to take another route where they became lost, living from hand to mouth in a deserted village until the spring, when they made their way towards Constantinople, joining up with the surviving refugees. That's all we know.'

Under the unwavering love and care of Sophia and his friends, Andreas slowly recovered his strength and little by little filled in the missing pieces of the horrors of the previous six months.

Making his way through the Rhodope Mountains, he had stumbled upon a small Turkish village. On learning that he was heading to Constantinople, the headman, an elderly, pious man known as Yusuf Bey offered Andreas hospitality in his home for a few days. Although he quickly realized that Andreas was a Greek, he told him that as a man of God he detested this war that had set brother against brother and bore no ill will towards him. Also, bound by his faith and tradition it was his duty to offer sanctuary to the stranger. Sometime before dusk on the evening before he was due to depart, the sound of artillery fire could be heard coming from the direction of the nearby fields. Yusuf Bey gave Andreas a pistol and ordered him to run to the safety of a nearby ridge on the outskirts of the village. Meanwhile, the fearful villagers armed themselves, bolted their doors, and waited for the onslaught. On the rocky outcrop, Andreas positioned himself under an oleander bush, where he had a clear view of the village below. There was not a villager to be seen when the Bulgarians stormed the village. Despite a few of the attackers being killed by well-aimed Turkish fire, the villagers were no match for the troops. Before long, this quiet sleepy village became a terrifying scene of slaughter.

Young girls and married women, some pregnant, were taken away and violated. Andreas watched with a mixture of fear and revulsion. The worst crimes appeared to be committed by a violent band of komitadjis—thugs that would make any mother ashamed to have borne them. The blind old hodja was dragged out of the mosque, beaten, had oil poured over him, and was set alight while the komitadjis looked on laughing.

In the square, the men were herded together under the plane tree where their ancestors had once watched the world go by. Insulted and tormented, a few brave souls hastened their deaths by trying to resist. Eventually, on the orders of a fearsome officer whose blood-spattered uniform spoke of other heinous crimes, they were gunned down.

Gradually, the screams of women and children ceased. Sporadic gunshots were heard amongst the alleyways. The Bulgarians looted the houses, taking whatever they could carry. As quickly as they arrived the men departed, leaving an unholy scene of devastation behind them.

With one hand on Yusuf Bey's pistol and the other on his own dagger, Andreas returned to the village feeling an overwhelming sense of shame at having deserted his hosts. Yes, they were Turks, and yes, he wanted to rid Greece of them, but the horror of what he had witnessed sickened him to the core. His enemy had offered him refuge. He tried to reason about what would have happened if the village had been Bulgarian: the Turks would have done the same thing and perhaps his life would not have been spared.

All around, the earth glistened with blood. In the moonlight, he picked his way through bodies that littered the village; many of them still had the look of terror on their faces. Dogs were already picking at the bodies. Arriving at Yusuf Bey's house, he found the old man and his wife hacked to death. Yusuf died while trying to protect his wife, but this elderly couple were no match for a band of war-crazed bandits. Horrified, Andreas ran back outside and turning a corner, he slid on a slippery mass. Putting his hand out to save his fall, he realized that he had slipped on the entrails of a once-healthy young woman. Next to him was the body of a small girl, her beaten head lying face down in the mud. He thought of his daughter, Maria, and suddenly lost control. His head in his hands, he screamed the scream of the insane. On the outskirts of the village he heard the braying of a donkey behind a wall and the soft whimpering of a child. Searching the long grass he came across a small boy clinging to the body of a young girl. Miraculously, the boy was unharmed and despite her ordeal the girl was still alive. He soon discovered that they were the only surviving grandchildren of Yusuf Bey. Assuring the children that they were safe, Andreas went to find water to bathe the girl's wounds.

The following day he salvaged what little food he could find, saddled the donkey, and together they left the village. After a few days the weather worsened, and this boy called Fikrit died of weariness, hunger, and cold. They buried him in a makeshift grave somewhere in the mountains. Already weak from hunger himself, Andreas gave any food he could forage to her. Resting in a hut one night, the girl went outside to relieve herself. The mountains were still full of bears and wolves and she took her grandfather's pistol for protection. In the darkness, she heard voices. They had been spotted. Unable to warn Andreas, she followed the two men closely. Andreas was fast asleep when the Bulgarians burst into the hut. As they stood over him, the girl came up behind them and fired two shots into their backs, killing one and severely wounding the other. Andreas, for the first time in his life, was forced to kill. With the quickness that the instinct for survival brings, he pulled out his dagger and thrust it into the Bulgarian's chest.

After the Battle of Lüleburgaz, the bodies of Turkish soldiers were everywhere. Andreas stripped one of them of his clothes, boots and all. For months they lived like hunted animals, until they joined the stream of refugees and made their way back to Constantinople. By this time, it was now evident that Gulay was pregnant.

Andreas never knew when his hair turned white. He only became aware of it when he returned. Sophia listened to his story with a pain in her heart. Her eyes filled with tears. Even Markos, as strong as he was, shed a tear for his friend.

'You know,' Andreas said to Sophia, raising his head weakly, 'in my exhaustion, many times I felt the sweet breath of the Virgin as she tugged at my clothes, trying to pull me towards her. I would wake in a sweat, only to find it was Gulay who tugged at my sleeve. I believe that if she had not woken me from those dreams, I would have happily followed the Virgin into Heaven.'

Sophia knew that he had been just a breath away from death. Concerned that the children should not see him until he had recovered, Andreas stayed with Xanthe and Georgos for a few more weeks, but when the time came to go home, something inside him prevented him from leaving Gulay's side. He owed it to her grandfather to care for her and he did not want to see her placed in the care of the mosque, as was happening to thousands of other orphans. With that longing for their own child still deep in their hearts, Georgos and Xanthe cared for her until the child was born.

On May 18, 1913, the First Balkan War formally ended with the signing of the Treaty of London.

Markos and the Etairia were among those angered by the agreement. They predicted that the peace would be short-lived. Within a few weeks the victors began to quarrel among themselves. The biggest issue of concern was Macedonia. Serbia—angered at losing territorial gains in the much sought-after Adriatic—refused to pull its troops out of the area of Macedonia that was gained by the Bulgarians. Greece and Serbia signed a defense alliance against Bulgarian and Austro-Hungarian aggression. King Ferdinand of Bulgaria, later known as the Bulgarian Fox, together with General Savov entered into negotiations with the Russians. The negotiations quickly disintegrated when Bulgaria accused the Russians of siding with the Serbs in order to defeat any Austro-Hungarian expansion.

Nikolai was still in constant contact with his Russian friends in Sofia, and he warned Sophia and Markos that as far as the Bulgarians were concerned, they had borne the brunt of the fighting and would never agree to carve up Macedonia. Even more worrying to them was that Bulgaria asked Greece to relinquish land west of Salonika.

On June 16, 1913, the day known forever afterwards as 'the day of criminal madness,' Bulgaria declared war on Serbia and Greece. Romania declared war on Bulgaria, and the Ottoman Empire—seeing that the Bulgarians were mostly deployed elsewhere—retook Adrianople and a section of Thrace. With enemies on all sides, Bulgaria was forced to back down. The Treaty of Bucharest was concluded on August 10. In a humiliating defeat, Bulgaria lost part of Macedonia to Serbia. Greece gained Southern Macedonia, together with a large area of Thrace. The island of Crete was formally handed over to her a few months later. Romania gained a portion of the Dobrugia lying north of the line extending from the Danube to the western shore of the Black Sea. The Second Balkan War lasted just under a month. It took the lives of thousands.

On July 29, 1913, as the Bulgarian army made its last attack on the Greeks at the Battle of Kresna Gorge, Gulay gave birth to a baby girl. It had been a long and difficult labor and it soon became clear that Gulay would not survive. Since the day she had arrived, Xanthe and Georgos had looked after her as if she was their own, and they were distraught. Gulay offered her child to Xanthe and smiled—the first smile in nine months. Weakly, she mumbled something in Turkish.

'She is giving the child to you,' Sophia told her, fighting back her tears. 'She begs you to bring it up as your own and not to give her to the mosque.'

Xanthe burst into tears again. 'Tell her I will love and care for her as if she was from my own womb.'

'She wants it to be brought up in the Greek faith,' Sophia continued.

'Tell her,' Xanthe replied, cradling the child, 'I will call her Ariadne, "the holy one," after the daughter of King Minos of Crete who aided Theseus to escape from the labyrinth after killing the Minotaur. It will be in honor of her bravery.'

Gulay listened, smiled for the last time, and closed her eyes.

'*To keimeni*,' wailed Xanthe. 'The poor girl.'

Sophia walked downstairs and gave the men the news. Xanthe's wails filled the courtyard. Andreas went inside to pay his last respects to the young girl who had suffered so much. For a while he stood and watched over her in silence. She was barely thirteen and yet lying there on the old kilim, she looked like a small child—a little rag doll. He bent down and held her tiny hand. No words could express his emotion.

In the courtyard the men gathered together. Someone sent for Father Yannakos and Yianni Mandakis brought out raki. They all needed a stiff drink. Sophia looked at the tattered rags tied to the branches of the plane tree.

'It seems, Georgos,' she said, 'Xanthe's prayers have been answered after all.'

# CHAPTER 9

*Constantinople, Summer 1913*

It seemed that the summer of 1913 would have no end. It was as if the people of Constantinople had woken from the dark days of a long winter and they wanted to savor each minute of peace after the nightmare of war. Before long, a sense of normality gradually returned to the Laskaris household. Andreas moved back home and threw himself into the fervor of work, intent on producing his finest exhibition yet. To Sophia's delight he spent time with the children, who were overjoyed at having him back in their lives again. Leonidas no longer had nightmares, and even Maria, with her taciturn and headstrong ways, began to blossom into a much more endearing child, mainly because she had become her father's 'little doll.' She was quite content to be at his side as he showered kisses on her and told her that his *kouklaiki* was the sweetest and most beautiful doll in Constantinople.

Sophia watched this excessive attention to Maria with unease; he was spoiling her far too much and she had to contend with whispers that too much praise would attract the evil eye. Worse still, it was as predicted: he was no longer the light-hearted man she once knew; the trauma of war had scarred Andreas forever. Only she knew how violently he thrashed about in his sleep, waking in a cold sweat. And she also had the feeling that in Maria he saw little Rose-mouth, as she probably was before the unspeakable events robbed her of her innocence.

Andreas never spoke to Sophia of the horrors of Thrace again. It was as if he had built himself a protective wall. What disturbed her was the fact that he no longer touched her. Once or twice she had reached out to him as she thought a wife ought, but he simply froze, the gates of the high wall slamming shut behind him. It crossed her mind that he might have thought that she too was not the woman he had known before Thrace.

Summer drew to a close and Nikolai's car arrived from Germany. As he knew she would, Sophia fell in love with it. To the surprise of everyone except Nikolai, so did Ali Agha. Under Nikolai's guidance Ali Agha became an excellent driver and the envy of his friends. Casting aside his traditional clothes for the smart chauffeur's outfit, he could regularly be seen outside La Maison du l'Orient lavishing great attention on the car, polishing its red body and its brass fixtures until they gleamed. To the amusement of everyone he steadily acquired a following of women who, if they didn't want to marry him themselves, offered their daughters to him.

'Don't they realize he's a eunuch?' laughed Munire one day as they watched him from the window.

'Any woman would be content to be caressed as he caresses that car,' remarked Nikolai.

'And he is very choosy about the off-cuts of cloth that I give him,' Munire added. 'He sorts through them, taking only the softest, complaining that some are too harsh and may scratch its body. It must be the only car cleaned with fine silk.'

They all laughed. An old man wearing a red fez approached him, admired the car and asked what it was.

'It's a Mercedes 10/20 HP Erdmann and Rossi Phaeton,' Ali Agha answered proudly, emphasizing the word 'phaeton' as it was the only word that he really understood.

The admirer praised Allah that he could create such a wonderful thing.

'I am like the eagle that soars above the mountain when I drive *her*,' said Ali Agha, drawing himself up to a greater height.

The man was astonished. 'It's a woman then?' he asked.

Ali Agha looked confused. He had never thought to question Nikolai when he referred to the car in the feminine form, even though he had given the car a woman's name. He called her Mestinigar—the Turkish name for intoxicating beauty. That is exactly what she was to him. The old man bid him farewell, muttering to himself something about women. Inside the atelier Sophia, Munire, and Nikolai laughed so loudly that Ali Agha heard them. He gave them a look of utter disdain and continued polishing.

Sophia and Nikolai took long drives into the countryside, making the most of the last warm days before winter began. Since Andreas's return, it was one of the only ways they found to be alone. Nikolai's zest for life was just the tonic that Sophia needed and through his love she started to live again. Andreas had become a recluse and she was not able to shake him out of it—and if the truth was known, did she want to do that?

On the occasion of the family's visit to Constantinople, Dimitra fell in love with the car.

'This is wonderful,' she said to Nikolai admiringly when he took her for a drive in it. 'I feel like the Valide Sultan herself. I will buy one for myself.'

The problem was that Iskender would not entertain the idea and the more Dimitra coaxed and cajoled him, the more he dug his heels in against it.

'Hanim Efendi, it is the devil,' he lamented. 'I know my horses like I know yoghurt, and I trust them. This machine is like a woman—she shines, looks beautiful, but you will never really understand her. And one day she may play tricks on you. Anyway, I would have to wear the Frankish clothing and where would I put my pistol and knives?'

'What do you know about women, Iskender?' asked Dimitra, tempting him with a plate of his favorite rose-flavored locum.

'Bah,' he cried, settling into a sulk.

'I want to beat him with a stick,' she said to Sophia. 'Perhaps then he will see sense.'

But Dimitra had no intention of beating him. Over the years she had grown to love and depend on him and he knew that only too well. Iskender probably knew her better than she knew herself. He also knew that she cared for her horses far more than she would ever care for any car.

La Maison du l'Orient was almost ready to launch the new collection when an incident happened that was to have far-reaching consequences for everyone. On a sunny June day in 1914, a nineteen-year-old Bosnian Serb, Gavrilo Princip—a member of a Serbian secret society—fired two bullets, killing the Archduke Ferdinand, heir to the throne of the Austro-Hungarian Empire, and his wife Sophie in Sarajevo. Fired with the same spirit of nationalism as that of the Etairia, Princip and his co-conspirators were outraged that the Archduke chose to visit the city on that most sacred of all days—June 28, the anniversary of the Battle of Kosovo in 1389.

The following evening, the Etairia called a meeting. Over forty members gathered in the courtyard of The Blue Eye—far too many to be cooped up in Georgos's small room on such a warm night. Instead, Yianni arranged his wooden tables and chairs under the plane tree. The somber mood of the occasion eased somewhat when Yianni brought out platters of *mezethes* accompanied by carafes of wine and bottles of raki.

There was much to discuss. Soterios was in Constantinople when the Archduke was killed and the assassination did not come as a surprise to him or other members of the Etairia. They knew there remained 'unfinished business' in the Balkans; they just didn't know when and where the finishing would take place. The Serbs had merely substituted their old Ottoman masters for new ones, the Hapsburgs. Consequently, they still suffered hardships. The Hapsburg officials had been warned of impending trouble and the evening's discussions centered on just how the Hapsburgs would react. The government in Belgrade sent condolences, but the assassination sent a strong message to the Austro-Hungarian Empire that the region was still unstable. It was concluded by most members in the group that the incident would be contained. After all, they reasoned, no one had the appetite for another war at the moment.

Towards the end of the evening, Soterios broached the subject foremost in his thoughts. The Christian populations in parts of the Aegean region were forcibly being made to leave their homes. In 1913 the Office for the Settlement of Tribes and Immigrants had been established within the Interior Ministry, and thousands of refugees fleeing the war-torn Ottoman provinces were sent into the countryside, there harboring a desire for revenge for the huge losses in their old homeland. Tension between the Muslim refugees and the Christian minorities was high. So many military defeats had created deep wounds in the Muslim psyche. Soterios warned that the clashes would soon affect them all. Turkish Nationalism was steadily gaining momentum. Members of the Etairia were well aware of the stirring speeches of the Homeland Society. These were speeches that served to remind Turks of the heroism of their Ghazi forefathers—the Ottomans who struck fear into the hearts of the Western world. And revenge had been called for on more than one occasion.

Of immediate concern, especially for the merchant classes of which the Christians dominated—mostly Armenians, Greeks, and Jews—was the fact that the Turkish language was now required for all commercial correspondence. That would be enshrined in law within two years. It was one thing to speak Turkish, but very few Greeks could write in the Arabic script. This latest move was viewed by many as just another way to keep the Christians in check.

The evening drew to a close and Yianni brought out plates of halva and more raki. Outside the courtyard, a tambourine and finger cymbals could be heard. Minutes later the waif-like figure of Zaynab sauntered into the courtyard, accompanied by her mother the Egyptian dancer Khadiya, and her father Al Sayyid, leading a small brown bear on a chain. Al Sayyid was partially blind and his sole purpose in the troupe seemed to be to coax the forlorn animal to dance in a swaying motion to the music. His daughter, a curious girl of about thirteen with thick dark eyebrows and pale amber eyes, played the tambourine, while her mother, whose skin was as weather-beaten as a Bedouin's saddle, performed an oriental dance. Imbued with melancholy, she swayed her voluptuous hips towards the men with a flourish of sexual abandon, flirtatiously darting her eyes from one man to the other and making shrill trilling sounds. Venus she was not, but this serpent of the

Nile, her hair and skin glistening with sandalwood mingled with sweat, had a definite knack of making the men part with their tobacco, hashish, and raki money. Their blood warmed with copious amounts of raki, the men applauded wildly.

Ever superstitious, Xanthe brought out a tray of food for them. A curse from Khadiya would have been most unwelcome. Handing her a small piece of clothing belonging to Ariadne, Khadiya pressed it to her forehead, muttering incomprehensible incantations against the evil eye, spat on it, and gave it back to the grateful Xanthe.

Well fed and with a bag full of coins, the troupe departed, their jingles gradually fading into the dark night.

The servants had long retired to bed when Ali Agha brought Soterios back to the house. He made himself a nightcap and took it onto the verandah. The stars twinkled in the heavens and flickering lights dotted the Bosphorus. He sat in the white wicker chair listening to the sound of the cicadas. Somewhere on the dark water a ship sounded its horn. Glancing across the garden, he noticed a soft light in the pavilion and wondered who could be there at such a late hour. Putting his cup down, he went to find out.

The sound of his footsteps took Sophia by surprise. 'Papa, you startled me,' she said, pulling her robe around her body.

'What are you doing out here?' he inquired. 'Do you realize what time it is?'

He sat down on a cushion by her side.

'I couldn't sleep so I came out here to read. It's so peaceful. I must have dozed off.'

'I'm surprised you find time to read; you're always so busy. How is Andreas these days? He seems to have become something of a recluse; he's so withdrawn. He tells me he's working on his forthcoming exhibition but refuses to let me see anything.'

'Yes. He shuts himself in his studio all day. Maria is the only one who visits him. His work has taken on a somber feel—quite dark really. I don't know how the public will receive it.'

'Yes, I was afraid that the war would change him.'

They sat for a while. An overpowering scent of honeysuckle filled the night air. Soterios thought his daughter looked pale and drawn.

'Are you sure you're alright? Have you considered coming to stay with us for a while? Smyrna is so different to Constantinople; you used to love it as a child and you know we would all love to have you with us. Do you remember how we took excursions into the mountains and had wonderful picnics and you would chase the butterflies while your grandmother collected wildflowers for her dyes? Leonidas and Maria would love that. It would make your mother so happy.'

Sophia sighed. 'It all seems so long ago, Papa…Just lately I've become so tired.'

She lay back on the cushion. In the soft light, Soterios saw the incredible beauty in his daughter—the same beauty as her grandmother's. Such striking features made men's hearts miss a beat. Photeini had not possessed that same quality. Even in her sadness, Sophia was still beautiful.

'I'm tired of wars, Papa, tired of this hatred. Why can't we live in peace? Look at us…'

She became animated and gestured towards the house.

'We are Greeks, yet we live amongst Turks and some are like our family. I would never forgive myself if something happened to Zubeyde, or sweet Munire, who is like a sister to me and has given me the best years of her life. And look at Ali Agha. He has no living relatives. We are his family. I see no end and I'm frightened for my children.'

Soterios wished he could ease her sadness.

'Come, my dear,' he said after a while. 'Go to bed and try and get some sleep.' They walked arm in arm towards the house.

'Are you sure that's all that's on your mind? I'm your father and you know you can confide in me.'

There was something about her, something that he had seen many times before. Sophia was pregnant. For the moment, neither one of them wanted to acknowledge that.

# CHAPTER 10

*Constantinople, Summer 1914*

The hopes of many were dashed when one month after the assassination of the Archduke, Austria-Hungary declared war on Serbia. The next day Russia—Serbia's greatest ally—mobilized her troops. Three days later Germany—Austria-Hungary's ally—declared war on France, who refused to remain neutral. After cutting off resources to Germany, Britain joined the Russians and the French. One by one, other countries were dragged into the mire, while in Turkey many feared another war and wanted to remain neutral.

Markos called at La Maison du l'Orient to keep Sophia abreast of the Etairia's discussions.

'This doesn't look good,' he warned Sophia, pacing the room. 'They're afraid that the Ottoman Empire may side with Germany.'

Markos was an expert at hiding his emotions, but today Sophia thought him unusually agitated. She offered him a cigarette.

'But the Sultan has expressed his desire that the empire remain neutral,' she replied. 'And if the people don't want another war…?'

'The Germans have vested interests in keeping Turkey on their side. The Berlin to Baghdad railway is only one of them, and then there is the fact that they are helping to modernize the army. Enver Bey is very close to them—war may suit his ambitions.'

'What about Bulgaria and Greece?'

'Bulgaria is still angry at having lost territories gained in the last war. They'll do anything to get them back.'

'And Greece, where does she stand? Queen Sofia is the Kaiser's sister. That makes it very difficult for King Constantine.'

'Yes, his sympathies are known to be with the Central Powers even though he believes it's better for Greece to stay neutral.'

'Yet the Prime Minister is staunchly pro-Entente.'

'Therein lies the problem for Greece,' he answered, throwing her an anxious look. 'I believe that the views of Venizelos will win over in the end.'

The Cretan Eleftherios Venizelos had proved himself a force to be reckoned with in Greek politics. A powerful orator and possessing great charisma, he was staunchly pro-British and French.

'And...' Markos added, 'he has great empathy for the Greeks still under Ottoman domination. Your father has the greatest of admiration for him.'

'I can't say that my grandmother agrees with him. My father has tried to coax her round to his way of thinking. He even has the bird's "milk" is what he tells her; that is, something special that others don't have. It doesn't make the slightest of difference. My grandmother thinks no good can come of his smooth talk.'

They both laughed.

'Your grandmother has seen many changes in the empire but one thing is for sure, the Ottoman Empire is not what it was, and...Greece is getting stronger. Perhaps we will live to see the new Byzantium and a Greater Greece after all.'

Sophia looked at him. Did he really believe that, or was it just wishful thinking?

'How is Andreas?' Markos asked, changing the subject. 'I rarely see him at The Blue Eye these days.'

'I think he lost faith after Thrace, and he certainly has no interest in the war or politics any longer. Anyway, he'll soon be ready to have his exhibition.'

'Will it be at the Academy or here?'

'He wants it in the Grand Salon.'

'Well, I hope he has it soon. If this war worsens, no one will have the appetite for buying paintings.'

Sophia brushed her hair away from her forehead and straightened her back. Munire entered, bringing them small goblets of apricot sherbet and chilled water.

'When do you expect to have the child?' he asked, studying her carefully.

'In February. Let's pray that the situation improves by then.'

Despite the people's prayers events took a turn for the worse. On November 3, Russia declared war on Turkey. Two days later Britain and France declared war on Turkey. The Ottoman Empire was once again at war. Sophia now found herself at society functions seated next to high-ranking German officers sent by the Kaiser to command the Sultan's army. For the most part she enjoyed their company, finding that the arts gave them a common ground for social discourse. Discreetly, she began to use her charm to glean as much information as she could about the war, which she readily passed on to the Etairia.

From December onwards, Photeini arrived in Constantinople and aided by Munire and Nikolai took over the running of La Maison du l'Orient, while Sophia spent the last few months of her pregnancy in the confines of her home.

In February 1915, Sophia gave birth to a baby girl. She named her Nina. It was an easy birth, and from the moment she held her in her arms she knew she would love this child as she did Leonidas. From the moment his mother told him that the pigeons had brought him a beautiful sister Leonidas was fascinated by her, saying that when she grew to be as tall as him he would let her carry his parrot. The women laughed. Carved out of wood and attached to a long stick, the parrot was his prized possession. Andreas had realistically painted it in gold, crimson, and cobalt blue. It never ceased to amuse the adults when they saw it move through the bushes long before Leonidas came into view.

Maria took the birth as expected. Jealous of the attention the child received, she refused to have anything to do with her. Dark-haired and with a perfectly formed almond-shaped face, Nina was loved by all. Her great-grandmother traveled from Smyrna especially for the occasion and gave thanks to God that the child did not have flaming hair.

In March, Allied ships attempted to bombard the Dardanelles; an invasion was imminent. Shortly after, Andreas held his exhibition. His work was held in great regard by the establishment in Constantinople and the opening was eagerly anticipated. Invitations were duly sent out and journalists vied with each other to cover the event. Not since the launch of Sophia's Oriental Collection had the atelier been so extravagantly decked out.

The Italian Ambassador was among the first to arrive, as it was he who would formally open the exhibition. Andreas took him aside and gave him a briefing on the paintings. His face drained pale. He pulled Sophia aside and whispered in her ear.

'My dear Sophia,' he said, searching for the right words. 'I'm sure this isn't what the people are expecting. I fear that this time his work will not be well received. It will be a disaster for you both.'

Sophia knew very little about the works; they had all been executed behind locked doors.

'I'm afraid, sir,' she answered, taking a deep breath, 'it's too late now.'

As the Ambassador had predicted, the evening was a disaster. The people expected Andreas's work to be in his usual style: academic, romantic subjects meticulously rendered and executed with a fine yet subtle impressionist hand. It was the classical aesthetics and oriental imagery of his subject matter that had previously fascinated the public and it was this that his admirers wanted to see—more of the same. Instead, they were subjected to a new and controversial art style: Expressionism. Even more shocking was the subject matter: the horror of war. With its heightened and exaggerated imagery and vivid symbolic splashes of colour, the guests thought the paintings reflected his state of mind rather than the reality of the external world. Never in their wildest imagination had they been subjected to such unbearably brutal images. Distorted faces screamed from the canvas. Death, destruction, and torment were blatant in this collection. Here was Andreas's tormented inner self. In the spirit of Edvard Munch with his powerful work *The Scream*, Expressionism had arrived in Constantinople.

At first the guests were silent, trying to absorb it all. Then they began to show their disgust. Women turned away and men swore. One pasha, a hero of the war against the Bulgarians, threw his wine glass at a work entitled *Sacrifice in the Olive Grove*. In it a woman was depicted covered in blood and kneeling over her dead child, tearing at her own face in despair.

An hour after it opened the Grand Salon was deserted and the floor was a mess of torn brochures and broken glass. Throughout the horror of it all, Sophia noticed that it was the Germans who appeared to admire his work the most.

The following day, Munire and Sophia arrived at the atelier to find rubbish strewn across the steps. To add to their misery the critics panned the exhibition; the reviews in magazines and newspapers were relentless in their attacks. They labeled his work 'a travesty in the art world' and 'profoundly immoral and a disgrace to our society...When morale is already low, and our brave men are compelled to save the land of our forefathers from the *giour*, this artist seeks to humiliate us.' One reporter even went as far as to suggest that he seek the services of Herr Freud.

Even Andreas's closest admirers considered the exhibition bad timing. Colonel Liman Von Sanders, in charge of the Fifth Division on the Gallipoli Peninsular, was preparing his men for an Allied invasion. Also posted to the headquarters at Maidos was the newly formed Nineteenth Division, headed by a charismatic leader, Lieutenant-Colonel Mustafa Kemal. It was essential that morale should be boosted; nobody wanted to be reminded of the horrors of war.

Wounded and tormented by his apparent failure, Andreas avoided everyone. Several weeks later Sophia woke with a deep sense of unease in the pit of her stomach. As expected, Andreas was not beside her. She had long become accustomed to waking without him, knowing that more often than not he preferred to busy himself with his painting than to be with his wife. But this morning was different. She threw on her dressing gown, went down to his studio, and knocked on the door. He was nowhere to be seen. After searching the house she concluded that he must have taken an early morning walk to the seashore—a habit that he had recently taken to, saying it 'calmed his nerves.'

During breakfast she spotted him coming up the garden path, but instead of joining the family as he usually did, he made for his studio. When he failed to join them, she turned to Maria and asked her to go and fetch her father. Maria did as she was told. Ten minutes later they heard the unmistakable sound of a gunshot coming from the studio. Leonidas looked at his mother, his face as pale as a ghost.

'Papa!' he shouted, making a dash for the studio.

In his studio, Andreas's body lay on the couch, his eyes wide open and his left arm dangling lifelessly over the side. Blood steadily seeped from a gunshot wound in his chest. Beside him stood Maria, holding his pistol in her trembling hands. 'Papa! Papa!' she screamed. 'I didn't mean to! It was an accident!'

Sophia felt the room spin and fell to the floor in a faint. When she revived the room was filled with people. Maria was screaming hysterically and Leonidas sat next to her rocking to and fro, calling for his Papa. Within a matter of hours, Andreas's body had been removed to the bedroom and laid out on the bed.

'It was an accident,' the doctor informed Sophia. 'You must not blame the child.'

Andreas's death mobilized the Greek community: large crowds gathered on the streets to watch the funeral procession as it made its way to the Greek cemetery in Pera. Sophia stood by the graveside clad in black, the colour she hated the most—the colour of Charon. She listened to the dulcet voice of Father Yannakos talking about redemption in another world and of Andreas's soul now being in the hands of the Archangel Michael, as though he were talking about someone else. Surrounded by family and friends, she watched his casket being lowered into the earth as if in a dream; a real-life Greek tragedy that had changed all of their lives forever. In the churning turmoil of her mind she felt a deep sense of guilt that somehow it had all been her fault.

Sophia learned that Andreas's death had indeed been an accident. When Maria entered his studio, the exhausted Andreas had fallen asleep on his couch and Maria was unable to wake him. Seeing his pistol on the table nearby, she picked it up and pointed it at him.

'Papa,' she called out, intending to frighten him. 'Please wake up or I will shoot.'

It was meant as a childish prank to get his attention and it worked. Andreas opened his eyes, and seeing her standing over him he told her to put down the gun. She was just about to do as she was told when a maid accidently dropped a tray outside the door, startling her, and in the process causing her to fire the pistol.

'I didn't know it was loaded,' Maria cried. 'I never meant to kill my papa—I was just trying to get him to wake up.'

But no matter how hard Sophia tried, the nagging guilt continued to plague her that none of this would have happened if she had gone to her husband. Andreas had not been himself since Thrace; he was vulnerable and she should have taken better care of him.

After the obligatory forty days of mourning Sophia returned to work. By then, everyone had come to terms with the tragic accident and all were willing to forgive Maria—except Dimitra.

'Kismet,' she told Sophia. 'There are no accidents in fate; our lives are written on our brow. That Maria was the one who pulled the trigger was not an accident. It was meant to be.'

Slowly, Sophia's grief began to heal. But unable to comprehend the enormity of her actions, and losing her father who doted on her more than anyone in the world, Maria's heart had been ripped apart forever.

A few weeks after Andreas's death, Franz Von Straumbacher, a German general whom Sophia had met at several social functions, sent her a newspaper cutting from an avant-garde arts magazine in Berlin. It praised the talents and imagination of a 'new' artist in Constantinople: '*In the mould of our own German Expressionism, Herr Andreas Laskaris is a force to be reckoned with. We look forward to seeing more of his work.*'

How she wished he could read those words.

With the war taking a toll on business once again, Sophia was struggling to maintain the atelier. Most of her time was taken up with helping the war effort, preparing blankets and warm clothing that were collected weekly by the authorities and sent to soldiers on the front lines. She was not alone; people everywhere were struggling. Gangs of unemployed people were sent out of the city for fear of a revolt. Food shortages became a daily occurrence. When the Ottomans joined the war, families waited in dread as the distant beating of drums heralded the arrival of the town crier slowly walking through the streets, calling their men to present themselves to the local authorities in readiness to be sent to the Front.

'*Masallah*; Allah is punishing us,' wailed the Muslim women in the workroom. 'God's curse is upon us. Haven't we suffered enough?'

The Greek women muttered prayers to the saints, throwing their outstretched arms towards the sky and then clasping their heads as if to rid themselves of a never-ending pain. Just as heartbreaking was the fact that a law had been passed ordering all the Christians to report for duty, when previously they were exempt. All the Greeks knew perfectly well that these men would never reach the front lines. They were the infidel and the soldiers were fighting the infidel. Fearful of arming the Christian minorities, the government chose instead to send these recruits to the newly formed Labour Battalions. In the countryside, Turkish soldiers and gendarmes swept through villages, taking men and sending them to the camps to dig trenches and build roads. Under such harsh conditions, most would never return. The only way for the Greeks to escape this fate was to pay an exemption fee. Not all Greek families could afford this and the Etairia found itself helping families by donating funds. Some of the Greek women in the workroom secretly approached Sophia, begging her to help them. She never failed them.

Munire reported that the atmosphere in the workroom was tense. Some of the Turkish women considered it unfair that their sons were sent away to fight for their country, while Greek mothers were able to sleep at night knowing that their sons were safe.

'This is your land as well as ours,' they screamed at each other. 'Must my son die for yours to live?'

The tension saddened Sophia, as the women had spent many harmonious years together. Now they were being torn apart.

In January the withdrawal of the Allies from the Gallipoli peninsular was complete. Mustafa Kemal was hailed as the savior of the Turks and the people were jubilant. Greece was not united over whether to join the war and the Etairia in Turkey looked on in despair. However, in 1916 public opinion began to change. Venizelos—with the backing of France and Britain—set up a provisional government in Salonika. The young country was now on the brink of a civil war. The Etairia was frustrated. Markos desperately wanted the Greeks to show unity in the face of the Ottoman Empire. They staunchly backed Venizelos, and in particular Soterios was convinced that he would win. When Dimitra, politically astute despite her years, warned her son-in-law that Mustafa Kemal was a force to be reckoned with, he became angry.

'You will see,' she cautioned him. 'You praise Venizelos, but Mustafa Kemal also has the bird's "milk." There is a lucky star over him.'

It was unlike Soterios to show anger, but he was desperate, and at that moment the Central Powers had the upper hand. Bulgaria had already reversed her losses. With Serbia and Eastern Macedonia lost, who would be the next to fall? He had no time for superstition. For a person who constantly praised the logic of Plato, Socrates, and Aristotle, superstition was anathema to him.

The year 1916 was one bogged down in trench warfare. On the western front, the Battle of Verdun had begun, with no overall gains by either side. In July the Battle of the Somme began. British troops suffered sixty thousand casualties in the first hour. On April 4, Alexei Busilov took command of Russia's southern front. This was an offensive which destroyed the Austrian army two months later. Bulgaria invaded Greece in May. And in August, Turkey joined with its previous enemy Bulgaria and declared war on Rumania. There seemed no end in sight to this turmoil.

# CHAPTER 11

*Constantinople, Summer 1916*

Sophia was finding it even harder to make ends meet and there was still a constant stream of women approaching her for help. Nikolai could not stand by and watch her lose everything; something had to be done. He asked if he could use the Grand Salon to host a party for a few of his Russian friends and, as the room had rarely been used for anything except a storeroom since the outbreak of the war, she agreed. A party would cheer her up, he told her. In the meantime, she and Munire were to take the rest of the day off and return later that evening in their finest evening gowns. Sophia was too preoccupied with thoughts about her impending meeting with Markos at the Zaharoplasteion Olympia to argue and she welcomed the diversion.

Over *baklava* and *galatoboureko*, Markos told Sophia he had received information from a reliable source that the Turkish Secret Police had Russian spies working for them.

'Are you suggesting that Nikolai has something to do with all this?' she asked, suddenly losing her appetite. Markos lit a cigarette for her and she took it willingly.

'No. We have complete trust in him, but…it would be wise to keep an eye on his associates. As yet we have no information on who these people are.'

Sophia looked at the people in the café. She had a faraway look in her eyes.

'Thank God Andreas is not here to see what is happening,' she said quietly.

Markos lit another cigarette and studied her carefully.

'Is there something else bothering you? You seem preoccupied.'

Sophia flicked back a lock of hair and sighed. 'I've just learned that Munire has received several letters from her father. He's concerned that she won't give him grandchildren and since she's not been lucky enough to find a husband here, he has someone in mind at home who he is sure will make her very happy. He urges her to consider it before he loses face. She's worried because his relatives are blaming her mother, who, as you know, is

French. They are saying she is responsible for her daughter becoming too westernized. Of course, Munire doesn't want a loveless marriage and refuses to go. With the situation as it is, I fear I have no choice but to send her home.'

For the first time, the reality hit Sophia that she was about to lose Munire. She couldn't even begin to think about it.

Sophia prepared for Nikolai's party with a sense of optimism; a party was just what she needed to lift her spirits. She looked at herself in the mirror, picked up a fine brush and dipped it into a porcelain jar of dark powder and emphasized the arch of her brows carefully. As she dabbed attar of rose on her wrist and behind her ear lobes, Leonidas entered the room. She stood up, smoothing away the creases of her magnolia cream silk dress and reached for her jewelry box.

'Which necklace do you think I should wear, *mataikia mou*?' she asked, opening the inlaid casket that Dimitra had given her on her engagement to Andreas. 'Shall I wear this one…or this?'

She held a diamond and sapphire necklace against her smooth skin.

'Why don't you wear the locket, Mama?' replied Leonidas.

Sophia put the necklace down. She had forgotten all about it. It had been another gift from her grandmother and Sophia had worn it only once before—on her wedding day.

'It's not so fashionable,' she answered, opening another compartment and taking out a black velvet purse, emptying its contents into the palm of her hand.

'But it's so beautiful.'

Sophia opened the oval gold locket edged with tiny diamonds, and looked at the two portraits inside. 'Yes, darling, you're right. I should wear it more often.'

Painted in watercolor on ivory, one of the portraits was of a raven-haired woman wearing a dark green sash intertwined with a rope of pearls around her head. Her soft curls tumbled over her shoulders onto a fine chemise of the palest rose, embroidered in gold silk interspersed with small pink roses. The embroidery reminded Sophia of Dimitra's earlier work. The woman's oval face was as smooth and as pale as alabaster and her lips were full and sensuous.

'She's beautiful isn't she?' Leonidas remarked, examining the face. 'But I think she looks a little sad. Who is she?'

'I don't know, Leonidas. When Grandmamma gave it to me she said that it was the one thing she valued most in the world, and I was to take great care of it. The man is equally handsome. Don't you agree?'

'Isn't he dressed in the old Turkish fashion?' asked Leonidas inquisitively. 'Why would Great-grandmamma give you a picture of a Turkish man?'

'I don't know that either. Perhaps they aren't anyone in particular. Grandpapa was always painting portraits.'

'Wouldn't she have told you if Great-grandpapa had painted them?'

'Perhaps Grandmamma doesn't even know who they are herself. Anyway, the locket is so beautiful even without the portraits.'

'Look at the back, Mama.'

Sophia turned it over. The center was engraved with a small tulip.

'That's Great-grandmamma's favorite flower?'

'Yes it is,' she answered, realizing that she hadn't noticed the fine engraving before.

She put the locket around her neck. 'You're absolutely right. It is wonderful and it complements my dress to perfection.' She drew her son to her and kissed him. 'I will make you a promise. The next time I see Great-grandmamma, I *will* ask her who they are.'

Returning to La Maison du l'Orient later that evening, Sophia could be forgiven for thinking that she had arrived at a party thrown by the smart set of the Nevsky Prospekt. A doorman dressed in scarlet livery greeted her with a polite yet stern smile—a smile that Sophia recognized could turn nasty if he were provoked. The doorman—who she later discovered was an infamous gun smuggler in the exiled Russian community—consulted his list for her name. She was just about to inform him, rather indignantly, that *she* was the owner of the premises and that it was *she* who should be asking *his* name when Nikolai appeared at the top of the staircase. After a few words in Russian, the doorman put down his guest list, bowed graciously and wished her a good evening. Ali Agha, who had watched this stranger in amazement, gave him a scowl and promptly returned to the car where he settled down for the evening to wait for his mistress.

'Let me be the first to compliment you on your dress,' smiled Nikolai, taking her arm and escorting her into the Grand Salon. 'There is not another woman here tonight who can compete with your beauty.'

The Grand Salon had been transformed into a lively dancehall and Nikolai's soirée was in full swing. The room was filled with guests dancing to the sparkling and intoxicating rhythm of American-style music.

'Ragtime,' said Nikolai. 'It's all the rage in Europe.'

Sophia cast a quick eye over the guests. 'You certainly know how to throw a party.'

Already she felt her mood lift. It was not hard to be drawn into the fun of the evening. Nikolai led her onto the dance floor.

'I saved the first dance for you. The things I have to do to hold you in my arms,' he whispered.

'Then it has all been worth it,' Sophia replied.

Nikolai introduced her to his friends, many of whom had once lived a privileged life in their homeland. Despite their great titles and adverse conditions, their countenance belied the fact that many of them were now impoverished.

Sophia was particularly intrigued by the women. Looking strikingly beautiful and attired in stylish gowns—some of which she recognized from her collections—they emanated the similar freedom and *joie de vivre* that she had always admired in Parisian women. And she noticed how their sensuous perfumes competed with each other, enveloping the room with a sexually charged atmosphere of gay abandon. She found them quite captivating.

A waiter offered her *Zakuski* and vodka. She was startled to see such good food in a time of rationing. A woman of impeccable taste and devastating beauty dressed in a red velvet dress with a low décolleté whispered discreetly in her ear: 'Courtesy of the black market.'

She introduced herself as Helene Sumarakov.

'Even in wartime there's always someone with something to sell. You would be surprised how many people still want to buy jewels and the occasional antique,' she added, inhaling her cigarette through an amber holder and gently blowing the smoke into the air. She eyed Sophia's locket. 'This exquisite piece, for instance, would fetch a very high price from the right buyer.'

'How long have you been in Constantinople?' enquired Sophia, observing Helene's exquisite diamond necklace and matching aigrette neatly arranged in her swept-up fair hair. She wondered if they too were for sale to the right buyer.

'We left Russia at the same time as Nikolai and lived here for a short while until my brother Sergei was offered a job in Sofia. When Bulgaria joined the war on the side of the Central Powers we returned.'

'What line of work does your brother do?' asked Sophia, recalling her conversation with Markos earlier.

Helene took another draw on her cigarette, and holding her head back blew out the smoke as if she had all the time in the world. The diamond aigrette in her blonde hair glinted like stars under the chandelier. When she didn't answer, Sophia sensed it was a question she shouldn't have asked.

'Is your brother here this evening?'

'Yes, of course; you must meet him.'

Helene looked around the room. She indicated to a couple standing next to the red brocade curtains that hid the Petit Salon. 'He's over there. In fact he seems quite taken with the pretty girl in the apricot dress.'

Sophia couldn't believe her eyes. Helene noticed Sophia's reaction.

'Do you know the girl?'

It was Munire and she was clearly captivated with the man. He was flirtatiously engaging her in a conversation. Sophia was reminded of a wild animal who had snared his prey and was about to play with it before devouring it completely. She wanted to meet him. Making their way to the other side of the room, the orchestra began to play a tango. Someone asked her to dance and she tried to excuse herself by saying that she was unfamiliar with the steps, but the man refused to take no for an answer, assuring her that he would teach her. The next time she looked around, the mysterious man had disappeared…and so had Munire.

The next day, Nikolai entered Sophia's office, planted a kiss firmly on her lips and proceeded to empty a large brown bag of money onto her desk. When she saw the contents she was astounded.

'And this is not all,' he told her, picking up a handful of coins and notes and letting them drop through his fingers. 'There is vodka and enough smoked salmon and caviar left over to feed an army.'

Sophia stared at the money in disbelief. 'Where did all this come from?'

'Where do you think?' he said, flicking a banknote.

'Did you sell one of your paintings—an antique perhaps?' she asked, thinking of Helene.

'My dear Sophia, everyone who attended the party last night paid a *charitable* donation to be there.'

He smiled at her as he stressed the word charitable.

'You mean that you actually charged your friends to come to a party on *my* premises?'

'Well everyone, that is, except yourself and Munire.'

She suddenly thought of Munire. She had not seen her this morning.

'I wanted to talk to you about Munire.'

Nikolai ignored her.

'Sophia, we exiles are used to helping each other out in times of hardship.'

'I'm not exactly penniless,' she said indignantly.

'No, but you soon will be if you continue to give away what little you have. Regardless of hard times, people still have to live. They want to forget their troubles and have a little fun. By throwing lavish soirées as we did last night, where we can offer our guests fine wine and food and allow them to let their hair down by dancing to the latest music in a secluded atmosphere of like-minded people, we will have them beating their way to our door. And the Grand Salon is never used these days. Why not use it for such evenings?'

'And do you intend to charge every time?'

'But of course. By charging a high admission fee, it makes the evening all the more exclusive…and then there's the fine food and drink—the black market isn't cheap you know.'

Nikolai pulled up a chair next to her desk and leaned forward.

'In fact, I believe these evenings are a popular way to raise money throughout Europe. Just think about it, Sophia. Payments will be discreet.' He picked up a handful of money again as if to tempt her. 'Think what this means. It's not in your nature to turn people away when they come to you for help. With this money you can do some good. And it's not only money that we can get, but black-market goods—and that includes travel passes and guns, not to mention the odd snippet of information gleaned from loose lips.'

She grew alarmed.

'You're putting us in a dangerous situation, and your talk of guns scares me. Christians are not allowed weapons; the repercussions don't bear thinking about.'

Nikolai smiled. 'You of all people can see how this will help your people. If you asked Markos and your father about this, what do you think they would say? Of course their organizations would like to get their hands on such things. When things return to normal, well…you can revert to concentrating on the business again. And…' he stressed, 'it's not as if you're going to give it up is it?'

He stood, walked across the room, and looked across the road towards the Pera Palas. Sophia studied him. He radiated optimism and courage.

'I have even heard that Mustafa Kemal is not averse to a good time,' he added, turning towards her and giving her a wink.

Sophia picked up a few Turkish notes and looked at them. She mulled things over in her mind. The lira was becoming worthless. Before her were also gold and silver coins: Reich marks, francs and rubles. The war showed no sign of ending. A united army of Germans, Turks, and Bulgarians had invaded Rumania. She became despondent. Who would have thought that Turks and Bulgarians would be fighting together when the atrocities of the last war were still fresh in the people's minds? In Eastern Anatolia, the Russian army was still proving to be a problem. The news that Trebizond on the Black Sea had been captured by the Tsarist army in the spring was greeted with delight in the Christian community. However, they also knew that the Russian success had further angered the Turkish government.

Mustafa Kemal had already been dispatched to check their advances with a counter-offensive; his spirits were high after the Dardanelles. Even Nikolai thought it was only a matter of time before the Russians retreated and that rising discontent in his homeland threatened to destabilize Allied gains.

Sophia worried about Greece; the situation was deteriorating rapidly. In Athens the future dictator Ioannis Metaxas founded a paramilitary group, which undertook systematic violence against Venizelist supporters.

Nikolai waited for her reply. 'Well?' he said. 'What's your answer?'

'Who do you intend to invite?'

He turned and walked towards her.

'All nationalities—Christians and Muslims alike. All will be welcome. Money is money no matter whose hand it comes from.'

'You have a point. Let me think about it. It's a big step.'

'By the way, what was it that you wanted to discuss with me about Munire?' Nikolai asked, preparing to leave the room.

'It can wait. It's not important.'

He closed the door quietly behind him, leaving Sophia alone with the money. She was tempted to count it but that could also wait. Instead, she bundled it back into the bag and locked it in her safe.

A few days later Sophia received news that Xanthe and Georgos had been murdered in their beds and their home set on fire. As the fire took hold, Yianni Mandakis managed to save Ariadne, who had been asleep when the incident happened. The perpetrators—thought to be Turks—were never found and within a week, the investigation was called off.

Sickened by the deaths of her close friends, Sophia wasted no more time in giving Nikolai her blessing. He had known all along that she would agree; it was in her interest and she trusted him. Yet again, he had his own way.

# CHAPTER 12

*Constantinople, Winter 1916-1917*

It had been more than a year since Sophia had formally used the Grand Salon. The last occasion, for Andreas's exhibition, had left a sour taste in her mouth. Now she was happy to have a good excuse to use it again. She was astute enough to realize that in a relaxed atmosphere, where good food was plentiful and the wine flowed freely, discreet and intriguing stories would flow freely and could be put to good use. Before long, the lavish soirées held at La Maison du l'Orient became the talk of Constantinople and people vied with each other to be invited. It was now commonplace to see an assortment of bodyguards waiting outside La Maison du l'Orient. In the Grand Salon their masters and mistresses enjoyed a game of baccarat or joined in the latest dance crazes, improvising to ragtime and embracing their partner in the daring, pensive, yet passionate and sensual tango.

By January 1917, Sophia and Nikolai had amassed enough money to purchase the warehouse adjoining the atelier. With this latest acquisition, they set about transforming it into a spacious dance studio offering classes for those who wished to become accomplished in the new dance steps. The tango classes run by the Argentinean couple Carlos and Inez, whose orchestra it was that entertained them at the soirées, soon became fully booked. An American of Creole ancestry took the energetic ragtime classes that were equally popular. And for those who still preferred the waltz and the foxtrot, and especially for women for whom being out after dark was strictly unacceptable, afternoon tea dances were organized. For the first time in ages the money rolled in.

The popularity of the soirées meant that more help was required as Sophia's work was steadily growing again. Nikolai urged Sophia to put her trust in Helene as she had extensive contacts in the Russian and Levantine community that could prove to be invaluable.

'She's well educated, intelligent, self-assured and always surrounded by admirers,' he told her. 'And she is a loyal and trusted friend and has exceptional organizational skills, and…she's sympathetic to the Greek cause.'

Sophia's relationship with Nikolai had deepened to such an extent that she accepted his word without question. If he trusted Helene, then it was good enough for her. Besides, it would give her time to concentrate on her collections again. Women required the latest clothes for these occasions and many competed with each other to be the best dressed. The war had disrupted fabric supplies, especially silk, and she began to create simple dresses with sleek fluid lines that were ideal for the freedom of movement needed for the new dances. In keeping with European fashions she shortened the hemline to just above the ankle. With the occasional embellishment and her lavish use of color contrasting with the darker monotone colors of her European counterparts, Sophia's creations were once more in demand. Further, she was now able to give more work to the employees who had remained loyal to her in difficult times.

And so it was that Sophia, through her regular soirées with Nikolai, entered the shadowy world of espionage and intrigue. Seizing the opportunity to help those needier than herself, she would soon have to call for all the courage and resources possible to get her through the next few years.

In her office, Sophia discussed the final arrangements for the following evening's soirée with Nikolai. The softly stirring music of the bandoneon could be heard through the adjoining wall of the dance studio. The music was infectious. Suddenly, he pulled her away from her desk and embraced her in a sensual tango, smothering her neck with passionate kisses. Sophia felt her heart race and she returned his embrace. Theirs was a relationship hidden well away from the prying eyes of friends and family and they grabbed with open arms whatever chance they had to be together. It was a fleeting moment. Munire knocked on the door, prudently waiting for a moment before entering to inform Sophia that another order of tango shoes had just arrived from Lame Nick. He was only one of many friends who now prospered from her regular soirées. Hagop the Armenian supplied the leather and Lame Nick made the shoes—she couldn't be happier.

Still flushed from their embrace, she returned to her desk, smoothing the folds of her dress.

'I'm going to send her away,' she said to Nikolai, after Munire left the room. 'I don't like the way this is developing.'

He threw his hands into the air in despair. They had discussed the issue of Helene's brother many times. It had become a bone of contention. Nikolai saw nothing wrong with their friendship, but Munire's father had repeatedly asked her to consider his proposal to marry a man of his choice back home.

Sophia now felt a great weight of responsibility to her family.

'You should know full well, Nikolai,' said Sophia, 'her father would never allow her to marry a Russian. He is already beside himself that she has not returned home to marry the man of his choice. If it had not been for the devotion and influence of his French wife, he would have been here in a rage. And, I might add, there is still a possibility of that happening. Besides, I don't trust Helene's brother. I can't put my finger on it, but I assure you that something is not right—and he has an eye for the women. She will be hurt.'

Nikolai laughed. 'I've known him for a long time. He has eyes only for Munire and he truly cares for her. He has my trust. But if you insist...'

'My mind is made up,' replied Sophia firmly.

The next day she called Munire to her office and informed her of her decision. Munire protested. 'It's for the best. I don't want to lose you, but I have a duty to your family. Your father is losing patience with you.'

'I'm pleading with you. I cannot marry a man I know nothing of. My father will not let me return, and I don't want to leave Sergei.'

Sophia wiped away the tears from Munire's cheeks.

'At least appease your father by meeting this man. You have nothing to worry about; if Sergei cares for you he will wait.'

Munire was even more distraught when Sophia told her that she was to leave the next day. Sophia wiped her friend's tears with her finger.

'It's for the best,' she said. 'If it doesn't work out, I will welcome you back with open arms.'

From his office, Nikolai watched Munire tidy her desk and say farewell to the girls. She was still sobbing when she left. Sophia dropped a catalogue onto Nikolai's desk.

'Are you satisfied?' he said quietly as she turned to leave.

Sophia walked away, refusing to let him see the tears welling in her eyes. Letting Munire go was like losing a sister.

*Smyrna, August 1918*

With the outbreak of the Russian Revolution and the abdication of the Tsar, Russia was now out of the Great War. In Constantinople a wave of White Russians fleeing the tyranny of the Bolsheviks began to flood into the city. In Smyrna, Soterios surrounded himself with his associates in the Etairia but the atmosphere at home had become unbearable. He could still count on the support of his wife but Dimitra had become increasingly difficult. Her fears of an impending catastrophe fell on deaf ears; Soterios did not want to know. Ever the optimist, he was convinced that Constantinople would soon become the great capital of the Hellenes. In the end, of her own accord,

Dimitra decided that it would be better if she moved to her other house. Her daughter begged her to stay but Dimitra was adamant.

For many years, Dimitra had lived in the large family home in the Greek quarter of Smyrna where she had brought up her family. As was the custom of the day when Photeini married Soterios, the couple elected to live in the family home. But Dimitra had kept her first home on the outskirts of the Turkish quarter; she frequently stayed there, accompanied only by the faithful Iskender. This was the home that she and Jean-Paul built together when their fortunes improved and she was still very attached to it. In this Ottoman-style house with its overhanging timbered balconies and central courtyard, Dimitra was at her happiest. It was here in the vermillion room with its silk divans and sumptuous carpets that she had created her finest embroideries: the sash for the Valide Sultan that launched her fame, and the beautiful wedding dress for the Qajar princess. And it was here that she had once kept her horses that were then her passion. As far as she was concerned, her son-in-law with his foolish ideas of the glory that was Greece was more than welcome to the family home. What few years she had left she wanted to spend in peace and harmony. Photeini—caught in the middle—pleaded with Iskender to help her convince her mother to return. He remained resolutely faithful to Dimitra.

*Constantinople, November 1918*

In September, Greek forces participated in the massive Allied offensive, which broke the Bulgarian front and led to the collapse of the Central Powers. In October, the armistice was signed: the Ottomans had lost the war. Great empires lay in ruins and the upheavals had far-reaching consequences. Yugoslavia, Hungary, and Poland declared their independence and new countries were being formed in Europe and the Middle East. Almost nine million people had been killed and twice as many wounded.

From the verandah of her house, holding Nina in her arms, accompanied by Leonidas, Maria, Nikolai, Markos, and her father, Sophia watched the sixteen-mile convoy of Allied warships enter the Bosphorus and anchor off the Golden Horn. This was a momentous occasion and Soterios was beside himself with joy. Leonidas found the pomp and ceremony thrilling, pointing out the various ships to his grandfather and asking questions which Soterios was only too happy to answer.

'Look carefully,' Soterios said to him proudly. 'This is something you will remember for the rest of your life. The city has been liberated and you will grow up to be part of a new world. It is the Greek world that belongs to your forefathers and where all Greek-speaking peoples will be unified.'

'This is only the beginning,' cautioned Markos. 'If we are to achieve our final ambition then we must win over the Turkish people, and with all the distrust and resentment built up over the past few decades that will not be easy.'

Wartime conditions had given way to a simmering hatred and in the cold, dark days of winter, the atmosphere in the city was one of foreboding. After the armistice the Turks were humiliated and fearful of the future. They left the city in droves, heading for Anatolia and the eastern provinces. Returning from the war, thousands now found themselves destitute. All this was in sharp contrast to the exuberance shown by the Greeks who welcomed the Allies into the city with great joy and bravado, flaunting the blue and white flag, and provoking the Turks mercilessly.

'Until the Peace Treaty is signed, we know nothing for sure; truth is hidden at the bottom of the well,' Markos told them. 'There is disunity amongst the Allies as to the spoils of the empire.'

'The British have assured Venizelos they would accommodate his wishes for a Greater Greece,' replied Soterios optimistically. 'Our hopes are with Lloyd George; he is a true philhellene. The Great Ottoman Empire is no more, Markos. The Sultan has no real power and the government is in disarray.'

'We will see,' Markos replied. 'Time will tell.'

Later that evening, Sophia received a visitor at the house. Zubeyde announced that Ali Hodja wanted to speak with her.

'*Iyi aksamler*, Hanim Efendi Sophia.'

'*Hos geldinez*,' she replied. 'What brings you out on such a cold night?'

Ali Hodja clasped his hands together on his lap, his stern countenance belying his compassionate nature.

'I come in peace, Hanim Efendi Sophia. I have known your family for many years and together we celebrated the good times and mourned the bad. Allah has looked favorably on you and you have reaped his generosity. Yet I fear for the future. It is common knowledge that your people are desirous of the area first colonized by the Greeks of old in Asia Minor, and of the dream to take this city of our great Sultan Mehmet II, but...' he cautioned, 'be assured that our people will never allow it. It is said that he who passes through Gordium will untie the Gordian knot and conquer Asia. Eleftherios Venizelos is not Alexander the Great. Much blood has already been spilt. Let the past sleep peacefully in its grave. I do not want to spend my last years bathed in blood. I want to see the sons and daughters of our children live in harmony, as we have done for centuries. Your people have unprecedented wealth in the community, in many cases far exceeding those of the Muslims.

Do not let our blood mingle in this great earth of ours.'

He paused a moment to allow her to digest his words. 'I know that there are some in our communities who seek revenge, but they will reap what they sow in heaven.'

'Why are you telling me this, Ali Hodja?' asked Sophia, alarmed at the seriousness of his speech.

'Because you are a well respected member of our community, and your influence means something. I exercise caution in these turbulent times. I respect your father greatly, but it is impossible to say these things to him.'

'Our future will be decided by the Allies,' remarked Sophia. 'No one wants more bloodshed.'

'The Allies are fickle.'

'Man's destiny is Allah's will,' replied Sophia. 'Isn't that what you tell us? The river must run until it reaches the sea.'

Ali Hodja stood to take his leave. 'We will speak no more of this matter, Hanim Efendi Sophia,' he concluded with finality. 'I wish you and your family peace and a long life.'

Ali Hodja's visit weighed heavily on her mind. Having been schooled in both the Western and Eastern traditions, he was a wise and learned man and she valued his judgment almost as much as her grandmother's. That he should have paid her this visit at all spoke volumes.

When the German military left Constantinople, Von Straumbacher was among the first to leave. The day before he was due to depart, he paid a visit to La Maison du l'Orient to say goodbye to Sophia. He brought her a present, which he asked her not to open until after he left. She in turn gave him a present for his wife: an embroidered sash that he had admired on her at her first soirée. He was visibly moved to receive the gift, as he knew that she had made it herself in the style taught to her by her grandmother.

'Frau Sophia, your companionship has lifted my spirits enormously… much more than you will ever know. Words cannot express my gratitude. Perhaps one day we will meet again in happier times.' Von Straumbacher gestured towards the present. 'Keep it somewhere safe; you may need it one day.'

Bidding her family a good life, he bowed and left.

Sophia was saddened at his departure. He had hated the war almost as much as she did. In the short time that she had known him she had learnt to trust him. Under his ever-watchful eye, he had passed on sensitive information that he knew she would put to good use. After he left she removed the wrapping and to her great surprise found a mahogany box with his initials engraved on the lid in gold German script. Lifting the lid, she looked at the contents with alarm. Inside was a leather holster containing his Luger. She picked it up. It felt strange in her hands; it was heavy and out of character, and she wondered why he had felt the need to give it to her. She would never know. On the way back to Germany, Von Straumbacher was killed when his convoy was blown up by partisans near Belgrade.

She put the box away in the lower drawer of her desk and locked it, placing the key back in its position, hidden in the back of the silver frame that contained a photograph of her children. Nikolai walked into the room lamenting the departure of a good man. She decided not to tell him about the Luger.

Since the occupation and the ever-popular soirées, La Maison du l'Orient had experienced a welcome burst of activity and with Munire still away, Sophia engaged the services of her close friend Anna as vendeuse. Anna's father was a wealthy banker and a prominent member of the Etairia, frequently donating large amounts of money to the Greek cause. Anna had married a Greek ship-owner the year after Sophia and Andreas married, but the relationship was a disaster from the beginning. Her husband was a notorious womanizer and with the stigma of divorce inconceivable to her family, she was desperate to find suitable work outside her home. Anna's elegant naturalness combined with her delightful and lively personality, fluency in languages, and familiarity with high society made her a first-class vendeuse. Much to Sophia's delight she also got along well with Helene and the two became good friends. In many ways they were similar; both were ravishingly beautiful with a great zest for life, yet Sophia recognized one great difference. While her friend kept a certain dignity for her family's sake, Helene enjoyed unparalleled freedom, answerable to no one but herself, often taking lovers and leaving them without the slightest hesitation when she tired of them. Sophia was also aware that Helene was capable of far more treacherous acts than those of which Anna could ever dream.

Shortly after Anna's appointment Sophia received a letter from Munire stating that the man her father wished her to marry was a respected bey from a nearby town. His wife had died and left him with five children, the eldest being a girl ten years younger than Munire. She wrote that although he was much older he was a good and kindly man and she had grown fond of his children, describing them as well behaved and respectful to their father. In the end she had consented to marry him and concluded her letter by asking Sophia to explain the situation to Sergei.

Sophia kept the contents of Munire's letter to herself. Since her departure, Sergei had professed his deep love for his sweet Munire on several occasions, but with each passing week his loneliness seemed to diminish as he discovered fresh pretty faces to whom he turned his attentions. After a while he stopped asking after Munire.

Sophia angrily discussed Sergei's fickleness with Nikolai, who seemed to defend his friend's behavior by saying that he was drowning his sorrows. Gradually she began to detest Sergei, and over coffee one evening at Zaharoplasteion Olympia, she decided to confide in Markos something that had been on her mind for a while. Some time before she went away Munire casually let slip that Sergei had noticed the door to the Hellenic room behind the red brocade curtains. Standing next to it one evening, he moved the curtains aside and tried to open the door. Finding it locked he asked Munire what use was made of the room. At first Munire refused to answer but he was persistent and she finally told him that it was only ever used by the family, and even she had never been inside. Munire had found his preoccupation with the room alarming, admonishing his behavior as impertinent. One evening when he thought no one was looking, he tried the door again. 'It's always locked,' whispered Munire, imploring him to move away. 'Only Kyria Sophia has the key.'

His curiosity had caused Sophia unease. Markos listened to her concerns and asked her not to dwell on it any longer; he would look into it.

# CHAPTER 13

*Constantinople, Spring 1919*

After the Russian Revolution the Bolsheviks and the Nationalists became allies supporting each other's cause, particularly against any interference by the Western Powers. Constantinople, already home for many White Russians, was now being infiltrated with Bolshevik spies. The city's finest hotels and nightclubs became fertile ground for political intrigue. In this web of deceit, Markos informed Sophia that people in Greek villages in and around the city of Bursa had noticed several Russians asking questions of the Greek community. Being highly suspicious of outsiders, they concluded that they were Turkish sympathizers colluding with the local Turkish gendarmes to obtain information which threatened their survival. It was his intention to go there to check it for himself, but he had one thing to discuss with her—he wanted to take Nikolai. If they were Russian spies then his help would be invaluable.

Sophia gave it some thought. Bursa—the first capital of the Ottoman Empire, situated on the slopes of the Uludağ mountain range, some sixty miles south west of Constantinople—was the center of the empire's silk industry; she and Nikolai had been there on several occasions, but since then war bandits made the countryside a lawless place to travel. It was a dangerous mission and she was apprehensive. More importantly, she could not bear the thought that something terrible might happen and she would never see Nikolai again. She had always loved Andreas, even when they became estranged after Thrace, and his death affected her deeply. But Nikolai was different. She had fallen deeply in love with him from the very moment she laid eyes on him. They understood each other; she loved him like no other man and never would again. With him she found the courage to carry on through such turmoil. He was her rock, her very reason for living. In the end she concluded that the decision was his alone to make. She called him into her office, desperately hoping that he would say no. It was not to be—he was only too eager to help. She did not voice her disappointment but instead suggested that as speed was essential, Ali Agha should drive them there.

At dawn the next day they left Constantinople for Bursa. With a deep ache in her heart Sophia stood on the steps of La Maison du l'Orient and watched the car until it disappeared from view, leaving a cloud of gray dust in its wake. In the distance dark clouds gathered, threatening to unleash a violent thunderstorm. It was a bad omen and a sense of foreboding clouded her thoughts. The Greek villages lay scattered throughout the mountains and she estimated that they would be away about a week, two weeks at the most. After a few days she received a call to say that they had arrived safe and well and, weather permitting, would be leaving the following morning for the far side of the mountain.

Several days later, and shortly after she had retired to bed for the evening, there was a knock on the door. Downstairs she heard muffled voices in the hallway. Moments later Zubeyde knocked on her door saying that two of her friends were waiting in the reception room and that they needed to speak with her urgently. When she saw Lefteris and Panayiotis standing there, the blood drained from her face.

'What has happened?' cried Sophia, alarmed. 'My God, please tell me.'

The men's eyes avoided her. There was no way to soften the blow.

'There has been a terrible accident,' said Panayiotis.

Sophia tried to speak, but the words would not come. A pain ripped through her heart like a dagger and the room began to spin.

'They reached the outlying villages without incident but on the way back the Turks became suspicious of their presence,' he continued. 'It was a hazardous drive made even worse by a torrential downpour that turned the road into mud. For a while low mists afforded them valuable protection, but when the Turks began to fire at them Markos urged Ali Agha to go faster. By this time the winding road and hairpin bends had become even more treacherous. And then a bullet struck the front wheel, bursting the front tire. The car skidded and careered off the road, hurtling down the mountainside. The mangled wreckage lay strewn across the gulley.'

'News reached the Greek villagers straight away,' said Lefteris. 'But when they reached the wreckage it was burnt almost beyond recognition. The charred remains of Ali Agha were still in the burned-out car. Another body lay some feet away and they identified him as the Russian—Nikolai. After some time they found Markos. He had been thrown out of the car as it began to tumble down the mountainside. He was unconscious and suffering from badly broken bones but, thank God, he is still alive. The villagers managed to get him back to Bursa. He will remain there with a Greek family until he's recovered enough to return.'

Sophia felt as if her life had stopped. A constant thrumming at the base of her skull made her nauseous and the pain in her heart now wracked her whole body. First Andreas, now Nikolai. How would life ever be the same again?

A few days later Helene called at La Maison du l'Orient to see Sophia. 'The night before he went away, Nikolai called at my apartment saying that should he not return, I was to give you this letter.' She handed over a brown envelope. 'He said it was important.'

Seeing Sophia's trembling hands, Helene excused herself, saying that she had an urgent appointment in the Grande Rue de Pera. Once alone, Sophia read his letter.

> Dear woman of my heart,
>
> If I never return do not fret. Only know that the first moment I gave in to my desires was the moment I started to live. My heart bursts when I think of you but no one can expect such perfect happiness for too long. Sooner or later the spell is broken. These are treacherous times. No one knows where fate will take us. Do not weep. Be strong and courageous and know that I have loved you more than life itself. I remain yours always.
>
> Your lover, your obedient servant, and your true friend,
> Nikolai

Sophia held the letter to her lips and kissed it. It bore the faint scent of ambergris.

*Smyrna, May 14, 1919*

Dappled sunlight danced across the cobblestones as Dimitra sat on the chaise-longue underneath the Judas tree, enjoying a dish of fragrant rose-petal conserve. Clad in a pale rose and apricot chemisette, she closed her eyes and lay back listening to the gentle trickling sound of water from the fountain. In just three years she would turn one hundred and, despite exceedingly good health, she felt a strong premonition that the angel of death was soon to call on her. Strangely, she did not feel sad; she had lived a long and fortuitous life. God had seen fit to endow her with richness in life for which she was eternally grateful.

With the late afternoon sun warming her cheeks, Dimitra relived her memories. 'The heart that loves is always young.' Isn't that what Aunt Kuzel always told her? Dear Kuzel; how she often thought of her, and how she missed her still…even after all these years. The images of her childhood were as clear as if it were yesterday, yet she still kept them locked away in her heart, hidden even from her family. In many ways it was these memories that had sustained her after the loss of Jean-Paul. Her thoughts turned to her daughter. Photeini had never really understood her mother. The nearest anyone came to that was Sophia. There was a deep bond between them—something that words could not express. Somehow, Dimitra saw in Sophia the image of her own mother. She was beautiful, intelligent, creative and headstrong; she was everything Aunt Kuzel had said her mother had been. Her daydreams were interrupted when Iskender informed her that Photeini had arrived with an urgent message.

'Mama, I bring you good news. Earlier today Soterios, along with other Smyrniot notables, was called to a meeting by Captain Mavroudis. They were read a proclamation sent by Venizelos himself. The Greek army is on its way and will arrive tomorrow.'

Photeini was so excited that it was impossible to contain her joy. General Mavroudis was Greece's representative in Smyrna. Allied attachments had already arrived and taken possession of the Smyrniot forts and at first some believed that it was the British who were to take command of the city.

'This is such a wonderful thing for us,' she continued. 'Finally the Christians will be liberated and Smyrna will once again be a part of the Kingdom of Greece. We'll never be called *rayah* again. Soterios always knew the Allies would stand by us.'

Dimitra had neither the energy nor the will to argue with her daughter any longer. She desperately wanted to ask if she had felt like common *rayah* when she was openly accepted by the women of the palace, or by the wives of wealthy pashas when they had patronized the atelier, helping to make her rich. That in turn enabled her idealistic husband to buy books which helped to fire his nationalistic fervor. Instead she just listened.

'My daughter, my life is almost at an end. If the occupation of the Greeks from the mainland will give you a better life, then I will be happy for you.'

Photeini took her mother's hand. 'Mother, they are not simply "Greeks from the mainland." We are one and the same.'

Dimitra sighed. 'What do you know of Athens, Photeini? I have heard that it is a small city...without culture. Perhaps centuries ago, yes, but not now. It is nothing compared to Smyrna.'

Photeini threw her hands in the air in desperation.

'I want you to go home now, before it gets dark,' said Dimitra, exasperated by her daughter's talk. 'The Turks are angry and it would be unwise for you to be away from your home.' She called out to Iskender. 'Take Kyria Photeini home.'

'I will call again tomorrow, Mama,' said Photeini, taking her leave.

'My home will always be open for you, my daughter.'

As Iskender left the neighborhood a noisy commotion was taking place outside the house. Indignant Turks were running from door to door announcing that there was to be a protest that evening, and they urged all Turks to be there.

At the break of dawn on May 15, 1919, thousands of Greeks converged on the seafront in Smyrna. The atmosphere was that of a public holiday. A sea of blue-and-white flags fluttered in the early morning sun. Dimitra stood on the hotel balcony looking down at the mass of people below, their elation tangible. Beside her stood a small, conservatively dressed middle-aged woman, her head partially covered in a fawn silk veil. The two women watched in disbelief, the colour draining from their faces. The younger woman moved closer to Dimitra, holding her arm.

'Look at them, Aunt. This is the day for which the Greeks of Smyrna have long waited.'

It was almost seven and the quayside was completely filled with jubilant Greek families intent on being a part of this momentous and moving occasion. In the distance wisps of smoke could be seen at the far end of the Gulf. Soon the transport ships came into sight, and as they approached the quayside steamers sounded their hooters and the crowd went wild.

Dimitra saw the Metropolitan of Smyrna, dressed in his richly embroidered robes, walk forward and bless the first men to disembark. Some of them looped arms and performed a Greek dance. The onlookers cheered and wept with delight.

'How tactless is that?' said the veiled woman. 'Why do they humiliate us more? The whole episode is making me ill.' She tried to compose herself. 'Perhaps they expect you to be out there with them, Aunt? You're a prominent citizen and maybe people expect you to play a visible role.'

'To watch from this balcony is enough for me,' replied Dimitra. 'I have no desire to be a part of this great folly.'

Dimitra was in the minority. Very few Greeks there on that sunny morning doubted that the occupation would be anything less than a triumphant success. Someone caught her eye in the crowd.

'What is it?' asked the veiled woman, seeing her distress.

'Over there…next to the Metropolitan. That foolish son-in-law of mine and his friends are greeting the officers. Look at him, puffed up like a peacock. He's blind to the danger he makes for his family. If you join the dance circle, you must dance; he who acts without care shall remember with sorrow.'

'We are being divided and it is beyond our control. Your son-in-law has staked his fortune with the Greeks and my two sons are talking about taking up armed resistance. I pray to God that they never face each other.'

They discussed the events that had taken place the night before. Several thousand Turks, many of them from the neighborhood close to Dimitra's house, met on the heights of Bachri-Baba, next to the Jewish cemetery, to protest the invasion of the insolent, infidel Greeks. All through the night, fires burned and drums could be heard for miles. The noise sent a shudder through all those who heard it.

Shortly after ten, the two women left the hotel just in time to witness Greek soldiers, followed by a cheering crowd of onlookers, mercilessly poke and prod their unarmed Turkish prisoners with bayonets, forcing them to shout, 'Long live Venizelos! Long live Greece!' A terrified man was rifle-butted to the ground next to the hotel. Undeterred by onlookers, the soldier simply bayoneted him to death. Throughout the day groups of civilians took advantage of the chaos to plunder the shops and homes of Turks and the carnage continued well into the next day. Almost immediately the violence spread out into the countryside; soon hardly a town or village would be spared.

*Constantinople, August 1919*

Sophia made her way through Pera towards Galata. The streets were almost deserted. The Greek celebrations were coming to an abrupt end and they now feared a backlash from the Turks. She walked past Zaharoplasteion Olympia and found Constantine in the process of boarding up the windows.

'Where are you going?' he asked, continuing to hammer nails into the boards. 'Haven't you heard of the crowds gathering in old Stamboul? Soon they will be in Pera wreaking their vengeance on us.'

'I'm on my way to visit Markos.'

'I heard he's recovering well,' Constantine said, putting the last board in place.

'Yes, *doxa sto Theo*. The doctor says he'll soon be able to walk again and will eventually make a full recovery.'

'Come inside a moment. I'll prepare a box of his favorite cakes for him.'

Constantine had seen little of her since the accident but he couldn't fail to notice how the glow had faded from her cheeks. Yet for all her sorrow, she still possessed the most beautiful eyes he had ever seen; they were a deep amethyst that sparkled in the sunlight, emphasized by thick dark lashes. He could still clearly remember the first time he met her. Young and in love, she had the world at her feet. How happy and excited she and Andreas were as they discussed their plans for the new premises. That was when she was at her loveliest. Years later he observed that same youthful beauty

111

when she met Nikolai. Poor Sophia, he thought to himself as he tied the ribbon around the box; she needed love like the nightingale needed the rose garden. Without it, that brilliant light would fade forever.

'Here, take this also,' he said to her. 'It's a bottle of my finest raki. And take care—the streets are not safe.'

It had been over six months since Sophia last saw Markos and he was well on the way to a full recovery. He still found it hard to talk about Bursa and for a while they sat in silence. The deaths of Ali Agha and Nikolai preyed heavily on his mind and he blamed himself for taking them. He told her they had learned that Greek villagers often disappeared without a trace and while most were happy with the Greek occupation of Smyrna, there was a growing sense of unease. If anything was going to rally the war-wearied Turk, this would be it. They saw the Peace Treaty, still unsigned, as a betrayal, and viewed the Allies with contempt.

'You should replace Ali Agha,' he said after a while. 'I'll find you a Greek chauffeur myself. There are plenty of good men without work who would be only too willing to work for you.'

'Ali Agha was family to me. He is irreplaceable.'

Markos knitted his brows in a frown. 'He will never be forgotten. You must move on; it's far too dangerous for you to be unaccompanied and we'd never forgive ourselves if anything happened to you.'

Reluctantly, Sophia agreed.

The next day, Sophia received a telephone call at La Maison du l'Orient.

'Kyria Sophia, my name is Kapitanos Vangelis Karageorgos. I have been informed that you are in need of a chauffeur and bodyguard and I would like to offer my services. I have references, and should you consider me suitable I am available to start immediately.'

Sophia smiled to herself. Markos had certainly wasted no time in looking after her interests. 'Kyrios Karageorgos, I'm sure you will be most suitable. You may start tomorrow.'

Sophia put down the phone and glanced at Anna busily sorting though a mound of fabrics.

'Is everything alright, Sophia?' asked Anna.

'Tomorrow I will have a new chauffeur—but then you probably knew that already didn't you, Anna?'

Anna smiled and continued her work.

# CHAPTER 14

*Constantinople, 1920*

In the winter of 1919 and 1920 the Etairia kept watch on Sergei and discovered that he not only worked for the Nationalists, but for the Bolsheviks too. Being a part of the first wave of Russian aristocrats to the West, his Russian friends had considered him an enemy of the Revolution. He was an ambitious and ruthless man and recent events had forced him to reconsider his loyalties. Sergei was a gadfly, enjoying the fruits of an extravagant life. His instincts told him that his fortunes now lay elsewhere. The Nationalists and Bolsheviks would pay handsomely for information—especially when it concerned the Greeks. Sophia's first thoughts were of Helene. Was she involved in this game of deception with him? Markos assured her that Helene knew nothing of her brother's involvement. They had little to do with each other since leaving Bulgaria; something to do with a disagreement over a will after the sudden death of their aunt. The Dowager Duchess left all her money to Sergei, and Helene accused him of foul play.

Markos discovered that Sergei's monthly cash transactions had suddenly stopped. They assumed that his benefactors had demanded more for their money and just lately he had not been forthcoming with information of any substance. The idea of clawing a living, as his fellow Russians were forced to do, was a terrifying thought to Sergei and he was becoming desperate. With desperation came a lack of caution. Fearing trouble, several in the Etairia discussed getting rid of him. It was Sophia who asked them to wait. She couldn't shake it from her mind that it was because of her that he had entered their lives. More than anything, she needed to know for sure if he had anything to do with Nikolai's death and asked Markos to give her a little time to see if she could find out anything. Reluctantly, he agreed, but he warned her that she was playing with fire and should things turn sour, his days were numbered. In the meantime, she in turn resolved to put her distaste for him aside and try to win his trust.

In March 1920, the British disbanded the Ottoman parliament and formally placed the city under military occupation. The long-awaited Treaty of Sèvres was signed in August, just over a year after the Greek army landed in Smyrna. There was to be an independent Armenia and an autonomous Kurdistan; the Smyrna zone was ceded to the Greeks; and Anatolia was to be divided into French and Italian zones. The Turkish armed forces were to be under Allied supervision and the strategically vital Dardanelles and the Russian port of Batumi would be under international control. The Turks were outraged and their long-standing hatred of the Christian Greeks and Armenians was about to explode into further bloodshed from which there would be no turning back. The fragile treaty had merely served to push the war-weary Turks into the arms of the Nationalists. Under the determined guidance of Mustafa Kemal they would fight with renewed vigor to preserve their land. Ali Hodja had been right when he cautioned Sophia of the events to come—and so had her grandmother. In just a few short months, Ottoman Turkey was a country divided.

The situation plunged into further disarray when in November, Venizelos fell from power in Greece and King Constantine was brought back from exile. Remembering his reluctance to join them in World War I, the Allies threatened to cut off supplies and to give no further financial aid to an already beleaguered nation, thus greatly diminishing their chances of ever winning the struggle in Asia Minor.

*Constantinople, July 1921*

Towards the end of the year, Munire married Ismail Bey. She wrote to Sophia telling her that Allah in his goodness had seen fit to bless them with a child and they were very happy. What Sophia didn't know was that shortly after receiving her letter, Ismail Bey's village came under attack from Greek irregulars ahead of the army, who terrorized the Turkish inhabitants. In this small village where Turks and Greeks had lived peaceably for generations, attending each other's celebrations, the Greeks set fire to the centuries-old mosque and moved into the Turkish neighborhood, destroying the houses and tormenting the inhabitants.

Ismail Bey had been tending his fields when the attack happened. Munire and the children cowered in the house, fearing for their lives. As dusk descended the village became cloaked in an eerie stillness, followed some time later by a low wailing sound. Somehow, Munire sensed that it was for her. Finally, she could bear it no more and ran to the door, flinging it wide open and stumbling into the street. Out of the dark shadows a procession of men slowly approached the house. She stood as if nailed to the cobblestones. On their shoulders the men carried the lifeless body of Ismail Bey, and on his bloodied chest they had placed his red fez.

During the next few months, Sophia put all her efforts into winning Sergei's confidence. The soirées were still immensely popular, and after Nikolai's death Helene took over running them, allowing Sophia to concentrate on her design work. More and more, she was seen in the company of Sergei. To outsiders, she appeared to show a keen interest in him. Only a few members of the Etairia knew the truth behind her liaison. But Sergei wanted more from Sophia and it troubled him greatly that he had never been invited to her home to meet the children, as Nikolai had. He persistently asked when he would meet them but the answer was always the same.

'My children are still grieving and it would be unwise for them to see their mother in the company of another man,' she told him.

Observing his exasperation, Sophia felt a tinge of cold delight.

Driving back from a day's outing to Scutari on the opposite shore of the Bosphorus, Vangelis observed Sergei's face in the mirror. She is playing him like a cat plays with a mouse, he thought to himself. And soon she will tire of you. Arriving at his apartment, Sergei asked her if she would join him for tea. Feigning disappointment, Sophia assured him she would do so next time. He squeezed her hand tightly.

'I'll hold you to that,' he told her sharply.

Going home, Sophia leaned back in the seat, fanned herself with her glove and sighed. She caught Vangelis looking at her.

'Achhh,' she said to him. 'Such an offensive and tedious man, and we have absolutely nothing in common.'

Vangelis did not reply, but he did wonder just how much more of this deception she could take. In the short time during which Sophia had known Vangelis he had become a trusted member of her family, and he watched over her like a hawk. Like Ali Agha, he was resolutely loyal, but that is where the similarity ended. Ali Agha had been a quiet introvert, content with his own company. He had also been a deeply religious and superstitious man. Vangelis, on the other hand, had a jovial outgoing nature and was a captivating storyteller. He had once been the captain of a boat that plied the waters between Mytilene and Ayvalik, but after an altercation with the Turks his boat sank. As he had no money to replace it, he decided to try his luck in the city instead. There he worked on odd jobs until Markos offered him the job as Sophia's chauffeur. Her children loved him immensely and always referred to him as Kapitanos—something that both amused and delighted him greatly. He was an accomplished laouto player, often entertaining them in the evenings with popular Greek songs. With few other men in their lives, Vangelis filled a deep void and Sophia was eternally grateful to Markos for sending him to her.

Maria, now aged thirteen, was showing signs of blossoming into a strikingly beautiful young woman. Her sunset red hair had deepened into the lustrous rich shades of copper and chestnut, of which she was immensely proud. Her moody temperament had mellowed somewhat, slowly being replaced with an extraordinary vanity that Sophia considered unhealthy. When she wasn't studying, she whiled away her time dressing up and brushing her hair incessantly, trying out the latest styles. She told anyone who would listen that she would soon be the belle of the ball and would marry the richest, most handsome man in the city. She began to show an interest in music and dance and begged her mother to allow her to take lessons with Carlos and Inez. At first Sophia resisted. Maria resorted to her old tactics, shutting herself in her room and sulking for days on end until the tension in the house was unbearable. Leonidas, who showed no interest in dance whatsoever, agreed to accompany her as a dance partner and chaperone. Reluctantly, Sophia agreed.

Inez and Carlos informed Sophia that her daughter showed great promise and it might be a good idea to allow her to attend an afternoon tea dance, where there would be other young ladies of good standing. Once again Sophia gave in, but that was not enough for Maria: she then wanted to attend one of her mother's soirées, of which she had heard such wonderful stories. This time her pleas were met with a resounding no. She was becoming a handful. Without Andreas and Nikolai, Sophia felt the anguish of not having a man in whom to confide. She considered talking with Markos, but it had been a while since she had seen him and now was not the time.

To Sophia's great surprise Maria changed her mind. Instead, she told her mother that she had another idea. Would it be possible for her to stay in the Hellenic room and listen to the music? She suggested that Leonidas could be with her and out of sight and it would give her a chance to practice her dance steps. Once again Leonidas came to her rescue, promising his mother that they would remain quiet, and that anyway it would give him a chance to paint in his father's favorite room.

'That room hasn't been used for ages,' said Sophia. 'I'll have to think about it.'

'But, Mama, I'm sure that Papa would be only too happy to see us use it again,' urged Maria wistfully. 'What harm can it do?'

'I agree,' added Leonidas. 'He always enjoyed it when we were there with him, and his murals inspire me so much.'

Sophia thought about the times her son had twirled around the room in the Grand Salon, pretending to be an eagle. It had been a while since he'd been there.

'Alright,' she agreed reluctantly, 'but on one condition. You must promise me faithfully that you will keep absolutely quiet. I don't want other people going into that room.'

Maria threw her arms around her mother's neck and kissed her.

'Thank you, Mama. We will be as quiet as mice—even you will forget we're there.'

On the evening of the next soirée, Sophia confided in Anna that the children would be listening to the music in the adjoining room. She placed a tray of their favorite food in the room, making sure that they were comfortable.

'Promise that you will keep quiet,' Sophia said to Maria one more time.

'Don't worry, Mama,' replied Leonidas, reassuring her. 'We'll be quiet alright.'

She hugged them both and walked back into the Grand Salon, pulling the red brocade curtain back across the door. Soon after, Carlos and Inez arrived to set up the band along with Helene, bringing in the evening's food and wine.

In the adjoining room Maria settled down on the divan, placed a mirror by her side, and began to comb her hair, humming gently to the music. Leonidas opened his sketchbook, prepared his paints, and studied his father's murals. His thoughts wandered to his mother. Being in this room reminded him of how his mother always smelt of Damask rose, yet just lately it seemed that she never wore it. He missed her scent; it reminded him of happier times.

It wasn't long into the evening before Maria, completely exhausted, fell asleep on the divan. Covering his sister with a quilt, Leonidas continued painting until he too drifted off. Sometime later Maria woke to find the band still playing. She looked over towards her brother—he was sound asleep. Out of curiosity she decided to take a peek into the Grand Salon. Tiptoeing silently across the room, her bare feet sinking into the Kashan hunting carpet, she opened the door slightly. Momentarily, the plaintive sound of the bandoneon filled the room. Leonidas stirred and Maria quickly closed the door. Seeing that her brother slept soundly, she carefully opened it again. Her view of the Grand Salon was blocked by the red brocade curtain. Cautiously, she slowly pulled it aside until she caught a glimpse of the guests. Maria gasped with delight. The fashionably dressed women looked even more beautiful than she had ever imagined. Mesmerized, she watched them as they danced past, holding their partners in a way that she had never seen before. Even to her young and inexperienced eyes the dancing appeared flirtatious and beguiling, and the sound of their laughter was quite contagious. Maria thought it the most delightful sight she had ever seen and vowed that one day soon, she too would dance in the arms of a man like that.

Suddenly, a man's hand reached out and began to draw back the curtain. Alarmed, Maria quickly jumped back into the room and closed the door. Her heart thudded. What if someone saw her? Her mother would never forgive her. She saw the door handle turn. The door was unlocked, yet no one entered. Someone must have seen her. Afraid, she put her hand to her mouth wondering whether to call Leonidas. A few minutes passed and still no one entered. Relieved, she turned to walk back to the divan when the door opened. A man entered, quickly closed the door behind him and, leaning back against it, looked at her in silence. He surveyed the room, taking in every detail. His eyes narrowed when he saw the murals. Overcome by fear, Maria stood as if rooted to the ground. The man was quite dashing and very well dressed and she was surprised she hadn't noticed him. He must have been standing near the curtain and realized that someone was in this room, she told herself. The man forced a kindly smile and held out his hand.

'It's quite alright, my dear,' he whispered. 'There's no need to be afraid, I'm not going to harm you.'

He noticed Leonidas curled up on the divan and put his finger to his mouth.

'Sshhh, we don't want to wake him, do we? You're Maria, aren't you?'

She found herself nodding.

'I'm a friend of your mother and I recognized you from the photograph on your mother's desk. You're even prettier than your photograph. Why don't you come over and sit with me and we can get to know each other.'

He sat on the divan and patted the cushion, urging her to sit next to him. She looked over towards Leonidas—he was sound asleep.

'My name is Sergei,' said the man. 'Come, tell me about yourself.'

Carefully, and through flattery, Sergei gained Maria's trust. She told him about her love of music and dance, all of which he listened to attentively. He asked her about the room. Why did her mother always keep it locked? Perhaps she knew why? Was it because of the magnificent murals, which in his opinion far surpassed the ones in the Grand Salon?

'My papa painted them,' replied Maria proudly. 'This was his favorite room and he and Mama often spent time here.'

'And do you think that is why no one is allowed in here, because of your father?'

'Perhaps. She still misses him very much.'

'And did Uncle Nikolai ever come here?'

'I think so. After Papa became ill, Uncle Nikolai took great care of us, especially after Nina was born.'

As Sergei expected she would, Maria told him what he wanted to hear: that she often overheard them talk about meetings, sometimes held in the Hellenic room, at other times elsewhere, especially when her grandfather came from Smyrna.

'Sometimes they would come home very late and my brother and I would know they'd been to one of their meetings, especially before the war ended. But of course we were never allowed to talk about it.'

'Does your mother still attend any of these meetings?' he asked bluntly.

Maria tried to think. 'I don't think so; not here anyway. In fact, just lately she has spent much more time at home.'

Sergei stroked her chestnut hair and told her what a beautiful child she was—just like her mother.

'Do you think so?' she asked, surprised. 'Mama says I'm always naughty and that she doesn't understand me...and my great-grandmother Dimitra avoids me. I've often heard her say bad things about me.'

'Such as?' asked Sergei, showing concern.

'That I have the devil inside me and that I bring bad luck; too many things that make me sad.' Maria looked downcast. 'But...' she paused for a moment and looked across the room at Leonidas, 'everyone loves my brother.'

'Your great-grandmother is from a generation when superstition ruled people's lives. Don't take any notice; you mustn't believe those silly things. Anyway, I think you're wonderful...and very pretty.'

Maria's face lit up with his compliments. Sergei scrutinized the murals again.

'They are simply works of art; quite powerful. It's no wonder your father was proud of them. But they should not be hidden away.' A smile crossed his face as he contemplated their significance. 'Do you know what they depict?'

'Oh, yes,' she said innocently. 'They're of ancient Greece...we learn about them at school. That one is the Parthenon in Athens...and that one over there is the oracle at Delphi.'

'I see you know your history well,' Sergei smiled.

'Papa always told us that they were special.'

'Did he now?' Sergei replied. 'I agree with him. They are very special indeed.'

Leonidas began to stir and Maria ran to his side. He looked distressed to find someone else in the room.

'It's alright, this is Sergei,' Maria whispered. 'He's a friend of Mama's.'

Leonidas pushed his sister aside, jumped up from the divan and confronted the stranger.

'You have no right to be here. Please leave now.'

Somewhat shocked at the boy's reaction, Sergei declared that he was indeed a friend and meant no harm.

Outside, the band stopped playing and the last guests were just about to leave when the door opened and Sophia walked in. She let out a gasp when she saw Sergei, but her first thoughts were for her children. Thankfully they were safe. Then her fear quickly turned to anger.

'I've been looking for you for the last half an hour. I thought you'd gone home.'

'Dearest Sophia, I would never leave without thanking you for such a wonderful evening,' he said with a sardonic smile. 'And tonight has been quite special indeed.'

She saw that cold look in his eyes again.

'Finally, I have met your charming children.'

'You have no right to be in here,' she replied angrily. 'It's quite impolite of you to enter a room which you knew very well was out of bounds.'

Sergei turned to leave. As he did so he brushed by her and whispered in her ear, 'I thought I could trust you, but I see that you have hidden quite a lot from me.'

'Get out immediately, before I have you thrown out,' she said defiantly.

The veins in his temple swelled. 'Is this the gratitude I get for our friendship?' he answered menacingly.

'Get out!' she screamed, without even giving him a second look.

After he left the room, Maria ran to her mother in tears.

'I'm so sorry, Mama. I didn't know he would come in.'

'It's alright,' replied Sophia, holding her daughter tightly in her arms. 'It's quite alright.'

Leonidas looked down at the floor. He felt ashamed. If only he had not fallen asleep, none of this would have happened.

Downstairs, Helene was saying goodbye to the last guests. Sergei rushed past her and out into the street. In the Grand Salon Anna had been talking with Carlos and Inez; they had overheard everything. Sophia came out of the room with the children.

'Is everything alright?' Anna asked anxiously.

'Where is Vangelis? I need him immediately.'

Vangelis was waiting for her in the reception hall. He could tell by her face that something serious had taken place.

'Take the children home,' she told him. 'I have something important to do first.'

*

120

Markos shook his head gravely when Sophia recalled the events.

'All of those months of hard work wiped out by one incident,' she said, putting her head in her hands in despair.

The thought of courting a man whom she detested more than anyone in the world, and that it had all been for nothing, made her feel ill. Worse still, her deceit had aroused Sergei's suspicion—and certainly his anger. There was no telling what he would do now.

'Pull yourself together, Sophia,' said Markos firmly. 'You're no good to anyone like this. 'It's a setback, yes, but if we act quickly it may not be too late to regain the upper hand.'

'But how?' she asked, looking up at him searchingly.

'Listen carefully to what I have to say. I want you to make contact with Sergei as soon as possible.' He pulled his chair closer to her and leaned forward. 'Go to him and apologize for your outburst.'

'What!' exclaimed Sophia. 'Are you mad?'

'Listen to me. Make up an excuse—anything; you were feeling ill, you were worried about the children—anything. You must assure him that the last thing you intended was to take it out on him.'

'What are you saying? I can't do that. He'll know I'm lying.'

'You can, and you must.'

'But why? What will this achieve now?'

'There's no doubt that the room has aroused his curiosity, but more than anything, it's his pride that's hurt at the moment and only you can fix that. We have to act quickly and get rid of him as soon as possible before... before things turn nasty for us all. In the meantime woo him back.'

Ignoring her ill feelings about confronting Sergei, he told her what she should do and how.

'In a few days all this will be over. For the moment you must trust me. Have I ever let you down?'

'No...you haven't.'

'You're like my sister—my own flesh and blood. Trust me.' He clasped her hands tightly; his strength empowered her. 'Go home,' he told her. 'Get some sleep. Tomorrow you'll need a clear head.'

# CHAPTER 15

*Constantinople, August 1921*

The following afternoon, Sophia arrived unannounced at Sergei's apartment and found a black car parked in his driveway. The butler ushered her into the drawing room, apologizing that his master was presently occupied with someone else. She sat down, took off her gloves, and placed them on a small marble table, trying desperately to compose herself. A thin trickle of sweat ran down her spine. After a few minutes the butler returned carrying a tray of tea and cakes.

'Monsieur will be with you as soon as possible,' he told her and put the tray down beside her.

She poured herself a cup of tea and waited nervously, aware of the grandfather clock ticking soothingly in the stillness of the room. The afternoon sun streamed through the window, showing up particles of dust floating effortlessly in the air. The room was tastefully decorated, full of Russian and European antiques. On the marble table beside her stood a porcelain figurine of the Great Russian ballerina Tamara Platonova Karsavina in an *attitude en pointe*. She thought of Nikolai. He had called her the most graceful ballerina who ever lived. The clock chimed four. She heard voices in the hallway and caught a glimpse of Sergei escorting three men to the car. One of them had a limp. Another she recognized as Omer Suleyman, a Turkish officer known for his Nationalist sympathies. And she overheard him congratulate Sergei on a job well done.

The drawing room door opened and Sergei entered.

'To what do I owe this honor,' he asked icily.

Sophia steadied her nerves, smiled sweetly and beckoned him to sit next to her. She was here to apologize for her appalling behavior, she told him. He did not deserve to be treated so badly and she owed him an explanation.

'You must understand, Sergei, that room holds many memories for me—memories of happier times.'

'That, my dear Sophia, is perfectly understandable; but why the utter contempt? After all, I have tried hard to bring a little happiness back into your life, and…' he pointed out, 'I was only too happy to strike up a friendship with your children—especially the girl who, I might add, is a sheer delight. Unfortunately, due to your little outburst I did not get the same chance with the boy.'

'My son is an artistic and sensitive boy; he used to spend hours with his father in that room.'

'That I also understand, but…' he said, reaching for a cigarette. 'But you're still not telling me the whole story are you?'

'What do you mean?'

'You led me to believe that you had very little interest in politics.'

He lit his cigarette, leaned back into the sofa, and blew the smoke into the air.

'That's true.'

He tapped his fingers rhythmically on his knee, almost laughing at her.

'Come now, what do you take me for? We both know full well that the overt adoration portrayed in those murals would have seen you targeted by the Turkish officials, who in my opinion have shown extreme tolerance to such unpatriotic Greeks. Frankly, I admire your audacity. To entertain people who you obviously despise, knowing that in the next room there are images that are publicly explosive, takes a lot of gall. Your husband was applauded for his magnificent scenes of Constantinople in the Grand Salon. Surely, you must have known the Hellenistic murals would be seen as a flagrant display of dissention against the Sultan—and that to have them there at all was most unwise.'

'It's part of our history; no one can take that away from us.'

'History, yes…but what about the dream of tomorrow? Isn't that what's taught in the Greek schools? Union with Greece?'

Sophia understood full well that he had gleaned information from Maria. He narrowed his eyes, waiting for her to answer. She wanted to tell him how much she detested him; how he could never hope to step into the shoes of the only two men she had ever loved. And now, after manipulating her daughter, she wished he were dead. Quickly, she pulled herself together, afraid that her body language would give her away.

'I know I've hurt you, Sergei,' she said, feigning deep sorrow. 'More than anything, I wish I'd confided in you earlier. But something is troubling me and I haven't known which way to turn. I know now that I should have come to you in the first place.'

'Go on,' he said, unsure of whether to believe her or not.

'I don't know where to begin,' she said, searching in her bag for a handkerchief.

'Let me see if I can make it easier for you.' He lit another cigarette. 'It wouldn't have anything to do with the Etairia would it?'

'You knew all along!' she exclaimed, allowing him the upper hand.

'Of course!'

It was a blatant lie. She was well aware that if he had known anything at all, things would have come to a head long ago. It was his conversation with Maria that had aroused his suspicions, and now he was testing her. She felt the sweat trickle down her spine and her pulse quickened. He was like a lion waiting for his prey to falter. The consummate actress in her took over, and like a spider she began to weave her silken thread around him, pulling him towards her until there was no turning back.

Over the next few hours, she told him that yes, the Etairia had regularly used the Hellenic room for meetings; that he was correct when he had said the murals were inspirational, and that was one reason why they loved to meet there. But she insisted that she had always been the innocent victim in this. After all, she could not go against the wishes of her husband and, for that matter, her father. Sophia hated herself for bringing up Soterios, but she reasoned that he was far away in Smyrna, now under the control of the Greeks, and he would remain untouchable by the Turks. She assured Sergei that since Andreas's death, the Etairia held their meetings elsewhere and she had no idea where.

'And now,' she said, dabbing her eyes with the handkerchief, 'the group is pressuring me to let them use the Hellenic room again. It's hard for me to say no. I want nothing to do with all this any longer. I detest the situation.'

She moved closer to him and in a soft voice pleaded with him. 'Please help me, Sergei. What am I to do? I need your guidance.'

He listened attentively. Something inside him told him that if he could bring down the Etairia, his standing amongst the Nationalists would soar. Sophia turned his face towards her and kissed him with a deep intensity. He held her tightly, feeling the curves of her warm body close to his. She pulsated with sensuality. Sergei had known many women, but none had got under his skin like she had. She brushed her lips over his cheeks and eyes, knowing that she was giving the performance of her life—what harm was there in sealing it with a kiss? It would be the kiss of death.

*Constantinople, September 1921*

Inside the Church of the Holy Cross, Father Yannakos delivered the divine liturgy of St John Chrysostom. Sophia knelt before the small icon of the Virgin of Tenderness, murmured, and asked for forgiveness for what she was about to do. In his piety, the artist had understood his subject's sorrow and painted a glistening tear on her left cheek. It comforted Sophia to know that the mother of Christ had cried tears of joy and sadness too. She walked over towards the door and lit a candle. Someone came and stood next to her.

'It's arranged for tomorrow evening,' whispered Markos, lighting a candle and placing it next to her own. 'Tell Sergei the Etairia plans to have a meeting in the Hellenic room and find some excuse to meet him at the Pera Palas where we can keep an eye on him. Don't make any mistakes or you will put our lives at risk.'

Sophia made the sign of the cross and turned towards him but he was already walking out of the door. She followed him outside only to find that he had disappeared, lost among the crowd as they clamored to buy confectionary from the street sellers.

Later that day, she telephoned Sergei saying that she had news for him and would tell him over dinner at the Pera Palas tomorrow evening. All she would say was that the Etairia had requested another meeting at La Maison du l'Orient.

'I will book a table for seven-thirty,' he said, hardly able to contain his excitement.

'No,' Sophia replied quickly. 'I have fittings booked until quite late. Let's make it as late as possible; perhaps around nine-thirty.'

On the following afternoon, Sophia mentally made a note of everything she had to do. Next door, the dance studio had remained closed all day except for Vangelis depositing several barrels of olives from Mytilene in the morning. After sending the girls home a little earlier than usual, Sophia unlocked the door to the Hellenic room, walked over to the window and looked down onto the street below. She was half expecting the premises to be watched. Apart from a street vendor selling sesame rings to a child, the street was empty. She saw nothing out of the ordinary; it was just another day. Heading back down the stairs she walked through the empty workroom towards the rear entrance. She was to leave the door unlocked. In the yard outside, the early evening sounds of the city were punctuated by the competing calls of the muezzins from nearby mosques. A cat ran out from under a pile of wood and scrambled over the wall that divided the atelier from the dance studio, startling her fragile nerves.

Sophia returned to her office. In an attempt to keep a check on Sergei's whereabouts, she had tried to telephone him throughout the day but he was nowhere to be found. In the end she telephoned Helene, who hadn't seen him either. She checked her watch. It was almost time to leave. Picking up the photograph of her children, she looked at them affectionately, recalling her happy childhood in Smyrna. In doing so a small key fell out of the back of the silver frame onto the desk. It was the key to the bottom drawer of her desk; she had completely forgotten about it. So distracted was she by recent events that the drawer had remained locked since Von Straumbacher's departure. She unlocked it and took out the mahogany box, clearly recalling his words. 'Keep it somewhere safe—you may need it someday.' Without knowing why, she took out the Luger, loaded it, and hid it under a piece of red silk behind the photograph.

'All I know is that it has something to do with news of the Greek army and the Allies,' Sophia told Sergei over dinner later that evening. 'Something about the naval base in Constantinople and the supply of war materials.'

After observing his appetite well and truly whetted, she added that the meeting was scheduled for later that night.

'In fact, they might even be gathering as we speak,' she added innocently.

Sergei started at the news. He was perplexed. Whatever these men knew, he must find out. It was just possible that his fortunes would take a turn for the better. His associates would pay handsomely for this information. What better than to catch these seditious Greeks in action?

Sophia observed him deep in thought. He was in a dilemma and he knew it. Like Judas, she planted a kiss on his lips. 'But we won't worry about all that, will we?' she said coyly. 'We're having such a wonderful evening; why sully it with such talk.'

As the evening wore on, Sergei became more agitated. Unable to contain himself any longer he excused himself. He said he had to make an important telephone call. Calling the waiter, he asked him to bring Sophia another bottle of champagne. He would be back as soon as possible.

She waited for almost half an hour, digesting the sad fact that it was as Markos had predicted—he had been involved all along. He must have gone to notify his friends of the meeting. After an hour he had still not returned and she went to look for him. He was nowhere to be found. La Maison du l'Orient was still in darkness and she began to worry. What if it all went wrong? Even Markos could not always be sure that things would work out. A shooting star shot across the night sky, disappearing into the Milky Way. It was an auspicious sign.

At that moment a figure fleetingly appeared in the window of the Hellenic room but she was unable to see clearly who it could be. Seconds later she saw what appeared to be two people caught up in a scuffle. Overcome with fear for her friends, Sophia could not simply stand back and watch. She ran towards the atelier. The door was locked. After fumbling in her bag for

126

her key, she quietly unlocked it. Once inside she stood and listened, acutely aware of her heart pounding loudly in her chest. Upstairs one of the doors to the Grand Salon was slightly ajar and the light was on. In the stillness she could just make out the continuous scratching sound of the needle on a gramophone record. The place appeared deserted and she couldn't help wondering why someone would leave without taking the arm off the record and turning off the light. Cautiously, she made her way up the marble staircase towards the Grand Salon. At the top of the staircase, she suddenly heard the back door of the workroom slam shut with muffled sounds coming from the dance studio next door. She stood on the landing in terror. A part of her wanted to run away. Another part of her told her to go forward.

Apprehensively she pushed open the door to the Grand Salon to have a better view. The red brocade curtain lay strewn across the floor and an antique table lay on its side alongside the broken pieces of a fine porcelain vase. Trembling, she walked over and took the needle off the record. The rest of the records lay smashed near the torn curtain. Pools of blood on the floor glistened under the light of the chandeliers. The door to the Hellenic room was slightly ajar and as she put out her hand to push it open, someone inside moaned in pain. Before she could enter, she heard footsteps behind her.

'Sophia.'

Spinning around she was confronted by Sergei, standing in the doorway pointing a gun at her. His left hand clutched a wound in his side. Callously ignoring the cries in the next room he indicated for her to go back downstairs. Retracing her steps she saw fresh signs of his blood smeared along the banister, staining the white marble staircase. She knew that his injury was severe.

His eyes were filled with hatred. 'In there,' he said, waving the gun towards her office.

Once inside, he switched on the light and locked the door.

'Sit down.'

Afraid for her life, Sophia did as she was told. Sergei walked over to the window, anxiously checking the street.

'Why did you have to come here?' he asked angrily. 'Tell me.'

'I was worried,' she stammered, 'and I came to look for you. Then I saw someone in the window upstairs.'

He checked his watch and muttered something under his breath. Sophia realized he was waiting for someone. In a fit of anger he pointed the gun at her again.

'You're a liar. Your smile has deceived me. It's because of you that I'm here—in this condition.' He looked down at the blood steadily seeping through his clothes. 'You—the woman I thought I could trust—you betrayed me. They were right when they said I should know better than to trust a Greek.' Sergei continued to vent his rage at her. 'I let my feelings for you get the better of me and now I'm finished.'

Shaking with resentment he began to pace up and down the room. They heard a loud crash coming from the Grand Salon.

'What was that?' asked Sophia, jumping up from her chair. 'Sergei, I implore you—someone is still up there. We must go to him.'

The thought that one of her friends lay dying was more than she could bear. She turned, making a move towards the door.

'Stay where you are,' he hissed.

His face was drenched in perspiration and he was becoming weaker. He wiped his brow as he clutched his wound, desperately trying to stem the flow of blood. Sophia reached out to him.

'Let me help you.'

His anger rose again. 'I wish you'd never come here,' he stammered, knocking her hand away with the gun.

The telephone rang, startling them. Instinctively, Sophia moved to answer it.

'Leave it,' said Sergei.

They both looked at it until it stopped ringing. Sophia took a deep breath. She looked over to the door and then at him. The unmistakable smell of burning seemed to be filling the air. Terrified, she screamed at him.

'In the name of God! Something is on fire! We have to get out of here!'

Ignoring him, she ran to the door, trying desperately to open it. Turning to face her, he twirled the key in his bloodied fingers, taunting her. In vain, she pulled at the door knob. Sergei came up behind her and pushed her away roughly. She stumbled, landing heavily against her desk, knocking over a pile of papers and the photograph of the children. She put out her hand to catch it but it fell to the floor, smashing the glass. The faces of her children looked up at her. Pulling herself up, she saw the outline of the Luger under the silk cloth. It was only a few inches away from her hand.

The smell of smoke became stronger. Sergei steadied himself against the door. Racked with pain, he began to mutter to himself in Russian. Sophia glanced at the silk. She dare not reach for it for fear of him seeing her.

'Please, Sergei,' she implored. 'I don't know what you've done but I beg you, leave now, before it's too late.'

For a moment it seemed that he would do just that, but as he was about to put the key in the lock they heard the sound of the atelier door opening and footsteps coming towards her office. Sophia wanted to scream but Sergei pointed the gun at her, motioning her to be quiet. They watched the door knob turn as someone tried to enter. Seizing the moment, Sophia carefully reached out and grabbed the Luger from under the silk. Hiding it behind her back she waited. Finding the door locked, the stranger quickly walked away.

Smoke began to permeate the room and Sophia found it hard to breathe. With a look of hatred, Sergei walked over to her and raised his gun, ready to shoot. If he was going to die, he had no intention of dying alone.

'I curse the day I met you,' he said bitterly, his eyes moist with tears.

The sound of a gunshot resonated from the workroom and as Sergei momentarily turned his head, Sophia raised the Luger and shot him through the heart. His heavy body slumped over her and she screamed for help. She pushed him off her just as someone unlocked the door. It was Helene. Stooping over the lifeless body of her brother, she crossed herself. Still holding the gun, Sophia's hands shook like a leaf. Neither woman spoke. Helene gently took the gun from her friend's hand and put it in her pocket. Numb with shock, Sophia could only stand and stare down at Sergei's lifeless body. The enormity of what she had done suddenly hit her. Tears streamed down her cheeks.

'I'm so sorry, Helene.'

Helene took off her coat, wrapped it around Sophia's shoulders, and guided her out of the room into the street. Firefighters had begun to unload their ladders and were pumping water into the black smoke. Before long a large crowd had gathered across the road, and guests in the Pera Palas were being evacuated.

'I'm so sorry,' Sophia repeated.

'He had it coming to him,' replied Helene, in a matter-of-fact way. 'I cannot shed a tear.'

Dazed and disoriented, Sophia watched the smoke billow from the window of the Hellenic room. A group of men brought the covered body of Sergei outside and quickly drove away. The Grand Salon was now burning out of control and the fire had spread to the workrooms. The women turned to walk away when a loud crash reverberated in the street. The ceiling holding the magnificent palatial chandelier that hung in the reception hall had weakened, causing it to crash to the ground, shattering its large crystal pendants into a myriad of sparkling fragments. For a few seconds, Sophia stood with her back to the atelier. Then, gathering her dignity, she pulled herself together and walked away.

# CHAPTER 16

*Constantinople, 1921, several days later*

Sophia ate breakfast in her room, giving orders not to be disturbed. Pushing the tray to one side, she picked up the numerous daily newspapers lying scattered on the bed and reread the headlines.

CONSTANTINOPLE'S PRESTIGIOUS COUTURE HOUSE DESTROYED IN MYSTERIOUS BLAZE, wrote the *Turkish Daily*. ONLOOKERS WATCH AS FLAMES LEAP FROM THE WINDOWS OF PERA'S MOST EXCLUSIVE FASHION HOUSE—LA MAISON DU L'ORIENT, wrote another.

Each headline was like a dagger through her heart, but it was the last headline that distressed her the most: THIRD GENERATION OF THE GREAT EMBROIDERER "DIMITRA OF SMYRNA" LOSES EVERYTHING IN MYSTERIOUS FIRE.

> The famous granddaughter of Kyria Dimitra, whose finest creations have graced the ladies of the Ottoman Court, is said to be heartbroken by the loss of her atelier La Maison du l'Orient in a devastating fire during the early hours of the morning. Season after season, Kyria Sophia Laskaris, wife of the renowned painter Andreas Laskaris, has enthralled us with her glamorous collections, which were as acclaimed in London, Paris, and Vienna as they were in our own great city. Firefighters are still trying to determine the cause of the blaze, which is believed to have started in the Grand Salon.

Tears rolled down her face. 'I have let my family down,' she cried to herself.

More than anyone, it was Dimitra she feared the most. Her grandmother had shown such faith in her. How would she take this loss? She was almost a hundred years old now and Sophia doubted that her heart was strong enough to bear the disappointment.

Downstairs, she heard Zubeyde answer the telephone. It had not stopped ringing all morning.

'I'm sorry, but the Kyria has asked not to be disturbed,' said Zubeyde. 'She thanks you for your well wishes and will return the call when she is well again.'

This time, however, it appeared that the caller would not take no for an answer.

'But, Kyrios,' Zubeyde pleaded, her voice raised, 'you'll get me into trouble.'

Whoever it was was putting enormous pressure on her until she could not take it any longer. She ran up the stairs and knocked on her mistress's door.

'Kyria,' she cried, wringing her hands nervously. 'Kyria Anna and her father are coming over this very minute. They told me they will break the door down if you don't let them in. What am I to do?'

Hearing her pleas, Leonidas came out of his room. 'Please tell them they'll be welcome,' he replied. 'My mother will be ready to receive them.'

Stunned, Zubeyde stood for a moment looking at him.

'Go on,' continued Leonidas. 'Tell them we're waiting.'

Zubeyde bowed and ran back downstairs. Leonidas entered his mother's room, sat on the bed, and reached for her hand.

'Please, Mama. I want you to put on your prettiest dress and come downstairs. We will be waiting for you.' He bent over and kissed her forehead. 'You will get over this—we will all get over it and...' He paused to pick up a small translucent green bottle from her dressing table. 'Put on some of this. The time for grieving is over; it is time to wear it again.'

She watched him leave the room, looked at the perfume bottle in the palm of her hand and pulled out the stopper. With her eyes closed she held it to her nose. Slowly, the air began to fill with the exquisite fragrance of Damask rose. How could she have known that it would all end like this?

Anna and her father waited patiently in the drawing room. Sophia was desperate to know how it had all gone wrong, but she was even more anxious to learn of the fate of her friends. The fact that she had killed a man was the last thing on her mind. When she entered the room Leonidas rose and walked over to her.

'I will be in the next room if you need me, Mama,' he whispered to her.

'Have you news of our friends?' asked Sophia, when they were alone.

'We can report to you that everyone is safe and sound. Panayiotis suffered a minor injury, but he will recover,' replied Anna's father.

Sophia breathed a sigh of relief. '*Doxa sto Theo*,' she said, crossing herself hastily.

'Due to the close proximity of the atelier to diplomatic buildings, the officials are conducting an inquiry. They are concerned that the fire may have been politically motivated and they want to be sure that it was not an act of terrorism.'

'What about Sergei's body? Won't that make them suspicious?'

Anna's father paused for a moment.

'There were two bodies, Sophia.'

Sophia remembered the groans of someone in the Hellenic room.

'One we know for sure was Sergei. The other—which was practically unidentifiable—is the man with the limp. He was one of the most important Russian secret agents in the pay of the Nationalists.'

Sophia looked confused.

'It was Helene who recognized him and she alerted us immediately,' continued Anna's father. 'She knew there would be trouble. He and Sergei had been close friends at the time of the Dowager Duchess's death in Bulgaria. At the time it was widely suspected the two had poisoned the old woman after destroying her old will and forging a new one. Nothing was ever proven, but rumors continued to surround Sergei until he left Sofia for Constantinople. Sometime later the pair met again—during the Great War. The Russian was then working for the Germans and it was through him that Sergei was recruited as a spy. He was already a devotee of the Young Turks when you met him.'

'And Nikolai was not aware of any of this?' asked Sophia.

'Nikolai, God rest his soul, would never accept that Sergei's integrity was doubtful.'

Sophia thought of Munire. How glad she was that she'd sent her away.

'When Sergei left you, he notified his associates. Shortly after, they arrived and followed him to the atelier. One of the men was the Russian, the other Omer Suleyman—the Turkish officer. The rest we learnt from Markos. The trap was already set. Thinking there was a meeting in the Hellenic room, the men quietly made their way upstairs towards the Grand Salon. In order that all should appear normal, Lefteris played the gramophone. The door to the Hellenic room was left ajar and unbeknown to the intruders Markos had placed a mirror near to the door in such a position as to allow them to see anyone entering the room. They were ready for them. Believing that this was a surprise attack, the men quietly crossed the Grand Salon towards the Hellenic room. Omer Suleyman was the first to enter but before he could utter a word, Konstantine Mandakis—waiting behind the door with his dagger at the ready—quickly severed his throat. The intruders quickly realized it was a trap and turned to escape. It was too late. The men burst out into the Salon and attacked them with devastating consequences. In the ensuing struggle Lefteris spotted Sergei running out of the door towards the staircase and followed him. Taking aim he fired at him, sending him careering into the banister and toppling down the last few steps. He was about to pursue him when one of the assailants attempted to tackle him. Lefteris was far too agile and the man was soon overpowered. When Lefteris looked again, Sergei was nowhere to be seen.

'All of Sergei's accomplices were dead—or at least they thought so at the time. One by one the bodies were dragged through the workrooms and outside into the yard. They were then hauled over the wall and into the dance studio where Vangelis, along with two other men, waited to dispose of them. Returning for the remaining bodies, the men failed to notice that one was missing. Sergei's friend—left for dead when the first bodies were taken next door—had managed to crawl into the Hellenic room and hide behind a large cabinet. And then there was Sergei. Markos ordered everyone to search the premises for him but when they heard someone at the door, they thought it was the gendarmes and made a hasty retreat to the dance studio.'

'So it was Sergei's friend who I heard moaning in agony?' Sophia asked.

Anna's father nodded. 'Yes.'

'And all that time, Sergei remained hidden in my office?'

'We think so. Everything happened so fast. They had no time to check.'

'But the fire? And the gunshot—the one I heard from my office? I don't understand!' exclaimed Sophia.

'Anna had booked a room in the hotel and was keeping a close eye on you,' Anna's father continued. 'When it was reported to her that you'd left your table, she suspected that you might have gone to the atelier and she tried to telephone you. No one answered. Fearing for your safety, she alerted us.'

'It was then that Helene entered the atelier,' said Anna.

Sophia recalled her shock at seeing Helene. She was even more shocked to find out that she had risked her life by going to the studio alone. What was she doing in all this?

'At the time we had no idea it was her,' said Sophia sadly. 'If only she had called out, perhaps Sergei would have come to his senses if he knew that the person on the other side of the door was his sister.'

Anna shrugged.

'She had no idea that we had set a trap for Sergei, but she did have her reasons for following him. Unfinished business, I suppose. And when you telephoned her earlier that day looking for her brother, she suspected that he was up to no good. By the time she entered the atelier the fire was already starting to take hold. Thinking there was no one in the building, she was about to leave and call for help when she heard a noise inside one of the workrooms. Helene never went anywhere without her pistol. In the semi-darkness with smoke spreading through the building, she took the gun out of her handbag and went to investigate. Following the trail of blood she found the Russian slumped against the wall. Somehow, he had managed to make his way out of the Hellenic room while Sergei had you locked in your office, and in doing so he knocked over an oil lamp. That's what started the fire. Helene told us of the fear in his eyes when he recognized her. He pleaded for his life, but Helene—full of hatred for the man—held her pistol to his head and shot him. That's when she heard your shot. By that time the fire engines had arrived.'

'My God. All this bloodshed,' said Sophia miserably.

The three sat in silence, contemplating the enormity of the situation. Sophia was relieved that none of her friends had been killed.

'They were lucky,' she said.

'No, Sophia. Luck did not play a part,' replied Anna's father. 'They were well prepared.'

'And consumed with hatred for what Sergei had done,' added Anna.

'What have they done with the bodies?' Sophia asked. 'Omer Suleyman was an important man. There are bound to be reprisals over their deaths.'

'Somehow I doubt it,' smiled Anna's father, looking at something out of the window. 'Why don't we ask Vangelis? He's just returned.'

Sophia called for him to join them.

'What bodies?' he laughed. 'Apart from Sergei and his associate, there are no other bodies.'

'What are you trying to say?'

'Due to Helene's fine work, when the Russian's body was discovered he was unrecognizable—and badly burnt. And of course, there was nothing on the body to identify him.'

'But Sergei...*his* body was recognizable.'

'That's so,' replied Vangelis.

He was unsure of what to say. Anna's father came to his aid.

'The body was covered and removed from the office by two firemen—two of our men. When it was examined at the morgue, the examining officer reported that the man brought in was a beggar who had apparently died from hunger and cold. They were baffled as to how a beggar had found his way into the building.'

Sophia was aghast. They had exchanged Sergei's body for some other poor unfortunate soul.

'And the others?' She looked away, afraid of what she might hear.

Vangelis threw his head back and roared with laughter.

134

'They were thrown into the olive barrels! And under the very noses of firefighters, gendarmes, and onlookers, they were moved out of the dance studio just before dawn. In the manner of our own good rulers of the past, they are now at the bottom of the Bosphorus.'

Sophia forced a smile. They had thought of everything.

'I want to see the atelier,' she said.

'Why don't you leave it until tomorrow?' replied Anna. 'Try to rest now.'

She would not take no for an answer.

Sophia stared at the gaping hole that used to be the ornate ceiling of the Grand Salon. Charred black beams exposed the steely gray thunder clouds rolling by that were threatening to empty themselves on the city. The Hellenic room was completely destroyed. The floor had collapsed into the workrooms below and there was nothing left of the murals that once depicted Andreas's dreamscape of ancient Greece. The fire had destroyed most of the murals in the Grand Salon. Here and there she could just make out an image or a scene: a dome of the Topkapi, a section of the old Byzantine wall, or part of a sailing ship on the Bosphorus. The blackened marble staircase had withstood the impact of the fire and rose majestically out of the ruins. In the workrooms, the firemen were busily clearing away the rubble. Exquisite fabrics had been reduced to ashes.

Picking her way through the ruins, her eyes rested on a fragment of carpet hanging from a fallen beam. In the grayness of its surroundings, the colors were as wonderful as they were on the day they were woven. This was all that remained of the famous hunting carpets. Sophia picked up the fragment, brushing her hand across the soft velvet pile as if it were a lover.

'The weaver is a poet,' Dimitra had once told her. 'He breathes life into his work. What you are looking at is his soul.' A pain ripped through her chest.

'Come on,' said Anna's father. 'I think you've seen enough.'

Outside Vangelis waited patiently by the car. The bravado had gone and the sight of the atelier filled him with grief. Sophia stood on the doorstep and took one last look. The brass plaque was still firmly attached to the wall and she asked him to remove it and put it in the car. Solemnly he did as he was asked.

A few weeks later a meeting was called at The Blue Eye. Speaking on behalf of the entire group, Anna's father said that a great threat to many lives had been removed. Turning to Sophia, he told her there were no words to describe her courage and patriotism to the cause. Furthermore, he expressed great sadness at the loss of the La Maison du l'Orient and assured her that everything in their power would be done to rebuild it.

'We want you to have this,' he said, giving her an envelope.

The room grew silent as everyone waited for her reaction. In the envelope was a bank check. Her hand began to shake.

'I can't accept it,' she said, handing it back to him.

'Why ever not? It's for you to begin again. There's more than enough to rebuild your business or to relocate if you wish. We know that you're insured, but this is a gesture of our gratitude. We're all here to help you. La Maison du l'Orient will be like the phoenix that rises from the ashes.'

Sophia looked at their faces. They had been at the center of her life in Constantinople and she loved them all. Markos asked the question again. 'Why not, Sophia? It's the least we can do.'

'Because…' She wavered for a moment. 'Because I could never recapture those dreams again. I have decided to go back to Smyrna.'

# PART II

# CATASTROPHE

# CHAPTER 17

*Athens, September 1972*

Eleni sat spellbound. That her mother's family had been so accomplished and well connected came as a great shock. She felt immense pride in their achievements and at the same time was deeply saddened by the devastating impact the wars had on their lives. To lose so much in such a short time was incomprehensible.

Chrysoula entered the room to give her aunt her medicine. Maria's eyes became languorous. 'Let her sleep awhile,' whispered Chrysoula, smoothing a wisp of Maria's white hair back into place. 'Come into the kitchen. I'll make you a drink.'

'Did you know what she wanted to talk to me about?' Eleni asked, as she watched Chrysoula stir the coffee in the copper *briki*.

'I had a good idea.'

'It's all so tragic. How different their lives must have been before the wars.'

'Yes, my dear,' said Chrysoula, pouring the foaming coffee into a tiny porcelain cup. 'Especially if you were wealthy, as your grandmother once was.'

Eleni had only ever read about the lives of the sophisticated bourgeois milieu of the Belle Époque in books. She never dreamt that her family had been a part of it. Maria's story fascinated her. Here was luxury beyond her wildest imagination, together with romance and a passion for life. All this was combined with the horror of war and the dangerous world of political intrigue. Not only had her grandmother lived through those turbulent times, but she had flourished in a man's world.

'Grandmother Sophia was certainly a woman far ahead of her time,' said Eleni.

'The uncertainty of the times challenged and toughened them—especially your grandmother.'

Eleni thought about her mother. 'And *my* mother, Chrysoula—did she inherit that strength of character?'

Chrysoula looked uncomfortable. 'Yes,' she answered reluctantly. 'Perhaps that was her downfall.'

Eleni was intrigued by her remark. She was about to ask what she meant when the tinkle of a bell coming from the bedroom told them that her aunt was awake. Chrysoula breathed a sigh of relief. The last question was not one on which she wanted to elaborate. They hurried back to Maria's side.

'Are you sure you want to continue?' Chrysoula asked her. 'I fear all this talk about the past will do you harm.'

Maria pursed her lips. 'I will finish what I began,' she said in an irritated tone. 'Hand me the mirror.'

Chrysoula passed her the silver hand mirror and a powder compact, tidied the bedcovers and left the room. Eleni resumed her seat by the bedside and sat quietly until her aunt finished powdering her face.

'Tell me, Aunt Maria; what happened next?' she asked softly.

*Smyrna, April 1922*

Vangelis gathered together the crockery, folded the picnic rug and walked over the hill back to the car. He hummed a little tune to himself, a new composition that he would perform for the first time that evening to a packed house at the Café Aphrodite—one of the smartest music venues on Smyrna's elegant waterfront. Putting the hamper into the boot of the car, he pushed aside the sheepskin and took out his laouto.

It was an idyllic spring afternoon; there was not a breath of wind, but warmth that melts away the troubles of the soul. Everywhere trees displayed their blossoms, tiny buds that sprang into life with the warm glow of the sunshine. Birdsong and the gentle hum of bees filled the air. Vangelis sat beside the car, and turning his face towards the sun he closed his eyes as if in prayer and began to sing. Every now and again he interspersed his composition with the plaintive lament—*Aman*—giving him time to ponder the next line. The music was emotional, composed in the style of classical Turkish with its variations of makams and self-improvisation. The warmth of the sun's rays on his face and hands seemed to inspire him.

> In the mountains of Smyrna
> I look for my love.
> I wander about and my soul suffers.
> Only you can ease this torment.
> Aman...Aman...
> Bitterness and sorrow are in my eyes.
> I waste away because of you.

Have pity on this wretched soul.

Only you can free me from this torment.

Aman…Aman…


Not far away, Sophia sat on a large rock with Leonidas. Next to them lay Maria, curled up asleep on a rug. The sound of Vangelis's music drifted through the air and touched her heart. She found his presence reassuring and deep down was glad that like her, he had chosen to leave Constantinople and begin a new life in Smyrna. He was still her chauffeur but since discovering that he was an accomplished musician, she had encouraged him not to waste his talents. It had been her idea that he join the *Kumpania* at the Café Aphrodite. Although not one for modesty, Vangelis had thought it out of his league; after all, there were many talented musicians eager to advance their fame and fortune in Smyrna at that time. After a word to the right person by Soterios, Vangelis was given an audition and hired on the spot. That was three weeks ago. In such a short time he had gained a reputation as something of a virtuoso.

'If only Markos could see him,' Sophia said to Leonidas. 'He would be so proud of him.'

Leonidas looked up from his painting. It was the first time his mother had mentioned any of her old friends since leaving the city. There was a time when he thought she would never smile again, but just lately he saw signs that made him think her spirit was healing. At first he had been apprehensive about the move to Smyrna but the family had rallied together and both Soterios and Photeini rejoiced at having their grandchildren with them again. It gave them a new lease of life and took their minds off more serious concerns—including the fate of the Greek army in the hinterland. Most of all Leonidas saw the enthusiasm with which his mother threw herself into her new atelier on the Rue Franque—Smyrna's equivalent of the Grande Rue de Pera. And it gave him great cause for optimism. In his young mind he had no doubt that she would soon reach the same heights as she had once done in Constantinople.

While Soterios nurtured his grandson, taking him to the Greek Club or to political meetings, Photeini fell under the spell of Maria's charms. The girl quickly learned how to twist her grandmother around her little finger to have her own way. Photeini was awake to Maria's manipulative ways but decided to overlook this, as she felt she might benefit from a little more attention. She had always believed that much of Sophia's inability to communicate with Maria came from Dimitra and the prophecy of the girl with the flaming hair. No one ever spoke about it, but Dimitra's rejection of the child from the day she was born had left a profound impression on Sophia.

Maria soon became the belle of the ball. There were parties and gala balls to attend; there were theatre and music recitals in the homes of Smyrna's wealthiest families, and she was adamant that, as the daughter of a famous couturier, she must live up to people's expectations. That meant wearing the most fashionable clothes. She refused to wear the same dress twice. Rather than cause an argument with Sophia, Photeini took all this in her stride, tirelessly attending to Maria's every little whim.

Nina, on the other hand, was a happy child with an inquisitive nature. On the day that Sophia returned to Smyrna with the children, Dimitra felt instantly drawn to her, taking her under her wing and teaching her embroidery. Nina idolized her. In Dimitra's company Nina blossomed and it became something of a ritual that after school Iskender would arrive at the house to collect the child and take her to her great-grandmother's home. Dimitra noticed how Nina learned easily—just as she had done when she was the same age.

'The child has a special flair,' she told Sophia. 'She was born with a needle and silk thread in her fingers.'

Each afternoon the pair would sit in the vermillion room surrounded by boxes of cloth, needles, and skeins of multi-colored silk threads. Dimitra liked nothing better than to watch the child's concentration as she practiced her stitch work. Occasionally, she would stroke her hair murmuring soft words that Nina found hard to understand. There was a familiarity in her perfectly formed almond-shaped face, with its heart-shaped rose-pink lips and gently arched dark eyebrows—expressive eyebrows that moved as her concentration intensified. Often the child would chatter away lightheartedly, hardly pausing to take a breath. Her gaiety filled the room. It was at times like this that Dimitra would reach out and cup the child's small face in her hands and lavish her with kisses.

As Sophia had done years earlier, Nina took note of everything her great-grandmother told her: how the red dye is obtained from crushed roots, beetles, and pomegranates; yellow from turmeric and saffron; and black, browns, and grays from the leaves and shells of nut trees.

'Dyeing is an art,' Dimitra told her. 'Each recipe is jealously guarded and passed down from father to son.'

'Like you teaching me how to embroider,' replied Nina. 'And like you taught Mama and Grandmamma Photeini?'

'Exactly,' answered Dimitra.

Nina thought about this carefully. 'And did your Mama teach you?' she asked innocently.

The question caught Dimitra by surprise. Nina failed to notice the sudden faraway look in her great-grandmother's eyes, or to comprehend the pain that tore through her heart like a dagger. Her question remained unanswered.

Sophia pulled her knees under her chin and listened to the sound of Vangelis's laouto. A small striped lizard slithered out of a crevice, basking in the afternoon sun. For the past two hours Leonidas had been preoccupied with his painting.

'May I look?' Sophia asked.

He put down his brushes and showed her. Sophia looked startled. It was a portrait of Maria. 'It's lovely,' she said nervously, 'although her hair isn't quite as red.'

Leonidas looked at it again.

'Oh, but you're wrong, Mama. Look closely; see how the sun catches it.'

The intensity of the fiery redness of Maria's long tresses dominated the painting.

'It's only the sunshine; her hair isn't normally like that. It's usually a deep chestnut,' she said with conviction.

But the more she looked, the more she saw that her son was correct and it unnerved her. She looked at her daughter sleeping peacefully in the warmth of the afternoon and thought of the prophecy. How silly, she told herself, that I should let a meaningless prophecy cause me unease. My daughter might be a difficult child, but surely that is no cause for alarm.

Putting her thoughts aside, she praised her son's talent.

'Grandpapa asked me what I want to do when I finish school,' Leonidas continued.

'And what did you tell him?'

'That I want to be an artist like Papa. Grandpapa suggests that I should study law at the new university. He says that when the Greeks win their struggle, we will need good lawyers.'

Sophia's attention turned to the small figure walking through the grass towards them. Nina had been playing among the ruins of the Temple of the Two Nemeses. As she came closer, they saw that she was cradling something in her arms.

'Did you find Ali Baba's treasure?' shouted Leonidas.

'No, silly,' she laughed. 'It's something much better than that. It's a tortoise.'

Nina was immensely proud of her find. Its legs thrashed about and it hissed angrily at her when she spoke to it.

'What are you going to do with it?' Sophia asked. 'You can't take it with you. It belongs here.'

Nina sat on the rock beside them and frowned. Leonidas laughed at her.

'Can you imagine what Grandmamma Photeini will say if you take it home?'

'It's not for her. It's a present for Great-grandmamma Dimitra.'

Sophia and Leonidas smiled at each other.

'What will she do with such a present? She can't possibly look after pets. No, it's best to leave it here,' said Sophia sympathetically.

Nina put the tortoise on the rock and gave her mother a big grin.

'I think she will love it, Mama. She told me that she used to have a few when she was my age, and that on summer evenings they would attach candles to their backs and watch them walk through the garden. She said it was such a wonderful sight—like large fireflies.'

Sophia looked surprised. She had never heard this story before.

'Please, Mama,' Nina pleaded. 'It won't be any trouble for her. Iskender will feed it.'

'Well, I tell you what we'll do,' Sophia replied, with a hint of sternness. 'If your great-grandmamma accepts it, alright…but…if either she or Iskender refuses to look after it, then we bring it straight back here. Is that a promise?'

Nina threw her arms around her mother's neck and kissed her.

'Does it have a name?' asked Leonidas.

'Umm…let me think,' replied Nina, putting her finger between her teeth thoughtfully.

She picked up the tortoise. It hissed at her again, quickly shrinking its long wrinkled neck back under its hard shell.

'I think I'll call it Aladdin because he had a wonderful lamp and it will remind Great-grandmamma of the days when her tortoises glowed.'

Sophia smiled for the second time that day. Leonidas saw the happiness in his mother's eyes.

Café Aphrodite was already full when the family arrived later in the evening. The manager ushered them across the room to a table that had been reserved next to a raised platform with a row of seven empty high-backed chairs.

'Drinks are on the house tonight,' he said to Soterios. 'The Kapitanos draws a large crowd and we have you to thank for that.'

He clicked his fingers at a passing waiter who promptly brought over platters of *mezethes* and two bottles of his finest wine.

The air was heavy with smoke and an obvious sense of excitement filled the room. There was nothing that the Christian population of Smyrna loved more than to dress up for an evening of entertainment in a convivial atmosphere, accompanied by plentiful food and good music. Over the past decade a number of such establishments had sprung up to cater for this growing demand. Café Aphrodite was considered to be the best. Every musician and chanteuse aspired to play here.

Maria helped herself to a borek stuffed with spinach and pine nuts. Leonidas—uncharacteristically nervous—couldn't eat. This was the first time he'd seen Vangelis play in public and the mixture of anticipation and anxiety was almost too painful to bear. He fidgeted incessantly on his chair until Sophia put her hand on his shoulder to calm him. Moments later the audience began to applaud, as each member of the *Kumpania* wove their way through the tables and took their seat on stage. Leonidas jumped up and clapped loudly. Vangelis, seated at the far end of the row, looked over and gave him a wink.

'Sit down,' said Maria angrily. 'We can't see.'

Embarrassed, Leonidas resumed his seat. One by one the musicians were introduced to the audience.

'Ladies and gentleman,' began the compere, 'tonight I present to you… Georgos on the santouri; Stratos on saz and baglama; Kayseri Katsiyannis on bouzouki; and, ladies and gentleman…' he continued, with the flourish of a showman, 'our own *tragoudistria*—the beautiful Nitsa from Smyrna.'

At the very mention of her name, the singer—a sultry young woman in her early twenties—stood up and took a bow. The audience applauded.

'And on our left we have Mikhaili on the dog-skin drum; Ayvali Apostoli on the violin; and finally, ladies and gentleman, the newest member of our group.' His voice grew louder. 'From Constantinople…Kapitanos Vangelis on the laouto.'

The audience clapped wildly. During the first part of the evening the group played a selection of old favorites, interspersed with Neapolitan *Cantalides*. Nitsa—with her lilting and seductive voice—sat with her legs crossed, tapping out a rhythm with her foot and occasionally shaking a tambourine. She held her admirers spellbound. Every now and again she rose, moved away from the group, and began to dance the *Tsifteteli*—a slow, sensuous dance in the same rhythm as the belly dance. Clasping her finger cymbals over her head, she moved her hips to the rhythm in a swaying motion. Before long the stage was awash with long-stemmed flowers thrown to her by ardent admirers, each one hoping that she would pick up his flower—a sign that they had not gone unnoticed.

Nitsa was a slip of a woman with a mesmerizing presence. She wore her thick dark hair cropped, with a low, full fringe that served to emphasize her seductive eyes. She was dressed in a calf-length ivory satin dress, bordered in beaten silver threadwork that shimmered under the soft lights. Maria was fascinated. Nitsa reminded her of a Hollywood screen goddess—the very ones who she watched in the Theatre de Smyrne next door. She noticed how easily the men succumbed to her charms and vowed that one day, she too would have her name in bright lights and be the object of every man's desire. That evening would remain etched in her memory for the rest of her life.

With their slicked-back hair, waxed glistening moustaches, and freshly manicured fingernails, the musicians had their share of admirers. Vangelis told Sophia many stories of the near-death fights that some of these men found themselves in with many a green-eyed husband. Ayvali Apostoli, a notorious womanizer, was still recovering from a knife wound inflicted upon him by his fiery girlfriend.

Finally, the part of the evening that everyone had anticipated began. With the same plaintive cry of *Achhh...Aman...*Vangelis sang his new composition. Not a soul stirred as he poured forth his heart in the verses that Sophia had heard earlier that afternoon.

> Have pity on this wretched soul.
> Only you can free me from this torment.
> Aman...Aman...

She felt the same shiver run through her spine. His rendition of the words combined with the mastery of his instrument reduced his audience to tears. They gave him a standing ovation. The family shone with pride and none more so than Leonidas.

As the evening progressed, every conceivable space between the tables was filled with dancers. Couples clasped arms around each other and men danced alone, wrapped up in a world of their own. No one wanted the evening to end. Sophia noticed a group of men standing by the door, deep in conversation with the manager. Minutes later he came over and whispered something in Soterios's ear. His face paled. Sophia and her mother exchanged glances.

'Please excuse me, my dear,' he said to Photeini, his voice trembling. 'I have urgent business. You mustn't leave on my account. Stay and enjoy yourselves.'

Photeini reached out to touch him. 'What is it, my husband?'

He could barely find the words to answer her.

'The Paris Peace talks have broken down. Greece accepts an armistice but the Turkish Nationalists refuse to sign without the assurance of a Greek evacuation of Asia Minor. Time is running out for us.'

# CHAPTER 18

*Smyrna, July 1922*

When Sophia returned to Smyrna in the early spring of 1922, she had not realized the gravity of the situation. The Greek army's push into Anatolia nine months earlier had given rise to an optimism that was to be short-lived. They had fought bravely but Mustafa Kemal, sensing their broken spirit, issued a counter-offensive which saw the Greeks retreat to the town of Eskişehir, which was where they had been a month earlier. When King Constantine was told of the retreat he suffered a nervous breakdown.

The Greek army was in a pitiful condition. The march across the inhospitable great central Anatolian Salt Desert with its parched landscape and scorching heat had taken its toll. Army vehicles consistently broke down in the choking dust. Malaria and dysentery were rife. Throughout the winter a stalemate existed. In Greece, the people began to resent the war. The economic burden caused the drachma to fall and inflation to rise and they had grown tired of losing their husbands, sons, and brothers to what many now perceived as a lost cause. The Megali Idea—that great dream of uniting the Greeks—was disintegrating.

With the Turks refusing to sign the armistice and the treaty providing no guarantee as to the safety of the Christian populations, the Greeks had nowhere to turn. The Nationalists, on the other hand, had used the winter months to rest and rearm.

For days there was no sign of Soterios. He and his close associates had been using their influence to exert pressure on Smyrna's High Commissioner and the Greek and British governments. He knew that should the Nationalists regain the Smyrna territories, their anger would be unleashed on the Christian populations with chilling consequences.

When he returned he was in a state of near collapse.

'We're trying our best,' he told them. 'But we have it on good authority that the Greek army will soon leave. If the people get wind of this, they'll panic and there's no telling what will happen.'

Iskender was not only Dimitra's bodyguard but he was also responsible for certain other household duties with which no one dared interfere. Sophia once commented that he was like a much-revered old piece of furniture that always had its place and yet no one ever knew its origin. He was always the first to rise and the last to retire. Each day, before sunrise, he would head to the market and haggle over the price of a piece of meat, pick out the choicest unblemished fruits and vegetables, and sample the cheeses for just the right amount of saltiness. He was never idle and could always find something to do: sharpening knives, preparing charcoal burners to heat the rooms or for Dimitra's narghile, or meticulously tending the vines that cascaded across the balcony, dripping with bunches of dark plump fruit in late summer.

One particular afternoon in late July, Leonidas accompanied Nina to Dimitra's home. As was his habit, Iskender made sure that there was a slice of cinnamon-and-clove-scented baklava and a jug of chilled cherry juice waiting for them on their arrival. Leaving Nina to her embroidery lesson, Leonidas sat on a rug under the Judas tree and settled down to read. Iskender brought over an extra slice of baklava and then began to sweep the courtyard. The swishing of the broom made Leonidas unable to concentrate. He put down his book and studied Iskender. He was a man of few words—even fewer than Ali Agha—and he wondered what sort of a man he really was. Certainly he had a fearsome presence, even without his knives and guns. Yet Leonidas suspected that his looks masked the gentle giant that he really was. He had always shown great tenderness towards Dimitra, and his undying service for her was never in question. His mother once told him that he had been Dimitra's bodyguard and manservant since Mehmet left after the episode with the 'seer', and after the death of his great-grandfather.

Leonidas took a bite of baklava. Nearby the tortoise slowly clattered over the cobblestones towards the rug. It stopped and raised its head towards him and, as if sensing that it was in the wrong place, then turned and disappeared in a bed of herbs next to the pomegranate tree. Iskender finished sweeping, put the broom down, and disappeared into the old stables. Minutes later, the smell of tobacco drifted into the courtyard. Leonidas stood and followed him. The stables were cool and dark, and in the dim light he saw Iskender sitting on a stool smoking his narghile.

'Peace be with you, Iskender,' said Leonidas.

'And with you, my boy,' replied Iskender.

'Do you mind if I join you?' asked Leonidas, placing a stool next to him.

Iskender nodded his approval. They sat in silence. After a while their eyes grew accustomed to the light and Iskender picked up a broken basket, took a long length of twine, and began to mend it.

'You do that well,' said Leonidas, trying to engage him in conversation.

Iskender—deftly weaving the twine in and out of the basket—did not answer.

Leonidas cast his eyes around the stables. An array of bridles and two saddles hung on a wall and several wooden trunks and two large sacks stood against another wall. A partition divided the empty stalls from the main stable and the shiny terracotta-tiled floor was spotlessly clean. He got up and walked over to inspect the saddles. They were beautifully crafted and far superior to many he had seen before.

'Where did this one come from? It has Great-grandmamma's name worked into it,' he asked, running his hand across the smooth mahogany-colored leather.

'That was a present to Hanim Efendi Dimitra from a friend of your mother's,' Iskender answered. 'An Armenian by the name of Hagop Vartinian.'

'And this one?' he asked, pointing to the one with indentations that suggested it may once have been adorned with precious stones. 'This is even older.'

Iskender put down the basket and watched Leonidas carefully.

'It even has an inscription on it.' Leonidas turned the saddle towards the light. 'It's written in the Arabic script. I can just make out the date…1826. Do you know who this belonged to? How did Great-grandmamma get it?'

Iskender stood up and took a deep breath, drawing himself to an even greater height.

'Leonidas Efendi,' he said, in a very serious voice, 'as the son of a gentleman and a student of learning, surely you must know that it is impolite to pry.'

Iskender put the saddle back in its place, flicked away a non-existent speck of dust, and walked out of the stable, leaving Leonidas bewildered. Undaunted, Leonidas set about investigating the stables further. Thin shafts of light streaked across the stalls where the horses once lay. Lanterns hung from the rafters. The sacks contained dried pulses and all except one of the chests were empty. Even that held little of importance: a copper dish and a few simple unadorned earthenware containers. He wondered why Dimitra bothered to keep them.

His curiosity satisfied, Leonidas was just about to leave when he spotted an old leather portmanteau that had fallen behind one of the boxes. Carefully, he lifted it out and brushed away the dust. The brown leather was cracked and faded and its clasp was badly tarnished. On one side were initials: J M L. Looking over his shoulder to make sure that Iskender was out of sight, he opened it and to his astonishment found it to be full of artist's materials.

There were brushes, powdered paints, gums, and oils. Leonidas realized the bag must have belonged to his great-grandfather Jean-Paul, although it puzzled him why the initials were not J P L. What did the M stand for? One by one, he took out the items and examined them. He picked up a brush and ran his thumb through the fine bristles. Specks of red pigment were still visible. A feeling of guilt came over him; he should not be snooping. Quickly he put everything back in the bag. He sensed someone watching him.

'What are you doing, my son?'

Leonidas jumped back in fright, dropping the bag. Dimitra, her hands firmly clasped in front of her, stood in the doorway. Behind her was Iskender. Leonidas lowered his head in shame.

'Please forgive me. I didn't mean to pry.' Iskender threw him a stony look. 'I was curious, that's all.'

Scarlet with embarrassment, Leonidas cast his eyes downward, but instead of chastising him Dimitra lifted his chin and forced him to look at her. She was a diminutive figure but he felt small in her presence.

'I'm not angry with you,' she said. 'I watched you from the balcony and I sensed your curiosity. It shines in your eyes.'

She turned to Iskender and murmured something to him in Turkish. He hurried back to the house and returned with a key.

'Come with me. I want to show you something.'

Leonidas followed her across the courtyard and up an old timber staircase so worn he feared it would collapse under their weight. At the top, a narrow balcony led to a blue door, next to which stood a large terracotta storage jar. Partially obscured by the pomegranate tree, Leonidas had always thought it a storeroom.

Dimitra unlocked the door, took off her slippers and beckoned him inside. Leonidas felt a thrill of excitement.

'Close the door behind you,' she said, walking over to a window and throwing back the shutters to let in the light.

A swallow darted out from under the eaves and the scent of jasmine filled the room. The view over the rooftops of the Turkish houses towards Nymph Dagh and the Velvet Castle was magnificent.

'Except for me, you are the only other person to enter this room since he died,' said Dimitra, settling herself down on a kilim-covered divan. 'Not even Iskender is allowed in here.'

Leonidas could find no words to express his emotions. He felt as if he'd stepped back in time. This long narrow room with its whitewashed walls, low roof, and highly polished wooden floor was Jean-Paul's studio and it remained just as it was when he left on that fateful journey to Palmyra all those years ago. A collection of assorted busts stood next to a pestle and mortar on an upturned crate. There was not a speck of dust anywhere. Fresh flowers filled an agate vase on the table next to his easel. Leonidas half expected his great-grandfather to walk into the room at any moment, pick up his palette and brushes, and finish the painting that stood on the easel. A feeling of serenity enveloped the room. Dimitra had kept it as a shrine to his memory; he felt deeply honored that she saw fit to share it with him.

'It's so long ago and yet I still feel his presence,' said Dimitra, her eyes filled with emotion. 'In life, my son, you will realize there is happiness and there is sadness and they are intertwined. I feel both here.'

She opened a small decorative box containing 'tears' of Chian mastic, took a piece out, and began to chew it.

'You are young and have your future ahead of you. More importantly, you have a thirst for knowledge and a gift for painting that runs through your blood. When you returned from the city with your mother, I knew then that in you my husband's legacy would live on, and...' she added, 'your father's. God rest his soul.'

Leonidas felt his chest tighten at the mention of Andreas.

'I have not long on this earth, and when I go what will happen to all this?' she said, moving her arm in a grandiose sweeping gesture. 'He would want me to share it with you.'

Leonidas looked at the unfinished canvas on the easel.

'That was the last of a series,' said Dimitra. 'All except one was sold. It's exceptional, wouldn't you agree?'

Still overwhelmed, Leonidas nodded in agreement. The painting, executed in oil in the early Orientalist style, depicted the traditional way of life at the portal of a majestic caravanserai. In the distance rose a range of snowcapped mountains. Jean-Paul's attention to the intricate architectural details of the stonework, exuberant carvings, and ornamental inscriptions was superb.

She told him of the many trips she had once made with Jean-Paul, and as the sun slipped silently over the summit of Nymph Dagh, he saw that in reliving those memories his great-grandmother was young once more. But thrilled as he was with everything she had shown him, Leonidas was even more taken with the portrait of a woman on the wall over the divan where Dimitra sat. He waited for her to say something. Finally, he could bear it no more.

'Great-grandmamma, you have told me so much about Great-grandpapa and his work, and yet you purposely avoid speaking of this magnificent portrait where you are sitting.'

As he spoke he remembered his mother's locket. He was sure this was the same woman. She had the same mysterious allure. Not only that, but she bore an uncanny resemblance to his great-grandmother. Leonidas stared at the woman as if possessed. She was the most beautiful creature he had ever seen. She was even more beautiful than his mother, if that was at all possible.

'Such beauty invokes comparison with a Greek goddess!' he exclaimed. 'She could be Helen of Troy—the face that launched a thousand ships.'

The painting was approximately 19 by 23 inches and was set in a simple ebony frame which enhanced the woman's cascading raven hair. Her face was hauntingly sensual; it was almond-shaped with a flawless alabaster complexion and a small yet perfectly formed mouth. A narrow, dark-green silk sash intertwined with pearls and the occasional gold bead was wrapped around her forehead, tied at the side with a small knot and left to tumble through her shining tresses. The fabric of her delicately embroidered silk chemise was so fine that Leonidas felt his eyes drawn to the luminous skin exposed on the curves of her barely visible breasts. But it was her deep amethyst eyes that captivated him. Their intensity made him think of the amethyst amulets worn as a protection against drunkenness. Her gaze seemed to meet that of the artist. He wondered what thoughts had been in her mind, or whether she had made the artist drunk with desire, just as she did him. To Leonidas, she was so alive that he could smell her. The style of painting was much finer than Jean-Paul's and he looked for a signature. In the border of her gold embroidered chemise, as if part of the embroidery itself were the initials J M L, the same as those on the portmanteau. It could not have been painted by his great-grandfather. And anyway, he always signed his name in full. He looked at Dimitra, waiting for a response. She was twirling the rings on her fingers.

'Won't you tell me who she is and who painted her? Who is "J M L"?'

Dimitra stood and closed the shutters. 'That's enough for today, my son. I'm feeling rather tired now.'

Leonidas could not understand her reluctance to answer when she had been so forthcoming with everything else.

'Well,' he said, trying to conceal his disappointment, 'the artist certainly had an eye for beauty.'

# CHAPTER 19

*Smyrna, July 1922*

'It *is* her, Mama,' said Leonidas excitedly. 'I knew it was.'

Nina leaned over to take a better look at the locket. He pointed out the similarities.

'She's so beautiful,' said Nina, taking it from him. 'I wonder why Great-grandmamma didn't want to tell you who she is.'

That question weighed heavily on all their minds. Leonidas's account of the previous afternoon with Dimitra had left them reeling. Long after the children had gone to bed, Sophia and Photeini talked until the early hours of the morning. They knew that the room had once been a studio, but they had no idea that it still held such an important place in Dimitra's heart.

'Do you think that's why she wanted to return to the old house?' Sophia asked her mother. 'And were her arguments with Papa over the Megali Idea just an excuse to leave?'

'No. Her feelings on that subject were well known. Anyway, she didn't need an excuse to leave. She often made regular visits back to the house. You know your grandmother, Sophia. She's always clung to the old way of life.'

Sophia felt saddened. 'It seems as though time really did stop for her when her grandpapa died. How sad she must have been for all those years; and to think that she couldn't confide in us. It doesn't bear thinking about.'

'I remember the day she received news of his death,' said Photeini. 'She was so ill that we thought she would die of grief. For the first few months she wore the obligatory black clothing, covered the mirrors with a black cloth, and fasted. Then one morning we woke to the smell of burning. She had taken down all the black cloths and was burning them, along with her mourning clothes. It caused a scandal but she didn't care.

'"I never want to see black in my house again," she told us. "How can I create such beautiful work surrounded by the colors of Charon?"'

Photeini laughed. 'She's always shown great passion and determination. In that way, you take after her. Not long after, the matchmakers began to arrive. She received them warmly, always telling them she would think about their offers. She was a wealthy woman in her own right—she didn't need to remarry.'

'Wasn't there anyone at all?' asked Sophia. 'After all, she was still young and extremely beautiful.'

'Oh yes! Your grandmother was considered to be one of the most beautiful women in Smyrna. She had admirers of all nationalities, not only Greeks—Levantine businessmen, an Armenian silk merchant, and even a few pashas. In fact there was one person who came to the house more often than anyone else—a pasha. I can't recall where he was from; it was somewhere in Anatolia, not far from Kayseri, I believe. Anyway, he sent her wonderful gifts and her face lit up at the mention of his name. It may have been his family who sent her the blood-bay foal that she treasured so much.'

'Then why did she never marry him? Was it because he was a Muslim?'

'Possibly. Certainly that would have been frowned upon in our community, especially with a person of such good standing as your grandmother. After a while, his visits stopped. We never saw him again. I don't know what happened.'

'Perhaps she realized that no one could replace grandpapa' said Sophia wistfully.

'Perhaps. I agree with you—we know so much about her and yet we know very little, and it's always puzzled us as to why she never talks about her life in the times before she married. She certainly is an enigma.'

'She wouldn't be the first person to keep her past a secret, and she certainly won't be the last,' said Sophia, thinking of Constantinople.

Photeini looked at her. She understood exactly what her daughter was saying.

'Leonidas is right though, she does seem to feel the need to talk now. Spend some time with her. If she's ever going to reveal anything, then it will be to you. You are much closer to her than I ever was. Anyway, I must stay here with your father. He needs me more than ever now.'

For more than three weeks Soterios remained bedridden with severe depression, resulting in aches and pains for which no one could find a remedy. Photeini feared that this time it would take far more than her herbal potions to cure him. His last hope for an Ionian State had gone. Without the support of Greece—by now, virtually bankrupt, and with the Allies eager to support Mustafa Kemal's Nationalists—an autonomous Smyrna could not survive. In desperation there had been discussions of Smyrna being run by a committee involving all the other non-Muslims, in particular the Levantines and Armenians. However, the will to pursue this idea was as doomed as all the others.

'She's waiting for you,' Iskender said, his eyes indicating the blue door at the far end of the balcony. 'You will not be disturbed. The children are asleep.'

He returned to his duties, leaving Sophia alone in the courtyard. The familiar splashing of water from the fountain punctuated the stillness of the afternoon. She made her way up the staircase. The door was ajar, a sign that her grandmother was expecting her. Sophia removed her shoes before entering. Dimitra sat on the divan, waiting. She smoked a cigarette.

'Come in, my dear.'

Sophia was surprised to see her grandmother with a cigarette.

'I'm trying to be a modern woman,' she smiled, blowing out a cloud of smoke.

Sophia sat beside her. She had always wondered when Dimitra would give up the narghile, yet seeing her with a cigarette seemed so out of character. 'I want to thank you for what you did for Leonidas.'

'He's a young lion,' replied Dimitra. 'The son I never had.'

'It's your blood that flows through his veins, Grandmamma. He's as much a part of you as he is of me.'

Casting her eyes around the room, Sophia looked at the unfinished paintings. Like Leonidas, she felt as if Jean-Paul would walk in at any moment and finish them. Joining her grandmother on the divan she saw the portrait hanging on the wall behind her. Leonidas was right—it was definitely the same woman. Sophia had purposely used this occasion to wear her locket. She took it off and placed it in her grandmother's hand, closing her fingers over it. The exceptional brilliance of the Burmese sapphire in Dimitra's ring sparkled in the light.

'When you gave me this locket, you told me that it was your most prized possession.' Sophia indicated to the portrait on the wall. 'It *is* the same woman isn't it? Who is she, Grandmamma? Won't you please tell me? Who are the couple in the locket? And why do they remain a mystery to us?' The questions tumbled out. 'And why do we know nothing about your life before you came to Smyrna? What could be so terrible that you were never able to tell us?'

The pain on Dimitra's face was all too evident.

'There were reasons for my silence; perhaps they were selfish ones. For years my past was something that I thought only concerned me. Now I realize that I was wrong.'

Dimitra searched for the right words, but try as she might the words would not come; the part of her that had remained locked away for a lifetime refused to surface. Sophia thought of Constantinople and her own decade of suffering. She knew there were parts of her life that she would never talk about again, and that she would take her secrets to her grave. What right did she have to put her grandmother through such agony?

'Forgive me, Grandmamma, I didn't mean to upset you. If the memories are too painful, I'll never ask you again.'

'No!' replied Dimitra, standing up and giving her back the locket. 'I just ask you to be patient. In time you will understand everything.'

Throughout the scorching heat of August, Dimitra shut herself in Jean-Paul's studio and began to write down the words that she found so difficult to say. Each day a jumble of memories emerged from her private world, and each day a weight was lifted from her shoulders. But there was something that bothered her greatly. Occasionally, a raven landed on the windowsill. It cawed three times and flew away. One afternoon the window slammed shut due to a freak wind, and on that particular day the raven appeared again and tapped its beak on the window pane, determined to go inside. Dimitra tried to shoo it away. For a few seconds, it tilted its shiny black head and looked at her, before flying away. It was a bad omen—a sign of death.

At dawn on August 26, 1922, Mustafa Kemal—the man Lloyd George had once called 'an enigma; a carpet seller in a bazaar'—stood before his troops and announced, 'Soldiers, your goal is the Mediterranean.' Four days later, almost half the Greek army had been wiped out and half a million troops were taken prisoner. The rest fled towards the Sea of Marmara and Constantinople. In their wake whole villages were razed to the ground and thousands of civilians were slaughtered. On both sides this was a war of extermination. The Nationalists cut the lines of communication and for days the Turkish victories were virtually unknown.

Rumors did reach Smyrna and Constantinople, but were dismissed as idle gossip. While thousands perished, the citizens of Smyrna—largely unaffected by war—went about their daily lives much as they had always done. Theatres were filled to capacity and people continued to queue outside Café Aphrodite, where Nitsa and the Kapitanos still drew large crowds.

One morning, Vangelis arrived at La Maison du l'Orient with a letter from Constantinople. Sophia opened it, eager to hear news of her friends. It was from Anna's father and her expression quickly changed from joy to apprehension as she read it.

'What is it?' he asked. 'Is everything alright?'

She read him the contents. It stated that the family yacht—the *Medusa* —would be anchoring in Smyrna's harbor in a few days' time. The captain had been authorized to take on board eight members of her family: Soterios, Photeini, Leonidas, Maria, Nina, Dimitra, and herself; Vangelis was included. They would be given safe passage back to Constantinople, where his family would be honored to have them as guests until the situation had blown over. Anna's father urged her to give the evacuation some serious thought. He had it on good authority that should the Turks enter Smyrna victoriously, the Allies could not be relied upon for protection; the life of every Christian would be in danger.

The letter shocked Sophia. What information did he have access to that they didn't know already? Could the rumors of such a catastrophic Greek defeat be true? And if so, why did the Greek military continue to give an upbeat assessment of the situation? Only that day they had received news that the Greek forces had secured a great victory, and some even said the Ghazi himself had been taken prisoner. They discussed the possibility of telling her father about the letter but Vangelis advised her against it, fearing that he may have another breakdown.

'Let's keep it to ourselves,' he said.

'Perhaps you're right. Keep an eye out for the yacht and we'll see how things develop. The letter says that it will remain in the harbor for a week. Hopefully, there will be no need for an evacuation at all.'

Vangelis agreed, yet neither of them could dismiss the nagging doubts that threatened to destroy their optimism.

At the beginning of September, Vangelis reported that the *Medusa* had arrived. Together they made their way to the port where they hoped the captain would be able to shed light on the situation. But he revealed very little, saying that his orders were to drop anchor in the bay for a week. After that, with or without her, he was to return to Constantinople.

The three stood on the deck surveying the lively scene around them. The sea breeze was invigorating and the sounds of the busy port filled the air. Despite the fact that camel trains from Anatolia were virtually non-existent, trade had revived. This was one of the busiest times of the year. Crates and sacks of tobacco, licorice, figs, and raisins were being loaded into waiting merchant ships destined for Europe and America. Life went on as usual, but a quick glance out towards the harbor was unsettling. It was ringed with foreign warships.

The captain looked in their direction. 'It doesn't look good does it?'

'They're here to protect us. The eyes of the world are on the Allies. It's inconceivable that they will allow us to be slaughtered.'

The captain showed her a Turkish newspaper dated May 10. It declared that the country had been good to their minorities and gave an ominous warning—*Beware: We have no intention of repeating the same mistakes.*

'Think carefully,' the captain replied. 'You have one week.'

Deep in conversation, Sophia and Vangelis made their way back to Rue Franque. Neither of them noticed the Greek hospital ship slip quietly into the gulf.

It did not take long after the fall of Uşak to realize that the rumors had been right all along. Uşak was the empire's major carpet center, and for centuries its fine carpets with their distinctive medallions and bird motifs graced the palatial homes of the world's wealthiest families. The fall of Uşak came as a great blow to the citizens of Smyrna. Panic hit the city and shops began to empty of foodstuffs. At home Photeini tried her best to calm the servants. Behice the head cook fell to the floor in a faint at the news. Others wailed, crossing themselves and beseeching God to save their families. Soterios spent most of his time in heated discussions behind closed doors with his colleagues; their angry voices resonated through the house. When he did emerge, his breath smelt of alcohol and his face was like thunder.

'The British have advised their nationals to evacuate,' he told Photeini angrily.

With the same discipline that had made her an accomplished embroiderer, Dimitra composed and rearranged her words as if they were delicately spun silks on the finest cloth. Where she would deliberate over the subtle shading of a rose, she deliberated over a phrase. Throughout the past few weeks she had felt Jean-Paul's presence. He breathed life into her, caressing the nape of her neck whenever her emotions threatened to overwhelm her. She savored every moment. Now the task was almost completed and his presence began to fade. She blotted the last line and placed the pen in the portable writing case. The room suddenly became cold and silent. The raven no longer appeared. She looked at the woman in the portrait, uttered a prayer, and walked out of the studio.

While Dimitra put down the final paragraphs of her memoirs, a woman wearing a fawn veil arrived to see her. She took great delight in watching Nina embroider, talking to Leonidas about his impressions of Smyrna, and discussing the French society magazines which Maria flicked through.

'Ahh…what splendid clothes,' she said to her. 'Are you going to follow in your mother's footsteps and be a famous couturier?'

Maria was unsure of what to say. Who was this woman who appeared to know her mother? She deliberated over the answer.

'Yes,' she replied, though that was far from the truth. How could she tell her she wanted to be a chanteuse like Nitsa? Her mother would be embarrassed.

'Do you know my mother?' asked Leonidas.

'Very well…although I'm afraid she doesn't know me.'

Leonidas thought nothing more of her reply. After all, there were few women of good standing who hadn't heard of his mother or La Maison du l'Orient. The two women greeted each other effusively and promptly disappeared into the vermillion room. Dimitra gave Iskender orders that they were not to be disturbed.

'It has been three years since I last saw you, Aunt,' said the woman, placing her veil on the divan beside her. 'How time flies.'

Dimitra asked as to what she owed the honor of her unexpected visit.

'I bring you important news from Anatolia.'

The 'lady with the fawn veil', as Nina referred to her, stayed for a few hours. The children were still on the balcony when she waved them goodbye.

'Who was that?' Leonidas asked Iskender.

Iskender stood with his feet apart, his hands firmly placed on his hips and drew himself to a formidable height again.

'Leonidas Efendi…you're prying again.'

The children burst out laughing.

# CHAPTER 20

*Smyrna, the first week of September, 1922*

One minute the lilting voice of Nitsa held her audience spellbound, the next minute pandemonium broke loose. A man burst into the room screaming, 'The troops! Our defeated troops are here!' Within minutes Café Aphrodite was empty; tables and chairs lay upturned and the floor was covered in broken glass. It had been a stampede and Nitsa was visibly shocked.

'*Christos kai Panayia*,' she cried. 'If they panic like this at the sight of our troops, what will it be like if the Turkish army arrives?'

She stormed angrily from the stage. The manager bolted the doors and peered out of the window.

'Give me a cigarette,' she said to him. 'It's going to be a long night.'

The rest of the *Kumpania* joined them. In sheer disbelief they watched the unfolding scene outside. A ragged column of Greek soldiers passed along the quay towards the port. Within hours, fifty thousand sick and exhausted soldiers congregated along the promenade waiting for Greek ships to take them away from this wretched land.

It was little more than three years since these same troops had been welcomed so enthusiastically, in exactly the same spot.

'What will happen to us if you go?' they heard a man shout.

A soldier turned and stared at him, his eyes hollow as a corpse. 'We just want to go home,' he answered weakly.

'Cowards!' an onlooker shouted, shaking his fist in the air. A scuffle broke out.

'Look. We're fighting between ourselves now,' said Nitsa in disgust.

Vangelis tapped her on the shoulder. 'Come on. You can't go home alone. Come back with me.'

The rear entrance to Café Aphrodite opened into a narrow alleyway leading to Rue Parallele. In the darkness they managed to make their way across the city to Sophia's home. Everywhere, columns of gaunt, ghostlike soldiers shuffled through the streets, and with them came the first influx of refugees.

With the first light of dawn, Vangelis awoke to the sound of voices and the bleating of goats outside his window. To his utter amazement he saw that the garden was now full of refugees. Throwing on his clothes, he hurried downstairs to find out what was happening. Sophia and Photeini were already in the kitchen supervising a meal large enough to feed an army. Behice—her round frame covered with a white apron splattered with crushed tomatoes—stirred the contents of a huge cast-iron pot on the stove, while her assistant gradually added rice and an assortment of chopped vegetables. Next to them Photeini busily rolled out paper-thin sheets of filo to line a row of baking trays. As quickly as she finished, a maid filled them with mounds of a spinach, cheese, and pine-nut mixture. Sophia refilled the samovar. At the sight of Vangelis she stopped and wiped her brow.

'What's going on?' he asked, alarmed. 'Who are these people?'

'Most of them are Behice's relatives,' she said, handing him a glass of tea. 'They arrived yesterday pleading for help. What could we do? They have nowhere to go.'

She picked up a tray of glasses filled with steaming hot tea and went outside. There were at least fifty of them. They sat huddled on makeshift beds, and their condition was almost as pitiful as the soldiers'. Vangelis counted six goats and three donkeys laden with pots and pans tethered to the fruit trees. An old woman sat on a broken rush stool clutching a birdcage. She spoke to the tiny yellow songbird with such tenderness.

'Sshhh,' she said, poking her finger into the cage. 'Soon you'll have a home again.'

Vangelis was a strong man but he felt himself weaken.

'Come on. Don't just stand there,' Sophia called out, shaking him out of his despondency. 'There's work to be done. Help me with the food.'

Hungry mouths quickly emptied the plates. Photeini brought out more. 'Today a banquet,' she said to Vangelis. 'Who knows what tomorrow will bring?'

Seeing their plight, Nitsa offered to help. Photeini gave her a freshly starched white apron and promptly put her to work. The sight of Nitsa with her fashionably bobbed hair, eyes lined with kohl, red lips, knee-length cabaret dress and heeled shoes, smoking a cigarette as she sat amongst the goats, washing the children's hair and faces with her jeweled fingers, raised a rare smile in a sea of despondency.

'There's still time to evacuate,' whispered Vangelis, as Sophia replenished his tray.

'I know…It's constantly on my mind, but my parents would never leave and I can't go without them. At the moment there are far more pressing things to think about.'

Vangelis wondered what could possibly be more important than saving one's life.

Over the next few days trainloads of soldiers half dead with exhaustion continued to arrive in the city, heading towards the Chesme Peninsular—a stone's throw away from the island of Chios—where they were evacuated by Greek warships. In a scene reminiscent of Thrace, thousands more trudged alongside oxcarts, camels, mules, and emaciated horses. Smyrna was now choked with refugees, more arriving daily. All the hospitals, orphanages, schools, colleges, and even the cemeteries overflowed. Thousands more were forced to sleep in the streets. As quickly as they arrived the Greek troops embarked and were taken away, while the refugees looked on pitifully, praying that their turn would soon come.

Behice's relatives were the lucky ones. Sophia arranged for them to be given shelter in her grandmother's atelier in the street of the embroiderers. Boxes of silks, sequins, ribbons and bolts of fabric were quickly piled into a corner. In a space that normally held no more than thirty, sixty people now crammed together. Tables were turned into makeshift beds and families huddled dangerously around small cooking stoves. While Sophia and Photeini supervised their welfare, Vangelis, accompanied by Leonidas, did the round of shops, bringing back any foodstuffs on which they could lay their hands. No sooner were the refugees installed in the atelier when unfamiliar faces and more animals filled the garden again. Photeini was dismayed to find her beautifully kept garden completely destroyed.

In the evenings, Vangelis and Nitsa still performed at the Café Aphrodite. Despite the tumultuous events taking place, for most establishments it was business as usual. Even La Maison du l'Orient was still busy. In a bizarre situation, Sophia's wealthy clientele made their way to her premises through streets clogged with the homeless and starving, to leaf through the society magazines of *Femina*, *Gazette du Bon Ton,* and *Styl*, agonizing over whether to choose between the exquisite lines of Jeanne Lanvin or the irresistible chic of Coco Chanel.

On Friday 7 September, the Greek flag was lowered in Smyrna. At seven that night, High Commissioner Stergiathes left the building for the last time and to the booing and jeers of a hostile crowd, embarked on a launch that carried him out to the safety of a British battleship. With his departure the short-lived Greek state in Asia Minor ceased to exist.

From the Café Aphrodite, Vangelis watched Stergiathes leave. Even more alarming was the fact that the Greek gendarmes also departed. His instincts told him this could only end in tragedy. Again he urged Sophia to leave. Later that evening, Soterios called a family meeting and for the first time the subject of evacuation was discussed. Soterios's own position was that it was impossible to resist any longer. He did not trust the Turks but like others, he still tried to be optimistic. Such a formidable presence of foreign warships in the harbor assured him that despite their eventual lack of support for a Greek state in Asia Minor, the Allies would not stand by and allow a massacre. Above all, he was adamant that he would not leave Smyrna and a cause to which he had devoted his life. For him, it was only a matter of time before the Greek state would rise again.

Sophia felt that the time had come to tell him about the *Medusa*.

'Why not take a holiday in Constantinople?' she asked her father. 'The break will do you good and we will be among friends. Our departure can be arranged straight away.'

'Sophia has a point,' said Photeini. 'After all, many of our friends have already taken holidays.'

Soterios banged his fist on the table. 'And do you think that Mustafa Kemal will be content with Smyrna? No. His eyes are set on the bigger prize—Constantinople.' He waved his hand in the air. 'I give all of you my permission to go. I will stay here. I will not be called a coward.' His body began to tremble.

'Fate has many voices,' Photeini said, trying to calm him. 'Already the Turks are issuing proclamations that we have nothing to fear, and I've heard that the Italians will patrol the streets with them to ensure that everyone keeps the peace. What's more, many of the Allies have landed Marines. Doesn't that count for something?'

'They have landed them to protect their own interests,' said Soterios sarcastically.

'Well, if they are ashore, then they must mean to protect us also. What do you have to say, Mother?'

Dimitra's views on Venizelos and the Greek occupation were well known. She looked at her son-in-law with contempt. If you join the dance circle you must dance, she once told him when he was swept along with the euphoria of the Megali Idea. Now he was reaping what he had sown. But she could only feel sadness for her daughter, who she knew would stand by him, no matter what. And Sophia—how she wished she had never returned to Smyrna.

'You already know my thoughts. Smyrna is my home and I will die here. What use have I of foreign parts now? This time I'm afraid I agree with Soterios. A man does not seek his luck, luck seeks him. No matter what happens now, a thousand years hence, the river will run as it did. For now, we must keep our heads.'

Soterios threw Dimitra an angry glance. 'Bah…always talking in riddles,' he thought to himself. He had known all along that she would stay; she was one of the few Greeks in Smyrna who had been vehemently against the occupation and her views had often caused him embarrassment. There were times when he chastised Photeini for her mother's apparent tolerance of the Turks.

Photeini's reply was always the same. 'Through their patronage our business flourished.'

'No,' Soterios replied. 'There's more to it than that.'

Throughout the moonless night Smyrna lay eerily silent, but to everyone's great relief the city remained relatively calm. In the morning Vangelis made his way through the throngs of refugees to the *Medusa* and breathed a sigh of relief when he saw her still at her mooring.

'So...the Kyria has decided not to leave after all?' the captain asked, seeing the look on Vangelis's face. 'I was told she had a stubborn streak. The day after tomorrow, we will leave; if I don't see her again, please give her this. The Kyrios wanted her to have it.'

He handed Vangelis an envelope containing a large amount of money.

'It may come in handy.'

Vangelis walked back along the waterfront to Café Aphrodite. Outside, Nitsa and Ayvali Apostoli chatted to a group of men. At that moment the crowd began to panic.

'The Turks are here!' someone cried out.

Crowds of hysterical refugees began to flee in all directions. In tense silence, Vangelis, Nitsa, and Ayvali Apostoli watched a column of Turkish cavalrymen approach. Wearing the black kalpak of the Nationalists emblazoned with the red crescent and star, their scimitars held high, these battle-hardened cavalrymen trotting along on their magnificent horses presented a formidable sight. Vangelis saw that the commander's uniform was drenched in fresh blood and his cheek was bleeding. Terror-stricken women continued to shriek. Occasionally, a cavalryman called out, '*Korkma! Korkma!* Fear not! Fear not!'

Nitsa commented on their discipline, praying to God that it would stay that way. Suddenly, someone nearby threw a grenade at the captain, hitting him forcefully on the cheek. Immediately, the cavalrymen closest to him aimed their rifles in the direction from which the grenade had been thrown. Shots rang out and Nitsa let out a piercing scream. Ayvali Apostoli slumped to the ground. A bullet pierced the violin case that he held against his chest and entered his lung. By the time they dragged him into the café he was dead.

In the vermillion room, Nina prepared an assortment of threads in readiness to embroider a small kerchief. Throughout the morning a steady stream of ecstatic citizens from Smyrna's Turkish community made their way past Dimitra's house towards the Konak in anticipation of the arrival of Mustafa Kemal's troops. Turkish music blared out loudly. Nina knelt on the divan, opened the latticed windows, and peered into the narrow street below.

'Look at all those people,' she said to Dimitra. 'Where are they going?'

In the carnival atmosphere, a sea of red fezzes worn by a cheering crowd surged towards the quayside. Turkish flags fluttered alongside life-size portraits of Mustafa Kemal.

'The Ghazi's soldiers have arrived,' Dimitra replied.

'Who is the Ghazi? He must be very important for them to be so happy.'

'The Ghazi is an old Turkish word. It means the conqueror—the victorious one.'

Nina looked puzzled. 'Is there going to be a war?' she asked.

'Of course not, my child. Whoever told you that?'

'I overheard Mama and Grandpapa talking, and Maria told me that the Turks are going to kill us all and throw our bodies into the sea. Leonidas said that was a big lie and she only wanted to frighten me.'

Dimitra felt her anxiety. 'Your sister shouldn't say such things.'

'What will happen to all those people sleeping in the streets? Will they be able to go back to their homes?'

'Yes, of course.'

'Do you think the Ghazi will help them?'

Dimitra looked at her sadly. She envied her naivety.

In a moment in history that many thought would never happen, on Sunday 10 September, 1922, a victorious Mustafa Kemal arrived in Smyrna. To the jubilant cheers of thousands, his cavalcade of cars made its way to Government House escorted by lines of cavalrymen. Appearing on the balcony, he appealed for calm. Shortly after, local Greeks watched in amazement as he entered a nearby hotel and toasted his victory with a glass of raki.

With daylight fading over Smyrna, the Greek and Armenian communities cowered behind locked doors. In Sophia's home the servants checked the doors and windows and retired to their quarters. In the drawing room, Photeini, Soterios, Sophia, Leonidas, and Maria discussed a leaflet that had been handed to them during the day. It read:

Mustafa Kemal has given strict orders to the soldiers to harm no one. Those who disobey these orders will be punished by death. Let the people be assured of safety.

Upstairs, Sophia pulled the quilt over her youngest daughter and gave her a goodnight kiss. Since the influx of the refugees, Nina had cried herself to sleep every night, afraid of recurring nightmares in which she found herself in the sea, trying to swim. In the stillness of the room, Sophia watched the child's breathing. Her thoughts wandered back to the day when she was born. Over that time she had long ago learned that a mother's love is not enough to protect her child from the evils of the wider world. She turned down the lamp and returned to the drawing room. The tension in the air was very obvious. Maria leafed through a copy of *Femina* while Leonidas sat in the armchair, swinging his legs like he had as a child. Soterios paced the room nervously, eventually settling down to a book.

As the evening wore on, the silence was broken by sporadic bursts of gunfire and screams that seemed to pierce their very souls. Just after midnight they were startled by someone hammering on the door. They looked at each other anxiously.

'Perhaps it's Vangelis?' said Maria.

'No,' Leonidas replied, jumping up from his chair. 'He'll still be at Café Aphrodite.'

Soterios motioned them to be quiet and stay out of sight. Cautiously, he looked over the banister into the hallway below. One of the servants poked his head out of his room. Sophia told Leonidas and Maria to hide on the balcony.

'Open up,' a voice called out in Turkish. 'Open up before we break the door down.'

Soterios walked down the stairs telling the servant to go back into his room and bolt the door. Photeini stood on the landing trembling. She begged him not to open the door. He ignored her. A Turkish officer entered followed by soldiers carrying rifles.

'I'm looking for Kyrios Soterios Kostavaros,' he said sharply.

'I am he,' replied Soterios.

The officer waved a document at him. 'I have orders from the Revolutionary Tribunal for your arrest. You are to come with us immediately.'

Photeini rushed down the stairs towards her husband. 'No!' she screamed. 'Please don't take him! He has done nothing!'

A soldier blocked her way with his rifle.

'For what reason?' asked Soterios, outraged at the violation of his home.

Clearly hostile, the officer shrugged. 'It seems that you have compromised yourself, Kyrios Kostavaros.'

Photeini reached out to him and was swiftly knocked to the ground by a soldier who cursed and threatened to shoot her. Sophia ran to her side.

A deep sense of impotence cut through Soterios's pride like a dagger. 'In God's name, won't you at least allow me the dignity of saying goodbye to my wife?' he asked, shaking with emotion.

The officer ignored him. He stuffed the documents back into his jacket, turned to the soldiers and laughed. 'Take him away,' he said impatiently. He glanced back at Photeini and laughed again. 'The whore is better off without you.'

Sophia held her terrified mother back as her father was led into the street. Hiding on the balcony, Leonidas and Maria watched their grandfather being marched away at gunpoint.

Just before dawn, Vangelis donned his newly acquired fez, and with Nitsa he cautiously made his way home from Café Aphrodite. A few streets away from the house, they noticed several bodies slumped against the wall of the Greek school. With the curfew still in place the street was deserted, and they took a closer look. Twelve men had been bayoneted to death.

'*Christos kai Panayia*,' Nitsa whispered. 'They never stood a chance.' She tugged at Vangelis's jacket. 'Let's get out of here before someone sees us.'

Vangelis stood as if rooted to the ground. The crumpled body of Soterios lay just feet away from him. Reeling from shock, they discussed whether or not to tell Sophia. In the end they decided to keep it to themselves. What was done could not be undone and they did not wish to cause further heartache. The next morning, Sophia found them sitting in the breakfast room. They listened solemnly as Sophia recalled the events of the previous night.

'Where could they have taken him?' she asked. 'There's only one place I can think of and that's the Konak. If he's on an official list, someone at Government House must know something. I must go and find out for myself.' Vangelis looked aghast and tried hard to dissuade her, telling her the streets were unsafe.

'Nonsense. The tram cars are still running and there are people everywhere.'

Photeini entered the room. Her eyes were swollen and her hands shook.

'Did I hear you say you were going to the Konak? Is that wise?'

'Listen to your mother,' said Vangelis guiltily. 'Why risk trouble—at the Konak of all places?'

'I have to do something. I can't just sit around. I'll go mad with worry.'

'I'll stay here and wait,' Photeini replied. 'He could walk through the door at any moment and I would never forgive myself if I wasn't here to greet him.'

Exasperated, Vangelis stood up and pushed his chair away. 'I refuse to let you go alone. If you're stubborn enough to go to the Konak, then I will accompany you.'

He went to his room, picked up the red fez, and twirling his dark moustache looked at himself in the mirror. Could he pass for a Turk? It was worth a try. Sophia went to check on the children. Nina lay on the bed next to Leonidas. He wanted to go with her but she refused, saying that he was needed at home to look after his grandmother and sisters.

'I'll be back soon. In the meantime don't open the door to anyone.'

Passing Maria's room, she heard her crying. She was face down on the bed, the pillow wet with tears.

'Please don't cry, my darling. We must all try to be strong.'

Sophia touched her arm to calm her. Maria turned over and pulled away. Her eyes narrowed and she looked at her mother coldly.

'Don't touch me,' she said, knocking her mother's hand away. 'This is all your fault...'

Sophia reached out again. She was in no mood for one of Maria's tantrums.

'Leave me alone!' Maria screamed. 'If only we had stayed in Constantinople. Then we wouldn't be hiding like scared rats behind closed doors.'

'This will all blow over soon. You'll see; in a day or two everything will be back to normal and Grandpapa will be back with us again.'

'Don't lie!' Maria screamed.

'I'm not lying.'

'Yes, you are. Grandpapa is dead and he's never coming home again.'

Sophia tried once more to calm her daughter but she only screamed louder. In desperation and anger, she lashed out at her, slapping her across her face. Maria's screams could be heard throughout the house. Everyone ran to see what was happening.

'That's enough, Maria. Stay in your room until you come to your senses. I don't want to hear this kind of talk again. Is that clear?'

Maria buried her face in the pillow and Sophia walked out of the room.

'She is possessed by the devil,' said Sophia angrily.

She hated herself for saying such a thing. It was something that she expected her grandmother to say. Vangelis averted his eyes. Had Maria overheard his discussions with Nitsa?

# CHAPTER 21

*Smyrna, the second week of September, 1922*

Making their way to the Konak, Vangelis purposely tried to avoid the Greek school. He need not have worried; the bodies had long been carted away and the street was once again clogged with refugees. He was forced to take an alternative route which skirted past the Armenian quarter. Here, the full horror of the previous night's brutalities was all too evident. Looting—which had taken place immediately after the Greek officials departed and which was carried out by Christians and Muslims alike—had deteriorated into full-scale carnage. Shops and houses lay ransacked, shutters and doors had been forced open, and the streets were littered with broken glass, furniture, and mattresses. Everything that was not broken had been carried away. Bodies—already deteriorating in the warmth of the mid-morning sun—lay amongst the rubble and in doorways. Sophia realized that the proclamations of protection against the Christian population meant nothing. Out of sight of the Allies, the Turks were intent on taking their revenge. Death fouled the air and she was thankful for the veil which she had prudently thought to wear. She held it tightly over her nose. Still, the odor of death seemed to seep into her very bones.

A group of soldiers came towards them and ordered Vangelis to stop.

'Leave this to me,' said Sophia.

An officer approached, looked inside the car and then at Vangelis. '*Eger bir Turk var mi?* Are you a Turk?' he asked, looking at the fez.

Vangelis sat erect, staring straight ahead, avoiding the scrutinizing eyes of the officer. He kept one hand on the steering wheel and the other within reach of the gun in his jacket.

'He is as Turkish as you are, sir,' Sophia replied in perfect Ottoman Turkish. 'Do you want me to ask him to speak to you? Perhaps a story from *The Forty Viziers* will do?'

The officer looked at her. 'I beg your pardon, Hanim Efendi, but this area is out of bounds.'

'Then perhaps you can recommend an alternative route. I have an appointment with General Nureddin at the Konak and we are late as it is.'

Her apparent meeting with such an important person forced him to back down.

'One of my men will escort you safely out of here,' he replied. 'But for your own safety, find another route back.'

'Thank you kindly, sir. We will heed your advice.'

The officer shouted something to one of his men and indicated for Vangelis to follow him.

'You are two streets away from the boulevard. May Allah go with you.'

A trickle of sweat dripped from Vangelis's forehead. It had been a close call. Once on the Grand Boulevard, he removed his fez and wiped his brow. Gaining his composure he caught a glimpse of Sophia's face—the face that he had come to know so very well. He saw that deep in her heart she now knew that Smyrna was a lost cause.

They arrived at the Konak just as the gates opened and a dejected-looking group of prisoners were being led away by armed Turkish soldiers. Sophia got out of the car and asked Vangelis to check on the refugees in Dimitra's atelier. He was to meet her later in the bar of the Hotel Kraemer. Taking a deep breath, she covered her face with her veil and strolled confidently to the Governor's mansion, where a long queue had already gathered. Several Italian soldiers stood guard at the gate and she began to chat with them in Italian. They told her that they were there to keep the peace and protect the Christian population. Sophia asked why, if what they said was true, was it that the Armenian quarter had been ransacked? They looked at her in surprise.

'The Turkish soldiers have behaved admirably,' the Commander assured her. 'We have never witnessed such atrocities. It must have been the Armenians themselves—or the Greeks. They will do anything to discredit the Turks.'

It was useless to argue. Her father had been right all along when he said that the Italians sided with the Nationalists, especially after the Greek army landed. Yet whether out of guilt or simply because he could not resist a beautiful woman, the Commander offered to see if someone in the Konak would see her. Almost an hour later there was still no sign of him. The queue had lengthened considerably, snaking around the corner into the same side street that led to the Turkish bazaar. And the heat was becoming unbearable. Unbeknown to her, someone was watching Sophia from one of the upper windows of the Governor's mansion. She'd almost given up waiting when a small side gate opened and the Italian Commander reappeared, escorted by a Turkish official.

'Please follow me, Hanim Efendi,' said the official.

Sophia's spirits suddenly lifted. She could not thank the Italian enough. '*Arrivederci, Senora*,' he said, raising a salute. '*Il bocca al lupo.*'

'Thank you. I will need all the luck that I can get.'

The official led her to a small reception room where someone was replacing the portrait of King Constantine with an even bigger one of Mustafa Kemal. Sophia contemplated the face that had inspired so many. His steely eyes stared down at her. He seemed to be telling her that they had all underestimated him. Seeing her face flushed from the heat, the official brought her a chilled orange drink.

'General Nureddin is presently occupied, but General Nuri Pasha will see you soon,' the official told her.

He commented on the portrait, telling her that Kemal was his hero. Sophia hardly heard his words. Instead, she wanted to know who Nuri Pasha was. It was an unfamiliar name to her. She did not have to wait long to find out.

Nuri Pasha stood by the window with his back to her. Through a pair of binoculars, he watched a parade of soldiers leave the barracks. Sophia stood waiting. He seemed to be ignoring her.

'Sir,' she began rather indignantly. 'I am here on behalf...'

'I know why you're here,' he replied, replacing the binoculars on the window sill.

He turned towards her. 'Come over here.' Obeying his command, she walked over and stood next to him. 'Look out there. What do you see?'

Sophia thought it a strange question. Was he trying to trap her?

'Well...' she began, 'I see the esplanade, and...' She deliberately chose not to mention the thousands of refugees lining the quayside.

'What else?'

'I see the Turkish flag everywhere.'

'And the warships in the bay, do you see those?'

'Of course. Why do you ask such a question?'

'Why do you think they are there?' he continued.

Sophia could only reply with what was now beginning to sound like a hollow mantra. 'To protect the citizens of Smyrna and to see that no harm befalls the Christian population.'

Nuri Pasha smiled. 'No, Hanim Efendi. They are here for their own nationals...and for us Turks—who against all odds, have fought valiantly for the honor of our country. Where are the Greek warships? They have left. Greece never had any intention of protecting your people.'

Sophia turned to face him. A feeling of impotent rage surged through her. She wanted to slap him. A soft smile lingered on his lips.

'Take a seat. Let us discuss your situation.'

Over the course of the next hour, Nuri Pasha listened to Sophia's pleas regarding the whereabouts of her father. What had he done wrong? The General opened a large file on his desk, telling her that the Revolutionary Tribunal knew about his involvement with the Etairia.

'He has been pronounced an enemy of the State. This file was assembled by the Secret Organization. It was in existence long before I came across it.'

Sophia froze. She thought about Sergei. A feeling of panic overcame her. If the Nationalists took Constantinople, her friends were also doomed.

'I don't know anything about a secret organization. I just want to know if he's alright. What can I do to bring him home?'

'This war has caused much heartbreak,' he said, closing the file. 'Families and friends have been torn apart and the countryside is a vast wasteland. We have all suffered. I would like to help you but I cannot.'

His eyes bore a look of sadness; his vulnerability surprised her. He was powerful; a robust man with a gentle face, and mannerisms that told her he was well educated and from a good family. She guessed they were about the same age. In another time they could have been good friends.

There was a short pause. 'Hanim Efendi, I want to give you some advice. I speak to you as a friend. Take your family and leave Smyrna before it is too late.'

'But my father...we can't leave without him.'

'Perhaps one day you will be reunited with him. For the moment, you must save yourself.'

She got up to leave. There was nothing more to be said. Nuri Pasha escorted her to the door.

'Please heed my warning. I would not like to see anything untoward happen to you.' He looked at her with deep concern. 'I see that behind that veil is a beautiful woman. Others may not look on you as kindly as I do.' He offered her his hand and wished her the best.

After she left he returned to the window, picked up the binoculars and watched her head towards the Hotel Kraemer on the seafront. 'It's true what they say about her,' he thought to himself. 'She is even more beautiful in the flesh.'

Vangelis had been waiting for more than three hours when Sophia arrived. Consumed with guilt, he had drunk more liquor than usual.

'You look awful,' Sophia said to him as he ordered her a drink.

'How did it go?' he asked, ignoring her remark.

She told him about Nuri Pasha and the Revolutionary Tribunal, and about his ominous warnings for them to leave before it was too late.

'What do you think he meant by that?'

'I don't know…but it's not good is it? How did you go at the atelier? How are the refugees?'

'For the moment they're safe, but I don't know for how long. Most of the shops have been looted and picked clean.' He stared into his glass for a few moments, swirling the contents around distractedly. 'I have some bad news. Metropolitan Chrysostom is dead.' Sophia felt the blood drain from her face. 'Yesterday he was summoned to the Konak, where General Nureddin called him a traitor and gave him a dressing down. When he left, the waiting mob seized their chance to attack him. Like a pack of dogs, they carried him away until they reached the shop of Ismael the barber. After dressing him in the barber's white coat, someone shouted out, "Give him a shave." The rest is too terrible to contemplate. He was tortured mercilessly before someone finally put an end to his misery. And all this under the eyes of a dozen French Marines who were powerless to help him.'

Sophia felt her spirits crushed. The Archbishop was their spiritual leader and Sophia's family had known him for more years than she cared to remember.

'He was a good and kind-hearted soul. If they can do that to him, what will they do to us?'

'Exactly,' replied Vangelis.

'Do you think that the *Medusa* is still here?' Sophia asked.

Vangelis sat bolt upright. Now, he thought to himself, she is beginning to see sense.

'It may be too late. She was supposed to have sailed yesterday, but the captain told me that he would wait until the very last moment.'

'Let's go. If we hurry we may just catch him.'

With more and more refugees crowding the quayside, it took what seemed like an eternity to reach the port. The area was blocked off by foreign Marines watching porters load the few remaining merchant ships. Vangelis persuaded them to let him through.

'You'd better be quick,' replied one of the Marines. 'Most of the yachts have gone.'

Leaving Sophia in the car, Vangelis raced along the jetty. His efforts were in vain. The *Medusa* was nowhere to be seen.

'She sailed this morning,' a sailor called. 'About four hours ago.'

'Damn!' yelled Vangelis, letting out a volley of expletives. He slumped down on an empty crate with his head in his hands. 'We are doomed,' he said to himself. 'And it's my fault. If only I had told her the truth about her father's death. At least she would have realized what the Turks were capable of doing and she would have had the chance to leave.'

Sophia knew by the look on his face that they had missed their chance. When they returned to the Greek quarter, the streets were already swarming with armed militia harassing the refugees. They knew that it was only a matter of time before the streets would resemble those they'd driven through earlier in the day.

Taking matters into her own hands, Sophia called everyone in the house together.

'Please do as I say. I want you all to go to your rooms and pack a suitcase. Pack a change of clothes and a few of your most valuable possessions. Everything else must be left here and we must pray to God that when we return everything will be as we left it. Hurry! There's no time to waste. It's imperative that we leave as soon as possible.'

At that moment a loud banging on the door startled them. Vangelis peered through the shutters.

'It's Iskender,' he called out, hurrying to let him in.

Sophia's first thoughts were for her grandmother.

'The Hanim Efendi is safe,' Iskender assured her. 'She has put me at your disposal.'

His timely arrival gave Sophia an idea.

'Vangelis, see to it that the servants obey my instructions. When they're ready, have them assemble here.'

Sophia took her youngest daughter's hand and headed for the bedroom. The child sobbed as Sophia prepared a small knapsack for her to carry. Leonidas appeared on the landing. He tried hard not to look dejected when Vangelis took the suitcase from him.

'Don't worry, *kriso mou*,' Sophia said to him. 'It won't be for long. Now, please go and help your grandmother. I will be with you in a moment.'

Paying little attention to the goings on around her, Photeini had spent the day in her room rocking to and fro, calling out her husband's name. Leonidas began to fill a suitcase for her. To ease her pain, he put her wedding photograph in with the rest of her clothes.

'See, Grandmamma,' he said. 'A photograph of Grandpapa to keep you company while we're away.' Photeini smiled emptily.

Vangelis called out to say that the servants were all ready.

'Good,' replied Sophia. 'Have them assemble in the drawing room. I'll be with you in a moment.'

She rushed to her room to pack her things. It was an impossible task. She took one last look around the room and headed downstairs. It was then that she realized Maria was nowhere to be seen. With so much on her mind, she had completely forgotten about Maria's angry outburst.

'Maria!' she screamed loudly. 'Where are you?'

She ran to her room. Maria sat with her back to her mother.

Sophia recoiled in horror. 'My God, Maria, what have you done?'

Scattered on the floor were long locks of chestnut hair. She had deliberately cut her hair in an attempt to give herself a 'bob'.

'You can't force me to go,' said Maria insolently. She looked at herself in the mirror, picked up her silver hairbrush and began to brush her newly cropped fringe.

Sophia angrily walked over to the dressing table and stood next to her daughter.

'Look at me,' she said, turning Maria's face towards her.

Maria stared defiantly at her mother. Her eyes were heavily outlined in black kohl and her naturally thick eyebrows had been plucked into thin curves and accentuated with a dark brown pencil. Her normally pale cheeks were smeared in rouge and her lips glistened with lipstick the colour of ox-blood.

Leonidas, Nitsa, and Vangelis ran to see what was happening. The room filled with tension. Sophia snatched her daughter's hairbrush out of her hand and flung it at the mirror with such force that it shattered into small pieces.

'*Aman!*' Nitsa muttered under her breath, looking at the fragments scattered across the carpet. 'Such bad luck!'

'You look like a *putana*,' Sophia cried, shaking with anger. She slapped her daughter hard across her face. 'Wipe it off. You have five minutes to pack.'

Even in her darkest days in Constantinople, Sophia had never lost her temper as she did now. She stormed out of the room, throwing Nitsa a cold look.

'What happened?' Vangelis asked Nitsa, when they were alone.

'I didn't know she would do that,' she replied miserably. 'After you left, I felt so guilty about last night I tried to comfort the poor girl. She asked if she could try out my make-up and I agreed, thinking it would take her mind off things. How was I to know she would go to such extremes as to chop off her hair? Now, Kyria Sophia thinks I'm to blame.'

'Don't be too hard on yourself,' said Vangelis wearily. 'The shadow of guilt has followed me all day.'

In the drawing room, Sophia addressed the servants for what she prayed would not be the last time.

'Despite proclamations to the contrary, the murder of our beloved Archbishop has clearly shown us that the Turkish authorities cannot be trusted. This neighborhood is no longer safe. We must all try to take refuge nearer to the quayside within sight of the Allied warships and in close proximity to the foreign consulates. There is nowhere else to go. Until the situation improves, you will all go to join Behice's relatives in my grandmother's atelier.'

They looked anxiously at each other. 'Can you guarantee our safety?' someone asked.

'I can guarantee you nothing. As for myself, I will go to La Maison du l'Orient. My mother, Nitsa, and Vangelis will come with me.' Sophia turned to the children. 'And you, my children, will go with Iskender to stay with your grandmother. You will be more comfortable there.'

There were loud gasps of disbelief. 'You're sending them to a certain death!' one of the servants cried. 'It's too near the Konak.'

At the mention of death, Nina ran to her mother, burying her head in her skirt. Sophia held out her hands to silence everyone.

'My children are my life. Contrary to what you may think, I am not throwing them into the lion's den. Yes, it is true that the old house stands at the edge of the Turkish area but, as my grandmother would say, the crow does not take the eyes of another crow. The Turks would never destroy their own neighborhood. Isn't that so, Iskender?'

Iskender, his hand on the hilt of his knife, stood erect and proud. He agreed with her.

'My grandmother is a respected member of the community there and I trust Iskender with my life to see that no harm befalls them.' She paused for a moment. 'There is one last thing. We can't all leave together; it's too dangerous. Vangelis will take us to the Rue Franque first and return for you as soon as possible.'

'Lord protect us,' someone called out.

'Kyria Sophia, how long will we have to wait?' asked Behice nervously.

'We plan to be out of here well before sunset. The sooner we leave, the sooner Vangelis returns. That gives you a little time to prepare one of your wonderful meals for everyone before you leave. We don't want you leaving on empty stomachs.'

The talk of food raised the mood a little. Sophia gathered the children together.

Leonidas protested. 'Mama, I'm no longer a child. I'm old enough to fight. Please let me return with Vangelis.'

'No, Leonidas, there will be no fighting and I want you to go with your sisters. This is only for a few days until calm is restored. I will come to you as soon as possible. Now hurry.'

She stood in the doorway and watched them leave. There was no time for sorrow.

Sophia returned to the house to say goodbye to all the servants.

'Don't forget,' she said one last time, 'don't open the door to anyone.'

# CHAPTER 22

*Smyrna, the second week of September, 1922*

On entering Rue Franque, Sophia was relieved to find most shops still open for business. She also noticed that many more men had prudently opted to exchange their homburgs and bowler hats for the fez. A group of Turkish soldiers had stationed themselves outside the street's largest department store in an attempt to create a show of normality. By nightfall they would be gone—replaced with marauding bands of irregulars or Turkish civilians, out for revenge.

Krikor Hartunian and his wife Meryam owned the premises directly adjacent to La Maison du l'Orient. This highly respected Armenian family had been in the Rue Franque since Sophia was a child. Fearful that the Turks would use this opportunity to strike out against the Armenian community, Krikor and Meryam—together with their two sons, their daughter, and their son-in-law— decided to leave their home in the Armenian quarter and take refuge above their shop immediately after the departure of the Greek Administration. Their only daughter, Anoush, was almost at the end of her pregnancy and they were not about to take chances. When Meryam saw Vangelis stop and begin to unload the car, she rushed to help. She had known Photeini all her life and was distressed to see her in such a terrible condition.

'My father was taken away and it has broken my mother's heart,' Sophia whispered to her.

'Come on, Kyria Photeini. Let me help you inside.' Meryam looped her arm through Photeini's, patting her hand reassuringly. 'It won't be for long. Remember, dear friend, you're not alone. We're next door should you need anything.'

Above the showroom, Sophia could hear the sound of Vangelis's heavy footsteps and the clatter of Nitsa's heeled shoes on the floorboards. Minutes later she heard his voice on the balcony above the entrance to the shop. Outside, passersby turned their gaze upwards. She ran upstairs to see what was happening. The French flag hung from the railing.

'What have you done!' cried Sophia angrily. She rushed across the room but Vangelis slammed the balcony doors shut and blocked her way.

'Take it down! This is a preposterous act. You have no right to do that.'

Sophia tried to push by him to take it down, but he caught her arm.

'Think of your family before your pride,' he said firmly. 'We Greeks are not ashamed of who we are. But we are now a target for revenge and the Turks mean to punish us. You must align yourself with the Allies. Much of this violence is committed by men who can neither read nor write, but they do recognize the different flags. If it causes them to think twice before committing a crime, then it's worth it.' He loosened his grip. 'I don't want to see a second business harmed.'

Sophia sighed heavily. 'You're right, Vangelis. I shouldn't have doubted you. I know you have our best interests at heart. Please accept my apologies.'

'Bravo!' Vangelis laughed loudly. 'Now come over here. I want to show you something.'

He opened his suitcase, took out the wad of notes that the captain of the *Medusa* had given him and handed them to her.

'Anna's father must have foreseen your stubbornness,' he said with a wry laugh.

Sophia was speechless.

'Keep it somewhere safe and close at hand.' He slammed shut the suitcase. 'I've wasted enough valuable time here. I must get back to the house before it's too late.'

Sophia followed him outside. He attached a small French flag to the bonnet of the car. 'Be careful. Don't do anything foolish,' she said.

He laughed and patted the breast of his jacket to indicate the gun. 'It's still loaded and I'm not afraid to use it.'

As he drove away, she looked up at the tricolor draped over La Maison du l'Orient and felt thankful she'd had the foresight to give her business a French name.

By ten o'clock that evening Vangelis had still not returned. Sophia went into the workroom to sew pockets inside her skirt in which to conceal the money. Nitsa followed.

'Do you mind if I sit with you? My feet are killing me,' she said, screwing up her face in pain.

Sophia saw that her feet were badly swollen. She put down her sewing and fetched a bowl of warm water. 'Put your feet in this. It should ease the pain.'

Nitsa closed her eyes with relief as Sophia gently bathed them. 'Ahh... sheer bliss; you have a soft touch. They feel better already.'

She poured a little orange-blossom water into the palm of her hand and began to massage Nitsa's toes—long toes with red nail varnish that matched the nails on her long, slender fingers. Sophia thought the colour a little too garish for her. Both women felt the tension between them fade. Whether they liked it or not, they had been thrown together through circumstances beyond their control and, at the moment, they needed each other.

'Do you think something has happened to him?' asked Nitsa, with a worried look.

Sophia reached for a cushion and placed it underneath Nitsa's feet.

'Vangelis? No. He's as cunning as a fox. If anyone can look after himself, he can.' She emptied the water and returned to her sewing. 'You're very fond of him, aren't you?'

'He's been a good friend if that's what you mean,' Nitsa replied. She lit a cigarette. The all-too-familiar sound of gunfire could be heard outside. The women tried to ignore it.

'There's no place in my life for any one man,' she continued. 'I'm unlucky in love. Sooner or later they become jealous and demand of me a life I can't give them. No. My only real love is the stage.' She threw back her head, slowly exhaling the smoke. Sophia was reminded of Helene. 'Besides, a man would drain me of my passion and there would be nothing left for my audience.' She turned towards Sophia. 'And you, Kyria Sophia, can you see the day when you will fall in love again?'

Sophia finished her sewing and began to place the money into the hidden compartments. 'Never,' she answered, in a matter-of-fact way.

'Never is a long time. You could have any man you desired.'

'My children are my life now.'

'Children are no substitute for a love between a man and a woman.'

'Maybe you're right. I have loved so passionately that it hurt, but...' Sophia's voice faltered. She looked across at Nitsa and smiled. 'In some ways we're similar—I, too, am unlucky in love.'

Nitsa could offer no comment.

Sometime before midnight they heard windows being smashed in the street. Cautiously, they stepped onto the balcony to take a closer look. A group of soldiers were systematically terrorizing the refugees, demanding money and tearing away women and young girls from the arms of their distraught families. In the dark side streets, blood-curdling screams pierced their ears. Somewhere below, a gun went off. The bullet splintered the shutters, narrowly missing Nitsa's head. Badly shaken, they hastily retreated to the safety of the room.

During the early hours of the morning, they were woken by the sound of voices and heavy footsteps in Meryam and Krikor's premises. Meryam's screams pierced the night air, making their hair stand on end.

'Lord have mercy on us,' Sophia cried out. 'Won't somebody save us?'

Dimitra opened the ivory casket, took out a fresh tear of mastic and bit into it, releasing its fragrant aroma. She attributed the fact that she still had a full set of teeth and healthy gums to a lifetime of chewing this highly prized resin with its health-giving properties. She closed the lid and ran her fingers over its smooth surface. The once-milky ivory was now a faded pale honey. It had been a gift from Aunt Kuzel. She recalled the day as if it were yesterday. The image faded. Putting the box aside, she picked up the child's embroidery and examined it. The crimson tulip was superbly executed. She noticed tiny droplets of blood in the unfinished border of hancesi leaves where the sharp needle had punctured the tiny fingers. The child had been too distressed to concentrate. Dimitra felt a great pride in the artistic achievement of her family, but it came at a cost. The blood of an artist was tinged with sensitivity—a candle flame that could be snuffed out by human frailty. Her life had been one of passion. There was no other way to live.

As she often did in summer before retiring, Dimitra took a stroll through the courtyard, kicked off her slippers, and sat by the fountain enjoying the night air. Still consumed with anger, Maria lay awake in her room mulling over her mother's actions. Hearing a noise in the courtyard, she peeked through the window to see who it was. Bathed in the glow of moonlight, Dimitra splashed the cool water from the fountain over her face and through her hair. Maria's feelings of hatred intensified.

'Why?' she murmured to herself, clenching her fists. 'Why has Great-grandmamma never shown me the same love as my siblings? What have I done to deserve such rejection?'

She watched as Dimitra let down her hair, wetting it completely and then wringing it out. Though it was a warm night, a fresh wind had picked up and a sudden gust of wind sent fallen leaves swirling across the cobblestones. She wrapped a shawl around her shoulders, picked up her slippers, and headed back to the house. Maria noticed something sparkle on the low wall beside the fountain. Waiting until she knew her great-grandmamma would be asleep, she tiptoed downstairs to see what it was. The sudden gust of wind had caught Dimitra off guard and in her haste to get back inside, she had left her rings on the wall. Maria picked them up. Dimitra's rings were worth a small fortune, especially the one with the Burmese sapphire. One by one, she tried them on.

'They are simply wonderful,' she said to herself, admiring them on her outstretched fingers.

Another gust of wind rustled through the trees. Something moved against her foot, startling her. It was the tortoise slowly making its way towards a bed of roses.

Maria kicked it angrily. 'Go away,' she hissed.

The tortoise pulled its head under its shell to protect itself. She kicked it again. It refused to move.

'Ugly thing,' she mumbled to herself.

Reluctantly, she removed the rings and replaced them where she found them. She thought how easy it would be to take them. No one would know and Dimitra would only have herself to blame if she lost them. Throwing caution to the wind, Maria quickly reached out, snatched up one of the rings, and hid it inside her bodice. She got up to return to her room and saw that the tortoise was still near her feet. Angrily, she picked it up and smashed it against the fountain. Safely back in her room, she put the ring on her finger. The Burmese sapphire was the most beautiful thing she had ever seen and now it belonged to her.

The next morning, Nina became anxious when Aladdin was nowhere to be seen. Iskender and Leonidas helped her look for him. It was then that Iskender spotted Dimitra's rings by the fountain and realized that the large sapphire one was missing. Perhaps it had fallen into the fountain? He peered into the water and saw a dark shape amongst the floating leaves. Nina was heartbroken when Iskender pulled the tortoise's broken body out of the water. Maria lay in her bed twisting the ring around her finger, listening to her sister's inconsolable sobs. She felt no emotion.

When she eventually left her room, Iskender was cleaning out the fountain. He appeared to be looking for something. Convinced that somehow or other she had something to do with all this, Iskender turned his back on her as she passed, feigning a spitting sound. That his mistress could be so ill-fated as to have such a wretched offspring did not bear thinking about.

Shortly before dawn, Vangelis returned to the Rue Franque to find most of the shops plundered. The rioters had long gone and people were slowly beginning to come out of hiding to clean up the mess. His heart missed a beat when he saw a sizeable crowd gathering outside Krikor and Meryam's shop. His fears for Sophia subsided somewhat when he saw that La Maison du l'Orient appeared to have been spared; the French flag still hung proudly from the balcony. The crowd parted and the bodies of Krikor, his two sons, and his son-in-law were carried into the street. Vangelis pushed his way into the shop. An antique grandfather clock lay smashed to pieces on top of upturned showcases. Everything of value had been taken. He ran upstairs just as two men were moving Meryam's body from the bed onto a stretcher. A pool of blood stained the mattress.

'Did you know them?' one of the men asked.

Vangelis nodded. Meryam's throat had been slashed and the look of terror was still firmly etched on her face.

'I'm sorry. It's better to remember her as she was,' the man said, covering up the body. 'These things can haunt you for the rest of your life.'

'What about the daughter?' Vangelis asked.

The men looked puzzled. 'There was no one else.'

'Are you sure? She was heavily pregnant; she must be here.'

'We searched the place thoroughly,' the men assured him while maneuvering the stretcher down the narrow staircase.

Vangelis decided to search the place himself. He noticed a small door hidden behind a large cabinet. Frantically, he called the men to come back to help him move it. Behind the door in dark and cramped conditions, Anoush, too terrified to move, stared out at them. Vangelis took off his jacket, wrapped it around her shivering body, and carried her back to La Maison du' l'Orient.

The three women had barricaded themselves in on the first floor. Sophia and Nitsa pushed the furniture aside to let him in. At the sight of Anoush, the women knew just how close they had been to death themselves. Vangelis slumped into the chair, his face ghostly white. Sophia knew something terrible had happened.

She scrutinized his bloodstained jacket. 'You're hurt!' she cried, trying to pull it open to get a better look. 'Nitsa—quickly, get some water.'

'I'm alright,' he said, angrily pushing her away. 'I'm alright, I tell you.'

'In the name of the Virgin, Vangelis, what happened? The servants... tell me, are they safe?'

He took the cigarette out of Nitsa's fingers and drew a deep breath.

'I was too late,' he began, his head downcast. 'When I arrived there was nothing I could do.'

Sophia put her hand to her mouth. 'Sweet Jesus, you mean—they're all...?' She couldn't bring herself to say the word.

'Yes,' answered Vangelis. Minutes passed before he could continue. 'The neighborhood had been overrun when I arrived. I couldn't even get the car anywhere near the street—such chaos; bodies swelling in the heat, animals wandering through the streets. By the time I reached the house, I already knew what to expect.'

Vangelis began to weep. Sophia had never seen him like this before. 'I have never witnessed such a sickening sight,' he told her.

Sophia stood as if turned to stone. The hopelessness of it all had finally sunk in. Vangelis couldn't bring himself to tell them of the grim picture that greeted him; how the maids lay violated throughout the house, some with their breasts sliced off. In particular, he couldn't tell her about Behice. Poor Behice! She'd put up such a fight, but in the end she was no match for the Turks. He'd found her in the kitchen. Trampling over mounds of broken crockery and foodstuffs, her partially naked body had been decapitated and her head was nowhere in sight. Violently sick, he ran from the room and in doing so knocked over a cauldron of freshly made stew, sending its contents flying across the floor. Behice's head rolled out in front of him. Vangelis fled the house in terror. Back in the street he doubted that he would ever get out of the neighborhood alive. By then it was evident that those men who had not been butchered had been marched away to so-called labor camps. Very few would ever get further than the outskirts of the city before they too would meet their untimely deaths.

Luckily for Vangelis, he was spotted by his old friend Abraham, the violin maker who once made violins for Ayvali Apostoli. Abraham had been deployed with a group of Jews to clear the streets. They took him to safety. It took him a harrowing seven hours of playing cat and mouse with the Turks through desecrated cemeteries and empty buildings to get back to Rue Franque.

'What are we going to do?' Sophia asked, her voice shaking with emotion.

'There is only one thing to do. Fetch the children and try to get to Greece.'

'But how? The Greek ships have already left and the Allies will only take their own nationals.'

'Use the money from Anna's father to buy your way out. Go to the passport office straight away. You should have no difficulty in obtaining travel documents.'

'You'll come with us, won't you?' she pleaded.

'Don't worry; you won't get rid of me that easily.' He got up to change his clothes. 'You'd better go before it's too late. In the meantime I'll collect the children and your grandmother.'

'She'll never leave,' said Sophia.

'Then you must go without her.'

Sadly, Sophia knew he was right.

# CHAPTER 23

*Smyrna, the second week of September, 1922*

With the acquisition of the travel passes, the realization that they were finally leaving was too much for Sophia and she stepped out onto the balcony to hide her tears. A never-ending flow of refugees passed. Women bent double under the weight of huge bundles on their backs carried a child in one arm and a heavy suitcase or their prized sewing machine in the other. All the time their weary offspring clung desperately to their mother's skirts. Where did they find such strength? And where would they go? Very few had even the money to buy food, let alone to buy a passage to freedom as she had done. She prayed that Behice's relatives were still safe in Dimitra's atelier. It was impossible to go to check.

Sophia sniffed the air. Her heart began to pound. 'Nitsa, come out here. Do you smell something?'

'What?'

'Over there...' she said, pointing in the direction of the Armenian quarter. The fear associated with the burning of her atelier had never left her. '*Theo mou*, the houses are on fire and the wind has changed direction. Let's pray to God they keep it under control or we'll all be wiped out.'

A few hours later Vangelis returned.

'Mama!' shouted Nina, running into her mother's arms.

Sophia looked at him expectantly, desperately hoping that her grandmother would walk through the door at any moment. Vangelis clicked his tongue and moved his head in an upwards direction—a familiar Greek gesture signifying a definite 'no'. She took him aside, wanting to know what had happened. He told her that Iskender showed him to the vermillion room where to his great surprise, Dimitra sat waiting for him.

'She received me like a Sultana,' he said. 'And in a dignified manner she indicated for me to take a seat. "I already know why you're here," she said to me calmly. "The children are ready to leave. I, however, will not be joining you." I pleaded with her to reconsider, but it was useless. She called the children and one by one whispered something to them and kissed them goodbye. I tell you, Sophia—it took all my strength not to break down.

'I couldn't hear what she said but it must have been something reassuring because both Leonidas and Nina smiled. I did hear her say something to Maria about forgiveness but I didn't understand what she meant. "Go with Vangelis," she told them. "You're going on a wonderful adventure." Iskender was waiting for us downstairs with their bags. Without uttering a word he escorted us as far as Rue Franque. I have never seen that man show emotion. I swear on my life that he fought back the tears, just as I did. For a while, he watched us. Every few steps, Nina turned back and waved to him—then he was gone.'

Sophia's body shook with emotion. She felt an enormous sense of guilt at not saying farewell to the woman who had had the most influence on her life. Yet something told her that this was too final. Neither of them could have brought themselves to say goodbye.

'She did ask me to give you this,' said Vangelis, handing her a leather satchel. 'The memoirs you've waited so long for. She said it explains everything.'

Sophia clutched it to her breast. She longed to read it, but for now her grandmother's past would have to wait.

'You had no difficulty getting the travel documents then?' Vangelis asked anxiously.

'No, I was one of the lucky ones. Many were turned away.'

'The money must have helped.'

Sophia shrugged. 'There's hardly any left now…but I do have my jewelry.'

'What are we going to do with Anoush?' Vangelis asked. 'We can't leave her.'

'She can have my grandmother's pass,' Sophia replied.

'Yes, but she could give birth at any moment. Besides, there's your mother—'

Sophia cut him short. 'My mother may be mentally ill but she's still able to walk, and if Anoush gives birth, well…that's a chance we'll have to take. If we have to carry her on our backs, then so be it.'

'When do we leave?' asked Vangelis.

'We are to assemble on the quayside tomorrow morning. The Americans are already gathering at the Smyrna Theatre.'

*Smyrna, 13 September, 1922, Dimitra's home*

In the early hours of the morning, Gizem, the wife of Ahmet the seller of leeches, made her way from her home in the street of the black mulberry to Dimitra's house. Iskender waited anxiously for her.

'*Salaam Aleikoum.*'

'*Aleikoum es Salaam,*' Iskender replied.

Gizem followed him into the kitchen and began to untie her coarsely woven *botcha* on the kitchen table. Iskender watched her like a hawk. One by one, she carefully spread the contents out in front of her. Iskender had known Gizem almost as long as he had known his mistress and, as her name suggested, she was a woman of mystery. Her skill in the art of folkloric medicine was well known and people treated her with a mixture of fear and awe. Gizem had a remedy for everything—from unguents for a jealous husband, to potions that ensured the safe removal of the unborn. Over the years, many had tried by deceitful means to steal her ancient recipes but she would divulge them to no one; the wily Gizem would take her secrets to her grave. A gust of wind blew out the lamp. Iskender relit it. With her lean, henna-stained fingers, Gizem picked up a dried bulb of autumn crocus and pounded it into the crushed oleander bark. The blue beads adorning her bracelet jangled rhythmically to her movements. Finally, she stirred in a little warmed honey, added a splash of sweet pomegranate juice, and poured the fragrant liquid into a delicate crystal goblet.

'My work is finished,' she said, washing any remaining traces from her hands.

'Praise be to Allah who gives us his blessing by sending this guest,' said Iskender. He reached into his sash and pulled out a small bag of gold coins.

'The Hanim Efendi wishes you to have this as a token of her gratitude.'

Gizem pushed the bag away. She wanted nothing from her old friend. When she had gone, Iskender picked up a long-handled ivory spoon, placed it alongside the goblet on a gold embroidered napkin and carried it up to the vermillion room. Placing it outside her door, he knocked once and retreated to the courtyard to pray.

Thick clouds of black smoke rose into the sky over Smyrna, making it difficult to breathe. Facing the direction of Mecca, Iskender fell to his knees and prayed as he had never prayed before.

'Allah is great,' he cried. 'Cradle her. Smile on her O Trusted One, and allow her to find acceptance in Paradise. Allah hears those who praise him. Allah is great.'

For the first time since he was a young boy, Iskender allowed his tears to fall freely, wetting the very earth on which he prayed.

During the early hours of Wednesday, September 13, the fires in the Armenian quarter began to burn out of control. Fanned by the stiff breeze, the flames rapidly spread towards the European quarter and the quayside and there was little that Smyrna's fire brigade could do to contain them. All those seeking protection in the city's churches, schools, orphanages, and hospitals were now faced with the choice of being burned alive or of fleeing into the hands of the waiting Turks.

As the sun rose on what should have been a magnificent autumn day, deafening explosions spewed forth flames and debris into an already smoke-filled sky. Knowing that they faced certain death if they stayed a moment longer, Vangelis and Sophia gathered everyone together and prepared to leave. One glance at the seething mass of people heading past La Maison du l'Orient for the quayside told them this short journey was fraught with danger, every step of the way. 'It's imperative that we stay close together,' Sophia warned them. 'One wrong step and we'll lose each other.'

Anoush clutched her belly in fear. 'Leave me here,' she implored. 'I'll never make it. I fear the child is ready to enter this world.' A sharp pain forced her to double up in agony. 'I can't burden you.'

She sank to the ground. Vangelis threw down his suitcase, fastened his precious laouto onto his back and pulled her up. She was like a rag doll in his strong arms.

Uttering a small prayer to herself, Sophia locked the door for the last time, pocketed the key, and picked up her suitcase. She took one final look at the familiar brass plaque on the wall: La Maison du l'Orient. It had been her life. This time she would have to leave it all behind. With the other hand, she clasped her youngest daughter's hand so tightly that Nina screamed in pain. For once in her life Maria lost her sense of self-importance—survival now being uppermost in her mind. She heeded her mother's words and stayed close to Nitsa, while Leonidas took care of his grandmother.

Like a tidal wave, the crowd swept them along Rue Franque and into Rue Parallele. They were almost there when she turned once more to check on Vangelis and Anoush. They were nowhere in sight. In the chaos and confusion they had become separated. Pushed forward by the crowd, it was impossible to turn back. She reassured herself that they were all heading in the same direction and was certain that they would reappear.

When they turned into the side street, Sophia caught a glimpse of HMS *Iron Duke* in the bay. Suddenly she heard screams. Turkish soldiers, their rifles aimed at the crowd, blocked their path. The people became hysterical, desperately showing their papers in an attempt to be allowed through.

'Quickly,' whispered Nitsa, looking towards Sophia for reassurance. 'The travel documents…'

She saw the blood drain from Sophia's face. 'I can't find them! Mother of God…they must be here!'

She searched her pockets thoroughly but they were nowhere to be found.

'Dear God!' she screamed out. 'We've been robbed!'

Somehow in the crush someone had picked her pockets clean. Without the precious papers they were doomed. The soldiers wasted little time in pulling the men and young boys aside as political prisoners, or tearing away the young girls and leading them into the alleyways. Shots rang out intermittently. Nitsa and Sophia were well aware of their fate if the soldiers got their hands on them. They were both strikingly beautiful—the men would fight like dogs over them. More than herself, Sophia feared for Maria and Leonidas. They would spare them no mercy. Tears rolled down Maria's cheeks and her body shook violently.

'Follow me,' said Nitsa, thinking quickly. 'The back entrance to Café Aphrodite is nearby. I still have the key. If we can make it, it will lead us to the quayside.'

Forcing their way through the crowd, they managed to reach the narrow alleyway. Minutes later they had locked themselves inside the empty building. The place was in darkness. Nitsa guided them through a series of rooms until they came to the café itself. The windows and doors were firmly boarded up. They could not get out. They could not go back.

Leonidas peered between a tiny gap in the boards. 'Mama, look! The Americans are evacuating.'

The American nationals had congregated in the Theatre de Smyrne next door. Marines lined the short distance to the waiting boats that would transport them to the safety of the warships. In sheer desperation, Leonidas tore at the wooden boards until his fingers bled.

'Help us!' he screamed, banging wildly. 'Won't anyone help us?'

It was useless. His cry for help seemed like a whisper amidst the cries of thousands of refugees. At the sight of Leonidas, normally so calm, so controlled, Maria screamed in fear. Only Photeini was able to block out the events: she had entered that world of madness where nothing around her seemed to matter any more.

Someone banged on the door. 'Thank God! Someone heard us after all!' cried Nitsa, running to the door. 'We're here!' she shouted wildly. 'Save us!'

Then as if struck by a blow, she took a step backwards. The man was Turkish and he called out for help to break the door down. In the semi-darkness they ran back through the rooms just as Turkish soldiers broke down the door. With nowhere to turn and soldiers swarming through the premises, Nitsa led them to a trapdoor that opened into a small space underneath the stage.

'Get inside,' she whispered. 'They'll never look under here.'

One by one, they crawled under the stage as Nitsa held open the trapdoor. Sophia was the last to enter, leaving little room for anyone else. She turned to help Nitsa just as the trapdoor slammed down on her. In the darkness, they heard the sound of her footsteps running across the stage above them. The soldiers were everywhere, tearing open every possible hiding place.

Minutes later a soldier called out, 'Look what we have here.'

Nitsa was led onto the stage at rifle point. The men laughed and jeered, making crude remarks.

'Where are the others?' the soldier asked.

Nitsa remained silent. Sophia's heart was beating so loudly that she thought they would hear her. 'In the name of the Virgin,' she prayed to herself. 'Please watch over her.'

'I know her,' one of the men shouted. 'She's the Greek singer—Nitsa of Smyrna. Sing us a song, lovely lady, a Turkish song.' He jabbed the bayonet of his rifle into the small of her back.

Nitsa turned to face him with a look of hatred. He was a hulk of a man with a hardened face, a fresh scar across his left cheek, narrowly missing his eye. She was determined not to show any emotion.

'I don't sing for dogs,' she answered curtly.

The man raised his rifle and struck her with such force that she fell heavily to the ground.

'We'll see who the dog is,' he cursed.

In the minutes that followed the men rushed forward taking their turn at violating the woman who had selflessly given her own life to save others. Underneath the stage, Sophia held Nina's head to her breast and covered her ears. Like Leonidas, Maria put her hands over her ears to block out the horror of the scene unfolding above them. Throughout the terrible ordeal, Nitsa never uttered a sound. Bravely, she refused to let her spirit be broken. Just above her head, Sophia caught sight of Nitsa's red fingernails gripping the floorboards. Tenderly, she put out her hand to try to touch them—to reassure her of their love. A gunshot rang out and blood dripped onto Sophia's arm.

'The nightingale sings no more,' laughed one of the men.

The soldiers left. As suddenly as it began, it was all over. When they were sure it was safe, Sophia, Nina, Leonidas, and Maria came out of hiding. Nitsa's body lay in the exact spot from where she had once stood and entertained her many admirers. A single bullet had pierced her heart, and her throat was severed with such force that she was almost decapitated. Leonidas pulled her dress down over her thighs.

By now the fire had reached the quayside and the sounds of buildings crashing to the ground terrorized them. By a stroke of luck, the soldiers had left the door ajar. With not a moment to spare, they made a dash for the quayside and freedom. The humanitarian disaster that greeted them was more than they could ever have imagined. The elegant buildings along the waterfront were on fire and the heat was so intense that they found it hard to breathe. Worst of all, the last boats evacuating all foreign nationals to the safety of the warships had left. They were stranded.

A sudden explosion blew out the windows of the Theatre de Smyrne. Sophia watched the flames dance around the large black sign displaying the name of the last movie shown: *La Tango de la Mort*. Seconds later, Café Aphrodite erupted into a ball of flames.

Inch by inch, they edged their way towards the water. The crowd of almost half a million was packed so tightly that even the dead were kept upright. Wedged between the sea wall and the burning buildings, many leapt to their deaths rather than subjugate themselves to the vengeful Turks. As darkness fell, the remaining refugees could only pray that the Allies would take pity on them.

'Listen, Mama,' said Leonidas. 'Do you hear that music? It's coming from the *Iron Duke*.'

With tears in her eyes, Sophia cursed the men who from the safety of their ships could mock her people by playing *Pagliacci* and *Humoresque*— music that she had so often danced to in Constantinople. Like her father, she questioned whether the Allies had ever really cared about the fate of the Asia Minor Greeks at all.

It all happened so quickly. Flames licked the quayside and the refugees struggled to free themselves from the burning embers. A horse stampeded into the crowd. Its saddle, laden with rugs and bolts of cloth, began to burn out of control. The crowd surged forward to escape being trampled to death. Precariously close to the sea wall, Photeini lost her balance and fell into the water, almost taking Maria with her. Unable to save her, Sophia watched helplessly as her mother slipped beneath the oily baggage-strewn surface. There was no time to think. Moments later the crowd pushed them forward again.

An unbroken wall of fire two miles long illuminated the night sky and the glow could be seen from as far away as Mytilini and Chios. Searchlights revealed a harbor full of floating corpses and upturned boats. For those still stranded, it seemed that further rescue operations had ceased. What they could not have known was that the Allies were under strict orders to remain neutral; they were not to antagonize the Turks by helping the Greeks or Armenians. Yet, as horrific stories of cruelty were quickly circulated by the returning sailors accompanying their nationals, a growing sense of shame at their lack of action began to turn the tide of opinion. Shortly after midnight, a flurry of activity saw boats lowered and quickly dispatched in a belated rescue mission.

The next day Sophia and the children remained stranded. Grief stricken and unable to come to terms with Photeini's tragic death, she had spent the night trying in vain to console her distraught children whilst at the same time avoiding marauding bands of Turkish soldiers and irregulars. A feeling of total unreality gripped her. There was no escape from this nightmare and they were near to exhaustion. At each end of the quay, the Turks aimed machine guns at the crowd. A group of soldiers prowled within feet of Sophia and the children. Maria's headscarf slipped off, revealing her thick bob of glossy chestnut hair. The soldiers spotted her and made their way over. Maria became hysterical. At that moment a cavalcade of Turkish officers on horseback passed by. Sophia recognized the man in charge—it was Nuri Pasha.

Sophia called out to him for help. Instantly, he recognized her. Turning his horse around, the crowd feared further harassment and started to panic. He fired several shots into the air calling for order. The soldiers backed away. Sophia stepped forward and thanked him. She considered it an act of God that his presence had saved them from a fate too unbearable to contemplate.

Nuri Pasha dismounted. Amid such squalor, and despite her disheveled appearance, he still saw the beautiful and proud woman who had sat in his office just days ago. Maria and Nina, their faces still streaming with tears, tried to hide behind their mother. Leonidas stood by his mother's side, watching the general with a mixture of fear and distrust.

'I warned you to leave,' said Nuri Pasha, shaking his head solemnly.

Sophia did not answer. Still reeling over the death of her mother, she could not possibly begin to tell him of the events of the past few days. He turned his attention to her children. Maria hid her face further. He scrutinized Leonidas, a handsome and sensitive boy in the first flush of youth. In his face he saw the thousands of his own young countrymen who had given their lives for their country.

'Our travel documents were stolen,' said Sophia anxiously.

Mounting his horse, he told them to follow him to the far pier. The crowd looked on fearing the worst. Despite her dishevelled and grimy appearance, Sophia held her head high. On the short journey she was acutely aware of Nuri Pasha's men eyeing them with suspicion. When they reached the narrow pier they saw that Turkish soldiers guarded the gates. Under the eyes of their officers, the men brutalized and robbed the refugees of their last few prized possessions. Many lost their balance and fell into the sea, suffering the same fate as Photeini. At the far end of the pier American Marines were on hand. They helped people who were fortunate enough to make it through the gates to the safety of the small boats. Nuri Pasha called to an officer.

'Make sure they leave safely,' he said, indicating Sophia and the children.

The officer made a comment about Leonidas. Surely he was old enough for deportation. Nuri Pasha's face grew red with anger. The officer would reap the consequences if he did not heed his words. The man saluted.

Nuri Pasha turned to Sophia. 'Go with him and may Allah protect you.'

Sophia thanked him. He watched her enter the first gate, tugged at the reins of his horse, turned, and left. Halfway along the pier a second gate slammed shut, forcing them to a standstill. A soldier had become suspicious and he called to the others.

'General Nuri Pasha has given us permission to leave,' said Sophia confidently. 'Ask the officer over there. It was he who personally escorted us through the first gate.'

The men laughed. Suddenly, Sophia's optimism turned to fear again. The man walked over to the officer and after a heated conversation, the officer threw his hands in the air and walked away.

'He has no knowledge of your claim,' the soldier exclaimed angrily. 'He knows nothing about you.'

Sophia was trapped. In desperation she took out the remaining money that Anna's father had given her and passed it to the officer. The man pocketed it hastily. With a bayonet pressed against his chest, Leonidas was ordered to stand aside.

'Deportation,' shouted the soldier angrily, pushing him away from the gate.

Sophia screamed. Instinctively she tried to hold on to him. The men pushed her back roughly.

'No! No! Please don't take my boy!' she cried. 'Take me in his place!'

In a superhuman effort to be brave for his mother, Leonidas put up no resistance. Someone at the first gate called out angrily, '*Aide*, get a move on.'

The gate opened and more refugees crowded through. Sophia, Maria, and Nina were pushed along the walkway with such force that Nina was almost trampled. In a frenzy of grief, Sophia felt herself being lifted into a boat by a man with an American accent.

The warship crammed with hundreds of refugees raised anchor. Sophia stood on the deck with her eldest daughter. The vision was apocalyptic in its scale. The great fire was beginning to burn itself out. Only the Turkish quarter and a section of the Jewish quarter remained of what had once been one of the finest cities in Asia Minor. The sea glowed a deep copper red. Shades of violet, scarlet, and orange streaked the sky. Long after the city had disappeared from view Sophia stared at the beautiful glow. The voice of a small boy with dark curls whirling around the Grand Salon like a dervish called out to her. 'Mama, I am an eagle and I can see Constantinople from the sky.'

Tearfully, Maria looped her arm through her mother's to offer a little comfort. When there were no more tears to be shed and the light in her eyes had dimmed, Sophia turned to look at her daughter. Her eyes said it all: Why did they take him and not you?

# PART III

# SURVIVAL

# CHAPTER 24

*Athens, September 1972*

The depth of Maria's suffering was all too evident. The years of pent-up emotions were suddenly released like a river in a spring flood. Tears smeared her heavily powdered face and she clutched at her breast, gasping for air. Eleni watched helplessly as Chrysoula tried to coax a small glass of thick amber liquid between her trembling lips.

'Hush!' whispered Chrysoula, gently dabbing the wet cheeks with her handkerchief.

The sobs subsided and Eleni clasped Maria's frail hands tightly. They felt cold and clammy. She was acutely aware of the sapphire ring pressing into the palm of her hand. Her aunt's heartbreaking story had left her reeling. Desperately, she searched for words of consolation but words seemed hollow in the face of such tragedy. Her mind was a whirlpool of thoughts; the life they had known lay in ruins. In a short space of time, they had lost everything and almost everyone dear to them. And then there was Leonidas—her grandmother's favorite—the uncle she never knew existed until now. All of them gone. They had lost more in one lifetime than most people could even begin to contemplate. Finally, she thought of Dimitra. What *did* happen in those last few hours as Smyrna burned?

Eleni felt a deep sadness for her aunt. She may have been a difficult child, but judging from what she had just heard, she had almost certainly been shunned. She thought about her own childhood, spent grieving over a mother she never knew and a father who, although she never doubted his love, was nevertheless too wrapped up in his sorrow to give her the love that she had so craved. She looked at the ring. Saturated in shades of blue with a subtle violet undertone accentuated by its border of exquisite tiny diamonds, the magnificent ring cast its spell over her. She looked up and caught her aunt's silent gaze. Maria pulled her hand away abruptly.

Once again, Chrysoula begged her not to continue.

'After what I have been through, do you think that I'm afraid of the final crossing?' replied Maria sharply, referring to Charon's boat ride to the other world.

'What is done cannot be undone,' replied Chrysoula. 'It makes no sense to rake up the past.'

Maria's face hardened. 'I have an obligation to her.'

Chrysoula left the room shaking her head.

'You suffered a great loss,' said Eleni softly. 'And your mother more so; her grief must have been unbearable…'

Maria cut her short. 'You don't understand,' she rasped, fighting for air. 'It didn't finish there.'

Eleni felt a sense of foreboding.

'What don't I understand, Aunt Maria?'

Maria's words were slow and deliberate. 'It was at that point that my mother suffered a complete nervous collapse. In her delirium she called for my brother…and for others whom she would never see again. Occasionally the ship's doctor came to administer drugs, telling us not to worry. But we did worry. She was one of thousands who suffered a living nightmare and, for many, their memories pushed them into a madness, or even worse, to suicide.'

'But you were the lucky ones. You managed to escape,' Eleni consoled her.

'Lucky! How lucky were we? At that point we had no thoughts of the future. At the end of each day we gave thanks to the Lord that we were still alive. And Nina, she was so traumatized she couldn't speak for days. An old woman, a rather diminutive figure with braided hair caked in a mixture of dried blood and dirt lay on a mattress next to us on the ship, rocking to and fro. Night and day she prayed for Mama, assuring us that we would soon return. She tapped her chest to indicate a pocket inside her jacket. "I still have my key," she told us. When I asked her what use was a key when her house was gone, she looked at me with such sadness that I realized my words had cut her like a knife. "Without hope, there is nothing," she said to me, full of emotion. That night, she curled up on her mattress and closed her eyes. The next day she was dead. I couldn't help feeling responsible. She was just like Grandpapa Soterios…always telling us how the Greeks had lived in Asia Minor for more than two thousand years, and that everyone would come to their senses and realize that we had a greater claim to that land than the Turks had. Thousands were like them—all believing that things would be as they were.

'On September 30, we took our first steps on Greek soil. Mama had recovered enough by then to take us in hand and I remember clearly what she said to us as we sat on our suitcases, awaiting papers to determine our refugee status. "From now on we must give all our thoughts to the future; there will be no looking back. That chapter of our life is closed forever. We have grieved enough and now we have been granted a new life. Our destiny lies in Greece and I never want to hear you mention the past again. Is that understood?" We both gave her our word.

'Looking back, it was really the best way to survive. As the year ended most refugees still held on to the idea that peace between Mustafa Kemal's Nationalists and the Greek government would see them return to Asia Minor. The Treaty of Lausanne signed in 1923 soon brought them the realization this was not to be. The League of Nations negotiated the first international compulsory exchange of minority populations, which saw a further two hundred thousand Christians forcibly removed from Asia Minor and Thrace to resettle in Greece. In return, three hundred and fifty thousand Muslims were compelled to settle in Turkey. The only people exempt from this forced removal were the Greeks of Constantinople and the Muslims of Thrace. Apart from the fact that the Greek Patriarch had been allowed to remain in Constantinople, the Greek civilization in Asia Minor ceased to exist.'

'With the country almost bankrupt and in chaos, how did the Greeks react to the arrival of over one and a quarter million refugees?' Eleni asked.

'I recall that we had been brought up to think of the mainland Greeks as our brothers—that we shared the same religion and history. But we refugees were a diverse group, varied in language and with important cultural differences. Both sides found it hard to come to terms with that. For instance it came as a great shock to some here that certain refugees only spoke Turkish. That caused great suspicion for the less educated. And then there were many among us, especially from Smyrna, who regarded Athens as a backward city. Smyrna had been far more cosmopolitan and, I believe, a more sophisticated city. In later years I grew to understand their anguish. After all, many Greeks had died trying to save Anatolia. To see us on their soil was a reminder of the failure of the Megali Idea.

'Yet for all our differences, most Greeks rallied together to support us. Committees were formed and every available space was requisitioned to house us. We camped in the municipal buildings, empty warehouses, schools, churches, and even the Opera House and the Parthenon. The government may have been close to bankruptcy but the people found it in their hearts to give donations to ease our plight. Every day, the newspapers published the amount of money collected.

'We were housed in a small hotel near the National Gardens along with several other refugee families. The owner, Kyria Angeliki, was very kind to us. She adored my mother and the two became quite close. I think my mother liked her because she never pried into our past. In return for her kindness, my mother borrowed a sewing machine and made her a dress. Kyria Angeliki was so delighted that she wore it to her next *Tea Chansant* in aid of the refugees. The very next day, Kyria Angeliki brought Mama an order for six more. Soon Mama was busily making clothes again.

'Kyria Angeliki had been a lyric soprano in her younger days and delighted in an opportunity to perform in front of an appreciative audience, no matter how small. She would usher us into her *saloni*, sit at the piano and clear her throat loudly, and begin to sing. You could hear a pin drop. *Madama Butterfly* was her favorite opera, and on these evenings she would assume a theatrical pose and transform herself into Cio-Cio San, acting out her despair with great flourish. Everyone in the room showed their appreciation by clapping enthusiastically, shouting "bravo!" and giving thanks to God that in his infinite wisdom he had seen fit to grant Kyria Angeliki the voice of an angel. Afterwards, we finished the evening with Smyrniot songs.

'Kyria Angeliki knew of my interest in music and asked Mama if she would allow her to tutor me. Happily, she agreed.

'Those first few months saw numerous "Gala Concerts for the Benefit of the Victims of the Smyrna Disaster, under the Auspices of the Refugees from Asia Minor." My mother was asked to create several more gowns. She never spoke to anyone about her life in Constantinople and Smyrna, although I am sure some people were aware of who she was.

'One day about a year and a half later, Mama told us that she had managed to put aside enough money to purchase a small apartment of our own. Needless to say, after living in such cramped conditions for so long, we were elated at the news. A few months after we'd settled, Kyria Angeliki asked Mama if she could find work for an orphan girl sent to her by the church. That orphan was Chrysoula. She was two years younger than me, could neither read nor write, and she certainly couldn't sew. Mama was struck by the warmth of her personality and took pity on her. That was almost fifty years ago and she has been a part of our family ever since.'

*Athens, Spring, 1929*

Sophia opened the shutters and gazed out at the breathtaking view before her. It was a view that could have been lifted from Andreas's wall paintings in the Hellenic room. It was partly because of this that she chose to buy the apartment in the first place. Nearby stood the magnificent Temple of Hephaistos, built in the fifth century BC and dedicated to Hephaistos, god of potters and smiths and to the goddess Athena. Beyond, bathed in the rose-tinted warmth of the late afternoon sun, the Parthenon rose majestically out of the craggy sacred rock of the Athenians—the Acropolis. Below the Acropolis the scattered marble ruins of a once-great civilization that had given the world democracy lay partially hidden in a landscape of wild myrtle, olives, laurel, and carob trees. It was hard to believe that less than a hundred years ago shepherds still brought their flocks from the outlying plains of Attica to graze on this land, much as they had done centuries earlier when offerings to the god Pan were left at the small cave on the slopes of the Acropolis.

Situated within walking distance of Keramikos, the city's ancient cemetery from the twelfth century BC to Roman times, Sophia's apartment was on the second floor of what had once been the home of a famous naval commander at the great naval Battle of Navarino in 1827. The building was an eclectic mix of fashionable neoclassicism with touches of local tradition and was only recently converted into apartments. Despite its dilapidated exterior and the lack of adequate plumbing, Sophia saw considerable charm in this once-grand home. With such a severe shortage of available properties on the market, she considered herself lucky to have found them a home at all.

Where once the house stood in a quiet picturesque square along with several other houses of notable charm, the influx of so many refugees meant that it was now situated in a lively and vital neighborhood. Makeshift dwellings, hastily thrown together during the first year of the Asia Minor Catastrophe, were rapidly being replaced with small businesses that seemed to spring up overnight. Except for the few hours each afternoon when workers stopped for lunch or took a short siesta, from dawn until dusk the cries of the street vendors competed with the *tack-tack-tack* of the artisan's hammer and the clatter of wooden carts as they rolled over the cobblestones, making their way towards the commercial districts of Psyrri, Omonia, and the center of Athens.

Sophia took a deep breath. This was the time of year that she had enjoyed so much in Constantinople. She closed her eyes and her thoughts drifted to her garden. She could hear the soft splashing of water from the fountain of the nymph as clearly as if she were there. She saw Selim the gardener clipping delicate pink rosebuds for Sevkiye's pilavs. She could see Ali Agha and his look of pride when he drove Mestinigar. She thought of Munire, Ariadne, Markos, Yianni Mandakis, Anna, and of the courageous Helene. If it hadn't been for the wars she would have been launching her new collection now. How fashions had changed in just a few short years. How life itself had changed. She had heard that Mustafa Kemal deplored the veil, urging the women of his new nation to become Westernized. She wondered what he would make of her Oriental collection now. 'Who would have thought that the Sultanate would have been abolished and replaced with a Caliphate?' she thought to herself. Now even that had been abolished. It was not only the Greeks who had paid a high price for these wars.

Leaning out of the window, Sophia looked into the quiet street below. It was three o'clock and still siesta time. In the *saloni,* Chrysoula laid out the dining table in readiness for the visitors, conscientiously arranging platters of baklava, hair-fine *kataifi,* and a freshly baked *karithopita* studded with walnuts—Kyria Angeliki's favorite. After adding a pot of freshly made quince preserve and a dish of ripe figs, she stood back and admired her handiwork. The Kyria had taught her well; this was a special occasion and she wanted to make her proud. After all, it wasn't often that the Director of the Athens Conservatoire came for afternoon tea. A car stopped outside the house and Sophia returned to the *saloni* to welcome her guests.

Kyrios Papayiannis took a sip of coffee, put down his cup and helped himself to another slice of walnut cake. 'Wonderful,' he said appreciatively. 'Just the right amount of syrup. My compliments to your cook!'

Wiping the crumbs from his mouth with a serviette, he patted his round stomach and lit a Cuban cigar. He was a small man nearing his mid-fifties, impeccably dressed and somewhat a dandy. According to Kyria Angeliki he had decided quite early in his career never to marry, stating that a wife would always be a poor second to his musical career. 'Although,' she added with a wink, careful not to tarnish his good name, 'he does enjoy the company of certain men known for—well, how can I put it…other talents.'

During the three years that she had known him, Sophia had often seen him in the company of an outrageously temperamental concert pianist known for his dark mood swings that occasionally reduced the poor man to tears. Today, however, Kyrios Papayiannis was in exceptionally good spirits.

'As you are well aware, Kyria Laskaris,' he said, arching his back and savoring the aroma of the cigar, 'our graduating students are given the wonderful opportunity of performing an opera at the Olympia Theatre. It's a very important stepping stone in their career, wouldn't you agree, Kyria Angeliki?'

Kyria Angeliki wholeheartedly agreed.

'Last year,' he continued, his chest bursting with pride, 'we performed Mozart's sophisticated comedy, *Le nozze di Figaro,* and the year before that…'

'*Peleas et Melisande,*' said Kyria Angeliki, before he could finish the sentence. 'Such exquisite music…' She closed her eyes and began to hum a little tune from Debussy's only completed opera.

Kyrios Papayiannis coughed politely. 'And this year we agonized over two great favorites—*Tosca* and *Madama Butterfly.*'

'And which did you finally agree to perform?' asked Sophia, eager to get to the point.

'Why, *Madama Butterfly,* of course.'

'Of course,' echoed Kyria Angeliki. She leaned closer to Sophia as if to divulge a great secret. 'And out of the ten finalists, Maria has been chosen to play the role of Cio-Cio San. *My* role,' she added, patting her chest proudly. 'Isn't it such thrilling news?'

Sophia's heart skipped a beat and she felt her chest burst with pride. It had been almost five years since Maria took her first singing lessons, and through sheer determination and hard work her daughter's dreams were finally within her grasp. It was Kyria Angeliki who was the first to recognize Maria's musical talents, but having purchased the apartment, Sophia was in no position to pay for private tutorials. Kyria Angeliki offered to teach her and refused to take a drachma. Aware that she had never been denied her own ambitions, Sophia agreed. After three years, Kyria Angeliki had taught her all that she could. For Maria to realize her full potential, she needed study with the maestro—Kyrios Papayiannis, who was the conductor of the Athens Symphony Orchestra and a director at the Conservatoire. Finally, all the hard work had paid off.

'You do us a great honor, Kyrios Papayiannis,' Sophia replied. 'We are indeed, indebted to you.'

Stroking his well-trimmed beard, Kyrios Papayiannis acknowledged her gratitude with an air of graciousness.

'Not since Kyria Angeliki's acclaimed performance some nine years earlier...just before the refugees arrived, has this opera been performed here. Yes, it is a popular opera. But the part of Cio-Cio San must not be underestimated. It has difficult arias that can wreck voices, especially one as young as Maria's. Over and over again the critics have panned international performances of this opera, so you will understand, Kyria Laskaris,' he said, his voice taking on a serious tone, 'we are putting great faith in the hope that Maria's performance will not meet with such a fate.'

He picked up his white gloves and amber-topped walking stick. 'And now, if you will excuse me, ladies, I must take my leave.'

'What was it you wanted to discuss with me, Kyria Angeliki?' asked Sophia, when they were alone.

'Do you remember Esther Rosen—the Jewish lady who owns Rosen Furs with her twin sister Rivka in Mitropoleos Street?'

'Yes, of course,' Sophia replied. 'She bought one of my best creations; the cotton tulle and golden metallic-lace evening dress with the fishtail train and silver beading. How can I forget? Nina and I worked until the early hours of the morning to finish it in time for her. Why do you ask?'

'Because,' continued Kyria Angeliki, 'she has informed me that Rivka is to be married to a fur merchant in Kastoria and will leave Athens to live there with him.'

Sophia had only met the Rosens twice, but she had been struck by how different they were from each other. They were in their early thirties and it had remained a mystery to many as to why such wealthy ladies had never married. The confident Esther was blessed with the sultry looks of Greta Garbo, whom she idolized. Tall and slim with slightly masculine looks, she was both elegant and stylish. Her twin, on the other hand, was considered to be the ugly duckling, with none of Esther's glamour and no interest in fashion. She was unfortunate enough to have been born with a birth defect that marred the left side of her face. Consequently, it came as a great shock when people learned that it was Rivka and not Esther who was to be married.

'I am happy for her,' replied Sophia. 'But what does this have to do with me?'

'This means that Esther will be alone in the shop and she has asked me to see if you would be interested in leasing a part of her shop from her. She tells me that with Rivka gone she would welcome the company of another person, and she considers you to be a very good designer and business woman. She also thinks your business would complement hers.'

The proposal was completely unexpected. Until now, working from home had suited her. She had managed to put a little extra money aside and this could be just the opportunity she needed.

'I am extremely grateful to Esther for her kind proposal but I will have to think about it.'

'Well, if I might be so bold, Sophia, don't think about it for too long. There are plenty of people out there who would jump at such an opportunity. Esther has an elite clientele and her premises, within walking distance of the Parliament and the Hotel Grande Bretagne in Syntagma Square, are second to none. I wouldn't like to see a good opportunity pass you by.'

'I agree,' Sophia replied. Her gaze fell on the dark storm clouds gathering over the Acropolis.

'Look, Sophia,' said Kyria Angeliki, in a concerned voice. 'I have never pried into your past and I never will. But one thing I know for sure is that you have exceptional talent and a good head for business. Don't let the past destroy your future.' She stood to leave. 'With the look of those clouds, I think I had better hurry.'

The soft patter of raindrops on the window pane threatened to turn into a downpour. Kyria Angeliki gave Sophia a peck on the cheek. 'Goodbye, Sophia. Give my congratulations to Maria, and do think about Esther's offer.'

After a convivial afternoon, the mood in the apartment darkened again.

Thunder clouds now shrouded the Acropolis from view and the thunder of cannon fire resonated through her body. A bolt of lightning momentarily lit the sky, the heavens opened, and for almost an hour Zeus reigned supreme. Then as quickly as they came, the clouds passed over. For a few seconds, a shaft of golden light drenched the Parthenon in molten gold. Sophia's heart raced at such beauty. Then it was gone. A sense of calm swept through her. Kyria Angeliki was right. She must move on.

# CHAPTER 25

*Athens, Summer, 1929*

Just three months after she accepted Esther Rosen's offer, fate dealt Sophia another bitter blow. It began innocently when she noticed a change in Chrysoula's behavior. Normally of an even temperament, she suddenly took to avoiding them, shutting herself in her room as soon as her chores were done. When Sophia confronted her Chrysoula shamefully admitted that she had visited Kyria Koula—the blind old crone in the Plaka who sat on her doorstep all day, offering to tell people's fortunes in exchange for a few drachmas to feed her lazy, good-for-nothing son. She knew Sophia had an aversion to fortunetellers but Chrysoula was a simple girl, and part of her was just as eager to know her future as other young women.

'And what did she tell you that could possibly have made you so miserable?' Sophia asked.

Ashamed, Chrysoula looked down at the floor, fiddling with the hem of her skirt.

'Well, that's just it. I thought the least she would say was that I also would find a good husband—after all, she tells all the girls that, but...' Chrysoula stammered, 'well, at first I thought she didn't like me; it was as if she tried to ignore me—like I didn't exist...and it wasn't like her to refuse a drachma! So I apologized and told her I wouldn't bother her again. Then she indicated for me to sit next to her. She was quite blunt, telling me that she could not see a man in my life. She said I was unlucky in love.' Chrysoula looked forlorn. 'As you can imagine, this was not what I expected to hear. The least she could have done was *pretend* to give me good news.'

'I have told you this many times, Chrysoula. Only God knows our future.'

'But, Kyria Sophia, that's not all. She told me I was living in a house surrounded by bad luck and the only way to avoid my fate was to move away. She gripped my arm so tightly that her nails dug into my flesh. "There is someone in that house who is possessed by the devil," she said. "No,"

I answered sharply. "That's impossible…there's not a kinder family anywhere." She hissed at me like a cat and spat on the ground. "Someone will betray you and when they do, you will remember my words." Then she pushed me away.'

Chrysoula looked at Sophia's face, half expecting her to laugh or put her at ease. Instead, she looked as if she'd seen a ghost.

'Did she say who would betray you?' Sophia asked.

Chrysoula was unsure if she should continue. 'She said, "Someone with hair the color of the wild mountain cherry—and like the fruit, the taste will be bittersweet." If she saw more, she was reluctant to say.'

Something in Sophia's demeanor frightened Chrysoula. For a moment she thought she would chastise her for her silliness—she almost wished she would. At least it would be a reaction.

'I'm sorry. I didn't mean to burden you with my actions,' Chrysoula said miserably.

'I'm glad you told me,' Sophia said. 'But you must put this nonsense behind you.' She got up to leave. Holding the door handle, she turned back to face Chrysoula. 'And I think it would be wise not to mention this again.'

Chrysoula nodded.

That night, Sophia found it hard to sleep. She had lived for years with her grandmother's fear of the child with the red hair, and Maria was shunned because of it. Yet Dimitra's fear was something she could never truly forget. She was far too clever and intuitive to dismiss her, although she knew she should ignore Chrysoula. She reasoned that a person with red hair could be one of many. Why, she only had to go outside and she would find red-haired women. Many of the Anatolian women stained their graying hair with henna—wasn't that red? And then there was Kyria Angeliki. Her auburn hair was streaked with shades of redwood. But that was also dyed. Reluctantly, her thoughts came back to her daughters. Nina's hair was the blue-black of the raven—a family characteristic. Only Maria differed. The day she gave birth to her and saw the mop of strawberry hair she thought there had been a mistake—a cruel joke. As Maria grew older, the color intensified until the vibrant copper tones deepened into an intense, beautiful chestnut. Yes, it was true that Maria was a difficult child. But surely there were plenty of other children like her. And these days, her wild, fiery temperament and her outrageous behavior had become less aggressive, and her misdemeanors were now few and far between. No, Sophia told herself, it could not be Maria. Angry with herself, she again reasoned that superstition belonged to the realm of make-believe and the uneducated. There was no place for it in her life.

On the following day Sophia found herself walking in the direction of Kyria Koula's house. The old woman was already sitting on the doorstep.

Sophia felt a strong urge to speak to her. Kyria Koula sensed someone approaching, pulled herself up, and shuffled back into the house, almost slamming the door in Sophia's face.

The auditorium at the Olympia Theatre buzzed with anticipation when Sophia and Nina arrived, accompanied by Kyria Angeliki. Kyria Angeliki was in her element, nodding graciously as the distinguished guests of Athenian society acknowledged her. In the crowd, Esther Rosen, surrounded by a group of admirers, waved to her. She looked radiant in the ice-blue gown that Sophia had made especially for the occasion.

'It's going to be a splendid evening,' said Kyria Angeliki. 'I wouldn't have missed it for the world.'

An attendant ushered them to one of the box seats usually reserved for royalty. A row of fresh flowers placed below the velvet rail filled the box with a sweet perfume. In the half-light of the gilded rococo chandelier, Sophia looked her best in years. It was the first time Kyria Angeliki had seen her so happy. The last time Sophia attended the theatre was that fateful summer of 1922, and in the rosy light of recollection she felt a pang of nostalgia. It was hard to imagine that only seven years ago this same theatre was overflowing with an audience of another kind—the refugees of Asia Minor. A hush descended and Sophia steadied her opera glasses, fixed on the orchestra pit. Kyrios Papayiannis stood and bowed to the audience. Tapping the edge of his music stand and raising his baton, he waited for absolute silence. With the flick of his wrist, the orchestra began to play the prelude. Slowly, the gold embroidered velvet curtains slid back for Act I, revealing an oriental garden high above Nagasaki. The audience was immediately transported to the world of the geisha.

If Sophia had any doubts about Maria's talents, they were quickly put to rest. As the delicate Butterfly, she was captivating. The love duet performed with up-and-coming tenor Manolios Bouras playing the part of Captain Pinkerton did not disappoint. In Act III, Maria's skill at portraying Cio-Cio San's undying belief that Pinkerton would return held the audience spellbound. Her rendition of 'Un bel di vedremo' brought the house down. Sophia and Nina glowed with pride. Kyria Angeliki, overcome with emotion, patted her chest while choking back the tears.

An attendant entered the box carrying on a silver salver a sealed envelope addressed to Sophia. Kyrios Papayiannis would be hosting a reception in the ballroom of the Hotel Grande Bretagne and he requested their company, adding that there was someone of great importance that he would like her to meet. When they arrived Maria was already basking in compliments showered on her from everyone in the room. Seeing her mother, she excused herself and came over to greet her.

'How was I, Mama?' There was only one compliment that was important to her and that was from her mother, but before Sophia could answer, Kyrios Papayiannis approached.

'Allow me to introduce you to Monsieur Maurice Marchand, the distinguished Director of the Paris Opera House,' he said to her.

Like Kyrios Papayiannis, Monsieur Marchand was a man of impeccable taste and she had the distinct impression that she knew him from her days in Constantinople. He, on the other hand, was in no doubt about who she was. Addressing her in French, he told her that he had once worked with Diaghilev and on the occasion of Serge's party—One Thousand and Two Nights—his wife Clarisse had worn one of her gowns.

'A magnificent oriental outfit,' he smiled, 'with a glorious pair of flowing silk harem pants in shades of pomegranate and aubergine. It was one of her favorite outfits and she has it to this day.'

Sophia thanked him for the compliment. He leaned forward a little, lowering his voice. 'We were dreadfully sorry to hear about the fire. *Femina* and *Gazette du Bon Ton* covered it in great detail. Arson is such a terrible thing and it is a great shame that they never caught the culprit.'

Sophia felt as if her cheeks were on fire. Nina moved closer to her mother as if to offer support. Despite Monsieur Marchand's lowered voice, several guests overheard and looked uncomfortable. For the first time since Sophia had known her, Kyria Angeliki was stuck for words.

'Well, well, Sophia,' she whispered, finally gathering her thoughts together, 'you are a dark horse.'

Esther smiled. 'Finally the secret is out. I always knew your clothes were far too fashionable and well made for a mere seamstress.'

Sophia declined to comment further. Fortunately, Monsieur Marchand and Kyrios Papayiannis pulled her aside.

'I want to talk to you about your daughter,' said Monsieur Marchand. 'When I first heard that voice—the voice of a goddess—my soul soared. With strict discipline she will shine like a diamond. To possess such a fine voice combined with a gift for drama is a rare talent. That is why I am offering her the chance of a lifetime: to study with the best…at the Paris Opera House.'

He straightened his back and held out his arms, palms facing upward in a sweeping gesture of generosity.

Sophia expressed her gratitude. Many questions raced through her mind. Was Maria still too young to be away from home? How could she afford to pay for her when she had just put all her savings into leasing a part of Esther's shop?

Kyrios Papayiannis saw the look of concern on her face. 'Money will not be an issue,' he assured her. 'The Conservatoire has an endowment fund, and for the first year we will cover all expenses.'

Sophia promised to discuss it with her daughter. 'If that is her wish, then I will not stand in her way.'

Searching the room for Maria she found her standing next to a potted palm, engrossed in conversation with the tenor Manolios. Maria caught her mother watching her and taking Manolios by the hand, came over and introduced him to her. It was not only Sophia who was in good spirits that night. Maria, flushed with the euphoria of the moment, looked radiant. Instinct told Sophia that Manolios had more to do with this than her success as a soprano.

The bustling sounds of the day had long given way to the sounds of the night and in the nightclubs of nearby Plaka, the half-oriental rhythm of the bouzouki accompanied by the sour-sad voice of a singer resonated through the night air. Maria lay in bed, her arms folded behind her head, thinking of Monsieur Marchand's proposal. She had set her sights high and here was an opportunity of a lifetime. Far from being happy, she felt miserable. A move to Paris would mean leaving Manolios and that was unthinkable.

It was because of Manolios that Maria arrived home late in the afternoons. After their studies a group of students made a habit of meeting at Zaharoplasteion Perikles in Akadamias Street, within walking distance of the Conservatoire. It was there that her liaison with the young tenor blossomed.

Within the strict constraints of morality that Greek society placed upon its womenfolk, there were few places that young men and girls of a marriageable age were able to meet without the ever-present glare of a chaperone. Traditions were fiercely upheld and families remained ever-vigilant. In Athens, as in Constantinople and Smyrna, the fashionable Zaharoplasteion was one of the few dignified meeting places where a decent woman was able to socialize away from home. Even then, their actions were watched with the keenest of eyes.

Sophia was well aware of the whereabouts of Maria but she considered Zaharoplasteion Perikles a café of distinction, just as she had Zaharoplasteion Olympia in the Grande Rue de Pera. What she hadn't been prepared for was that Maria would fall in love and that this was where the two lovers engaged in their secret romance, albeit in the company of others.

From the warmth of her bed, Maria looked at the pale crescent moon hanging in a starless sky. It reminded her of the Turkish flag, and she thought of her homeland and of everything and everyone she had loved and lost.

With steely determination she vowed that Manolios would not be added to that list. 'No,' she told herself. 'We'll go together or not at all.' However difficult this was going to be, she would tell her mother in the morning.

When the morning arrived, Sophia had already left for work, telling Chrysoula not to wake her as she deserved the luxury of a few hours' sleep.

'After all,' smiled Chrysoula, 'you have a long journey ahead of you in the next couple of days.'

Maria slumped onto the sofa. The day would drag painfully until her mother came home and with each hour that passed she knew that her nerves would get the better of her. Eventually, tiring of Chrysoula's chatter, she shut herself in her room and went back to bed.

Sophia had been at the shop for less than an hour when she received a visitor. The man introduced himself as the secretary of Kyrios Petros Sakellariou, a prominent figure in Athenian political circles, well known for his anti-Venizelos sentiments. Sakellariou and his wife extended an invitation to her for afternoon tea at their residence in Kolonaki.

'Kyrios Sakellariou understands that you are a busy woman and apologizes for any inconvenience. However, he would be most grateful if you were able to accept the invitation.'

Intrigued as to what could warrant such an invitation at such short notice, she agreed to go.

'Very good, Kyria. A car will come for you at two o'clock sharp.'

Bidding her farewell, he bumped into Esther as she entered the premises. She noticed the perplexed look on Sophia's face.

'What was all that about?' she asked, watching the black Mercedes drive away.

'I haven't got the faintest idea, but at two o'clock, I'm sure I'll find out.'

The Sakellariou home was surrounded by a well-tended garden of poplars and ornate shrubs nestled against the slope of Lykavittos, the most prominent hill in Athens. Kyrios Sakellariou's secretary awaited her arrival and led her through a large marble hallway and down a long corridor. Dark brooding oil paintings of the Sakellariou dynasty adorned the pale walls, and here and there marble busts of Pericles, Plato, Sophocles and Socrates stood at eye level on slender colonnades. At the end of the corridor stood a priceless black Attic krater, which Sophia deduced by the red figure work to be from the fifth century BC.

After her arrival was announced, she was ushered into an enormous sitting room bathed in a pool of afternoon sunlight from a series of French windows that opened onto a veranda filled with citrus tubs. The room itself was decorated with even more fine paintings and glass cabinets filled with an impressive array of weaponry from the War of Independence. Kyrios Sakellariou shook Sophia's hand with a firm grip. He was a small, well-built man, with an air of self-importance. He was a man who knew what he wanted in life and who would stop at nothing to get it. Sophia could not warm to him. Turning to the two women seated on a sofa next to a grand piano, he introduced her to his wife and his daughter Penelope.

Kyria Sakellariou stood and welcomed her to their home. Shy and ill at ease with pale melancholic features, she looked as if she carried the weight of the world on her shoulders. Sophia noticed that the daughter, a frail girl in her mid-twenties who appeared to take after her mother, had been crying. Her pale gray eyes were red and swollen and she twisted a lace-trimmed handkerchief nervously in her fingers.

Courteously, Kyria Sakellariou poured Sophia a cup of tea and handed it to her. As she proffered a selection of delicately iced petit fours, her husband started to tell Sophia why they had asked her here.

'The issue is a rather delicate one. Your daughter, Maria, has…how can I put it, a hold on a young man whom I believe you know—Manolios Bouras?'

Sophia looked surprised. 'I'm not sure to what you are alluding. I met him for the first time last night at the Grande Bretagne. Certainly, I was aware that he was to play the part of Captain Pinkerton in *Madama Butterfly*. Apart from that I know nothing of him.'

'I see,' replied Kyrios Sakellariou, uncomfortably. He glanced at his wife, who had resumed her seat next to her daughter. 'Are you telling me that you know nothing of the closeness between your daughter and this young man?'

Sophia hesitated. 'I will not deny that it had occurred to me that my daughter's happiness last night did not entirely appear to be due to her success in the opera, but I know nothing about a "closeness," as you so delicately put it.'

Penelope tried to stifle her sobs and her mother put a reassuring hand on her daughter's knee to calm her.

'Is this why I have been asked here this afternoon—to discuss my daughter? Because if that is so, then perhaps it's best if I leave. I fail to see what this has to do with you.'

Sophia felt her cheeks redden with anger and humiliation. If Maria had deceived her she could not bear to hear it from someone else, especially from a stranger, and especially from someone of such high standing in the community. Sensing her anguish, Kyrios Sakellariou softened his tone, begging her to hear him.

'Let me explain. You see Manolios is the son of a close family friend, and as such, it has been agreed that he shall be married to my dear daughter.' He looked at Penelope, who was now wiping away a steady stream of tears. 'The marriage proposal was agreed to by all of the parties concerned three years ago. Why, it is certain that the couple would have married well before now had it not been for Manolios's desire to pursue his career for a while longer before starting a family.' He sighed heavily. 'Please try to look at this from our point of view—the young man is spoken for and it would be a great breach of honor for our family if this marriage did not go ahead.'

Penelope began to sob and no amount of coaxing by her mother could stop her. Annoyed, Kyrios Sakellariou asked his wife to take their daughter into the garden; he would deal with the issue alone. Obediently, Kyria Sakellariou helped her daughter out of the room, apologizing for Penelope's distress.

'You see how the girl suffers,' continued Kyrios Sakellariou. 'Am I not justified in looking after the interests of my only child?'

'Indeed, that is a virtue,' replied Sophia. 'But if Manolios is already betrothed to your daughter, then what is the problem? Aren't you jumping to conclusions?'

Kyrios Sakellariou looked irritated. 'The problem is that he has told his father that he no longer desires Penelope and that he is in love with Maria, and wishes to marry her.'

Sophia remained composed. She now understood that, for whatever reason, Maria had hidden all this from her.

Kyrios Sakellariou implored again. 'We cannot lose face over this marriage. It must go ahead. Penelope possesses a handsome dowry—enough to set the couple up for life. That must not be overlooked.'

Sophia's eyes focused on a finely engraved gilt yataghan, set with enamel and precious stones. She recalled that she had also received a grand dowry and if the truth be known, equal to anything the Sakellariou family would give Penelope. Andreas had often told her that he would have married her despite her family's wealth. Yet Sophia was well aware that love alone was not enough for most Greek families; in fact, it was often looked upon as a curse. But a dowry put great strains on the family of a bride and she had known many a family reduced to poverty through marrying off more than one daughter.

'If Manolios does not love Penelope,' she asked, 'then why do you pursue this? Surely this won't bring your daughter happiness?'

'Ah, there I simply cannot agree. In time they will grow to love each other—through respect, just as I did with my wife. Anyway, he is young. He says that he loves Maria now, but in time he will forget her. I will not deny,' he added, lowering his voice, 'that Maria is an exceptionally beautiful young woman and I cannot blame him for falling for her. There are many who would desire her for a wife. Manolios, God help the boy…his nature is weak, and one day soon she will tire of him and break his heart. No good can come of this. It breaks my heart to say this, but my daughter does not possess Maria's looks. As you see, her features are plain and in personality she is shy and retiring, but she possesses a sweet nature and like her mother…will be a dutiful wife.'

Sophia felt uncomfortable. She wanted to be anywhere but here listening to this man's plight. She wondered if he had ever been through what she had. If he had he would know what real suffering was. With a poised dignity, she stood to leave. Kyrios Sakellariou escorted her outside. In the cool shade of the portico he thanked her for coming.

'As parents, we try to do the best we can. If you can persuade your daughter to see sense, my family will owe you a great debt, Kyria Laskaris. I have heard much about you since you came here, and I'm sure that I can count on you to manage this situation with the utmost discretion.'


Maria was lying on her bed listening to a recording of Caruso when she heard her mother's footsteps in the hallway. Hastily, she smoothed her skirt and prepared for what she knew would probably be another confrontation. Only this time, she was determined to stand her ground. However, when she entered the dining room the look on her mother's face caught her by surprise.

'You're home early, Mama,' said Maria. 'Is everything alright?'

Ignoring her completely, Sophia called out for Chrysoula. 'I want you to take Nina and go for a walk.' She reached into her purse. 'Here, take this and treat yourselves to an ice-cream.'

Sensing something amiss, Chrysoula tried to defuse the tension by jokingly telling Nina that they would revisit the ruins of the ancient agora, and this time they might even be lucky enough to find buried treasure. Over the past few months, a team of American archeologists working in the vicinity had unearthed priceless fragments of sculptures in what they referred to as 'Hellenistic rubble'. Nina had shown a great interest in their work and, accompanied by Chrysoula, she often visited the site to check on their progress. Relishing an excuse to leave her homework, Nina was only too happy to find an opportunity to watch them at work again.

'I have something of great importance to discuss with you,' said Sophia to Maria, when they were alone.

Nervously, Maria told her mother that she also had something important to discuss. Sophia put one hand out to stop her. Not since Turkey had

Maria seen her mother like this. Her eyes spoke volumes. It was the same look that she had experienced so often as a child: the look of exasperation when she did not measure up to the same exacting standards as Leonidas did. It was a look which told her that no matter how hard she tried, she would always stand in his shadow.

'Tell me,' said Sophia, frostily, 'what do you know about a girl called Penelope Sakellariou?' Maria felt the blood drain from her face. 'I will come straight to the point. She is engaged to be married to the tenor Manolios Bouras—is that correct?'

Maria shuffled uncomfortably on her chair. 'Manolios is not engaged; in fact, that is what I wanted to discuss with you. I have known him for almost three years now and during this time he has declared his love for me. In fact, he was intending to come here and ask for your permission to marry me.'

Sophia looked at her daughter angrily. 'I trusted you and you have betrayed me and dishonored our family.'

'No, Mama—that isn't so!' Maria became hysterical. 'I beg you to believe me. Since I have known him, he has eyes for no one but me.'

Tearfully, she pleaded with Sophia to hear her out and she tried desperately to explain how Manolios's father had expressed his wish that his son marry Penelope—the only daughter of his childhood friend Petros Sakellariou—but that Manolios had no feelings for the girl. She said that he had implored his father not to push ahead with the arrangement, but that he and Kyrios Sakellariou simply would not hear of it—the marriage was to go ahead or Kyrios Bouras would disown his son. Thinking Penelope would tire of waiting, Manolios had asked his father at least to let him pursue his singing career for another three years. Reluctantly, he agreed. However, over the past few months, the Sakellariou family had started putting pressure on the family again to go ahead with the marriage. This time, Manolios refused, telling his father that his love for Maria was too strong to break.

Maria implored her mother to understand, eventually telling her that Manolios had told his father that he would rather die than be in a loveless marriage. Racked with sobs, she pleaded for forgiveness for keeping their love a secret.

'I didn't want to worry you,' was all she could find to say.

Sophia told Maria of the humiliation that she had experienced at being called to the Sakellariou house. This was something she would not tolerate. One way or another the issue had to be resolved, and she asked her daughter to break the friendship. If Maria chose to throw away the opportunity of a lifetime with Monsieur Marchand, then her career in Athens would be in ruins. The Sakellariou family would see to that.

'They are a powerful family, Maria. If you don't break off this relationship, they will make sure you never perform here again.'

She found herself repeating the words of Petros Sakellariou. 'The boy is young; he must repair his grievances with his family.'

'You, on the other hand, have too much to lose by staying.'

Maria was forced to consider her mother's words. In the end the bright light of fame took precedence over her feelings for Manolios. She agreed to go to Paris as planned.

'Perhaps you're right, Mama. It would be terrible if I was unable to perform again,' she sniffed.

Handing her a clean handkerchief, Sophia told Maria to dry her eyes and to go and pack. 'The boat leaves in two days' time and there's much to do before then.'

In her heart, Sophia knew that Maria would always put herself first. Could she ever love anyone more than herself? God willing, time would change her.

The day before Maria's departure, Sophia asked for a meeting with Manolios Bouras and his father at the Grande Bretagne. What she told them was never revealed. Two months after Maria left for Paris, on the evening before he was due to marry Penelope, Manolios committed suicide. His body was found at the base of the Acropolis. Maria learned of his death from a short tribute to him written by Kyrios Papayiannis in the *Etude Music Magazine*. Blaming her mother for his death, Maria vowed to have nothing more to do with her. It would be several years before they were to see each other again.

# CHAPTER 26

*Athens, 1932*

It had been three years since Maria left for Paris and the only news Sophia had of her was from the occasional review in the foreign newspapers, or when Kyrios Papayiannis or Kyria Angeliki dropped by with a copy of *Etude Music Magazine*. If the truth were known, Sophia had spent many of those years worrying about more immediate problems. The Stock Market Crash in October 1929 saw the world spiral into the Great Depression. With the collapse of financial institutions and mass unemployment, combined with the problems already created by the influx of refugees, thousands of businesses closed. Others precariously struggled on by giving credit to their customers. When prices in the tobacco industry plummeted by almost seventy percent, thousands of families made their way to Athens and Salonika, desperately seeking food, clothing, and shelter. From their premises in Mitropoleos Street, Sophia and Esther witnessed the humiliation of poverty and unemployment first-hand. Night after night, month after month, families huddled together in doorways guarding their pitiful belongings.

When Sophia arrived at work one day and found Esther sweeping up shattered glass from a smashed window, with most of her expensive furs stolen, she knew she could not sit by idly. She offered her services in a nearby soup kitchen set up by one of the many charity organizations operating throughout the city.

By 1932, the worst year of the Depression, Sophia's income plummeted to the point where she was forced to consider giving up her half of the shop. When the premises was burgled for a third time, Esther decided to take the remaining furs off the market until the economy improved. She offered Sophia full use of the premises rent-free. With the situation at its bleakest, Sophia received a surprise visit from Kyrios Sakellariou requesting her to make two evening gowns; one for his wife and the other for Penelope. In better times she would have given him the cold shoulder but as he surveyed the half-empty showroom, he understood her predicament only too well.

'I will come straight to the point, Kyria Laskaris,' he said, in his usual abrupt, businesslike manner. 'I am here because I owe you a great debt. I have heard that you and your daughter are no longer on speaking terms and I cannot help but feel largely responsible for this. It was unforgivable of me to put so much pressure on you.'

The memory of that October afternoon flooded through Sophia's mind and she felt a surge of anger. She wanted to ask why he had waited three years to apologize. Instead, she asked him to take a seat; she would hear what he had to say. Surprisingly, he confided to her that he had almost been ruined when the stock market collapsed. However, his fortunes had recently reversed when the new government had offered him a position in the ministry and he was now in a position to repay his debt.

'You owe me nothing, Kyrios Sakellariou. You did what you thought best for your daughter.'

'No, I was wrong. I thought that such a union of two families would be beneficial to us. I know now that Manolios was not the right man for her. In fact she is now married to someone else and has given me my first grandson.'

'I pray that she has found happiness and the love that she deserves,' said Sophia coolly.

Again Kyrios Sakellariou laughed. 'Achhh…love again! I see you're still a romantic. The man I chose for her—although a good deal older—is a good man. More importantly he is prosperous, and he will care for her as a husband should. When we heard of Manolios's death, I must confess I breathed a sigh of relief. The boy was too weak; a true man would never kill himself over a woman.'

Sophia eyed him with loathing. Something about him reminded her of Sergei, of the arrogance, of the utter contempt for anyone but himself. He was a man without compassion. Manolios had done him a service by committing suicide and now he had the audacity to sit there in front of her and offer to pay for the guilt that had apparently consumed him. Something inside her snapped. She would make him pay for his callousness. With the same theatrical finesse that she had lavished upon Sergei, she thanked him for his kindness; it would be an honor to work on the gowns and she would begin immediately. If they pleased him, as she was sure they would, then perhaps he could see fit to arrange that the wives and daughters of other cabinet ministers also came to visit her. Her smile delighted him.

'Your smile lights up the room, Kyria Laskaris, and if I might be so bold, it is one of the most beautiful smiles I've ever encountered.'

'Your unexpected visit has made me a very happy woman. I look forward to our friendship.'

That evening, Sophia returned to the apartment with a choice leg of lamb and a box of Zaharoplasteion Perikles's choicest sweets. 'Cook it well, Chrysoula; seasoned with cinnamon and garlic, and surrounded by vegetables. Tonight we will eat like royalty.'

True to his word, Kyrios Sakellariou helped Sophia to get back on her feet again. It wasn't long before the shop was once again filled with customers eager to discuss the latest fashions of the day—the purity of Vionnet's line; the influence of Hollywood and the cinema, with the black and white silk crepe dress worn by Joan Crawford in the film *Letty Lynton* and of which Macy's claimed to have sold over half a million copies; the sophisticated costumes worn by Carole Lombard; and Esther's favorite, Greta Garbo in *Grand Hotel*.

Thankfully, Kyrios Sakellariou never returned to the shop. Surprisingly, it was Penelope who paid her regular visits, always to order a new outfit and impart a little news about her father, who now spent much of his time in Berlin. When Sophia inquired as to the nature of his work, Penelope could only reply that it was supposed to be top secret classified information—something to do with an industry and manufacturing alliance between the two governments.

Nina's enthusiasm for archeology made her a familiar figure at the excavation sites and although still young, her translation work from ancient into modern Greek, French, and English was considered to be among the best in Athens. Recognizing Nina's scholastic abilities, Sophia had hoped that she would attend university—the first girl in the family to do so. However, when the economy collapsed she could not afford to send her. Nina had always paid her way by helping her mother. When the translation work dried up she asked the American professor in charge of the excavations in the agora if he could find a full-time position for her. To her great joy he agreed to take her on, although he warned her that the pay was low as they were dependant on private donations from America. What with the Depression, the project could be cancelled at any time. Throughout the worst of the Depression Nina's meager wage always ensured that food was on their table.

Now Sophia wanted to repay her. She brought home samples of the latest satins—beautiful duck-egg blues, peach, and ivory—and asked her daughter to choose a color. She would make her an evening dress. Nina looked up from her work and told her mother that whatever she chose was alright with her. Sophia thought her unusually distracted.

'Is there anything you want to discuss with me?'

Nina remained silent.

'In that case, I will say goodnight. I have to get up early for a fitting with a client.'

'Wait! There is something, Mama.'

Sophia sat down again. 'I'm listening, *agapi mou*.'

'When we came here, you made it clear that we were not to bring up the past...but something has happened and I think I should tell you.'

'Go on.'

'I think he's here,' said Nina nervously. 'Here in Athens.'

Sophia looked startled. Her first thoughts were of Leonidas. 'Who? In God's name child, who?'

'The Kapitanos...Vangelis.'

'Vangelis!' repeated Sophia, stunned.

Nina went on to tell her how for more than a week now, she had been sent to help another group of archeologists working at the Theatre of Dionysus at the base of the southern cliff face of the Acropolis. Two days ago she finished work early, and instead of returning home by her usual route past the Temple of Hephaistos, she decided to take an alternative route through Anafiotika, where Chrysoula once lived. Not being familiar with the area, she became lost in the maze of narrow winding streets. The walk had taken much longer than she had anticipated and she stopped to buy a cool wedge of watermelon from a street vendor. Plastered on the crumbling stone wall behind where he stood was a collage of torn and faded posters. One of them caught her eye. In large bold letters were the words: CLUB ATTIKON PRESENTS BOUZOUKIA. Underneath were the names of the various artists playing that evening, and it was the last name which caught her attention: Kapitanos Vangelis. She took a closer look. Kapitanos Vangelis was featured as playing the bouzouki. There was no address and the date was missing. Judging by the state of the poster, she concluded that it must have been there for at least a year—perhaps longer.

Sophia listened, afraid of getting her hopes up only to have them dashed. If it was Vangelis, then why did the poster say that he was playing the bouzouki and not the laouto? She had never known him to play another instrument. And the name—there were hundreds of men called Vangelis, but surely only one musician called the Kapitanos.

'I didn't want to say anything until I was sure,' said Nina, 'so I went back again today but I couldn't find the street.'

Sophia was elated. 'We'll go back there tomorrow. And we'll take Chrysoula. She knows the area like the back of her hand.'

That night, Sophia found sleep impossible. The same thoughts kept running through her mind. If by the grace of God it was her Vangelis, then hope remained for Leonidas.

Sophia was disheartened to find that she too was unable to glean more information from the poster. Worse still, no one seemed to know anything about Club Attikon. All that the locals could tell them was that there used to be several clubs in the area but one by one most had either closed or moved to another suburb. Sitting outside a small bakery, a blind beggar overheard them and suggested that they ask Mikhailis, who ran the kafenion in Plateia Lysikatous in Plaka.

'He's been here since he was a young boy. Perhaps he can help you,' he said, holding out an old tin can.

Sophia dropped a coin into it and thanked him. The beggar insisted that he would take them there himself.

Kafenion Mikhailis was little more than a narrow cramped room situated at the far end of the Plateia, well away from the newer and brighter establishments. A small wiry man stood behind the counter with his shirt sleeves rolled up, cleaning the glasses.

'Mikhailis?' asked Sophia.

The man nodded. She ordered coffee and the women took a seat. Four men at the next table sat engrossed in a game of cards. Mikhailis came over and placed three small cups of coffee on the table.

'What can I do for you?' he asked.

'We're trying to locate Club Attikon,' Sophia replied.

The men at the table stopped playing and stared at her. Mikhailis threw them a quick glance.

'Why, that used to be Crazy Nick's old place.' He eyed Sophia carefully. 'Now why would a nice lady like you be looking for a place like that?'

'I'm looking for an old friend—a musician by the name of Kapitanos Vangelis. Perhaps you've heard of him? We saw his name on a poster in Anafiotika. He was playing there.'

Mikhailis laughed. 'Crazy Nick closed that place years ago. Or should I say, the police closed it down for him.'

'What happened to him?'

'I don't know! Knowing Crazy Nick, he probably set up somewhere else under another name. Isn't that right, Vassili?' The men nodded. 'Look, Kyria, that place was really a whorehouse.' The men sniggered. 'At the time, the police closed down most clubs in the area. The locals began to complain— you know what I mean?'

Sophia looked offended. 'My friend is an accomplished musician. He would have worked there because they offered him work.'

The men sniggered.

'It takes a certain type of man to work for Crazy Nick. What sort of friend can he be?'

Nina tugged at her mother's skirt. 'I think we'd better go,' she whispered.

'Now there's a little lady with some sense. Just forget Club Attikon; it doesn't exist any more.'

Mikhailis went back to his work. When the women had finished their coffee, Sophia went over to pay him.

'Thank you,' she said, putting a few coins on the counter. She placed her business card next to them and in a low whisper added, 'We didn't mean to bother you, but if you do hear of my friend, this is where I can be reached.'

Seeing the men distracted by their card game, Mikhailis picked it up, put it in his shirt pocket and continued wiping his glasses.

'What sort of a place could Club Attikon have been?' Nina asked when they were outside.

'Probably full of criminals,' laughed Sophia. 'No wonder no one admitted to knowing anything about it.'

Through the smoky haze of the darkened room, Sophia's eyes fell on the shadowy figure of a man seated on a wooden chair. With his back towards her, he smoked a narghile in front of a burning brazier. A young boy—not much older than nine or ten—crouched on the dirt floor next to him, tending the coals. The man leaned over and whispered something in the boy's ear. The boy discreetly went out of the room, leaving the pair alone.

Sophia would have recognized those strong muscular shoulders anywhere. After all, she had spent a good few years observing them from the back seat of her car.

'Hello, Vangelis. It's been a long time.'

Vangelis did not answer, nor did he turn to face her. She took a step towards him and in a gesture of tenderness, laid her hand on his back.

Sophia's heart pounded like a drum. 'Vangelis,' she said in a low voice. 'It's me, Sophia.'

'Don't!' he snapped, getting up and walking away. 'You shouldn't have come.'

His tone frightened her. Why wasn't he pleased to see her? And why wouldn't he face her? It felt like a bad dream. This dingy room at the back of a small lean-to in the seedy area of Piraeus—a place well known for its hashish dens and whorehouses—was the last place she had expected to find herself. Who was this man, hiding away in the shadows like a frightened animal?

Was this the same Vangelis who had looked out for her? The man who had disposed of her enemies in the olive barrels without a second thought? Was this the same man who had cared for her children as if they were his own?

She moved closer towards him. 'There was a time when you and I were like brother and sister. What happened to—'

He cut her short. 'You should leave now. The Vangelis you knew died in Smyrna. Remember him as he was.'

'A part of all of us died in Smyrna, but we carry on...if not for ourselves then for those we left behind.' Her voice shook with emotion. 'Look at me... After everything we've been through, do you really want me to leave?'

Vangelis turned around. His eyes were lifeless and hooded from years of hashish.

'How long have you been addicted?' Sophia asked.

He shrugged. 'Since I came here...It was the only thing that blocked out the past and eased the pain.'

Sophia collapsed onto the chair. Vangelis sat on the dirt floor opposite her, took a piece of hashish from a little packet that lay warming by the fire and placed it into the cup of the narghile.

'Ahh,' he smiled, his eyes beginning to close over. 'The best stuff is from Bursa; expensive, but worth it.'

Sophia looked on helplessly. Tears ran down her face.

'Not a pretty sight is it?' he said, taking another draw.

After a while, he began to unburden himself. 'As soon as we left La Maison du l'Orient, Anoush went into labor,' he told her. 'I thought we were doomed. How could a woman give birth in that crush and live? It was then we heard gunshots and screams in the next street and I knew that the crowd could go no further. With only minutes to spare, I managed to break open a shop door and drag her inside, just in time for the birth. Minutes later soldiers entered the premises. I tried to shield Anoush and the child with my body. I closed my eyes and prayed that the end would be quick. But luck was on our side. A group of American Marines passed by and came to our aid. The next day we made our way to Piraeus. By the time we reached Greece, news of the fire had reached Athens and the city was in mourning. Anoush and the baby were taken into care by the American Women's Hospital Service. Shortly after, they left for America.'

Sophia told him about their last days in Smyrna. On hearing of her loss he held his head in his hands and wept like a baby.

'If only we had left earlier,' he lamented.

Finding no work in Athens and Piraeus, Vangelis had made his way to western Thrace where he worked in the tobacco fields. In the evenings he played the laouto in the camps. One evening while returning from the tobacco fields, he was set upon by bandits. Leaving him for dead, they robbed him of his money and his precious laouto. It took him many months to save enough money to buy another. In the meantime he became enamored with the bouzouki, finding its rich and sharp metallic sound to be far more suitable for the type of music that was becoming popular in the cafes of Athens, Piraeus, and Salonika.

'In Salonika, I began to make a name for myself again,' he said, crushing another piece of hashish between his fingers and dropping it into the bowl. 'Then I met a dark-eyed beauty known as Roxanne—a dancer at the Beau Rivage…Something about her reminded me of Nitsa, a free spirit—owned by no one. How she pierced my heart—like a needle! *Aman…* What a woman!'

'What happened to her?' Sophia asked.

'A *putana*, or a *hanoumaikia* as we called them back in Turkey, belongs to no one. She was found in an alleyway—stabbed to death by a jealous lover… so they say.'

Sophia felt a chill run down her spine and a flash in his eyes told her not to pry.

'What happened to make you come back to Piraeus?'

'Ahh,' he smiled. 'I was befriended by a group of musicians. After hearing me sing "In the Mountains of Smyrna" they welcomed me into their group. I owe my life to them. It was them who brought me here.'

The two sat in silence for a while, taking in the enormity of what they had just learned. 'Who is this mysterious Crazy Nick?' asked Sophia. 'And why did those men in Kafenion Mikhailis try to warn us away?'

Vangelis looked at her thoughtfully. 'That man who brought you here…'

'You mean he's Crazy Nick?'

'None other…He took a great risk in doing that.' He fished in his trouser pocket and pulled out her business card.

*Sophia Laskaris*
*Haute Couture*
*48 Mitropoleos Str. Athens*

'That's a very impressive address, Sophia. Only a wanted man with the police in his pay would wait outside such a place in broad daylight.' He winked at her.

Sophia reached out and took his hand. 'Well, we have him to thank for bringing us together again, don't we?'

\*

222

With Sophia back in his life again, Vangelis was persuaded to get help for his addiction. Six months later, and well on the road to recovery, he moved into Sophia's apartment. He still kept his contacts with the underworld and never refused a request from Crazy Nick to play bouzouki in one of his establishments. Sophia never pried into his comings and goings. She was just happy to have Vangelis in her life again. She did, however, pay an early morning visit to the Kafenion Mikhailis in Plateia Lysikatous. Mikhailis was setting out the tables when she arrived. He acknowledged her with a nod.

'I want to thank you,' she said. 'Without your help, it's almost certain that I would never have seen Vangelis again.'

Mikhailis smiled. 'He's a good man. Take good care of him.'

Sophia shook his hand. 'Don't worry,' she laughed. 'This time, I don't intend to let him out of my sight.'

# CHAPTER 27

*Athens, Spring, 1939*

During the first half of the 1930s, Greece's political landscape oscillated between the Liberalist Venizelists and the Royalists. In 1935, with the Royalists firmly in power, King George returned to Greece and the fledgling republic was abolished. These were also the years when the communists began to gain a foothold in politics. Throughout Europe and further afield, governments would stop at nothing to wipe out the spread of Bolshevism.

With social problems and industrial unrest threatening to split the country, General Ioannis Metaxas, backed by the King, declared martial law. The Fourth of August regime, as the dictatorship came to be known, was to change the political landscape once more.

Sophia watched the turmoil with growing unease and when Esther arrived at the shop one morning with news that all newspapers had been suspended, her worst fears were realized. Esther paced the floor like a caged animal.

'We are doomed!' she cried. 'General Metaxas is a known admirer of the Third Reich.'

Esther's family had been in the fur trade for generations, and as she was fond of telling everyone, they had once supplied the Russian Royal Family and the Ottoman Sultans with the finest ermine robes on the market. As a prominent Jewish family, they had important business associates and family connections in Germany and Austria. They already knew of the harsh laws which affected Jews in those countries after Hitler came to power in 1933. With the rise in fascism throughout Europe Esther was convinced that anti-Semitism would spread to Greece, and she feared the consequences. For the rest of the morning she sat gloomily flicking through copies of *Hollywood* and *The New Movie*. Sophia watched her with sadness. She knew what she was suffering.

In the spring of 1939 Europe teetered on the edge of war. Night after night Sophia followed the downward spiral of events from the BBC World

Service—one of the only ways that she could get a balanced opinion. Greek media was still strictly censored. On the evening of the last day of March, she was alone in the apartment when she heard the British Prime Minister Neville Chamberlain announce that should Hitler attack Poland, Britain would declare war. She turned off the radio, contemplating the implications of his speech. Her experience of the earlier Balkan wars and of the three-year Greek occupation of the Smyrna territory told her that war was inevitable. Germany had become too powerful.

Her thoughts turned to her daughter. It had been almost six months now since the American archeological team began to scale back their work in the agora and Nina had found herself out of work. With little prospect of finding other work in the field, she applied for a position with the British Embassy as a translator. Within less than three months she was promoted to the office of the Diplomatic Mission in the Balkans, translating documents often stamped Top Secret. It was a world away from her career as an archeologist.

Sophia reflected on just how much her daughter had changed in that short time. Except for her embroidery, Nina had shown little interest in fashion until now. She no longer wore the thick cotton kerchief that had protected her from the hot summer sun and the dusty conditions in the agora. Her practical trousers were now replaced with pretty dresses, pencil-slim skirts, and elegant blouses—clothes that flattered her shapely body. Sophia was in no doubt as to the cause of this sudden transformation; the signs were unmistakable—Nina was in love. To Sophia, Nina was still the small child who sat next to Dimitra in the vermillion room. She remembered the intense concentration etched on her face as she mastered the fine *cin ignesi* stitch work on a long-stemmed tulip and she felt the pain of sadness. Somehow, she had failed to notice her youngest daughter grow up: one day a child, the next a woman. What happened to those in-between years?

Voices in the hallway brought her back to reality. It was almost midnight and Vangelis and Nina had returned from the ball at the British Embassy. In her steel-gray taffeta dress, Nina looked beautiful and the glow on her face only served to verify Sophia's earlier thoughts.

'It was such a wonderful evening,' said Nina, taking off her shoes and stretching out on the sofa. 'And Vangelis took great care of me…as always.'

'The Lord only knows what would have happened if I hadn't kept a watchful eye on her,' Vangelis replied, winking at Sophia. 'There wasn't a man in the room who could take his eyes off her.'

Nina blushed. 'Don't believe him, Mama. He's exaggerating as usual.'

Sophia thanked Vangelis for giving up his evening at the nightclub to chaperone Nina to the ball.

'She's the daughter I never had,' he told Sophia when they were alone. 'I was so proud of her…and I saw you in her. Suddenly, I was back in Constantinople…to those glorious soirées in the Grand Salon. My heart sinks when I think I might never have seen you both again.'

She told him about the news from London.

'I know,' he replied despondently. 'By the time we left the Embassy that was all anyone could talk about.'

When they left the Church of the Pantanassa, the rain had eased and the sun was beginning to break through the soft white clouds, bringing with it the promise of another bright spring day. In the Plateia, kafenia and taverna owners were busily setting up tables and chairs on the footpath. As they often did on Sunday after church, Sophia and Nina headed to Kafenion Bournabat for a plate of *loukomathes*—soft chewy fritters dribbled in honey and sprinkled with cinnamon. Like most refugees from Asia Minor, they looked forward to this Sunday morning ritual, much as they had in their homeland. When Nina caught her mother's arm and suggested that they forego this treat today, and instead take a leisurely walk up to the Acropolis, Sophia knew that she was about to tell her something. She braced herself for the inevitable.

The heady scent of acacia blossom filled the air as they made their way along the Panathenaic Way, through the east side of the agora towards the sacred rock. Steady streams of visitors were already heading in the same direction. At the foot of the Acropolis, Sophia paused to catch her breath. She wiped away the beads of perspiration from her brow, commenting on how the ancients must have been fit to have made this short trip on a regular basis. Entering the Propylaea—the imposing entrance to the Acropolis— Nina informed her mother that this masterpiece of classical architecture was designed by the architect Mnesicles, and built in the period from 437 to 432 BC on the site of an earlier entrance.

'If we look closer, we see how brilliantly the architect created a rare aesthetic blend of Doric and Ionic orders…and when Turkish rule began in 1458, the Turkish Commander lived here.'

Sophia had heard it all before but today was different; she detected a note of anxiety in her daughter's voice.

'And in 1645, the powder magazine was struck by lightning, destroying the building and killing Commander Isouf Agha and his family.'

'Well, I must say,' Sophia replied, 'when I see these buildings now, the marble so white in the sunshine, I find it hard to imagine that they were once brightly painted.'

They continued towards the top, past the small elegant Temple of Nike to the Erechtheion. Sophia suggested that they might sit for a while on the Acropolis wall and enjoy the splendid view below of Athens. Nina picked up a small stone and playfully tossed it from one hand to the other. The cast of her features, set in a half frown, looked almost oriental. Her finely shaped eyebrows arched towards the bridge of her nose, a nose that began straight in the classical manner yet turned slightly over her small mouth. Sophia was immensely proud of her and the two had formed a close bond.

'I have something to tell you, Mama,' said Nina, letting the stone fall over the side of the wall where it bounced from rock to rock until it reached the thicket where Manolios's body had been found. 'I have fallen in love.'

Sophia refrained from telling her that she had already guessed as much. Instead, she asked who the lucky man was.

'You may not like it when I tell you. He's an Englishman I met at the Embassy. He's here as part of the British Diplomatic Mission to the Balkans. Until last night we had hardly spoken to each other, but I knew when I first met him that there was something special between us.'

Nina was a private person who kept her feelings to herself. That she was spilling her heart out like this left Sophia in no doubt as to the seriousness of the situation.

'Please don't be angry with me,' she said softly.

'Why would I be angry with you, *agape mou*? Your happiness is my happiness.'

'Because I have chosen an Englishman.'

Sophia smiled. 'You are not the first person in the family to have chosen a foreigner. Don't forget that your great-grandfather was French and many years later, there was…' Sophia hesitated. Her thoughts drifted to Constantinople. 'Anyway, the important thing is, does this man have the same feelings for you?'

'Of that I am sure, Mama.'

'Then I would like to meet him. Next week is Holy Week—the most important holiday of the year. I can't think of a better time to show him how we Greeks celebrate. Can you?'

The two made their way back to Monastiraki, and in doing so turned into the street where Kyria Koula the fortuneteller lived. As usual, the old crone was sitting on the doorstep.

'I've heard that woman can predict the future,' Nina said. 'Perhaps I should ask her what the future holds for me.'

Before Sophia could stop her, Nina let go of her mother's arm and quickened her pace. She told her mother to go on without her. Dismayed,

Sophia watched Nina approach the woman. She was too far away to hear what took place, but the expression on Nina's face told her it was not what she wanted to hear. With her head bowed, Nina walked back to her mother. Warily Sophia asked her what she had said. Distressed, Nina said the woman wanted nothing to do with her; that there was no future to tell.

'When I told her that was impossible, she said something about a viper in the house and that my only salvation was to kill it first...before it killed me. What does it mean?'

'These people talk in riddles,' replied Sophia consolingly. 'Don't let such idle talk spoil such a lovely day.'

Nina looped her arm through her mother's again. 'Perhaps you're right; only God knows what's in store for us.'

Sophia agreed, yet no matter how hard they tried, neither of them could forget Kyria Koula's words.

'Kill the viper before it kills you.'

The Church of the Pantanassa was lit by flickering candles—hundreds of them—and in the fading light the congregation watched as the priest and monks took down the icon of Christ, wrapped it in linen, and put it on a great casket covered in flowers, symbolizing the tomb of Christ. Like some ancient rite of ceremonial magic, the priest delivered his prayers and the men picked up the bier and headed out into the night. Outside, a small crowd of true believers carrying candles began to follow the procession through the streets of Monastiraki. For three days the bells would toll; three days in the Orthodox year that symbolized the death of Christ culminating in his resurrection the following Sunday.

At home an enormous cauldron of *mayeritsa* bubbled gently on the stove, and in the *saloni* Sophia and Nina prepared the resurrection table with baskets of red dyed eggs and plaited *tsoureki* bread. By early afternoon the table was ready. A steady stream of guests arrived at the apartment to partake in the celebratory feast.

Sophia watched Vangelis teach the Englishman backgammon, and by all accounts he was a quick learner. Every now and again Nina offered him a small plate of food, explaining the significance of each dish.

'Try this,' she said affectionately. 'This pilav is a specialty of our family.'

She laughed heartily when he was challenged to crack the red eggs, each time winning against his opponent.

'The person whose egg lasts longest is assured of a happy life,' said Nina. 'Look, mine cracked on the first go; you still have yours.'

'And I still have mine,' shouted Chrysoula, waving her egg in the air.

'Now it's down to you two,' said Vangelis, encouraging the guests to place bets on the lucky winner.

Everyone cheered when Chrysoula won; none more so than the Englishman.

Vangelis slapped him enthusiastically on the back. 'But you are lucky in love,' he whispered. 'You have no need of red eggs.'

It was a silly, superstitious game, but in the pit of her stomach Sophia harbored a nagging fear when her daughter lost.

'Let's give thanks to God for a good Easter,' she said to everyone. 'Raise your glasses. *Christos anesti!*'

'*Christos anesti!*' the guests replied. 'Christ is risen.'

Earlier in the day the Englishman formally asked Sophia for her daughter's hand in marriage. That the couple were deeply in love was evident to all. Sophia gave them her blessing. He told Sophia that he wished to be baptized in the Orthodox faith and that when the couple married, they intended to live in Greece where Nina would still be close to her mother. Sophia welcomed the decision.

The festivities drawing to a close, the Englishman made a speech thanking Sophia for welcoming him into her family. Halfway through the speech a commotion began outside the house. Chrysoula opened the window and peered into the street. A large crowd surrounded a black car that stood outside the entrance to the house. People were running towards it from all directions. 'Welcome home,' the crowd cheered. Nervously, Chrysoula turned to face Sophia. Her face was as white as a sheet. The cheering grew louder.

'What's happening?' asked Sophia.

Before Chrysoula could answer, the door to the *saloni* swung open and silhouetted against the poorly illuminated light of the hallway stood a woman wearing an elegantly tailored woolen suit, with a fox fur draped over one shoulder. A wide-brimmed hat decorated with a ribbon into which two pheasant feathers were decorously attached partially covered her face. Sophia felt the blood drain from her cheeks. She recognized her eldest daughter instantly.

'Hello, Mama.' She swept her hand around the room in a grand gesture. 'How thoughtful of you to plan a little party for my return,' she said, with a hint of sarcasm.

Sophia reached out to Vangelis to steady herself. Ignoring the cool welcome, Maria continued. 'Isn't anyone going to offer me a welcome home drink?'

In a spirit of reconciliation Nina approached her sister, and taking her in her arms she kissed her on both cheeks.

'Welcome home, Maria. We're all happy to have you with us again. It's been too long.' She picked up her glass and turned to the guests. 'Please, everyone, take up your glasses. Let us make a toast that, finally, my sister is back where she belongs.'

'Welcome home, Maria,' said Chrysoula, regaining her composure. 'You're looking well. Paris has done wonders for you.'

She offered to take her fox fur and hat. Thanking Chrysoula for the compliment, Maria removed her hat, allowing her hair to shake loose over her shoulder.

'That's better,' she smiled.

Instinctively, Chrysoula pulled away, her mouth wide open.

'Whatever's the matter?' laughed Maria. 'I'm not going to bite you.'

A guest standing nearby let out a gasp. Maria's hair appeared like fire— the burnished red-gold of a Titian painting.

'What delightful hair,' she murmured to her companion. 'I've never seen such a head of hair before.'

Panic-stricken, Chrysoula looked at Sophia for reassurance and instinctively knew that she too was gripped by an irrational fear.

# CHAPTER 28

*Athens, November 1940*

When Germany attacked Poland in September 1939, Britain and France declared war on Germany. One by one, countries everywhere were dragged into the theatre of war. Greece remained neutral, but in October 1940 the unthinkable happened. Greece found itself at war with Italy. Almost a month later, Nina and the Englishman exchanged marriage vows in a small ceremony at the Church of the Pantanassa. Sophia signed the apartment over to them as a wedding present and bought herself a new house a few miles to the north of Athens. A week later the Englishman was informed of an urgent assignment in Cairo. He was to leave on the next boat for Alexandria.

'Damn Mussolini,' Nina cursed to herself as she watched his ship sail out of Piraeus harbor. 'Why did he have to attack us?'

She placed a hand over her belly, rubbing it gently in a circular motion. They had been together for barely two weeks, yet already she knew she was pregnant. There was never any question that she would tell him; his mission in the Middle East was far too important to burden him with unnecessary worries. Besides, he would be back in no time. Meanwhile, she busied herself with her work. With a war on, her workload had more than doubled. One afternoon, she was accidently given a set of documents marked MOST TOP SECRET. By the time the secretary realized the gravity of his actions it was too late—Nina had already glimpsed the contents.

Waiting until the secretary left for the evening, Nina discreetly entered the room, removed the file from his drawer, and read the contents. In front of her was the evidence that Hitler meant to occupy Greece. The plans for 'Operation Marita,' as it would later be known, had already been implemented at the highest level in Berlin. The revelation that Germany did not intend to stand by and see her Axis partner defeated caused her to feel nauseous and she clutched her belly, instinctively trying to protect her unborn child.

'What is to become of us, little one?' she asked. 'May God protect you from experiencing such horrors as I have witnessed. I would rather die than bring you into such a world.'

The enthusiasm with which the Greeks pushed the Italians back into Albania changed when the German army launched an assault on Greece on April 6, 1941. General Metaxas did not live to see that day. He died on January 21, having prophetically proclaimed that he would rather die than surrender to the Axis Powers. The euphoria gone and the country on the verge of disarray, the Greek Prime Minister shot himself. The King and his government fled the country. The Greeks prepared themselves for dark days ahead.

The road to Athens' main fishing port of Rafina was clogged with an unimaginable confusion of vehicles. Streams of tracer bullets streaked the night sky and in the distance German bombers could be heard on the way to their destination. Tonight, the port of Piraeus would take another pounding. It had been a wise move to embark elsewhere. At least there was less chance of a direct hit. The car maneuvered along the road and came to a halt at a police checkpoint.

'Documents please,' an officer asked.

Vangelis wound down the window and handed them over. The policeman pressed his face against the window and looked at the occupants in the back. Nina felt the child kick violently and reached out for her mother's hand.

'Have a safe journey,' he said, waving them on.

Further on they found the entrance to the port already blocked. Empty trucks lay abandoned and soldiers jostled with each other for the last places on board the boats.

'What a nightmare,' Vangelis muttered to himself. He honked the horn but it was no use. 'Better get out here or you'll miss the boat,' he told Nina. 'It's not too far.'

Remembering his failure to convince Sophia to leave on the *Medusa*, he vowed that this was one boat that would not be missed.

Tearfully, Nina hugged her mother goodbye.

'It's not forever, my darling,' said Sophia, wiping away her daughter's tears. 'You have a husband and a child to think of now. Your duty is to them. You leave with my blessing. At least I can sleep at night, knowing that you will be in safe hands.'

'Hurry!' Vangelis shouted. 'Let's go. The last boat is about to leave.'

'Write as soon as you reach Cairo,' Sophia called out as they made their way through the dense throng of soldiers.

Nina turned back and waved. Somewhere a scuffle broke out. Men cursed each other. Women sobbed. For a while, Sophia stared vacantly at the chaotic scene that bore a resemblance to her last days in Smyrna. She then walked back to the car and waited for Vangelis to return. Unlike the situation with Maria, Nina's absence was a void that could not be filled. But it was for the best. At least her grandchild would be born in safety. Sometime later, Vangelis returned with the news that Nina was safely on board.

'Let's go,' Sophia said to him. 'We have much to do. This time we stay and fight.'

No one seemed to know the real reason for Maria's decision to return to Greece. There were many who, quite rightly as it turned out, thought France's 'phony' war with Germany would turn into the real thing. Kyrios Papayiannis surmised that Maria might be one of them.

'But she could have gone to America,' said Kyria Angeliki. 'Far away from the troubles; she's popular there.'

'Or she simply could have stayed put. The Germans adore her. As Princess Elizabeth of Thuringia in Wagner's *Tannhäuser* she received standing ovations in Leipzig, Dresden, and Berlin…not to mention Vienna.'

'Well, you have to admit it, Greece welcomed her back and for a while the Metaxas press heaped a great deal of praise on her. And now that we have the Germans here, she's popular once again. From what I hear, she's always performing at some function or another, singing Wagner or German Lieder.'

Kyrios Papayiannis stroked his small pointed beard and thought of his partner—the temperamental Sophocles. Maria had managed to flatter him into accompanying her on the occasions on which she sang Lieder, saying that his virtuosity on the piano brought out the best in her, particularly when she sang Schumann. On such occasions, Sophocles needed the courage of drink to get him through the evening. He despised the Germans and it was a credit to his brilliance that no one suspected that he was often so drunk that he couldn't remember where he was. Maria suffered no such guilt. Whether they were Germans, Italians, or Greeks made no difference to her. She was paid handsomely for her appearances and that's all she cared about. Her admirers showered her with gifts and at a time when most Greeks suffered escalating hardships, she flaunted her acquisitions with no regard for others whatsoever.

'Of course, there's always the possibility that she returned to make amends with her mother,' suggested Kyria Angeliki. 'Have you thought about that?'

'Somehow, I doubt it. The way she parades herself tells me that she has little regard for the feelings of others. It's a great pity. I had such high hopes for that girl, you know. She has a rare talent, not to mention her striking looks, but I am afraid she is severely lacking in humility.'

Kyria Angeliki agreed. 'She is nothing like her mother. With everything that woman has endured, she still walks with her head held high...the woman is a saint. And neither is she like her younger sister. Such a quiet and unassuming person, and possessing a fine intellect to boot. The two are like chalk and cheese.'

Sophia was well aware of such conversations taking place behind her back. She had not understood the reason for Maria's return either. In a society where family honor was paramount, and where a daughter treated her mother with respect, Maria was an embarrassment. Nina had welcomed her back with open arms but for Sophia, she caused nothing but heartache.

The other thing troubling Sophia was that the older she was, the more superstitious she became. Over and over again she recalled Dimitra's fear of the child with flaming hair. Her grandmother was rarely wrong. And Kyria Koula's warnings harking along similar lines only served to reinforce these thoughts. She simply could not shake them off. Flaming hair, red hair—what did it matter? All thoughts led her back to Maria. In the end Sophia told herself that no matter how difficult her daughter was, she would never deliberately do anything that might harm them.

The news that Nina had given birth to a girl in October 1941 filled Sophia with great joy. As yet there was no photograph of the child, but in her letter Nina described her in great detail.

> She is the most adorable creature I ever laid eyes on; a sweet child with
> dark eyes and black hair. I have named her Eleni—my shining light.

Sophia transported herself back to the drawing room of their house in Constantinople. The image of a small boy rocking his baby sister's crib to and fro filled her with sadness. Yet at the same time, the birth of her first grandchild gave her cause for optimism.

Within hours of receiving the news, Sophia was kneeling in front of the icon of the Virgin and Child in the Church of the Pantanassa giving thanks for the safe delivery of the child and the health of its mother. And like her grandmother all those years ago, she gave thanks that the child did not have red hair.

During the first few months of the occupation, the Germans confiscated properties, cars, and valuable possessions. Esther's villa in Kifissia, along with the Bentley, was given to a Wehrmacht officer and his family. With accommodation in short supply, she was forced to rent rooms in Kyria Angeliki's house in the center of Athens. A few days later Sophia was informed that her old apartment—the one that she had given to Nina as part of her dowry—was being requisitioned. She was to present herself at the apartment the following day to hand over the keys. When she arrived, two officials had already let themselves in and were waiting for her. The elder of the two, a small overweight man in his mid-forties, sat at the dining table typing an inventory of the apartment's contents. The younger, a fair-haired man with an arrogant expression, stood next to him leafing through a set of documents.

'Sign here,' he snapped. 'You will be compensated in due course.'

'Would you mind if I take a few of my daughter's personal effects?' Sophia asked.

He nodded his approval. She began to fill a small box with a few books and several trinkets from her dressing table. It was then that she noticed her old suitcase tucked away beneath a pile of empty shoe boxes, the one she had brought with her from Smyrna all those years ago. In the turmoil of recent events, she had completely forgotten about it.

'Do you mind if I take this?' she asked. 'There's nothing of importance in it.'

The older man looked up from his typing, peered over his glasses at the battered case and looked amused.

'Alright, but hurry up, we haven't got all day.'

When she left the apartment she found Vangelis leaning against a shop wall, smoking a cigarette and reading a newspaper.

'Esther told me you were here,' he said, stubbing the cigarette out with his foot. 'Come on, I'll give you a hand. We'll take these to the shop. Mikhailis has called an urgent meeting at the kafenion for four. If we hurry, we can still make it.'

More than a dozen men were already crammed into the tiny room at the back of Mikhailis's kafenion when Sophia and Vangelis arrived. Someone offered Sophia his seat and joined two men sitting against the wall on upturned olive-oil containers. A bare electric light bulb hung from the center of the room over the wooden table, with its dim light emphasizing the copious clouds of yellow-tinged cigarette smoke that swirled effortlessly around the room. Glasses of aromatic ouzo, clouded by the addition of water, punctuated the staleness of the smoke.

Mikhailis sat at the head of the table waiting patiently for everyone to arrive. Next to him sat a clean-shaven man in his early forties. He had sandy hair and impeccable English public-school manners. He was introduced to them simply as George the Englishman. The only other woman in the group was a pretty girl in her late teens. Wearing a floral dress and matching scarf, she added a decorous touch to an otherwise dowdy room. Around her neck was a thin chain from which hung a silver cross. She occasionally fingered it nervously during the meeting.

Vangelis leaned over and whispered in Sophia's ear. 'Mikhailis's granddaughter, Effie,' he told her.

Mikhailis tapped his glass loudly with a knife. 'Friends,' he began. 'It's been over six months now since the Germans and Italians arrived. With a puppet government firmly under their control we have no alternative but to take matters into our own hands. We will not drown in a sea of helplessness. The Greek people are proud people,' he said, his eyes flashing and his voice rising with anger. 'All of you here today are well acquainted with the inscription written on the flag of our hero Theodoros Kolokotronis during the War of Independence against the Turks. "Freedom or Death" was his motto—the motto of our forefathers. And today that motto will once more give us the strength to defeat the enemy. One day soon, the Greeks will be free again. Freedom is our birthright.'

Everyone cheered. Sophia glanced towards Effie. Tears welled up in her eyes as she listened proudly to her grandfather's words. Mikhailis put his hand on her shoulder.

'She is too young to know the bloodshed we endured for our beliefs,' he said, looking into the eyes of everyone in the room. 'We owe our children a better life than the one we had.'

Sophia recalled Markos saying those very same words to her in Zaharoplasteion Olympia.

The rousing speech over, Mikhailis turned his attention to why the meeting had been called. 'There are already Resistance groups forming in the mountains and we must do everything in our power to help them. One of our objectives is to liaise with them, and furnish them with information which will support their basic operations of subversive activities and sabotage. For most of you here today, your work will be confined to the vital task of intelligence-gathering. I cannot stress enough the importance of secrecy and respect for your fellow comrades. Discretion is paramount. One wrong move will mean certain death for us.' He took a large sip of ouzo and cleared his throat.

'All of you here have in one way or another proved beyond doubt that you are invaluable to the cause, and I don't need to tell you that we must be vigilant at all times. Even the innocent among us can deceive us. With severe shortages of everything from fuel to food, the people are desperate.

Desperation could cause many to sell their souls to the devil.

'Most importantly,' he stressed, tapping the side of his head, 'you must learn to keep everything up here. This is not a game.' His words were slow and deliberate. 'It is a matter of life and death.'

Like many in the room that day, Sophia had never trained in clandestine communications of any sort. However, she did possess a natural talent for extracting important information from people which she had willingly passed on to the Etairia. Since those heady days, she had tried to distance herself from the disillusionment of politics. Building a new life was all she cared about. But now the circumstances were different. It was as Mikhailis said—their very freedom was at stake. Yes, he was right. She wanted to make a better life for her grandchild. The defiant determination of her days in Constantinople resurfaced. She would do whatever she could.

Mikhailis sat down and George the Englishman took over. Using his knowledge of ancient Greek and a smattering of modern Greek he thanked everyone for their support, in particular those who had helped to shelter the English and Commonwealth soldiers marooned in Greece after the German invasion. That work was ongoing; there were still hundreds more in hiding.

'Some people have chosen to stay and work alongside us,' he told the group, 'but we still rely on the support of the Greek people.'

Sophia thought of Esther. She had often used her villa in Kifissia to house Jews fleeing the tyranny of Hitler's Europe. Since the German occupation they had been replaced by Allied soldiers, and it was only the fact that her gardener had been seen snooping around that forced her to stop this. Kyria Angeliki's home was also a safe house. Even Vangelis hid the occasional soldier at the nightclub. Sophia felt a twinge of guilt for not offering her house, but after careful consideration she reached the conclusion that Maria's associations with the Axis leaders and members of the puppet government could put refugees in jeopardy.

The meeting was over. The men went their separate ways. George asked Sophia and Vangelis to stay behind.

'How do you feel about working with us, Kyria Laskaris?' he asked. 'Your previous work in Constantinople tells us that you are well suited to this kind of thing and we would value your involvement tremendously.'

His comment shook her.

George took out his pipe and filled it with fresh tobacco. 'We are aware of your involvement with the Etairia during the Great War and the subsequent role that you played in the demise of some special agents working for the Turkish Secret Police.'

Sophia watched him light his pipe. Nothing in her face gave her away.

George smiled. He liked that about her.

'Kyria Laskaris, you are a highly intelligent lady. You are as well respected in Athens as you were in Asia Minor. And with your excellent command of languages, you would be invaluable to us.'

George's manner was disarming. He tried to put her at ease by telling her about his earlier work with the Foreign Office in London, Paris, and Cairo.

'I was asked to recruit suitable agents to work behind enemy lines in the Middle East,' he said. 'People whose job it would be to relay information to the Special Operations Executive in Cairo and London. Kyria Laskaris, no one is asking you to act as you did all those years ago. But your business is an excellent foil for contacts, and at this point all we ask is that you use this to gather information and pass it to us. A meeting would be arranged to give you a little training which, given your attention to detail, would not be difficult for you.'

He held out his hand waiting for her handshake of acceptance.

'You have my word,' she replied. 'I am at your service.'

'Excellent,' he smiled. 'It has been an honor to meet you. And now that we are firmly assured of your allegiance, there is one more thing that I have to say.'

George's demeanor suddenly changed, his smile replaced with a look of deep concern. 'Your daughter…' he began.

'Do you mean Nina?'

'No, the elder one…Maria. I have to advise you that we have had her under surveillance for some time now.'

Sophia's fingers gripped the buttons she had been fastening tightly. She looked at Vangelis and Mikhailis. Neither could bring themselves to look at her.

'Why is that?' she asked calmly.

'I will come straight to the point. We believe that she may be working for the Germans.'

His words echoed in her ears.

'Were you aware of this?' she asked Vangelis coldly.

He wished he were anywhere but in that room, her face searching for answers.

'I had my suspicions. Until now they were never confirmed.'

Sophia picked up her gloves and turned towards the door. 'Thank you, gentlemen; will that be all?'

George apologized, saying that he had to be sure of her commitment before telling her this. 'I'm sorry to break it to you in this way,' he said in a matter-of-fact way. 'I understand she is your daughter; that is why you must be even more careful.'

Mikhailis saw them outside. 'Take good care of her,' he said to Vangelis in a low voice. 'She's a plucky lady. I still remember the day she walked into the kafenion looking for you. Nothing would stop her. That's something to be admired.'

Plateia Lysikatous bristled with Germans sitting at the outdoor tables. An officer approached the kafenion with a Greek girl on his arm.

'*Guten tag*, Herr Lieutenant,' smiled Mikhailis, pulling out a chair and flicking away specks of dirt with a white tea-towel. 'What can I get for you?'

# CHAPTER 29

*Athens, Winter 1941*

Maria turned in front of the mirror, admiring herself. The pale blue woolen suit that her mother had made for her fitted well and the new fashion of shorter skirts, due to a scarcity of fabric, showed off her shapely legs to perfection. There was no doubt about it: her mother's skills were equal to any of the top couturiers who had dressed her in Paris—and thankfully, they didn't come with an exorbitant price tag.

Picking up the silver hairbrush, she brushed her silky hair, swept it up into a mound of curls on top of her head, and with well-manicured hands, the brightly colored nails tapering to a fine curve, she deftly flicked each curl until not a strand was out of place. She rouged her cheeks, applied blood-red lipstick to her full lips, and dusted her face with a delicate layer of powder. Finally, she dabbed a little *Mitsouko* behind her ears and on her wrists. Checking the time, she called to Chrysoula to bring her coat.

Chrysoula laid the calf-length mink coat on the bed and placed her black gloves next to them. Preoccupied with herself, Maria failed to notice Chrysoula's disapproving look. Given the circumstances, such a display of luxury was in poor taste. The coat was a gift from Kyrios Sakellariou shortly after her return to Greece, and Maria remembered the occasion well. He was throwing a party in honor of an important German industrialist and on hearing of her return to Athens, he invited her to sing. His guests were most impressed and it was largely because of her that he succeeded in securing important business interests in one of the largest chemical plants in Greece. As a token of his gratitude, he sent her the mink coat—the most expensive that Rosen Furs had to offer. Maria was flattered. Sophia was appalled. He was the last person she expected to see in her daughter's life.

Throughout the Metaxas years and the Italian and German occupations, Sakellariou had managed to prosper where others struggled. On her return to Greece his patronage helped Maria enormously, and when the Germans arrived her prospects soared once more. Since her days in Paris the Germans had admired her singing voice; to them she was a diva. Those who once flocked to see her performances in the Reich now vied with each other for her private performances in Athens. With that came more gifts. How could she refuse them? Nor did she want to. In Maria's mind, to be adored was to be loved—something she had craved all her life. Yet for all the adoration she was still a lonely woman and no one sensed that more than Sakellariou. Because of her, his parties outshone all others and his gifts became more extravagant and expensive. Maria was like a moth to a flame.

It didn't take her long to realize that it was not simply his adoration for her that kept the gifts flowing, but his love. He had never told her as much. Since his wife's death six months earlier, she had waited for the day when he would say it. Sakellariou was old enough to be her father, with a daughter older than she was. What looks he had once possessed were long faded. He was grossly overweight and suffered from bouts of illnesses due to his extravagant lifestyle. Despite his attentiveness to Maria, he displayed a certain callousness towards women. She also found him abrasive and completely devoid of the finer charms of the European men she had met. Yet he intrigued her. More importantly, he was powerful.

Since the death of Manolios, Maria had rejected the idea of marriage. She was now thirty-three years old—the age at which most respectable Greek women had at least two or three children. Even she realized that her looks and fine voice would not last forever. If Sakellariou should propose— and if she could ignore his shortcomings—he could give her the lifestyle she so cherished. She didn't love him but the idea of becoming one of the most influential women in Athens appealed to her immensely.

She heard his car arrive outside the house. He had sent his chauffeur to pick her up again. From the window, Chrysoula watched her leave. Embarrassed, she knew that other unseen eyes in the street also saw her leave.

The winter of 1941 to 1942 saw Greece experience the worst famine in living memory. Conditions worsened when the Germans requisitioned quantities of foodstuffs that far exceeded their needs, either sending it home to their families in Germany or selling the surplus at exorbitant prices. Hampered further by the British blockade of supplies, and worthless occupation money, the population now faced mass starvation. By winter, what foodstuffs there were sold out within the first hour. The population died in their thousands and it was commonplace to see trucks collecting the dead that littered the streets every day. Charon was relentless. Death through starvation and disease would reach almost one hundred thousand in Athens alone, and the sight of emaciated children begging or sitting empty-eyed next to the decomposing body of a parent haunted the population. Suspicious of any well-fed person, the privileged felt anxious, lest they be labeled collaborators.

With images of the Great Depression still imprinted on their minds, Sophia and Esther decided to paper over the windows of the shop in order not to offend anyone or to attract looters. Not that it made any difference to Esther; her supply of furs dwindled to a standstill. Her nerves were shattered and she now felt that her Jewishness made her a target for the Gestapo. In the end she decided it was better to help Sophia and took charge of the sewing room, enabling her to continue with her charity work or to deliver garments to the clients.

Esther tidied away several bolts of cloth and laid out the last piece of a magnificent cherry-red fine wool-blend fabric that was to be made into a jacket with matching trousers for a local actress. She liked this new fashion which enabled women to ride their bicycles with ease. And if there was any left over she intended to ask Sophia to make her a pair of trousers. It would bring her cheer. One by one she checked the seamstresses' work. Several were engaged in attaching sequins to the bodice of an evening dress. They had been trained by Nina and their work was faultless. She recalled the early years when Sophia's only help was Nina. Now she employed more than a dozen women—a rarity in times of extreme unemployment.

On top of this, Sophia had taken to organizing knitting and weaving circles in the working-class suburbs inhabited by the Asia Minor refugees. There she would exchange black-market food parcels for much needed knitwear and blankets, which were quickly dispatched to various charities and orphanages. Occasionally, Esther accompanied her and watched in admiration as Sophia explained, often in Turkish, what could be created by unraveling old socks and vests. Sophia's energy was boundless and Esther had nothing but the highest regard for her. What she didn't know was that this was one way that Sophia gauged the people's discontent, and she regularly picked up little pieces of information that she passed back to the group.

Esther returned to the showroom and was surprised to find Kyrios Sakellariou's daughter Penelope waiting there. It had been a while since she had visited the shop and she hardly recognized her. She had lost weight and looked gravely ill. Surely it couldn't be due to the famine, Esther thought to herself. Her family was too well connected.

'How good to see you again; it's been a while since—'

Penelope cut her short. 'Kyria Sophia, is she here?'

'I'm afraid she's left for the day. Can I give her a message?'

Penelope looked downcast. Esther noticed the dark circles under her eyes.

'It's imperative that I speak with her. Please ask her to be in touch with me as soon as possible.'

'I'll ask her to call you first thing in the morning.'

'It might be better if she comes to see me. Tell her I'll be waiting.'

Outside, the weather was worsening. The temperature had plummeted to zero and a soft veil of snow gave the street a bleached look. Esther looked around for Penelope's car. It wasn't there. She watched her walk towards Plateia Syntagma. Penelope looked too ill to be out in such weather.

Penelope was tending to her collection of orchids when Sophia arrived. Next to the warm stove her younger child, a boy of two years, played happily with his toys. Outside, the garden was covered in snow, and icicles hung from the eaves of the conservatory; they were glistening jewels in the clear winter light.

'Thank you for coming at such short notice,' said Penelope. 'You're just in time for mid-morning tea.'

She reached over and picked up the teapot and poured them both a cup of tea. Platters of sandwiches and a freshly baked cake filled the table. Sophia tried to conceal her embarrassment. Outside, the population of Athens starved and many froze to death through lack of fuel, yet in the warmth of this conservatory, with its potted palms and wicker furniture, Penelope's life appeared untouched.

'As you see,' Penelope smiled, sensing Sophia's unease, '*doxa sto Theo*, we are not suffering as others are.'

Sophia ignored the remark. Instead she was more concerned with Penelope's health. It took her only a matter of minutes to realize that Penelope was in the final stages of consumption, the illness that had carried away the Grand Duchess Anastasia. She glanced at the small child playing innocently at her feet and wondered just how much time they would have together.

'How long have you known?' Sophia asked.

'A couple of years now; that's why I never came to visit you personally for fittings and I sent my maid instead.' Penelope smiled. 'You always knew my taste in clothes anyway.'

She cut a slice of cake, broke it in two and gave half to her son. He took one bite and left it on the floor. Sophia winced. She had lost count of the times she had seen children and adults alike fight over less.

'Esther told me that you needed to see me urgently?'

'I have some bad news,' replied Penelope, wiping her hands on a crisply starched napkin. 'You're not going to like this. My father came to see me two days ago. Apparently, he is in love with Maria and wants to marry her.'

Sophia stared at her in disbelief. 'That's impossible, he's old enough to be her father.'

'Exactly. The point is, what are we going to do about it? She may be your daughter, but after Manolios, I can't bear to be in the same room as her, let alone to have her as my stepmother. It's unthinkable.'

'How long has he had these feelings?'

'I believe it's been some time now…even before my mother died. In her unhappiness, she once let slip that she was the reason he traveled to Germany so often. They definitely knew each other when she returned to Greece.'

George the Englishman's words echoed in Sophia's mind.

'I was furious of course,' continued Penelope. 'Suddenly, it all made sense. All those parties. It was to impress her. I'm sure it was because of Maria that my mother became so ill. How could she compete with a beautiful young woman? He simply idolized her and my mother was pushed into the background.'

A myriad of thoughts raced through Sophia's mind. Sakellariou was a well-known Germanophile and had profited greatly from their presence. How much was Maria involved in that? Surely she couldn't take his proposal seriously; she was still a young woman. Sophia felt dizzy.

'I had no idea. She said nothing to me,' said Sophia. 'What does your husband have to say about all this? Can't he make him see sense?'

Penelope's face hardened. She looked down at the child playing next to her feet.

'We have lived separate lives since he was born. After giving him five children, he has lost all interest in me. Now he flaunts other women in my face. One of them—his secretary—has even moved into the house. It seems that I am doomed to share the same fate as my mother,' she said sarcastically.

Sophia saw the sadness in her eyes. It was ironic how fate had thrown them together.

'So you see, he sees nothing wrong with my father's actions. He even finds her quite charming himself.' Penelope paused for a moment, as if searching for the right words. 'Poor Sophia. You don't really know your daughter at all do you?'

'What do you mean? Is there something you want to tell me?'

Penelope walked over to the window. For a while she watched two crows scratching in the snow, searching for food. 'I shouldn't have said what I did. I was a little confused. Please forgive me.'

Sophia took her leave, promising to find out what intentions Maria had towards Sakellariou. Heading away from the house, she caught sight of a woman watching her from one of the windows.

Vangelis was the only one Sophia could truly confide in and she decided to pay him a visit. The Black Cat in Plaka was one of the most popular night spots in the city. It had been a favorite haunt of the British, and now the Germans and Italians sought relaxation there. The huge cocktail bar on the ground floor was filled with officers and civilians alike, and at the back there was a discreet gambling room where Axis personnel and black marketers traded anything from diamonds to coffee over roulette and blackjack. Posters of Vangelis and his dance orchestra lined the walls alongside photographs of musicians and popular cabaret singers with sultry eyes.

Vangelis was rehearsing when Sophia arrived and she was shown to the manager's office on the first floor. Yianni the Arab, as he was known because he was a Greek from Egypt, sat at his desk counting the previous evening's takings while listening to the music of Sofia Vembo. Sophia had known him ever since she was reunited with Vangelis. He was a tough character, always impeccably dressed in handmade suits. He wore a fedora over one eye in a rakish manner. He reminded her of a Hollywood gangster.

'How's that daughter of yours?' Yianni asked, still counting the money. 'Any time she wants to sing popular songs, tell her to give me a call.'

He put the money in a paper bag and locked it away in a safe behind a large poster of a singer; a beautiful doll-like creature with eastern looks. Nadya, as she was called, bore a striking resemblance to Nitsa.

'The Germans love her,' Yianni smiled, noticing Sophia's interest in her. 'Who wouldn't? And so versatile too—Dietrich, Rina Ketty, Hildegard, Rosita Serrano. You name them, she is their equal; even our own Sofia Vembo.'

'Quite a woman,' said Sophia, surprised that anyone could have such a voice range.

Yianni lit a cigar, sat back in his chair and put his feet on the desk. His smart white shoes with tan inserts and brown leather soles were spotlessly clean. Leather was a scarce commodity and Sophia marveled that Yianni still had access to such shoes.

'I'm serious, you know. Maria would make far more money here than she would singing at those parties...what do you call it—Lider?'

'Lieder,' smiled Sophia.

He laughed. 'I never was one for that highbrow stuff. All I know is that the people crave popular music—something that takes their minds off their troubles.'

'I'll tell her, but I'd be surprised if she would take your advice. Opera is what she does best.'

'Nonsense. If she has a voice she can sing anything.'

Vangelis arrived and Yianni picked up his hat and left the room. 'Don't you forget our little chat now, will you?' he said, giving her a wink.

'What was all that about?' asked Vangelis when they were alone.

'Oh, nothing. It's just a silly idea of his to get Maria to forget opera and sing here.'

Vangelis laughed. 'Working in this place is not for the faint-hearted. You have to be thick-skinned.'

He poured himself a whiskey.

'Pour one for me,' said Sophia. She took one sip and screwed up her face. 'I never could stand the stuff, but I suppose now's as good a time as any to start.'

Vangelis pulled up a chair and sat beside her. She asked why he hadn't told her about Maria being under surveillance.

'How could I tell you? I had no real proof of her treachery and I still don't. Whatever George the Englishman knew he kept to himself. Anyway, what could be so important that you came to see me today? Is something bothering you?'

'I saw Penelope today, for the first time in over two years. She told me about her father.'

'That old fool!'

'Well, it seems that "that old fool" is intending to marry Maria.'

If it wasn't for the tears welling up in Sophia's eyes, Vangelis would have burst out laughing. She told him the whole story; how Penelope was sure that the pair had met in Germany, well before she returned to Greece. Vangelis shook his head in disbelief.

'My head's spinning,' she said, the tears rolling down her cheeks. 'I can't think straight anymore.' Her eyes pleaded with him. 'You must help me.'

Vangelis pulled her to him in a brotherly embrace. It hurt him to see her like this.

'Look at me,' he said, lifting her chin to face him. 'I'm here for you. We've been through too much to give up now.'

Not for the first time he saw just how beautiful her eyes were. It was her amethyst eyes that had caught his attention when he first met her and now, after all those years, they were just as beautiful and her tears only served to deepen their intensity.

'I'm glad you came,' he said, gently wiping away her tears with his finger. 'Now, I want you to go straight home and get some rest. Don't worry, we'll work this out.'

Getting up to leave, she took another look at the poster of Nadya.

'Doesn't she remind you of someone?'

Vangelis smiled. 'You mean Nitsa? Yes, and if you saw her perform, you would think she was her twin.'

The following Saturday evening, the four women took a taxi to The Black Cat nightclub. In the foyer, Yianni the Arab awaited their arrival with great anticipation. He paced the floor nervously, shouting orders at any employee who happened to come near him. He had every reason to be nervous. Tonight Vangelis had organized the line-up for the cabaret, promising that it would be an evening to remember. He had better be right or he would find himself looking for employment elsewhere.

The tables in the dance hall were steadily filling and the band had already started to play when the women walked in.

'Welcome to The Black Cat, Kyria Laskaris,' smiled Yianni, dropping the familiarity of the previous week. 'How wonderful of you to join us; tonight's show promises to be one of our best. We have a superb line-up of talent and I'm sure you won't be disappointed.'

Yianni recognized Esther immediately. 'Ahh, the charming Miss Rosen. How good to see you again. Where have you been hiding yourself? It's been a while since you graced us with your company. Let me see, when was the last time?'

'Before the Germans arrived,' she answered curtly.

Yianni looked around uncomfortably. 'Unfortunately, we can't always choose who we do business with. I'm sure you understand.'

He turned to Chrysoula. It was the first time she had ever set foot in such a place and she was clearly overwhelmed. 'Let's hope we will see more of you,' he said to her.

'And this must be...' He fixed his attention on Maria. She was staring at a gilt-framed photograph of Nadya in the center of the foyer, with the words 'Tonight Only,' plastered across one corner. Far away in her thoughts, she had not heard him.

'Maria,' said Sophia.

She turned to face him. Yianni was accustomed to beautiful women, but something about her intimidated him. She had a cold type of beauty that he found disconcerting.

'Let me say what a great honor it is to have you here with us this evening. The Black Cat is not the opera and I confess to knowing very little about such music, but I can guarantee you an excellent evening of entertainment. And now if you will follow me, we have reserved a table for you.'

News that Maria Laskaris the opera singer was at The Black Cat had already circulated through the club. Patrons craned their necks to catch a glimpse of her. A bottle of champagne had been placed on the table, next to a bowl of red roses. Yianni uncorked the champagne himself and filled four glasses. Vangelis spotted them and smiled. Sophia lifted her glass to him. The band struck up a Tommy Dorsey number followed by a lively rendition of 'Sand in My Shoes' sung by Hariklia, the resident singer at The Black Cat. The dance floor began to fill with couples eager to display their technical expertise in a foxtrot. Tapping her feet to the music, Chrysoula looked on in awe as women dressed to perfection whirled across the floor in the arms of their impeccably dressed partners. That no one put a step out of place amazed her.

'This beats listening to the same records over and over again,' she said to Esther. 'Do you know, ever since Vangelis dropped a pile of records over last week, Sophia and Maria have done nothing except play them continuously, discussing the merits of each one. I know them so well, I could sing them myself—especially Nadya's latest hit.'

Esther laughed. 'Well, it shouldn't be long before we get to see Nadya in person.'

From the sidelines, Yianni lit a cigar and watched the women. He was joined by a journalist from one of the leading newspapers.

'Are my eyes deceiving me, Yianni?' he asked, looking rather surprised. 'Isn't that Maria Laskaris, the opera singer?'

Aware of admiring eyes, Maria tilted her head provocatively, twisting a curl around her index finger at the nape of her neck. She was dressed in a faded green rayon dress that clung to her body like a second skin. Around her neck she wore a magnificent necklace of subtle gold, studded with diamonds. Every now and again she crossed her long legs, aware of the glint of her silk stockings under the cabaret lights.

'I hear she has a rapacious appetite for extravagant gifts,' the journalist continued. 'Most of them from that wealthy industrialist Sakellariou who follows her around like a crazed lover. By the way, where is he tonight?' He surveyed the room and seeing no sign of him, laughed scornfully. 'She must have given the old dog the slip.'

'There's no doubt about her,' Yianni replied, 'she's some woman and no mistake.'

A Wehrmacht officer approached the table and asked Esther for a dance. Within his circle of friends, Günter's penchant for mannish women was well known and Esther fitted the bill perfectly. Hiding her disgust for Germans well, she accepted.

'Well, well. That's a turn up. The delightful Jewess, Esther Rosen, dancing with a German!' exclaimed the journalist.

'My dear fellow,' replied Yianni, feigning hurt, 'at The Black Cat, we try to leave matters of politics and race at the door—it's much better for business.'

During the interval the dance floor emptied and a tall and lithe dark-skinned woman dressed in skimpy leopard skin and introduced simply as Egyptian Voodoo Woman played a set of African drums with astonishing dexterity. Her act was followed by a juggler dressed as a clown and accompanied by a violinist. Meanwhile, patrons moved to the cocktail bar or mingled around the tables.

Before long a bell announced the second half of the show and everyone returned to their seats. Nadya was the reason that most people were there that evening, and no one wanted to miss her opening. The floodlights turned onto the stage and a hush descended on the room. After what seemed like an eternity, Nadya failed to appear. Vangelis took the orchestra through one song after another. Still there was no sign of Nadya. The crowd became impatient. Here and there shouts echoed through the room. People began to stamp their feet and men of impeccable character resorted to cat-calls.

The journalist began to scribble notes. 'Well, Yianni, the evening is turning out to be extremely interesting. I daresay that if Nadya fails to appear, you may find yourself in a sticky situation.'

The growing clamor of dissent made Yianni decidedly uneasy. Red-faced, he stormed onto the stage begging for calm.

'Ladies and gentlemen, please remain seated. We have a small hiccup. Nothing to worry about, I assure you. Unfortunately, Nadya has been delayed. We expect her here at any moment. In the meantime, dear patrons, please enjoy the music of Hariklia.'

The crowd refused to be quiet.

'What about the curfew?' someone shouted. 'We haven't got all night.'

A quarrel broke out at one table and threatened to turn what until now had been an amicable evening into something unpleasant. Sophia, Esther, and Chrysoula watched with growing alarm. Only Maria retained her composure. Despite the cries of 'Hush!' around them, the crowd threatened to turn nasty.

It was then that Maria stood up and with great self-assurance walked across the dance floor towards the stage. The crowd watched as if mesmerized. By the time she reached Vangelis the uproar had settled down, replaced by an expectant hush. Yianni stood paralyzed. Surely she wasn't going to add insult to injury by singing opera?

Maria whispered a few words to Vangelis and then walked to the center of the stage. She looked back over her shoulder to Vangelis and nodded for him to begin. The band struck up the first few bars and with a smile that warmed the audience in an instant, Maria launched into an unforgettable and spine-chilling performance of Hildegard's great hit 'The Touch of Your Lips.' The audience went wild.

Yianni stood at the edge of the stage, fanning himself with a souvenir program and trying to gather his thoughts. Vangelis looked at him and winked. 'Damn that bastard,' he cursed to himself. 'Is that what he meant when he promised a night to remember?'

The journalist leaned over his shoulder. 'Well, Yianni, this certainly is an unforgettable night. I wouldn't have missed it for the world. She's a sensation.'

Meanwhile, somewhere in the suburbs of Athens, an angry Nadya hurled abuse at her incompetent driver for getting them lost. And in a villa in Kolonaki, a despondent Petros Sakellariou entertained his guests… without Maria.

# CHAPTER 30

*Athens, Spring 1942*

Over the next few days Maria scoured the newspapers for reviews of her performance at The Black Cat. All spoke about her in glowing terms. She was ecstatic. Just lately, performing the same old thing at parties was becoming tiresome. And this was just what she needed to give her a new lease of life.

Chrysoula commented on the fact that for once, she understood what Maria was singing about. 'I never could get my head around opera,' she laughed. 'Far too highbrow for me!'

'I'll let you into a little secret,' replied Maria. 'I always wanted to be a cabaret singer.'

Chrysoula looked surprised. 'Then why did you choose a career in opera?'

Maria shrugged her shoulders. 'Perhaps a part of me wanted to please my mother. She thought opera a more acceptable path for a woman of good standing to take. After all, entertainers in nightclubs don't exactly enjoy a good reputation do they?'

'I don't know about that. Look at Vangelis. He's made a name for himself. It wasn't all that long ago that he was a bouzouki player. Now he's a band leader. I can name a lot more. Take Sofia Vembo for a start—no one would speak ill of her.'

'She's not exactly a nightclub singer,' laughed Maria, handing Chrysoula another cutting. 'When we lived in Smyrna, the whole family used to frequent the popular kafenia and nightspots along the quayside. I recall how much we Greeks loved our entertainment. It was a part of who we were, always enjoying life to the full. There was one particular venue— Café Aphrodite—which boasted the best entertainment in Smyrna. Anyone who was anyone played there, including Vangelis. That was where he first sang "In the Mountains of Smyrna."'

It wasn't often that Maria wanted to engage in conversation and Chrysoula listened intently.

'In those days he played the laouto. He often accompanied a singer called Nitsa.'

Chrysoula pricked up her ears. Was this the same Nitsa who she had overheard Sophia and Vangelis discussing a week earlier?

'Nitsa was a very beautiful and seductive woman who held her audience spellbound. She was like no other woman I've ever seen or I am likely to see again.'

Maria became despondent, and for the first time Chrysoula sensed vulnerability underneath the haughty veneer. 'From the moment I saw her, I wanted to be like her, but I knew my mother would never have approved.'

'Why ever not? Didn't your mother like her?'

'My mother certainly admired her talent and Vangelis adored her. I had only just started to get to know her when we had to flee.' Maria tapped the table nervously with her blood-red nails. 'It all seems like a dream now but I remember clearly that at some point we found ourselves hiding in Café Aphrodite. The Turks were scouring the place for us and there was no escape. It was then that Nitsa hid us under the stage and...'

Chrysoula put her hand to her mouth, as if anticipating what she was about to hear. Maria found it hard to say the words. She clasped the palms of her hands over her ears as if to drown out the sounds. 'And then they raped and killed her. She died saving us.'

Chrysoula had heard of the terrible atrocities committed in Smyrna but this brought home the horror of it all.

'So you see,' said Maria, pulling herself together, 'that's why I sang the other night when Nadya failed to show up. I took her place because I was doing it for Nitsa.'

From her apartment in Piraeus, Nadya's anger knew no bounds. Until now she had been the most sought-after singer on the cabaret circuit, and she didn't take kindly to competition. Her anger reached boiling point when Yianni the Arab informed her that he had signed Maria as top billing and Nadya would be relegated to second billing. Used to having her own way, Nadya considered this an insult. In a fit of anger she hurled a glass at him, knocking his fedora to the ground and causing a nasty gash on his forehead.

'I curse you!' she screamed hysterically. 'You will live to regret the day you dumped me for a collaborator!'

Keeping his anger in check, Yianni wiped the blood trickling down his face with his white handkerchief. 'I don't care who likes the Germans and who doesn't,' he answered. 'This is nothing personal. It's business and you would do well to remember that.'

Her hands on her hips, Nadya mocked him and spat on the floor.

'If you don't care to work for me,' replied Yianni, 'there's always The Athenian in Omonia.' He picked up his fedora, brushed its side with his well-manicured hands and turned to leave. 'But a word of caution, Nadya—don't listen to gossip. It's not wise to call someone a collaborator, especially when you have no proof. The Germans won't take too kindly to that. I don't want to see my club closed or, God forbid, anything untoward happen to you, so… keep that pretty mouth and that temper of yours in check.'

'Get out!' she screamed, picking up an ashtray in readiness to throw it. 'Get out of my sight!'

Back at the club, a pretty female usher attended to his wound with a cold compress. There was a knock at the door and Vangelis entered. Yianni asked the girl to leave them alone.

'That looks bad,' said Vangelis. 'Woman trouble?'

Yianni scowled. 'Listen to me,' he replied angrily, 'I have signed Maria Laskaris at your behest. There had better not be any trouble or both of you will be out. Is that understood?'

'Come on, Yianni,' he laughed. 'Think of the money she will bring in. And anyway, since when have women got the better of you?'

Yianni wagged his finger at him. 'You are a rascal, Kapitanos Vangelis. You are a likeable one at that.'


In the spring of 1942, George the Englishman called another meeting. He informed them that Cairo and London were more than pleased with their progress. As a result they would be expanding their operations throughout the rest of Greece. In particular, he praised the work of the individuals involved in the sabotage units which had successfully disrupted the flow of arms from Germany destined for Rommel's East Africa Corps in North Africa.

He singled out Sophia for her tireless work in recruiting individuals through her charity work in the urban areas where grievances of a disenfranchised population had the people at breaking point. Living virtually from hand to mouth, she found many families still harboring stranded soldiers, despite threats of death by the authorities if they were caught. Thanks to her new contacts, more safe houses and escape routes had been established and a number of men were safely smuggled out of the country. It had been noted that more and more men and women were fleeing to join the embryonic guerilla bands in the mountains.

George concluded the meeting by telling them that this would be the last time he would see them. His mission in Athens had been fulfilled and someone else would take his place. In the meantime, Mikhailis would coordinate further activities. As always, he urged caution. The Germans were stepping up their counterintelligence and for their own safety, each person was to choose a *nom de guerre*.

Sophia thought long and hard about her codename. For her, it must be as symbolic as Athos—the name given to their group in honor of the great capital of Byzantine monasticism. In the end she chose Helene, after her courageous friend in Constantinople. For Vangelis, it was easy. He chose Markos, after the great friend who introduced him to Sophia. A few hours later, George boarded a fishing boat taking him to an Aegean island and then on to Turkey. Sophia was bitterly disappointed that she hadn't had the chance to talk to him about Maria and, in particular, her connection with Sakellariou.

Vangelis saw the look of disappointment on her face. 'Come on,' he said. 'I'll walk you home. It's my night off.'

It had been a while since she had seen him and she looked forward to his company. There was a cold chill in the air when they left. Plateia Lysikatous was empty and the sound of their footsteps resonated through the square. Sophia looped her arm through Vangelis's to gain a little warmth.

'How's she going?' she asked, referring to Maria.

Vangelis laughed. 'Yianni the Arab never had it so good. The place is packed night after night. Even with more tables, he still has to turn people away.'

'Do you think she knows we set her up?' she asked.

He tapped the side of his nose and smiled. 'Our secret is safe. Yianni is too busy counting his money to ask any questions and the only other person who knows is Nadya's chauffeur, and he has been paid handsomely, and no longer works for her. However difficult it was, we did the right thing. Her interest in Sakellariou appears to have waned. In fact, if I am a good judge of character, she seems quite bored by him. The problem is that he will not give her up easily. In fact, he pays Yianni handsomely for his private table where he can be seen night after night, waiting for her to appear. Yianni has complained that the drink is beginning to get the better of him. If it wasn't for his money—and to some extent, his ruthless character—he would ban him completely. For a man with so much power, he has become a laughing stock.'

They walked along Athinas towards Plateia Omonia and on towards Kypseli. Despite the presence of German troops the hungry and homeless still huddled in doorways. By ten o'clock they would be gone, scattering like rats into the darkness.

'I often wondered what would have happened if I had taken your advice and left Smyrna on the *Medusa*,' said Sophia. 'Maybe we would still be living in Constantinople. To think we left all that behind. Turkey is not even in this war, yet war and discontent seem to follow us like a shadow.'

After the population exchange of 1923, an agreement was drawn up allowing a number of Greeks to live in Constantinople in exchange for Muslim farmers being still able to maintain their lands in western Thrace. It was viewed by many as a tenuous agreement. Many Greeks chose to leave rather than be at the mercy of the Turks, who still harbored a deep hatred towards them.

'We know nothing for sure; truth is hidden at the bottom of the well,' remarked Vangelis.

Sophia laughed. 'You sound just like my grandmother.'

He looked thoughtful. 'That leather satchel—the one she asked me to give you just before we left…did you ever read the contents?'

'I couldn't bear to open it and I forgot all about it until I found the old suitcase when Nina's apartment was requisitioned. It's still in it, next to my bed. Since then, I've often thought about it but something always stops me from reading it. I don't know what it is. Perhaps the fear of unlocking the past and not knowing if I'm strong enough to deal with it.'

'Don't wait too long,' Vangelis cautioned. 'Time doesn't always give us that luxury.'

After dinner, Sophia retired to her room early giving Chrysoula strict instructions not to disturb her. She picked up the tattered brown suitcase and placed it on the bed. It bore little resemblance to the one she had used on her sojourns to Paris with Andreas, or for her weekend on Prinkipo with Nikolai and Anastasia. In fact she marveled that it was still in one piece; the flight from Smyrna had almost destroyed it.

With great trepidation she unlocked the clasps and flipped back the top. For a few minutes she sat motionless, almost detached, staring at the remnants of her former life as if they had nothing to do with her. She opened the Damascene jewelry box. Its priceless collection was long gone, sold off to pay for the apartment in Monastiraki. The only thing that remained was the locket, carefully folded away in a silk wrap. Next to the box was a thick envelope containing family photographs. A deep pain pierced her heart. Even now she couldn't bring herself to look at them and put them to one side. Finally, she came to what she had been looking for: her grandmother's memoirs. With trembling hands she removed the manuscript and recognized her grandmother's handwriting. A strange thing happened. She felt Dimitra's presence and with it a deep sense of calm.

When Sophia came out of her room the next morning Chrysoula noticed that she looked different. 'I had the best night's sleep in a while,' said Sophia.

No sooner had she sat down to eat her breakfast when the telephone rang. Chrysoula went into the hallway to answer it. When she returned, her face was as white as a ghost.

'I've got bad news. That was Kyrios Sakellariou on the phone. Penelope has suffered a stroke and is not expected to live. She's asked to see you. His car is on the way.'

Maria had been asleep until the sound of the telephone woke her. Hearing the front door slam shut, she looked out of her bedroom window just in time to see her mother drive away. She recognized the car immediately. Slipping on her dressing gown, she called for Chrysoula.

'Do you know why my mother left in that car? Is everything alright?'

'It's Penelope. She's had a stroke. The prognosis is not good.'

Maria brushed her hair back from her face with her hand. 'Oh!' she exclaimed. 'The poor woman. I daresay she will get the best of medical attention. It's a miracle what doctors can do these days.'

Chrysoula shook her head at Maria's cold response. 'If there's nothing else,' she said frostily, 'I'd like to get on with my work.'

'Yes, of course,' replied Maria. She took off the dressing gown and went back to bed. 'I think I'll sleep a while longer. Too little sleep makes me irritable and I have a big night tonight. Oh, and if you hear any more news about Penelope, do let me know.'

Several cars stood in the driveway when Sophia arrived at the house, and two of them displayed cloth flags with the swastika painted on them. She was shown into the drawing room where friends and relatives gathered. A blonde woman with a German accent approached her.

'Such a tragedy. A young woman in the prime of her life,' she said. 'And those poor children, what will become of them?'

Her husband came over and joined them. Sophia recognized the single oak leaf tabs on the collar of his uniform as that of the rank of Standartenführer—a regiment leader of the SS. In his hand he held his peaked cap bearing the SS eagle and the death's head insignia. These were emblems to which she had by now become accustomed. That Penelope's husband's and father's affiliations were closely linked to the Germans was evident for all to see.

When Sakellariou entered the room Sophia hardly recognized him. He had aged so much. The lofty arrogance of his former years had all but disappeared and she thought him someone to be pitied rather than feared. He came straight over to her.

'Thank you for coming. She's been asking for you.'

She followed him upstairs and down a long corridor filled with heavy antique furniture and the occasional potted palm. A maid came out of Penelope's room carrying a pile of linen. Inside, the doctor stood by the bedside sorting out various bottles of medicine.

'The problem has been exacerbated by her tuberculosis,' Sakellariou said.

He drew up a chair next to the bed. 'Please,' he said to Sophia, 'take a seat.'

Penelope's eyes were closed and her mouth contorted. The stroke had paralyzed the left side of her body. Her eyes slowly opened and she forced a smile.

'I knew you'd come,' she murmured.

When she saw her father standing at the foot of the bed, her body stiffened and her face displayed a look of anxiousness.

'Please give us five minutes alone, Papa,' she said.

Sakellariou was reluctant to leave until the doctor assured him that five minutes could do her no harm. 'If you need me, I will be outside,' he told Sophia.

When they were alone, Penelope relaxed. She beckoned Sophia to come closer.

'I called for you because I want to tell you about Maria. I won't live much longer and you must know. It's something my mother told me—long before the war. Sometime in 1936 I think, when my father began to go away to Germany. During a function in Berlin he met your daughter. My father always had an eye for beautiful women, and they became friends. In exchange for acquiring several industrial contracts, the Nazis asked something of him in return. He was to recruit people sympathetic to their cause; people who could tell them of those whose political persuasions were either communist or anti-fascist. In other words, informers. In exchange for this information, they received tokens of gratitude—contracts like my father has, or in the case of Maria, money and jewels. Every time my father won a contract he boasted about it to my mother. She was much too meek to argue and stood by my father no matter what.'

Penelope forced a smile. 'My father has no idea that I know. It was a secret between my mother and me. It seems that he recruited sympathizers in several cities: Amsterdam, Prague, and of course, Paris. Maria was a willing participant. When Metaxas formed government in 1936, many Venizelists fled the country. Most of them ended up in Paris. As a Greek opera singer, she moved through the upper echelons of high society with ease. She knew all the prominent Greeks and their political affiliations. All this information was sent to my father. My mother found evidence of her letters in a file but it has since been destroyed.'

Sophia hung on to every word. She had no doubt that what Penelope was telling her was true—she knew her daughter only too well.

'Then why did she return to Athens if she was of more use to the Germans in Paris?'

'Several Greeks began to suspect that she was an informer. Berlin could no longer guarantee her protection. For her safety, they advised her to return to Greece—under the protection of my father.'

Listening to this, it all began to make sense. In her heart of hearts, Sophia always knew that Maria had not returned simply to be reunited with her family.

'I'm sorry, Sophia. I should have told you long ago, but how can a mother bear to hear such a thing about her daughter?'

Sophia choked back the tears. 'This is not the time for regrets,' she replied. 'I know how hard this must have been for you, but please…tell me one thing. Is she still an informer?'

'I don't know for sure. All I know is that she has no respect or use for my father any longer…especially since she started singing at The Black Cat.'

'Then doesn't that put her in danger if he knows her past?'

Penelope smiled. 'He still loves her; that alone binds him to her. To betray her is to betray himself, and he would be anxious to avoid a scandal.'

The voices in the corridor grew louder and Sakellariou and the doctor entered the room. Penelope gripped Sophia's hand. An expression of fear appeared on her face and she tried to speak but the words would not come.

'That's enough for today, Kyria Laskaris,' said the doctor. 'Penelope must have her rest.'

Sophia watched helplessly as Penelope gasped for breath and began to convulse. In a matter of minutes the convulsions stopped and a calm expression appeared on her face. Sakellariou broke down—his grief was more for himself than for his daughter. Sophia looked at him with contempt. Quietly, she slipped out of the room.

# CHAPTER 31

*Athens, Summer 1942*

After the funeral, Sophia told Vangelis about Maria's treachery. He was as shocked as she had been to hear the extent of her involvement. He also had news for her. Athos had discovered that Penelope's husband's secretary worked for the Gestapo long before the two became lovers.

'Penelope had few friends,' said Vangelis. 'And when he learned she had contacted you, he asked his mistress to keep an eye on you both. In fact, everyone in the household reported back to him. Penelope had every reason to be scared.'

'So she must have been the woman in the window who watched me leave.'

'Do you remember what she looked like?'

Sophia shook her head. 'Not much…other than she appeared to be of medium height and quite thin with short dark hair.'

The conversation turned to Sakellariou. 'He's become a laughing stock,' Vangelis told her. 'Since Maria started working at The Black Cat, he's gone downhill. He often arrives at the club drunk, and after the show he insists on going backstage to pay his respects to her. There he makes a fool of himself by giving her flowers and pleading with her to have a drink with him. A few nights ago the situation worsened. He went to her dressing room and begged her to reconsider his offer of marriage, threatening to kill himself if she refused. Maria warned him that if he didn't stop pestering her she would have him thrown out, once and for all. He became violent and by the time we were alerted, Maria was threatening to kill him with a knife. We managed to calm him and he apologized. Not until he was escorted out of the premises could I persuade Maria to give me the knife. "I would have used it," she told me. I believed her.

'When Yianni heard about this, he was furious. He called Maria to his office and gave her a dressing down, but because of his connections and the fact that Sakellariou spends a considerable amount of money at the club, he refuses to ban him. Instead, he ordered Maria to get her affairs in order. "Whatever it is between the two of you, sort it out—and quickly!" he said angrily. "Star or no star, I will tear up your contract."'

Sophia listened to this latest news with an air of someone used to receiving bad news. 'I don't like what I hear,' she told him. 'The character flaws of both Sakellariou and Maria are a lethal combination.'

'You may be right,' replied Vangelis.

Several weeks later, Vangelis broke the news to Sophia that Maria had fallen for a German. From the moment Vangelis saw Yianni seat him at the most prominent table in the cabaret, he knew he must be someone of importance.

'Yianni usually tells us who his most important patrons are so that we play their favorite tunes. In Maria's case, he had no need to tell her. As soon as she laid eyes on him she fell head over heels. It was as though she sang only for him. If I am a good judge of men, he feels the same. He is mesmerized by her and has been back every night. Needless to say, Yianni is overjoyed.

'As you can imagine,' he continued, 'Sakellariou is beside himself with jealousy but he must know who the man is, as he keeps himself in check. Eventually, I confronted Yianni as to who the man was. At first, he was reluctant to talk about him. Finally, he relented. "Ah well," he said. "You will find out sooner or later so I may as well tell you. His name is Klaus Reinhardt and he's the newly appointed counterintelligence chief. He's probably the most important man in Athens—the head of the Gestapo."'

Sophia thought she would faint. Two weeks later she received the news that Sakellariou was dead. His death was front-page news in all the papers. As a prominent businessman he had been well respected by members of the previous Metaxas government and by many in the quasi-government under the occupation. Little was said about the actual death, except that he was shot by an intruder while walking his dogs in the garden at his home in Kolonaki. The police issued a statement that no stone would be left unturned until the murderer was caught.

It was some weeks before Sophia discovered the truth about Sakellariou's death. Maria didn't want to talk about it. Vangelis left Athens with his band to play on the island of Syros. When she did see him again, it was at a meeting of Athos where they were introduced to George the Englishman's successor, Thymios, alias Balthazar. Thymios was an engineer from Arachova near Delphi. It was a mountainous and wild area, awash with wildflowers in the spring and snowcapped and inhospitable in the winter. He liked to say that he knew the area like a mountain goat—something that would prove invaluable for Athos.

He was an excellent organizer, ensuring that each recruit was allocated the job most suited to them. While many undertook extensive sabotage training in the mountains, Mikhailis's granddaughter Effie opted to train as a wireless operator. Sophia taught others how to memorize their messages and write them on silk, rice paper, and sheets of filo pastry—all of which could easily be hidden or destroyed at a moment's notice. Within weeks of Thymios taking charge, Athos was an effective espionage group capable of tackling the most complex of missions.

With Vangelis back in Athens, he and Sophia resumed their weekly lunchtime rendezvous at a taverna in Monastiraki. There was much to talk through together.

'What really did happen to Sakellariou?' she asked. 'Surely you don't expect me to believe the newspapers, do you?'

Vangelis lit a cigarette and took a deep breath. 'Night after night, he watched Maria fall in love with the German. After her performances, she took to joining him for a drink at his table—something Sakellariou could never get her to do. Not only that, but they often danced together and it was obvious to everyone that the pair had fallen in love. Finally, Sakellariou could no longer control himself. When no one was looking, he went backstage to her dressing room and waited for her. When she returned he confronted her. She tried to leave but he lashed out, knocking her into a vase of lilies and sending them crashing to the floor.

'The moment I noticed him missing, I rushed to her room and heard them arguing. He was wild with rage, telling her that he would let everyone know the truth about her. If he couldn't have her, then no one else would. Even my presence didn't deter him. She tried to run towards me and at that point he pulled out a gun. I knew that he would have used it and I had no alternative but to kill him. The commotion alerted others. Yianni ran into the room and seeing the body lying there, he slammed the door shut before anyone else realized what had happened. Suddenly we heard the Germans in the corridor and a loud knock on the door. The blood drained from Yianni's face. In a flash Maria snatched the gun from my hand. Reinhardt entered the room and surveyed the scene in front of him with absolute coolness. He turned to his associates and murmured for them to wait outside. For a few moments no one said a word and then Maria began to sob.

'"It was him or me," she whimpered. "I had to defend myself."

'By this time, the tears were streaming down her face and she was shaking. The German stepped over the body, wiped away her tears, and looked across at Yianni, telling him that no harm must come to her. "Get rid of the body as quickly as possible," he ordered, "and we'll pretend it never happened."

'He turned back to Maria, kissed her forehead and cautioned her to be careful of the company she kept. After he left, Yianni collapsed into the chair—we had all had a close shave. During the quiet hours of curfew we managed to dump his body outside a brothel near Athinas Street.'

Sophia thought about the morning of Andreas's death. This was the second time Maria had been witness to a death, and the second time that she finished with the gun in her hand. Thank God Dimitra was not here to hear about it. She also thought about the bodies in the olive barrels and of Sergei's body being exchanged for that of a pauper's.

'First Constantinople…now Athens,' she said with a smile. 'It seems you're becoming quite adept at disposing of bodies. But tell me one thing. Why Athinas? And why did the papers report him being found in his garden?'

'Think about it,' Vangelis replied. 'They could hardly report him found in the red-light district could they? This way, his fine reputation is still intact.'

Sophia was still puzzled. 'I don't understand. Why did Maria snatch the gun from you? She could have easily been blamed for his death.'

'I have to admit that was a shock to me as well. It was too late to take her home, and Yianni let her sleep on the couch in his office. Sometime later I went upstairs to check on her. She heard my footsteps. "I couldn't sleep and you startled me," she said.

'She asked me to come and sit next to her. "Why did you do it?" I asked. "Why did you take the gun and make out you were the one who shot him?" "Because I knew Klaus would believe me over you," she replied. "And because I couldn't let you take the blame for defending me."

'I assured her that this would have been my problem and I was quite capable of looking after myself. She laughed. "Oh, Vangelis. If only you knew. Then what would my mother have had to say? That it was *my* fault… again?" She pulled the blanket across her chest, leaned back on the pillow, and looked into my eyes. In the soft light, with her red hair tumbling over the pillow, she looked strikingly beautiful.

'"You know," she said, referring to Sakellariou, "he really was a horrible man." I told her I agreed. "You and I may not have always seen eye to eye," she continued, "but I have you to thank for getting me to work here. I know what you did to poor Nadya; I found out later." Her words took me by surprise, and she laughed again. "I am my mother's daughter. It's from her that I get my survival skills, although I don't think she'd like to hear me say that. It was a stroke of good fortune that I was able to pursue a career in opera, but ever since I first saw Nitsa I wanted to be like her. I adored her… and I have you to thank for all this—you have given me back my happiness."

'I asked her to tell me about Manolios. She said that he was the love of her life and the reason that she never bothered to marry. Then I asked her about Reinhardt and whether she realized who he was. She did. But what difference would that make? He had a job to do and that didn't affect their feelings for each other. She loved him—that was all that mattered, and after the war she intended to marry him. Nothing was going to stand in her way this time.'

Maria's relationship not only put her life in danger with the Resistance, but with the Germans too. For security reasons German men had been ordered to keep away from Greek women. Sakellariou had gone. Reinhardt posed a bigger problem.

At the end of April Sophia received a devastating phone call. Mikhailis's granddaughter Effie had been shot dead while resisting arrest outside the school where she taught. Sophia simply could not believe it. Sweet Effie. Just a child—dead. The words rang in her ears. With Effie's death, everyone in Athos was advised to be extremely vigilant. No one except the immediate family was allowed to attend the funeral. This news shook Sophia badly and made her realize just how precarious their lives had become. It was Constantinople all over again. Effie's death preyed on her mind and she couldn't help thinking about an incident which took place almost a week before her death.

It was a Tuesday afternoon, the day that Effie called into the shop to pick up any information that Sophia might have gathered during the week. Sophia always made sure that she was there. Effie never stayed long, just long enough for them to enjoy a quiet coffee and a chat about the latest fashions, and then she would leave. On that particular Tuesday, Sophia was out delivering a dress to a customer and she had been delayed. In the meantime a woman came into the shop and asked to see their latest collection, as she was thinking of having something special made. Esther quickly looked her up and down, surprised that such a badly dressed woman showed an interest in fashion. She wore an ill-fitting woolen coat with a rather garish enamel and gold brooch in the shape of a butterfly in the lapel, and her shoes were black and slightly scuffed, with wooden soles. All of this Esther found tasteless. At some point, Effie arrived and asked for Sophia. Esther apologized on Sophia's behalf but as she had seen her many times before, she asked her to wait a moment—she had something for her. Unaware of the real reason behind Effie's visit, Esther went into the sewing room and brought out a brown paper parcel.

'Here you are. She prepared it for you before she left and I'm sure she would want me to give it to you.'

Effie's cheeks reddened. She had been told never to accept packages from anyone other than Sophia.

'Go on. Take it,' urged Esther. 'It's the fabric you ordered several weeks ago. It arrived last week.'

With the other woman listening, she didn't want to argue. Effie thanked her and left. The woman watched her pedal away on her bicycle.

'A pretty thing,' she remarked.

Esther agreed and asked if there was anything else she could do for her.

'Thank you. I have seen all that I need. I'll return when Kyria Laskaris is here.'

'Who shall I say called?' asked Esther.

The woman turned abruptly. Instead of answering, she indicated a large sign over a display cabinet where Esther used to display her furs.

'Rosen Furs. That's a Jewish name isn't it?'

The woman's remark caught Esther by surprise and the obvious shock seemed to delight her. She left without leaving her name.

When Sophia returned, Esther was shaken. From her description of the woman, Sophia was in no doubt as to who the visitor was—Penelope's husband's mistress. Sophia waited for her to return but she never did. Now she couldn't help thinking that the two incidents were connected.

With an hour to spare before her Sunday lunchtime rendezvous with Vangelis, Sophia decided to take a stroll through the ancient agora. It was a beautiful spring day; wildflowers pushed their colorful blooms between the crevices of archaic rocks and marbles, and the scent of acacia and pine filled the air. Along the pathway, she heard the soft tinkle of a goat bell and noticed an old woman sitting under a tree watching her goat graze in a patch of yellow daisies. Sophia recognized her as the wife of Sophocles, the butcher who lived in the same street as Kyria Koula the fortuneteller.

'Good day, Kyria Laskaris. What a lovely surprise to see you again. How is that daughter of yours, the archeologist? I used to see her here all the time.'

Sophia told her that Nina was living overseas and had given birth to a daughter, Eleni. She omitted to say that she hadn't heard from her for a while now.

'God protect them. She's a good girl.'

The woman proceeded to tell Sophia of those in the neighborhood who had not survived the famine: Alexandros the cobbler and his parents, Maroulia the greengrocer's wife, and three of their children. The list went on and on. She retrieved a large white handkerchief from her skirt pocket and wiped her eyes.

'God is punishing us,' she wailed, 'for our sins in Asia Minor.'

Sophia wanted to tell her that that was over twenty years ago and even

God had more things to occupy himself with these days. Instead, she asked after Kyria Koula. The woman rolled her eyes and tutted.

'That useless son of hers…The rumor is that he went to live in Piraeus with a *putana*. No one has seen him since. Not even when we laid his poor mother in the ground.'

Sophia started at the news. 'You mean she died too?'

'*Aman*…She was one of the first to go. They found her emaciated body frozen to death on the doorstep where she used to tell fortunes.'

'I never knew what to make of her,' said Sophia. 'She was a strange woman and for some reason, she never wanted anything to do with me.'

The woman suddenly stopped wiping her eyes. She looked at Sophia and crossed herself again. 'That's not a good sign.'

Sophia looked puzzled. The woman stood up and untied the rope that tethered the goat to the tree.

'She once told me that some people are doomed from the moment they are born. She could never really explain it, but she always sensed when such people were in her presence. "Destiny does not look favorably on them," she used to say. I do know something though—she was never wrong with her prophecies.'

Sophia felt a lump rise in her throat.

'No one can tell the future. It's foolhardy to think otherwise.'

She had lost count of the times she had told herself this.

The woman detected a hint of fear in Sophia's voice. She made a shrill call, tugged on the rope, and the goat appeared, still munching wildflowers.

'I wouldn't let it worry you, Kyria Laskaris. You are a good woman. God is watching over you.'

When Sophia returned to the taverna the owner pulled her aside, telling her to get away as quickly as possible—there was to be a raid. She was about to leave when armored cars and trucks surrounded the Plateia. Within minutes the taverna was swarming with Germans. A group of men came and blocked her way.

'*Papieren!*' they shouted. 'No one leaves until all documents have been sighted.'

Sophia scrambled to find her identity papers. A man scrutinized them and asked her what she was doing in the taverna unaccompanied. Before she could answer, the taverna owner came over and gave her a neatly wrapped package tied with a white ribbon.

'Don't forget your baklava,' he said. 'And please tell your dear mother that I hope she gets well soon.'

The German looked at the box, hesitated, and then gave Sophia back her papers. With a sideways gesture of his head, he told her to get out. Crossing the Plateia, she made her way through the throng of frightened Greeks as quickly as possible. Many were being pulled aside and pushed into vans. When she reached home and opened the box she heaved a sigh of relief that the German had not asked to see its contents. Due to the difficulty in obtaining sugar, the taverna hadn't sold sweets since the war. Instead of baklava, it contained crumpled newspaper.

Almost an hour after curfew, Vangelis arrived at Thessaly Street. The fact that he had taken such a risk to see her told Sophia that something serious had happened.

'Good God! You look terrible.'

She took his jacket and hung it in the hallway. It was wet with perspiration and inside the inner pocket she caught a glimpse of his pistol.

'Where's Maria?' he asked in a low voice. 'Is she here?'

Knowing that Vangelis would never unburden himself in front of her daughter, Sophia assured him that they were alone.

'And Chrysoula?'

'You don't have to worry. She went to bed hours ago and she sleeps like a log.'

She led him to the drawing room where the last embers of a log fire were still burning. 'Come and sit by the fire; you're shaking like a leaf.'

'There's been a raid today in Plateia Lysikatous. In fact there's been several across Plaka and Monastiraki. You were lucky to get away.' He stared into the fire for a few seconds and then turned to face her. 'Mikhailis and Lina have been taken into custody.'

Sophia let out a silent gasp of despair.

'I found out by accident,' continued Vangelis. 'I was on my way to meet you when I suddenly remembered I had to pick up something from him. I'd almost reached Plateia Lysikatous when I saw the blind beggar. He recognized the sound of my footsteps and called me over. "Kapitanos," he whispered. "It's not safe here. The place is swarming with Germans and Greek militia."

'Then he told me that Mikhailis and Lina had been taken to the Gestapo Headquarters in Merlin Street. I took refuge in a safe house and it was from there that I telephoned the taverna. Later that afternoon I met Thymios. It seems that the Germans have wind of Athos.'

Sophia tried to stay calm but the thought of what the Gestapo would do to Mikhailis and Lina filled her with dread.

'Does this have anything to do with Effie's death?' she asked.

'According to Thymios, Effie told her grandfather that she thought she was being watched. He urged her to get rid of her transmitter and cease all activity for Athos until he could get to the bottom of it. She gave it to him. When the Germans came to the school for her, she knew what would happen if she refused to cooperate. That's when she made a dash for freedom and was fatally shot.'

Listening to Vangelis's story convinced Sophia even more that the woman in the shop had been watching them.

'It's just too much of a coincidence,' she told him.

'You may be right,' Vangelis replied. 'The point is we have bigger worries now that Mikhailis and Lina are in the hands of the Gestapo. They'll interrogate them until they get what they want. Mikhailis is strong, but Lina…God protect her, she could break down. And if she does, the consequences don't bear thinking about.'

Sophia reminded him of the years they were watched by the Secret Police in Constantinople. 'Didn't we learn to live with them? To always be one step ahead?'

Vangelis shrugged. 'We were young, idealistic, and single-minded then.'

'Don't disappoint me,' she said furiously. 'It's not like you to speak like that. We may not be young anymore, but we still have the same values. You and I are fighters. The blood still flows hot in our veins. That's what binds us together.'

Her burst of fury had the desired effect. Vangelis burst out laughing.

'Dear Sophia, what a proud woman! The day Markos sent me to you was the best day of my life.'

Mikhailis and Lina were detained at the Gestapo headquarters for several days. When they refused to cooperate they were removed to Averof Prison in Athens, where the harrowing interrogations continued. A few days later, Thymios asked to see Sophia—he had an assignment for her. She was to visit Lina and report back on her condition. The next day, armed with a package of clean clothes, Sophia joined the throng of distressed families gathered outside the prison gates. It reminded her of her last days in Smyrna when she went to see General Nureddin. Before long she found herself standing in front of a prison guard demanding to know the reason for her visit.

'I'm here to see my Aunt Lina,' replied Sophia. 'Lina Seviloglou.'

The guard discreetly slipped the money she had placed inside her identity papers into his pocket and indicated for her to go to the women's area.

'Over there—Block C,' he said tersely while waving the next visitor towards him.

She crossed the bleak prison yard to where several women sat on the cold stone steps leading to the upper floors. Listening to their conversations, she gathered that many of the women held there had been imprisoned simply for refusing to testify against their relatives. After an hour she was shown to a cell-like room and asked to wait. A shaft of morning light streamed through the small, iron-barred window onto the ochre-colored floor, illuminating two metal chairs and a wooden table. Some minutes later two female guards dragged Lina into the room and sat her on one of the chairs. Her arms and legs were blue and swollen. Her face was so badly beaten that she could hardly open her eyes. Sophia bit her lip to stop herself crying out.

'You have five minutes,' one of the women barked as they left the room.

'Lina,' Sophia said softly. 'It's me, Sophia. I've brought you a change of clothes.' She reached over for her hands—swollen to almost twice the size—and gently stroked them. The cloying stench of body fluids, mingled with fear, made her heave.

'Dear God, what have they done to you?'

Lina tried to speak but her lips could barely move. 'He's still alive you know. They'll never get anything out of him.'

Sophia wondered just how much more of this brutal treatment Lina could take. She didn't have to wait long for her answer.

'They're threatening to kill Mikhailis unless I talk…And they have names—Balthazar, Helene, and Markos, just to mention a few. I can't go on…I'm so very tired.'

Her voice tapered off; blood trickled from the side of her mouth.

Sophia reported her findings to Thymios. When he called her the next day, she already knew what her mission would be.

'If there was anyone else who I could get to do this, I would. The truth is you are the only one who can do it without raising suspicion.'

That evening, Sophia asked Chrysoula to bake a batch of *koulourakia*. The next morning she took one of them, laced it with cyanide, and placed it inside a woolen blanket. Securing the package firmly with string, she left once more for Averof Prison. Luckily, the same guard was on duty. Once again he removed the money from her papers, and without uttering a word he sent her across the yard. When Lina was brought into the room, her condition had deteriorated.

'I've brought you a warm blanket,' said Sophia, placing the package on the table and untying the string. 'Inside is a freshly baked *koulourakia*. I know you like them and I don't imagine you get anything like that in here.'

For a while, Lina stared emptily at the sweet. '*Koulourakia*…' she murmured.

'God bless you. You're a good woman…May the Lord watch over you.'

The look in Lina's eyes spoke volumes. She knew exactly what this meant. With a heavy heart and tears streaming down her face, Sophia left Averof and headed to a kafenion where she had earlier arranged to meet Thymios. By the time she reached there, Lina was already dead. At dawn the following day, Mikhailis and six other prisoners were executed by firing squad.

# CHAPTER 32

*Athens, Spring 1943*

The death of Effie, Mikhailis, and Lina hit Sophia hard. She couldn't shake them from her mind. This was the second time in her life that she had killed someone, but unlike Sergei, whose death had been accidental—the only way she could save herself—Lina's death had been meticulously planned. It didn't matter that Thymios had convinced her that they would all die if Lina talked. She was still a murderer. She had committed a sin and she would have to pay for it in the eyes of God.

On top of this was her growing concern for Nina. It had been well over a year since she had heard from her and she had no idea whether or not her letters to Cairo had been delivered. And then there was Esther. Since news reached her in February that Eichmann's trusted aide, Dieter Wislicency, had arrived in Salonika to implement the deportation of Greek Jews to Poland, Esther was on the verge of collapse.

During the week that Mikhailis and Lina were picked up by the Gestapo, Esther learned that her parents and her sister Rivka and her family had been sent to a concentration camp in Poland—Auschwitz. Esther had been an active member of the Jewish underground and Sophia had always thought that with anti-Jewish sentiment on the rise, one day soon she would leave for Palestine. That time had now arrived and she made one last visit to 31 Thessaly Street to break the sad news to her friend.

'You have made the right decision,' Sophia told her. 'I once had the chance to leave Smyrna before the catastrophe and I didn't take it. Not a day goes by when I don't regret that decision.'

'Tell me, do you really think the Germans will do the same thing to us in Athens as they have in Salonika?' Esther asked wearily.

'We can only hope not.'

'You're not a very good liar, are you, Sophia?' She reached for her briefcase and pulled out a set of documents. 'These are for you. I'm leaving the premises and the business to you. One day soon Greece will be free and

I know that your business will flourish once again—perhaps not to the great heights of La Maison du l'Orient, but enough to see you live out your days in comfort. Please accept this as a token of our friendship.'

Sophia never saw Esther again; she left Athens some days later. She had been a loyal and true friend and Sophia would miss her greatly. Among Esther's many attributes, it was her compassion and zest for life during those dark and difficult years after Smyrna that had kept Sophia going, and she could never thank her enough.

Armed with enough cash and forged documents to get her safely across to Turkey, it was Vangelis who took her to a tiny fishing village on Evia. From there, Crazy Nick—whose black marketeering and escape routes now spanned most of the Aegean—would smuggle her via the Cyclades to Chios and on to Smyrna. There, they would be met by members of the Jewish Resistance.

Three months later, Sophia received word that Esther had reached Jerusalem 'safely and without incident.'

At ten-thirty on the night of September 8, 1943, the brown radio hidden in Sophia's room, next to the battered suitcase containing the remnants of her life in Turkey, hissed and crackled as she tried desperately to tune into the BBC World Service. At long last, she heard the news that she had been waiting for: the Italians had surrendered to the Allies. With Italy out of the war, it was only a matter of time before Germany would be defeated. Sophia could not contain her joy. But Greece divided into the German and Italian zones was now plunged into chaos. Many Italian soldiers, fed up with war and even more so with the brutality of their German counterparts, sold their guns and ammunition to the Resistance. Two weeks later Mussolini, who had earlier been arrested and imprisoned, made a dramatic escape with the aid of the Germans. He set up a puppet government. Faced with the prospect of serving under the Germans or spending the rest of the war in detention camps, thousands of Italian soldiers fled into the mountains to join the Greek Resistance.

Angered by these actions, the Germans brought in battle-hardened troops from the Eastern Front and systematically began a campaign to hunt them down. All over Greece, villages, crops, and churches were razed to the ground. By the end of the war, thousands of innocent civilians and Resistance members would be brutally murdered by the Wehrmacht. Every Greek was now a suspect.

Once again Sophia's business was only just making ends meet and with hardly any fabric left and a diminishing clientele, her heart was not in it. The heyday of La Maison du l'Orient seemed a lifetime ago. She missed Esther's lively company, their chatter about the Hollywood stars and what they were wearing, and she saw very little of Vangelis.

At the beginning of summer Maria left home to live in a villa next to Klaus Reinhardt's in Kolonaki. Away from the public gaze, they were free to carry on their affair. Sophia saw her daughter once a week when they had afternoon tea together at Zaharoplasteion Perikles. It was on these occasions that Maria kept her mother up to date with her social life. She was still the main draw card at The Black Cat. The rest of the time she acted out the part of Reinhardt's mistress, entertaining his guests at the Hotel Grande Bretagne or throwing the occasional cocktail party at his home for important visitors from Berlin.

Sophia wondered just how long this romance would last. Klaus Reinhardt was already married with two children. 'Doesn't that bother you?' Sophia asked. 'The war will end one day and he will return to Berlin. What will you do then?'

'It's not a happy marriage,' replied Maria. 'That's why she stays in Berlin. He will divorce her after the war and then we can be married.'

Sophia wasn't convinced, but to argue would only alienate them again and she was much too shrewd to go down that path.

With the long hot summer drawing to a close, an atmosphere of acute sadness and melancholy hung over Athens. The prospect of another long winter without fuel and food drained the city of what happiness there was. An air of despair descended that was hard to shake off. This war had not ended as they had hoped, and morale was hard to sustain.

Delicate cooking smells wafted through the hallway when Sophia arrived back at Thessaly Street. It was the aroma of Constantinople—Sevkiye's pilav. It had been more than three years since they'd eaten such a delicacy—on the occasion of Nina's wedding to the Englishman. What would make Chrysoula cook it today? There was little to celebrate.

'I've got a surprise for you,' Chrysoula smiled, checking the seasoning in the rice.

She put the lid back on the pot and wiped her hands on her apron. 'Not the pilav, something much better than that.'

At that moment, Sophia suddenly became aware of someone standing in the doorway behind her. A familiar voice greeted her.

'Hello, Mama.'

Sophia spun around. For a brief moment she stared in disbelief, as if caught in a dream from which she did not want to wake.

'Are my eyes deceiving me?' she asked, almost inaudibly. 'Can this be true?'

Nina had come home. The surprise of seeing her daughter standing there before her filled Sophia with happiness and yet at the same time, she felt a rush of unease.

'Where are your husband and your daughter? Is everything alright? It's been so long.' There were too many questions and she didn't know where to begin.

Chrysoula interrupted. 'You can ask all those questions later. For now, the pilav is ready to be served.'

She piled the steaming rice streaked with lamb mince and studded with tender morsels of liver and dried wild cherries onto the serving platter, and stood back admiring her culinary delight. 'Well?' she asked, watching them take their first mouthful. 'How is it?'

'It's absolutely delicious; faultless, in fact. Well done! Sevkiye would be proud of you,' Sophia replied.

Chrysoula smiled with satisfaction.

When they were alone, Nina confided to her mother the real reason for her return to Greece. She had been recruited by the Special Operations Executive, SOE, to carry out an important assignment with Athos. Sophia's joy at having her daughter home suddenly turned to fear.

'Do you know what you've got yourself into?'

Nina laughed. 'A person does not seek his fate: fate seeks him. I learnt that a long time ago.'

Recounting the story, Nina said she was first contacted by SOE Cairo shortly after the birth of Eleni. During one of her visits to the archeological museum an English woman in her late forties approached her and asked if she would like to join her for afternoon tea and a game of bridge at the Gezira Club. This was an exclusive establishment frequented by a cross-section of expatriates and foreigners from around the world. On any given day, one could rub shoulders with generals and ambassadors, or a Russian prince down on his luck, or a coffee plantation owner from Kenya, or shady imposters trading on the black market. It was like Constantinople during the Second World War—a hotbed of intrigue and spies. Intrigued, Nina accepted the invitation.

The woman introduced herself as Mary Wilkins and told her that she was from London and was working for British Intelligence.

'She knew everything about me,' Nina recalled. 'All about Turkey, my life in Athens, and the fact that I excelled in Classical Greek studies and spoke several languages. All of this, she assured me, could be put to great use in assisting the war effort. When I asked how I could be of help, she said she had a mission in mind for me but that it would involve going back to Greece for a few months. She promised me that when the mission was over I would be safely smuggled out of the country again until the war was over. She asked me to think it over but under no circumstances was I to discuss this with David, as he was sure to dissuade me from leaving. Instead of telling him the real reason about returning to Athens, she suggested I make up a little white lie.'

'What did you tell him?' Sophia asked.

Nina shifted uncomfortably in her chair. 'That you were ill and needed me.'

Sophia raised her eyebrows. 'And, Eleni, how were you able to leave your child?'

'Among other things, I'm doing it for her...to give her a better future. You of all people must understand that.'

Sophia detected something odd in her voice. 'Tell me one thing—you say that they knew about your life in Turkey. Did she talk to you about me?'

Nina nodded. 'Mary didn't go into details, but she did tell me that I was from a family who fought for their convictions. When I asked what she meant, she told me about our family's involvement in the Etairia. I pressed her to tell me more. She simply said that you were a brave woman and had risked your life for others, but as you had never mentioned it, it was better left as a closed chapter.' Nina studied her mother's face. 'Is it true, Mama? Were you involved in things that you couldn't tell us about?'

Sophia took a deep breath. 'You were just children then...and it was so long ago. I never told you because it wasn't relevant. Mary Wilkins is right; some things should remain in the past. All I know is that I did what I had to do. They were difficult times and it was a matter of survival.'

'And us, your children—did you ever think about us when you did whatever it was you did?'

Sophia thought about it. 'If I look back now, I would like to say I did it all for you...but the truth is that I did what I thought was right. In doing so, I naturally thought we'd all have a better life.'

'Whatever it was, you did it for the right reasons. Now I'm asking you to trust me.'

Sophia felt an overwhelming sense of pride in her daughter. Perhaps all her sacrifices had not been in vain after all.

'And so I suppose you already know about my involvement in Athos as well?' she asked.

'Of course. Otherwise we would not be having this conversation. In fact, that's one reason why I wanted to become involved. We're in this war together, Mama. The sooner we are rid of the Nazis, the sooner we can start living again.'

'And Maria…are you aware of her treachery?'

At the mention of her sister's name, Nina stood up and began to pace the room. With so much to discuss with her mother, she had forgotten all about Maria.

'Yes. I can't believe it. How could she betray us?'

'And are you aware of who she is involved with now?'

Nina threw her mother a worried glance. 'It's been a while since I left Cairo. I came via Istanbul. During that time I had little contact with other members of Athos. I'm waiting to be updated with the situation here. The last I heard, Maria had just started working for The Black Cat nightclub. I presume she's still there?'

Sophia hesitated. 'She's fallen for a German and moved to a villa next to his to be with him.'

Nina shook her head and forced a wry smile. 'Well at least she's consistent. A German, you say. Who is he? He must be someone important for her to do that.'

'He's someone important alright! It's Klaus Reinhardt—the head of the Gestapo in Athens.'

Nina's face paled. 'Klaus Reinhardt!' She reached for her slim silver case and took out a cigarette. 'Of all the people, she had to become entangled with him?'

'I understand your reaction,' said Sophia, noticing her daughter's shaking hand. 'I felt exactly the same.'

Nina slumped back into the chair, took a long draw on her cigarette, and watched the smoke curl in the air. She avoided her mother's eyes. Sophia couldn't possibly feel as she did. Her assignment, codenamed Operation Icarus, was to assassinate Reinhardt.

The next day a car arrived outside 31 Thessaly Street. Two men in plain suits rang the doorbell. It was the call that Nina had been expecting. The Gestapo had wasted no time in contacting her. The men asked her to accompany them to Merlin Street. Trembling, Chrysoula watched her get into the car.

'Don't worry,' Nina assured her. 'I'll be back soon. It's just a formality.'

Whenever the Gestapo appeared, people deserted the streets, doors were locked and an eerie silence enveloped the neighborhood. Today was no exception.

# CHAPTER 33

*Athens, Spring 1944*

Nina was ushered into a packed waiting room. She stood next to a man trying desperately to soothe his heavily pregnant wife, who sobbed continuously into her handkerchief. One by one, everyone was called away until she was the only one left.

'Do you mind if I smoke?' Nina asked the guard, taking a cigarette out of her case and tapping the end on it.

'*Rauchen verboten.* No smoking.'

Nina put the cigarette back into the case and looked at the time. She had been at Merlin Street for over three hours. At that moment a minor SS official appeared and asked her to follow him. 'Wait here,' he said, and knocked on a door further down the corridor and disappeared inside the room. Seconds later, the door opened and he indicated for her to step inside.

It was a grand room with ornate décor dominated by a mahogany desk, behind which sat a middle-aged man wearing gold-rimmed spectacles. The officer clicked his heels. After giving the Hitler salute he left the room. The man behind the desk introduced himself as Dieter Wollstein. Nina already knew of him as Klaus Reinhardt's second in command.

'Thank you for coming, Kyria Stephenson. Please take a seat.'

Despite his polite smile—a smile devoid of emotion—Nina was under no illusion about the type of man Wollstein was. A fervent believer in National Socialism, he had joined the party in its early years. This was before Hitler came to power and rose to prominence after the annexation of Austria, playing a vital role in smashing anti-Nazi resistance with violence and torture. It was there that he and Reinhardt became close associates.

Wollstein wasted no time in telling her that they were aware that she had just returned from Cairo via Istanbul. 'You stayed there for just over two weeks…is that correct?' he asked, consulting his notes.

'That's correct.'

'And the reason for your return to Greece is…' Wollstein waited for an answer.

'I'm here to work with the German Archeological Society in Athens. I worked closely with their counterparts in Cairo.'

'And why exactly would you need to continue that work in Athens?'

Nina explained that a cache of Greek artifacts had just been found in the Mediterranean off the coast of Alexandria. The artifacts were lost during a series of violent earthquakes which destroyed the northern part of the city known as the Royal District. Many of the artifacts were of the Ptolemaic period and were clearly Greco-Egyptian. Several others bore similarities to certain artifacts she had uncovered in the agora, as well as those discovered in the vicinity of Alexander's birthplace in Macedonia. When the French and American archeologists left Greece, the Germans remained and Nina already knew one or two of them through her contacts in Cairo. If the Germans could unearth a connection between Alexandria's treasure and those in Greece, then the team would gain worldwide notoriety.

Wollstein listened attentively. 'I see,' he replied, after a long pause. 'As a Greek you have a right to return to your homeland, but there is one thing that puzzles me.' Wollstein leaned back in his chair, tapping his fingers together. 'Your husband is English—and you have a daughter called…' He leaned forward to consult his notes.

'Eleni,' Nina replied, before he could continue.

'So why would you want to leave them? Surely it is reprehensible to leave a small child behind, especially during a war. I cannot begin to imagine that a German woman of good character would consider doing such a thing.'

Nina bristled with indignation at his remark. 'Mr. Wollstein, it took a great deal for me to leave her behind but I know that she is well cared for. We will be reunited soon. My decision to return was motivated purely by my desire to contribute to the greatness of our profession and, hopefully, to discover something of importance that will serve to explain our civilization long after we have departed from this world.'

Dieter Wollstein smiled. 'A noble judgment,' he replied, with a tinge of sarcasm. 'And your husband…? We are at war with England. Doesn't that present a problem for you both?'

This systematic questioning was beginning to rile Nina, but she had been trained to hide her feelings well.

'I am apolitical, as is my husband.'

'But it says here,' Wollstein continued, tapping a finger on his notes, 'that he worked for the Balkan Section at the British Embassy before the war. Would you call that being apolitical?'

Nina smiled. 'That is correct. But he was against the war, as was I. In fact he strongly believes that England and Germany should have reached a peace agreement. If you care to consult your notes a little more, you will see that he no longer works in that field. Since we landed in Cairo he has been working in the commercial sector.'

'But he's still British!'

'Mr. Wollstein,' Nina replied, 'I understand your concerns but I can only assure you that my motives for returning must not be construed as anything other than for the good of our profession; and of course to help my mother, who is finding it hard to cope on her own.'

Dieter Wollstein flicked through his papers and read a few more notes to himself. He made no comment about Sophia.

'And if we need to question you further, we can find you at 31 Thessaly Street? Is that correct?'

'Correct,' Nina replied. 'After all, where else will I go? My apartment has been requisitioned.'

Nina had been questioned for almost two hours. She had remained cool and, paradoxically, garnered a little respect from a hardened man like Wollstein. Bidding her goodbye, he wished her well with her work, telling her that he would personally take an interest in the developments. After she left he added a few more notes to the file and delivered them to Klaus Reinhardt's office. Nina walked home to Thessaly Street, bitterly disappointed at not having met Reinhardt.

Maria was delighted to have her sister back again and Nina couldn't help but notice how happy she was. It was not just the relationship with Reinhardt, but her work at The Black Cat. She told Nina that however much she loved opera, the cabaret was where she had always wanted to be. And she praised Vangelis, who, she added, had encouraged her in this new endeavor and helped smooth away any doubts that Sophia might have had about it not being a respectable career. 'My only dream now,' she told her sister, 'is to conquer Berlin as I did with opera.'

Nina wondered if she was aware of the deadly bombing raids taking place across Germany. Soon there would be nothing left of Berlin.

'Anyway,' said Maria, 'enough about me. Tell me what brought you back.'

Nina explained the highly probable connection between Alexandria's sunken treasure and her work in the agora. Maria congratulated her on her intellect.

'I wish I had your capacity for learning,' she replied with a sigh. 'And

I never did have the skill to work with Mama. I can't even sew a button, never mind create wonderful embroideries as you do. I only have my looks and my voice and I wonder how long I will have those.'

Seeing her daughters getting along so well, Sophia hoped Nina might drum some sense into Maria and make her leave Reinhardt. But unbeknown to her, that was not what Nina had in mind. Instead, she decided to make use of her sister's relationship to carry out her assignment. It would be the perfect foil. The problem was that this time Maria really had fallen deeply in love and if she had the slightest inkling of her sister's involvement in an assassination plot, then their relationship would be ruined forever. It was a risk Nina was prepared to take. When she asked about her life with Reinhardt, hoping to store away useful information, Maria said little. She hadn't the slightest interest in his work and had never set foot in the Gestapo headquarters. Apart from The Black Cat—where they could be seen dancing together after the show—and her occasional appearances at a Reich function, she rarely went out in public with him. Reinhardt was careful to keep his private life to himself. In falling in love with him, Maria had well and truly isolated herself. For the moment it didn't seem to bother her. Next to most people in Athens she lived very well and, as long as he came back to her in the evenings, that was all that mattered.

The sisters planned to meet for afternoon tea once a week at Zaharoplasteion Perikles. As arranged in Cairo, Nina made contact with the German Archeological Society, where she devoted a few days each week to the sunken-treasure project. The rest of the time she spent helping her mother. More importantly she organized with Thymios to take over Sophia's work in the suburbs, allowing her to search out contacts for herself.

Throughout the winter the nebular cells that made up Athos stepped up their Resistance work. Vast amounts of intelligence were passed to Cairo, and regular raids against the Germans netted a considerable supply of weapons and ammunition which was hidden in various locations across the city, or smuggled to the Resistance. Nina's detailed knowledge of the area meant that much of the booty could be safely hidden in the numerous caves dotted around the base of the Acropolis, in long-forgotten crypts in the ancient cemetery, and in the network of underground cisterns that once supplied the now crumbling ruins of Ottoman hammams.

Further afield, Vangelis and Crazy Nick helped to scuttle German patrol boats and to ferry arms to Resistance groups on the islands. From his headquarters in Athens, Thymios coordinated parachute drops flown in by the Allies. Nina, codenamed Dimitra, supervised the dissemination of leaflets which countered propaganda from the German-controlled Greek press. But her expertise in code-work and as a wireless operator was the most valuable contribution to the group. She was the one who picked out and trained new recruits for this highly dangerous work. It was known that a wireless operator's life expectancy in the field was less than two months, and all new recruits were given the chance to decline the work, but very few did.

With her mother's consent, Nina hid one of her radio transmitters behind the racks of fabric in the workroom in Mitropoleos Street. Twice a week, after everyone had gone home, she pulled out the bulky machine, placed it on the cutting table, strung an aerial over the sewing machines, and began to type her messages to Cairo. Nina was a natural signaler but the fear of being discovered was never far away. The other transmitter—only to be used in emergencies—was kept in the attic over her mother's bed in Thessaly Street. At first she was reluctant to use her mother's home, but Sophia reasoned that the Gestapo would think twice before raiding the parental home of Reinhardt's mistress.

Nina agreed to take part in Reinhardt's assassination on the proviso that Sophia was not involved. Knowing as she did now of Maria's affair with him, she had been right to insist on that guarantee. The worry would have been too big a burden. Except for Thymios and Vangelis, no one else in Athos knew of the plot. If the plan succeeded, repercussions would be swift and brutal. Even Maria would not be above suspicion.

After settling back into the daily routine of Athenian life, Nina had still not met Reinhardt. Time was running out and she could not delay her mission much longer. Throughout Greece the Germans had stepped up their atrocities and the Jews of Athens now faced the same fate as those in Salonika. Collaborators were everywhere and thousands of innocent victims were netted in exercises of terror. Most ended up in the newly expanded detention camp at Haidari, a few miles outside Athens, where conditions were notoriously inhumane and prisoners soon became ill. Mass executions and deportations to Auschwitz were now a daily occurrence. Nina had to act quickly.

The Black Cat was the most popular nightspot in Athens. The entertainment was first-rate and whenever Maria and Vangelis had top billing, the place was booked out weeks ahead. Maria's popularity had not waned; she was still the number one draw card in Athens. Much to her disgust, Nadya, now the leading singer at The Athenian in Bucharest Street, was a close second. The rivalry was still there. Prudently, Nina waited several weeks before telling her sister that she wanted to see her perform. Besides, it was time she met her sister's lover. Until then, Nina had another urgent matter to which she must attend.

Sophia's instincts had been correct. Athos finally uncovered evidence that Sophia's shop had indeed been under surveillance by the Gestapo and it was there that they first became suspicious of Effie. After offering a tidy sum of money to the headmaster of the school, the Gestapo soon learned about her long and irregular hours. A few days before Effie was picked up, she suspected her transmissions to Cairo had been intercepted by the Germans. SOE Cairo also sensed that something was wrong after the line was scrambled. Effie's death had hit them all hard; it was now time for someone to pay.

It didn't take long for Nina to discover that the secretary known as Evdokia frequented the cocktail lounge at the prestigious Hotel Grande Bretagne every Thursday afternoon. Thursday was the day she met Maria at Zaharoplasteion Perikles, and when she suggested a change of venue to the Grande Bretagne, Maria was more than accommodating—it was her favorite venue.

Nina arrived at the hotel half an hour early and found herself a table in the bar with a clear view of anyone entering or leaving the room. She ordered a drink and waited. After some minutes, Evdokia walked into the room. Nina had no trouble in identifying her. She was exactly as Sophia had described her: of medium build, quite plain and conservative, with short wavy black hair. Esther had added a further compliment: 'completely without charm.' The woman now seated with a group of friends fitted the description perfectly, and on the lapel of her dark gray suit she wore the telltale butterfly brooch. This was the same one that Esther said she was wearing on the afternoon that she called into the shop. On the wall behind her hung an enormous French tapestry of Artemis, Goddess of the Hunt, aiming her bow at a fawn innocently grazing in the foliage. Nina did not fail to notice the irony.

Shortly after Maria arrived, making an entrance to which Evdokia could only aspire. Looking elegant in a tailored cream suit, she was as striking as Evdokia was dull. Wearing her hair down, the copper tones glinted under the crystal chandeliers, complementing the glossy red fox fur draped over her shoulder. All heads turned. There were few who failed to recognize her.

'What a good idea to meet here,' she said with a smile. 'I have entertained in this hotel more times than I care to remember.'

Throughout their rendezvous, Nina kept a close watch on Evdokia, waiting for the moment when she would leave. Eventually, Evdokia picked up her handbag and left the room. Nina quickly took out a few notes from her purse and placed them on the table.

'For the drinks,' she said to Maria. 'I really must be going or I won't get my work done.'

Maria looked disappointed but when a group of Germans came over and asked for her autograph, she quickly perked up.

In the corridor, Nina saw Evdokia pass the cloakroom and walk down a flight of stairs into the ladies' restroom. She followed her and seeing no one else there, quietly locked the door behind her and stood in front of the mirror powdering her face. After a few minutes, Evdokia emerged from a cubicle, stood next to Nina, and began to apply lipstick. Nina placed the compact back in her bag, took out a knife, and in an instant stabbed her in the back. Evdokia let out a gasp. Her small mouth with thin lips quivered, causing the lipstick to smudge as she slumped forward. In a flash, Nina spun her around and thrust the knife under her ribs, giving it a final twist. Evdokia silently sank to the ground, her startled eyes asking why. It all happened so quickly. She never even saw the glint of the blade. Wiping the knife, Nina quickly placed it back in her bag and calmly walked away and out of the hotel.

In a busy street not far from Effie's school, the headmaster walked home carrying a pile of books. He failed to notice the black car drive slowly past, or the passenger who lowered the window, took out his pistol and fired a fatal shot to his head. Effie's death had been avenged.

# CHAPTER 34

*Athens, Early Summer 1944*

Apart from Café Aphrodite in Smyrna, Nina had never set foot in a nightclub until she lived in Cairo. With a war on, there was never a shortage of famous singers willing to support the war effort and she and David regularly frequented many of the top nightspots, socializing with other members of the expatriate community and dancing until the early hours of the morning. Amid the seductive atmosphere of soft lights, music, and drink, people soon forgot their worries. But Nina was not at The Black Cat purely for her own entertainment, nor could she forget her reason for being there. Klaus Reinhardt was constantly on her mind. She was obsessed by him and not even the anticipation of seeing Vangelis and Maria perform could diminish that fact. And now here he was, seated at the very same table, waiting for his mistress to captivate everyone as she had captivated him.

The lights dimmed and a drum roll sounded. All attention turned to the stage. The red velvet curtains, embellished with the image of a slinking black cat, drew back to reveal Vangelis standing in front of his dance orchestra. His opening item—Jimmy Dorsey's 'Amapola'—immediately had couples scurrying onto the dance floor. Sophia was right, Vangelis was exceptional, but then Nina wouldn't have expected anything less of him. Music was his life blood. For a brief moment she allowed herself the luxury of nostalgia, remembering how proud they all were when he first performed at Café Aphrodite, especially Leonidas. A pain pierced her heart.

But it was Maria who most amazed her. The sheer enjoyment and emotion that she brought to her singing was astounding. Flowers carpeted the stage and the audience demanded an encore. When everyone had resumed their seats, she took the microphone from its stand and began to sing an electrifying rendition of 'Lili Marlene'.

Nina looked across the table at Reinhardt. For months now she had looked at his photograph, studying each detail until it was firmly etched in her memory: the way his short blond-brown hair parted just over the left eyebrow, the small mole on his left cheek, the intense blue eyes, and his soft full mouth. She had studied him so closely that in her imagination she could almost smell him. But nothing had prepared her for the real thing. He was much taller than she expected, not quite as handsome as his photograph suggested, but he possessed a certain confidence and charm. She was also struck by the beauty of his voice. Deep and rich, it was a voice that warned her that she was playing with fire. Unlike several of his entourage dressed in full uniform, he wore a dark tailored suit, and there was nothing about him that gave the impression of just how brutal and dangerous this man was.

'Finally I have the pleasure of meeting you,' he said towards the end of the evening. 'Maria speaks highly of you.' He held her gaze for a few moments as if trying to assess her. Maria joined them and he asked her if she would like to dance. Nina watched them glide across the dance floor to Cole Porter's 'Night and Day'. As if on cue, a young SS lieutenant asked Nina if she also would care to dance.

'Why not,' she thought to herself. Everyone else seemed to be having such a good time. The young lieutenant was an excellent dancer. She flattered him by telling him so.

He beamed with pride. 'I am from Vienna,' he told her. 'Until the war, I used to dance a lot. Perhaps after the war, it will be that way again.'

Nina agreed. At one point she found herself dancing close to Vangelis. He caught her eye and gave her a reassuring smile. She felt safe in the knowledge that he was there for her. If only David could see her now, she thought to herself. What would he make of her, dancing to American music in the arms of an SS officer?

A few days later, Nina received a phone call from Maria asking her to join them again the following Saturday.

'Klaus has been asking about your work at the Institute,' Maria said, 'and he would like to know more about what you do.'

Nina breathed a sigh of relief: no one had suspected anything. She told her sister she would look forward to it.

'What was that about?' Sophia asked.

'Apparently Reinhardt would like me to join them again next Saturday. It seems he's curious to find out about my work.'

Sophia frowned. 'And you agreed? Be careful. They are already aware of Athos and we are all under surveillance. One wrong move and we're finished.'

Nina tried to put her mind at rest. 'You don't have to worry, Mama. I don't intend to make a habit of it.'

'I hope not. By the way, I heard that the woman I suspected of being connected with Effie's death was found dead at the Grande Bretagne. Did you hear anything?'

Nina walked over to the stove, picked up a *briki* and began to make herself a Greek coffee.

'No, Mama,' she replied. 'Who told you?'

'Vangelis.'

Sophia watched her daughter stirring the coffee. 'Funny. I would have thought he would have said something to you.'

Nina poured the foaming coffee into a small cup, sat down at the table, and began to read the newspaper. Sophia could read her daughter like an open book. If she didn't want to discuss it, then it was better to let sleeping dogs lie.

'Oh, by the way, Mama,' said Nina, changing the subject. 'I can't possibly wear the same dress again on Saturday. Do you have anything that might fit me? Something glamorous?'

Sophia laid out several dresses on Nina's bed. She chose the pencil-slim cherry-red satin dress with a low slung cowl neckline that emphasized her firm breasts.

'Well, Mama. What do you think?' Nina asked, turning around in front of her.

Sophia was lost for words. Over the last three years her daughter had grown into a striking woman. With her dark and sultry looks, she was tall and elegant and she carried herself with a natural confidence.

'You look wonderful, *agape mou*. It fits you like a glove. But there's something missing.'

She went to her room and ten minutes later returned holding a folded piece of silk. Inside was her grandmother's locket.

'For you,' she said, offering it to Nina. 'I have very little jewelry these days but this is dearer to me than any of those magnificent jewels ever were.' Nina put the locket around her neck and looked into the mirror. 'Perfect,' said Sophia. 'Just perfect.'

At The Black Cat, Nina was pleasantly surprised to find Reinhardt and his entourage in high spirits once more. Dieter Wollstein was also there and he wanted to know more about her 'little project', as he referred to her work. This time, Nina sensed that Reinhardt took more than a fleeting interest in her. Throughout the evening, she felt his eyes on her and it unnerved her. Taking the bull by the horns, she asked if he also shared Wollstein's interest in archeology. She already knew the answer. He told her that before the war he studied it in Berlin and would probably have taken it up as a career if it had not been for the war.

'So you know about the project at the Institute?' she said, with a smile.

'Of course; nothing escapes me here in Athens. Herr Wollstein has been telling me all about it.'

Their conversation was interrupted by the applause from the audience. Maria took a bow and began another song. This time, Reinhardt hardly noticed.

'If you're interested in archeology, why don't you come along to the Institute and see what we're doing?' Nina continued. 'Better still, why don't you let me give you a guided tour of the Acropolis and the agora? Early summer is such a wonderful time to experience it. The light is perfect. I seem to recall that I gave such a tour when several of your countrymen came to visit in 1936. Dr. Goebbels was with them.'

At the mention of the Reich Minister for Propaganda, Reinhardt pricked up his ears. He was clearly impressed.

'Yes, we passed a pleasant two hours discussing the merits of the Peloponnesian wars.'

Nina had thrown him the bait, and from what she knew of him, he was extremely ambitious with an almost pathological need to distinguish himself above others.

'What did I tell you?' Dieter Wollstein said. 'A valuable asset to the Reich.'

Reinhardt refilled Nina's glass with champagne. 'By the way, I must congratulate you on your choice of dress. The color suits you perfectly.' His eyes fell on the locket. He took it in his hand, commenting on its beauty. 'May I?' he asked, opening the locket.

Nina was acutely aware of his long and supple fingers touching her skin. She detested the thought of him being so close to her. It was too intimate. He noted her concern and closed it again.

'Extraordinary,' he said, arranging it neatly above the curve of her breasts. 'Are they family portraits?'

'To tell you the truth, I don't know who they are. The locket belongs to my mother. It was given to her by her grandmother.'

'Most extraordinary,' he repeated, 'because you bear a resemblance to the young man.'

Nina was astonished. 'I'm afraid you have a vivid imagination,' she laughed. 'That's quite impossible! From what I gather by his dress, he was a Turk, and to my knowledge there aren't any Turks in the family. I'm sure I would have known if there were.'

Reinhardt couldn't fail to notice the indignant tone in her voice. 'I didn't mean to upset you,' he replied. 'But it wouldn't be such a bad thing if there were, would it? I have the greatest regard for the Turkish people. They were our Allies in the Great War.'

It was an awkward moment but Reinhardt was intrigued by her. He apologized for his lack of manners.

The orchestra struck up another tune, this time Hoagy Carmichael's popular 'Stardust.' The dance floor began to fill once more. Reinhardt asked if she would like to dance. He was a fine dancer and his timing was perfect. Under any other circumstance, she might have enjoyed herself. She felt his body press against hers. His scent was masculine and alluring.

'I do believe you're trembling,' he said softly.

She didn't answer.

Across the dance floor, Nina caught sight of Maria sitting at the table watching them. Eventually she pulled away, saying it had been a long day and she felt a little tired. They made their way back to their seats and Reinhardt told her that he might take up her offer of a guided tour after all.

Maria could hardly contain her anger. Reinhardt had never before asked anyone to dance in her company. Furthermore, she had been drinking too much. When Reinhardt failed to ask her to dance she poured herself another drink. Dieter Wollstein took the bottle away from her which made her even angrier. In a fury, she stood up and demanded that Reinhardt dance with her. Everyone looked embarrassed and Nina became alarmed when Reinhardt grabbed her by the wrist and pulled her back onto her seat.

'Sit down,' he said in a low voice. 'You're becoming quite tiresome.'

Shaken, Maria did as she was told. Nina could clearly see the marks left by his fingers reddening by the minute. At last, Reinhardt had shown his true colors.

'It's out of the question,' Vangelis shouted angrily. 'I saw the way he looked at you.'

Thymios put his hand up in a signal to quieten him. 'Let her finish.'

'And later he accepted my offer to act as his personal guide. This way I can get much closer to him.'

'And then what? We kill him in broad daylight? In the middle of the agora—with everyone looking on?' asked Vangelis, sarcastically. 'The idea's preposterous.' He turned to Thymios and pleaded with him to speak with Cairo. 'Someone else should do the job, not a slip of a girl.'

He got up and walked to the window, staring at the rooftops of Anafiotika and Plaka.

'In case you hadn't noticed,' Nina smiled, 'I'm no longer a slip of a girl.'

'Bah!' replied Vangelis. 'I couldn't fail to notice and neither did Reinhardt.'

Nina stood by his side. 'Look, I know that you're only trying to protect me, but you don't have to worry. I have my mother's steely determination. Trust me.'

Vangelis looked at her. He couldn't get the image out of his mind of her as a young child bent over her embroidery by Dimitra's side in the vermillion room.

'This is what I have in mind,' she said, resuming her seat. 'I have no intention of letting anything happen to him in Athens. It's too close to home. If he's killed here there will be reprisals, and not only will I be suspected, but my mother and Maria…even all of you.'

Thymios sat back in his chair with his feet on the table. 'No matter what happens there will be reprisals. We all know that.'

'Then we must minimize them. My plan is to get him to trust me and—'

'Reinhardt trusts no one,' Thymios interrupted. 'Not even his own shadow.'

Nina continued. 'After the Acropolis, I will suggest another visit outside Athens…perhaps the Temple at Sounion or even Corinth, somewhere not too far away but far enough for him to feel comfortable with me in the countryside.'

'And then what?' asked Thymios.

'And then I offer to show him the Sanctuary of Delphi.'

'Delphi!' bellowed Vangelis. 'What is this? A time-wasting exercise in tourism?'

Thymios sighed. 'Be patient. Hear her out.' He waved his hand for her to continue.

'If he is as interested in archeology as he claims to be, then he will never refuse to go to Delphi. That is where I suggest that the assassination takes place. Think about it. The terrain is mountainous—ideal for the Resistance. And the roads are narrow and winding—perfect for an ambush. Most of all, it's far away from Athens.'

Vangelis mulled it over. 'It has merits,' he said reluctantly.

'Bravo, Nina,' clapped Thymios. 'A brilliant idea. I know the area well and we will have no difficulty in recruiting the help of the local Resistance. There is just one thing.' His smile suddenly disappeared and his voice took on a serious tone. 'We cannot delay this for much longer. The Gestapo are closing in on Athos.'

Nina agreed. 'Delphi it is then,' she replied. 'Don't worry. I want to get this over with just as much as you.'

Maria's love life took a turn for the worse when Reinhardt's visits to her villa became more infrequent and he stopped going to see her at The Black Cat. Rather than confront her lover, she chose to take it out on Nina. She admonished her for trying to steal his attentions.

'I saw the way you danced,' she said to her angrily. 'And why did you have to wear that dress? Were you deliberately trying to seduce him? You already have a husband; isn't that enough for you? I think it would be better if you didn't come to The Black Cat again,' she said, hardly able to look her sister in the eye. 'In fact, it might be better if we didn't meet for a while.'

Nina looked at her with pity. The friendship that had blossomed over the past few weeks was now disintegrating. So smitten was she that she simply refused to see the sort of man that Klaus Reinhardt really was. There was little more to say. Nina now had no need of The Black Cat. She had achieved her aim but she felt a deep sense of guilt, and she hoped that in time Maria would find it in her to forgive her.

It was no more than two weeks before Nina saw Reinhardt again. She had just left the building of the Archeological Society when she saw the young Viennese lieutenant waiting for her with the car.

'Good afternoon, Frau Stephenson. Herr Reinhardt has requested that you meet him at the Prison of Socrates at two this afternoon. He has asked me to take you there.'

It was clear that by giving her no notice, Reinhardt was being cautious. He was going to prove to be a wily fox.

The lieutenant stopped the car at the entrance to the agora and indicated for her to walk on alone. The place was deserted and Reinhardt was nowhere in sight. She sat on a rock and covered her head with a scarf to protect her from the hot sun. Some minutes later, she saw him walking along the pathway towards her. Without as much as an apology for asking her to meet him without notice, he informed her that they had one hour.

'I'm all yours,' he said with a smile. 'Shall we begin our little tour here—with the death of Socrates?'

Nina thought his choice of venue a little ironic. Was he playing games with her?

'This is the cell where Socrates is known to have died after being given hemlock,' she began.

'And his crime?' asked Reinhardt.

'He was charged with corrupting the young.'

'Interesting.'

His deep, rich voice seemed to draw her out and it made her nervous.

'We know that while in here, he received a visit from a friend—the old and wealthy Critos, who had bribed the guards to enable him to escape.'

'And why didn't he leave?' Reinhardt asked, casting a glance around the dark cell.

'Because he considered that two wrongs don't make a right. The laws that he was being asked to violate were the same laws that had educated and enriched him. He had sworn an oath to the gods saying that he would accept the jury's verdict. To die was to prove his innocence.'

'Hmm,' Reinhardt replied thoughtfully.

'And by dying,' Nina continued, quickly regaining her composure, 'he changed the course of history. The development of science and the ideas of political reform later discussed by Plato were as a direct result of his death.'

'Impressive,' smiled Reinhardt. 'Most impressive.'

They made their way to the site of the Bouleuterion, the Council House, where Nina explained that each councilor, after being chosen by his team, held office for a year.

'And over there we have the Metroon, where births and deaths were recorded along with all of the decisions made by the people.'

'True democracy,' Reinhardt replied.

He congratulated her on a first-rate tour; he had enjoyed himself enormously. Nina suggested that he might like to see more another day. They returned to where his limousine was waiting. At the sight of Reinhardt, the Viennese lieutenant, who had been leaning against his car smoking a cigarette, jumped to attention. Reinhardt shook Nina's hand and departed, telling her that he looked forward to another tour. He contacted her twice after that. Each time it was without warning and always for no longer than an hour.

# Chapter 35

*Athens, Summer 1944*

It was a sunny July morning when Nina left Athens for Delphi. As predicted, she received no prior warning. During her meeting with Thymios the week before, he assured her that Athos had everything under control; she was being watched day and night. They would know exactly when she left and there would be several signs along the way. They fixed the place where the assassination was to take place. She was to carry no weapons but just in case, a gun would be hidden at the Turkish fountain about three miles south of Delphi. She was to make a quick stop on the way there to check it, but so as not to attract suspicion, she was not to attempt to retrieve the gun. That was to be done on the way back. That was when the ambush would take place.

Knowing that the assignment would take place at any time, Nina told her mother that she was going to Delphi for a few days on fieldwork. She also tried to make radio contact with Cairo from the workroom but for some reason she couldn't get the radio to work. When she did succeed, a high-pitched sound almost deafened her. It was not a good sign and she prayed that the frequency hadn't been jammed by the Germans. That evening, she told her mother about the problem.

'Use the one in the attic,' said Sophia. 'Chrysoula has gone to bed. You'll be quite safe, and just to be on the safe side we'll get Thymios to have a look at it tomorrow.'

At first, Nina was hesitant. It was too dangerous. Over the past six months, several other networks had been blown due in part to the transmitter being picked up. So far she had been lucky.

Sophia was insistent.

'It's your decision,' she told her, 'but if you don't radio in, Cairo will wonder what happened. By the way,' she said, before retiring to bed, 'there's something I've been meaning to talk to you about. Do you remember the leather satchel your great-grandmother gave me?'

'Until you mentioned it, I'd completely forgotten about it.'

'Well, I finally read it while you were away.'

'What did she have to say, Mama? I can't wait to hear.'

Sophia smiled. 'I'll tell you all about it tomorrow. For now you must get some sleep.'

That night, Nina had one of her recurring nightmares. Again, she found herself being thrown into the sea, arms flailing about frantically trying to cling onto the flotsam and jetsam to stay afloat. Around her, she could just make out the faces from her past: Leonidas with his wooden parrot, her great-grandmamma hanging colored threads over the branches of the Judas tree. Like a mirage the faces faded away and she woke in a sweat, unable to breathe.

The next morning, she found herself alone in the house. Her dream had left her with a deep sense of unease and she decided to take Sophia's advice and radio Cairo. The message was brief:

OPERATION ICARUS ALMOST COMPLETE. DIMITRA.

She was in the process of lowering herself out of the attic when the doorbell rang. Hastily she climbed down, pushed the bed back into place, and hid the ladder behind the cupboard. Tidying her dressing gown, she went downstairs to answer the door. It was the Viennese lieutenant. She glanced over his shoulder and saw Reinhardt in the back seat of his limousine.

'Good morning, Frau Stephenson. I believe that today we are going on a long journey.'

'I can't go like this!' Nina exclaimed, looking down at her dressing gown. 'Please allow me the courtesy of dressing appropriately.'

His eyes traced the shape of her body under the flimsy fabric. He smiled with approval. 'Hurry,' he said, 'we can't keep Herr Reinhardt waiting.'

Nina ran upstairs and quickly changed into her trousers and walking shoes and pulled a cardigan out of the drawer.

'Hurry,' shouted the lieutenant. 'We want to get an early start.'

Reinhardt's Mercedes with its Reich flag fluttering in the wind headed north towards Thebes. From there it turned west and at the town of Levadia they were joined by two other cars belonging to the Reich. After passing through numerous German-patrolled road blocks, the three cars began to make their way up into the mountains.

An hour later the road narrowed, hugging the wild mountains on the one side and falling away into the valley below on the other. Except for the occasional shepherd tending his flock, they saw no one. The car came to a halt outside a plateia in the mountain village of Arachova. Reinhardt got out and went to speak to the patrol officers in a nearby building. Two elderly Greeks sat outside a taverna playing backgammon. When they spotted Nina in the back of the car, one of them called to his wife to offer her something to eat. The woman came over to the car carrying a small chunk of bread and a slice of salty goat cheese.

'The Turkish fountain is two miles further on; it's halfway between here and Delphi,' she whispered.

Nina thanked her. Several minutes later Reinhardt returned and they resumed their journey. Nina thought him unusually preoccupied. In fact he had not been his usual self all morning. When she spotted the fountain at the side of the road she asked to stop and get a drink, saying that the salty cheese had made her thirsty.

The car pulled over and Nina walked over to the fountain. An old man stood next to it, attaching two panniers of grass to his donkey. She cupped her hands together, scooping the water splashing into the marble trough, and caught the man's eye. At the back of the trough was a decorative wall in the shape of a mihrab bordered with ornate scrollwork and an inscription in Turkish giving the name and date of the person who commissioned it.

'It's behind there,' the villager whispered, 'covered with fresh wildflowers.'

She took another drink and returned to the car, commenting on the freshness of the water.

Five minutes later the road curved around the mountainside and there in front of them, clinging to the terraced slopes of Mount Parnassus, stood the ancient site of Delphi.

The three cars stopped outside the entrance and amidst the spectacular landscape of resin-scented pines and the occasional tall cypress, Reinhardt and Nina began their tour. First he wanted to see the Athenian Treasury, built after the battle of Marathon. From there they covered the Sanctuary of Apollo, ending at the Sybil rock, a pulpit-like outcrop of rock along the sacred way, thought to be the place of the Oracle.

'It was here that the god Apollo spoke to the worshippers through a priestess,' said Nina. 'Would you like to ask her a question? After all, you'd be following in the footsteps of many a hero before you.'

Reinhardt laughed. 'There's nothing here.'

It was the first time she'd seen him smile all morning. 'Then use your imagination,' Nina replied.

She sat down on the remains of a marble column, fanning her face with her hand and watching him as he wandered around, sensitively running his fingers over the marble fragments and breathing in the beauty of the place.

At this moment he was no longer the ruthless, cold-blooded killer. This was a side of him that few had seen. She thought of her sister. She, too, must have once seen this side.

Nina looked at the mountains around them; mountains that were alive, with the Resistance watching their every move. In less than an hour he would be dead. She felt no remorse.

Towards midday Chrysoula returned to Thessaly Street and found Maria's suitcases in the hallway. In the kitchen sat Maria, crying into her handkerchief.

'He finally did it,' she sobbed. 'He threw me out—like a piece of old rubbish.'

Chrysoula was lost for words. She had never approved of the relationship but she hated seeing her in such a state. Her eyes were red and swollen and her normally coiffed hair was disheveled.

'Perhaps we should telephone your mother and let her know that you're here,' Chrysoula said.

'No! I'm not ready to face her yet. I doubt that she will offer me sympathy.'

'Don't judge her too harshly,' Chrysoula replied. 'She only has your welfare at heart. What happened to make him do such an unkind thing anyway?'

Maria shrugged. 'I don't know. It all went wrong a few weeks ago... after he met Nina.'

'Nina!' exclaimed Chrysoula. 'What has Nina to do with all this?'

'I suppose he found her attractive and far more interesting than me. I found out that they shared a common interest in archeology. He wanted her to show him around. After that, I hardly saw him. Then last night he sent someone around and asked me to vacate the villa. He didn't even have the decency to tell me himself.'

'Perhaps it's for the best.'

'I did love him, Chrysoula, but I'm so tired and confused I can't think straight,' she said tearfully. 'I think I'll go to my room and lie down for a while.'

'Your mother has given that room to Nina. She didn't think you were coming back. If you give me a minute, I'll prepare the guest room.'

'She's even taken over my room,' Maria said, with a hint of sarcasm. 'For the moment I'll lie down in my mother's room. Nina can move her things out of my room when she returns.'

She took off her shoes and lay down on Sophia's bed, mulling over the events of the past few months. How had it all gone so wrong? And what would Sophia say when she found out she'd also been sacked from The Black Cat?

'There are complaints about you,' Yianni the Arab told her. 'You're drinking too much and it's beginning to affect your work.'

That was more than two weeks ago. Eventually he pulled her into the office and dismissed her, telling her that he was bringing back Nadya from The Athenian. The humiliation was too great. How would she ever live this down?

Sleep would not come easily. The heat was stifling and she lay on her back wondering what to do next. Looking up at the ceiling, she noticed the trapdoor to the attic. It was the first time she'd seen it. What's more, it was open. She stood on the bed to take a further look but it was far too high to reach. Searching around for something to stand on, she spotted the ladder behind the wardrobe. It took only minutes to discover the transmitter concealed under an old gray blanket. Maria was horrified. There was no doubt what this meant—someone in the house was working for the Resistance. Looking for answers, she searched her mother's room and found nothing to implicate her. Then it dawned on her—it had to be Nina. All those weeks she had tried to get close to her. It was for one reason only—to get at Klaus.

Angrily, she ran to her room to search it. She must find the evidence. Throwing Nina's belongings to the floor, Maria searched the room thoroughly. She had almost given up when she saw a small notebook wedged in the back of one of the drawers. It appeared to be in code. Sitting on the bed, Nina's clothes and books scattered around her, she tried to decipher it, looking for any clue that would connect her with the radio. The writing was in Classical Greek, much of which Maria found hard to understand, but she persevered. Throughout the notes, she came across the name of Reinhardt several times. The other name she recognized was Athos. 'Athos,' she said to herself. 'Where have I heard that before? Of course!' She had overheard Klaus mention it to Dieter Wollstein. It was one of the biggest Resistance groups in Greece.

Maria clutched the notebook wondering what to do. Her instinct told her to go to Merlin Street. Her heart warned her of the repercussions. It was an easy choice. Her sister had betrayed her and she could not get away with it. She raced down the stairs and picked up the telephone.

'Dieter Wollstein please,' she said to someone at Merlin Street. 'Tell him it's Maria Laskaris. I have something urgent to report to him.'

Within fifteen minutes the Gestapo had Thessaly Street and the surrounding neighborhood blocked off. When Wollstein arrived Maria pointed to the attic and gave him the notebook. A bewildered Chrysoula was ordered into the kitchen at gunpoint. On seeing the radio, Wollstein telephoned Gestapo headquarters with orders to notify all German checkpoints between Athens and Delphi. He also asked for a translator from the Institute straight away.

Hysterical, Chrysoula was taken away as the Gestapo tore the place apart. Wollstein thanked Maria for her service to the Reich and suggested that for the time being she move into the Grande Bretagne for her own protection. There they would make sure she was well looked after. For now, 31 Thessaly Street was out of bounds.

When the three cars left Delphi, Nina spotted two other cars in the distance heading towards them from Arachova. Two miles out of Delphi, she asked Reinhardt if they could stop at the Turkish fountain again for one last drink of cool mountain water. He agreed. The car in front carried on, turning around the bend out of sight. As Nina got out and walked towards the fountain, they heard a loud explosion coming from the direction of the first car. At that moment a hail of bullets from the mountainside rained down on the remaining two cars. Nina threw herself to the ground behind the fountain wall. The gun was still there. She reached for it when a second explosion rocked the earth. The Resistance had thrown a grenade at Reinhardt's car, blowing apart the bonnet and sending shrapnel flying everywhere. A piece of metal ricocheted off the fountain and embedded itself in her thigh. She screamed in pain. Lying on the ground she looked up. Several men protected by heavy gunfire swarmed down the mountainside onto the roadway, heading towards the last car. She tried desperately to pull herself up but she couldn't feel her legs. Just a few feet away she saw Reinhardt crawling towards the fountain. He was badly injured and he had his revolver in his hand, trying to reach her. With superhuman effort, she pulled herself up against the fountain and aimed her gun at him. For a brief moment he looked at her with hatred. She took aim and fired.

By now the members of the Resistance were everywhere. Two of them dragged Reinhardt's bullet-riddled body into the car and set it alight. Another two pulled her out from behind the fountain.

'Quickly,' one of them said to her. 'We've got to get you away from here as soon as possible. Patrol cars are heading this way from Arachova.'

The men carried her down the mountainside out of sight. From a safe distance they watched the patrol cars approach the burning cars that were blocking the road. More grenades hurtled down from behind the rocks. As quickly as they had appeared, the Resistance members disappeared, melting back into the wild landscape with the ease of a wild animal. The few who stayed behind made a makeshift stretcher and carried her away in the opposite direction, towards the Gulf of Corinth. By nightfall they reached the harbor at Itea, but the Germans had already been alerted and were swarming all over the place. Nina's leg was swollen and was becoming infected. Skirting the town, they headed for the old port of Galaxidi. From there the group parted ways. A fishing boat ferried Nina and two of the Resistance across the gulf to Akrata, where she found Thymios waiting for her. He informed her that they were taking her into the mountains where she would be airlifted out of the country on the night of the full moon, in two days' time.

Within hours of Dieter Wollstein learning about the transmitter and the notebook, most of the members of Athos had been arrested. The network was finally broken. Sophia and Vangelis were amongst the first to be taken, and when a thorough search of her premises uncovered the broken transmitter the seamstresses were taken for questioning.

Despite being subjected to physical and psychological torture, neither broke down. Several others, however, proved less strong and Wollstein learned of the possible whereabouts of Nina and Thymios. Further road blocks were set up in the mountains south of Akrata. On the evening that Nina was due to be flown to safety, the Germans closed in and she and Thymios were caught and brought back to Athens.

After being interrogated at Merlin Street, the group was transferred to the Haidari Concentration Camp. Vangelis and Thymios were kept in solitary confinement in the notorious Block 15. Sophia and Nina were sent to the women's block. During the following few weeks, all of the suspects were taken backwards and forwards to Merlin Street for further interrogation.

On the morning of August 27, 1944, more than one hundred members of Athos and their associates were taken out into the yard at Haidari, where their sentences were formally read out. With the exception of Nina, who had to be carried on a stretcher, the condemned men and women climbed into the back of the waiting trucks and were driven to a nearby clearing not far from the camp. There they were executed by firing squad.

Chrysoula, who had been released earlier due to intervention by Maria, was asked to collect the family's belongings. Amongst those executed—along with Sophia, Nina, Vangelis, and Thymios—were Kyria Angeliki, Yianni the Arab, and Nadya—condemned mainly on evidence concocted by Maria.

Walking back along the quiet dusty road, Chrysoula passed the fifth-century Byzantine monastery of Dafni. A monk sat outside the gate. He had lost count of the hapless figures who had walked this way since the occupation.

'Can I offer you a prayer?' he asked.

Chrysoula followed him into the church where he led her to a beautiful mosaic depicting the resurrection.

'*Kyrie, elysian,*' he began to chant, in a mellifluous voice. 'Lord have mercy.' Chrysoula felt an overwhelming sense of peace.

Walking away, she thought of something Nina once told her after reading the works of the great German dramatist, poet, and historian Friedrich Schiller. '*And thus their crime has yielded them no fruits. Revenge is barren. Of itself it makes the dreadful food it feeds on; its delight is murder; its satiety despair.*'

PART IV

# THE HIDDEN PAST

# CHAPTER 36

*Athens, September 1972*

Eleni felt as if her head would burst. She jerked her hand away from her aunt's and backed away from the bed, knocking over a small table covered with figurines. Unable to get to grips with what she had just heard, she paced the room, crying out like a wounded animal.

'Why? Oh why did you do it?' was all Eleni could find to say. Her aunt's story had taken so many twists and turns she was emotionally exhausted and confused. In the end, the only image that remained was of her mother and grandmother facing the firing squad.

'How could you?' Eleni cried, looking at her in disgust.

Holding out her frail hand, Maria's eyes pleaded for forgiveness. Instead, Eleni backed away further.

Hearing the sound of Eleni's raised voice, Chrysoula rushed into the room. 'I knew it would end like this,' she cried, applying a wet cloth to Maria's brow in an attempt to calm her. She turned to Eleni and pleaded with her.

'In God's name, can't you see that she's dying? I beg you, if not for her sake then for your mother's. Forgive her. Absolve her of her sins.'

'I am not a priest!' Eleni exclaimed, the tears finally beginning to break.

Chrysoula was distraught. 'What is done cannot be undone. Forgive her and let her die in peace.'

Maria's breathing worsened and her eyes began to roll upwards. Eleni took one last look and ran out of the house. It was the middle of the night and she had no idea where she was going. She just had to get as far away from 31 Thessaly Street as possible. Through her tears, the neon lights of the night flickered like candle flames in the wind. And like a moth to a flame, she walked in their direction until after some time she reached a small plateia, surrounded by tavernas and kafenia. The merriment of late-night revelers only served to deepen her despair. Finally, out of sheer exhaustion, she sat down at an outdoor table at a small taverna in a quiet side street. A young waiter came over and placed a menu in front of her. She pushed it aside and ordered ouzo. Minutes later he returned, setting down a small glass in front of her, along with a carafe of water and a small plate of *mezethes*.

Eleni sipped her drink and through her tears stared at the dark shapes of ancient columns that lay scattered in a large area of long grass bordering the length of the street. The plaintive sound of the bouzouki drifted across the tiled rooftops of Plaka and in the distance, high on a rock, she could just make out the outline of the Parthenon, dark and brooding under the silvery moon. Never in her wildest nightmares had she expected things to turn out like this. She called the waiter over and ordered another drink.

The waiter raised his eyebrows. 'Are you sure you wouldn't like to see the menu?'

Eleni shook her head, avoiding his eyes. This time he returned with a larger plate of *mezethes*.

In the blurred chaos of her mind, Eleni tried to make sense of everything. No matter how hard she tried, she couldn't come to terms with the fact that it was because of her aunt's actions that her mother and grandmother met with such violent and untimely deaths. She now understood why her father never spoke about the past, why he always refused to take her to Athens, and why after Maria arrived in London they had quarreled the night before she left. Somehow, he must have known that she had something to do with their deaths. Now she had no way of ever knowing what he really thought.

After a while, her pain eased. Whether it was due to the ouzo or the warm night air filled with the soothing fragrance of jasmine she wasn't sure, but the tears stopped flowing. Inside the taverna, the waiter watched her. He should have closed long ago, but she was his last customer and he felt concerned about her. He prepared a platter of the evening's leftovers and took them to her table.

'I've been watching you for a while now. And if you don't mind me saying so, you look very unhappy. On such a beautiful night, it's not good to be alone like this. I usually eat before I go home,' he said, sitting down at the table with her, 'and it would please me greatly if you would join me.'

Eleni watched him as he tucked into the food, mopping up the oil from his moussaka with his bread. After a while, she picked up a fork and took a few mouthfuls.

'I was hungrier than I thought,' she said.

'By the way, my name is Markos,' he smiled, offering her his hand.

'Eleni,' she replied.

'You're English, aren't you,' he said, wiping his mouth with a napkin.

'I arrived from London today.' Eleni looked at her watch. It was four-thirty in the morning. She had lost all sense of time. 'Well actually, I arrived yesterday,' she said, clarifying herself.

Markos poured himself a beer. 'I don't mean to pry, but that's a short time in a country to be so sad. Was it a lover's tiff?'

'Certainly not,' replied Eleni, defensively.

Markos put his hands up and apologized. He continued eating.

'Are you superstitious?' she asked, after a while.

'What a strange question!'

'It's a perfectly serious question. What I mean is…do you believe in the evil eye and all that?'

'Well, let me see…No, I don't think I am superstitious. It's not rational to think that one can see into the future. But my mother, on the other hand, has the blue eye attached to her purse—just in case anyone tries to steal her money.' He laughed. 'And almost every female in my family reads the coffee cups. Is that what you mean?'

'And do they take it seriously enough for it to be a matter of life and death?'

Markos looked at the young woman in front of him. He guessed she would be in her late twenties or early thirties. Most likely they were the same age. Her hair was long and black and she had the pale-olive complexion of a Greek.

'What are you getting at?'

Eleni sighed. 'It's really too hard to explain; you wouldn't understand.'

'Try me. I'm a good listener.'

Her eyes reddened again. 'My mother was Greek and I came here because my aunt is dying. She has just told me things about my family, things I had no idea about and now…' Eleni paused. Once more she was plunged into her mother's past. 'And now I am no longer the same person who left England. My life has changed.'

Markos looked perplexed. 'You have only just arrived. Surely you're not trying to tell me that you've changed in such a short space of time? It's impossible. What's more, you're beginning to sound like a Greek—talking in riddles. What's this all about?'

'I have just learned that my aunt was responsible for my mother's and my grandmother's deaths,' she blurted out.

Markos's eyebrows shot up. 'Are you saying that your aunt is a murderer?'

'In a way, I suppose I am.'

Markos was beginning to wonder what he'd got himself involved with but something about her made him think she was sincere.

'Look,' he said, checking the time, 'I think we should call it a night.

I have to be at the university in a few hours. I must get some sleep. I'm going to get a taxi to take you home. How about we meet here again this evening? That way, you can tell me everything and I'll see what I can do to help you.'

Eleni thanked him for his kindness and apologized for keeping him up so late. 'I would like that.' She looked around. 'I'm afraid I have no idea where I am,' she laughed. 'These columns, what are they?'

'You're in Monastiraki,' replied Markos. 'This is the Roman Agora.'

Eleni felt the hair on her neck stand on end. It was as if she knew the area already.

When she arrived back at Thessaly Street sometime after six in the morning, the front door was wide open. On the pavement propped up against the wall was the lid of a coffin. Her heart raced. In the hallway, two old crones dressed in black wept loudly in an overt expression of grief. In the bedroom, surrounded by the paraphernalia of death, a priest stood at the foot of the bed chanting prayers from a large leather-bound bible, making the sign of the cross with dramatic sweeping gestures over Maria's body that had been laid out on the faded red coverlet. Her arms—folded after death—had been placed over a silver icon of the Virgin. The enormous and valuable rings on her long bony fingers with their manicured nails sparkled in the dim light. The room reeked of death and incense.

Chrysoula sat next to the bed, her eyes closed and her hands clasped in prayer. Eleni walked over to her and put her hand on her shoulder to comfort her.

'She's gone,' said Chrysoula, with a heavy heart. 'O allos kosmos—to the other world.'

Eleni stood transfixed before the body; she felt nothing. Even in death, Maria's pallid face looked full of anguish and torment. She sat in the chair where she had listened to the story unfold and resigned herself to her duty. As the only living relative, it was left to her to remain by the bedside until the following day when the funeral would take place. In the meantime, the old crones began to prepare the body for burial. Eleni looked on in awe at the biblical scene taking place in front of her. After removing her precious rings and stripping the body naked, they washed the corpse in wine, wrapped it in long lengths of white cloth and placed it in the coffin, along with thirty-three coins to appease Charon on the boat ride to the other world. Eleni could bear it no longer and went into the garden for air. She thought about Markos and how he would be expecting to see her again tonight. It was impossible to meet him now. Perhaps after the funeral—if he was still there.

Aunt Maria's body was laid to rest in the first cemetery of Athens, near

Pangrati, just fifteen minutes' walk away from Plateia Syntagma. 'May God forgive her sins,' the priest proclaimed.

Eleni was acutely aware of the lack of mourners. Apart from the odd bouquet of flowers left on the doorstep, even the neighbors had stayed away.

'To remember is to reinstate life,' Chrysoula told her, and clearly no one wanted to remember.

'People say that those who led evil lives do not die easily,' said Chrysoula. 'Their souls are reluctant to leave.'

'Do you believe Aunt Maria was evil?'

'It's not for me to say, God rest her soul. But perhaps we all have the capacity to do things we later live to regret.'

'Were you close? I mean afterwards, when there were just the two of you?'

'I suppose you could say we were. After all, neither of us had anyone else. We became much closer after she returned to Athens.'

'You mean after she returned from Paris?'

'Good lord, no!' exclaimed Chrysoula. 'Didn't she tell you?'

Eleni's eyes widened. 'Tell me what? Is there more?'

Chrysoula fixed her eyes on Eleni. It was obvious that Maria had not told her everything. 'After the death of your mother and grandmother, word spread through Athens that Athos had been betrayed by someone with links to the Gestapo. While some suspected Maria, others were convinced that she'd never betray her family. Penelope's husband Georgos was also a suspect. When his car was ambushed and his body strung from a balcony, Maria thought she would be next. After the executions, Dieter Wollstein had no intention of protecting her forever, and when the Germans eventually left in October 1944 she begged to leave with them. That was impossible. Almost two months later Greece was plunged into a bloody civil war. No one was safe. It was about that time when Maria disappeared. I never heard from her again until a year after that dreadful war ended in 1949.'

'And she never told you where she went or how she survived during that time?' Eleni asked, still reeling in disbelief.

'Nothing—but you have to remember that your aunt was very resourceful. She didn't exactly come back looking emaciated and years older, as others did.'

'Do you think she found a lover—someone to protect her again?'

'What else are we to think? She would do anything to survive. After your mother died, your father tried to find out what happened. He wrote many letters to her but I had no address to forward them. When she returned, I gave them to her.'

Eleni wanted to know if her father ever did find out the truth.

'I don't know what she told him,' Chrysoula replied. 'All I know is that they stopped communicating after she returned from London.' She paused for a moment. 'What will you do now? Go back to England or spend a few days here in Athens? There's the will to be dealt with of course, but the lawyers will keep you informed about all that.'

Eleni pondered the question. 'I suppose there's little reason to stay longer. This whole episode hasn't exactly put me in the mood for sightseeing—and there's my work.' At the mention of her work, Eleni wondered how the exhibition had gone. Had it been a huge success as anticipated? And what sort of exhibition would the gallery be working on next? She loved her work and the thought of putting together a new collection excited her.

'What is it that you do?' Chrysoula asked.

'I'm an historian, an art historian.'

Chrysoula nodded her head from side to side in a knowing way.

'So not only do you look like her, you also have her interests.'

'But I'm not an archeologist. And I've never embroidered anything in my life other than a school apron in simple cross-stitch.'

'Ah, but you share the same interest in history and, from the little I know of you, you also share her thirst for knowledge.'

# CHAPTER 37

*Athens, September 1972, four days later*

In the morning Eleni found herself alone in the house. On a tray in the kitchen, Chrysoula had thoughtfully laid out her breakfast of dried rusks, marmalade, and small plaits of *koulourakia* biscuits. Beside it was a note.

Dear Eleni,

I will be out until late this afternoon. Please help yourself to breakfast.

In the drawing room you will find a brown suitcase that once belonged to your grandmother. A few weeks before her capture, she asked that in the event of anything untoward happening to her, I was to look after it for her.

When I overheard Maria telephone Dieter Wollstein, I thank God I had the quickness of mind to hide it before the Gestapo arrived. Sometime later your aunt asked me what happened to it. After such treacherous action on her part, I am not ashamed to say that she died thinking it had been taken away by the Gestapo.

Wishing never to betray your grandmother's trust, it has remained hidden away for all these years. Now it is yours. I know that is what she would have wanted.

Chrysoula

Looking at the suitcase saddened Eleni immensely. She thought of her grandmother, faced with the unenviable task of deciding what to take and what to leave behind. In her mind's eye she saw it being dragged through the streets of Smyrna, the handle gripped so tightly that her knuckles were white with the fear of losing it in the crush. All their worldly possessions reduced to one suitcase.

She stroked the battered leather gently as if it were a book in Braille, each mark telling its own story. She unlocked the stiff metal clasps until the lid sprang open. Her stomach churned. Inside was another world—the old world. When Chrysoula returned she found her sitting on the carpet. Scattered around her were a pile of photographs, documents, and newspaper clippings, several *objets d'art*, and various other items.

'I'm afraid I've opened a Pandora's Box, haven't I?' she said to Chrysoula. She opened her hand and showed Chrysoula the locket. 'It's the one Aunt Maria referred to in her story and the one that my mother wore on her wedding day.'

Chrysoula looked at it closely. 'I can still remember that day as if it were yesterday,' she said with a heavy heart. 'When she gave it to her, I overheard your grandmother say that her own grandmother gave it to her when she married Andreas. It was her most prized possession. I believe the only other time that your grandmother wore it was for Maria's debut as Cio-Cio San.'

'If you wouldn't mind helping me, Chrysoula, I'd like to go through all this with you. You may be able to shed light on some of the people in the photographs and the significance of some of these objects.'

Chrysoula looked at the photos. 'I'm afraid I'm not going to be much help there. It's the first time I've seen them myself.' She picked up a bunch of keys. 'Perhaps I can help you with these though. I imagine that they belonged to the family home in Smyrna. Almost everyone took their keys with them. They did this in the expectation that they would return one day.'

There was a Damascene jewelry box inlaid with ivory and mother of pearl which Eleni surmised belonged to Sophia, possibly received as a gift on some important occasion. Inside was an engraved glass perfume bottle and although empty, it still retained a heady perfume of Damask rose. Underneath was a calling card with the name Grand Duke Nikolai Orlovsky. Its scent struck her as strange—sweet and earthy with a trace of musk.

There was also a silver cigarette case with the initials NO engraved on the back and a gold Breguet pocket watch—the movement and case made in Paris, with numerals that Eleni thought had been designed for the oriental market. And there were several pieces of embroidery, including an exquisite robe in shades of lapis, edged in silver, and a pair of ornately embroidered turquoise velvet slippers. On the back of them was a tiny crimson tulip, no bigger than a sixpence. There was a long sash decorated at each end with three complicated sprays of flowers and leaves rising from a stylized bow, all of which were almost the same. Eleni gasped at the sheer beauty and artistry of such work. Among the more obscure items was a fragment of hand-knotted carpet, so finely woven that Eleni was able to distinguish in the floral landscape the partial image of a leopard being chased by a horseman.

That night, Eleni found it hard to sleep. She was haunted by the faces in the photographs—ghosts of the old world whose whispering voices beckoned her like the Sirens in the Iliad. Was she following in the footsteps of the ancient mariners, washed up on some rocky shore from which there was no return? She was beginning to feel superstitious, something she had never been inclined to feel before this.

The following day Eleni and Chrysoula finished sorting through the photographs and various other contents of the suitcase. With Chrysoula's help, Eleni managed to identify Sophia's immediate family. The shy boy with the cherubic face and shiny dark curls—of which there were several photographs—was most likely Leonidas, although Chrysoula couldn't be too sure as until now she knew nothing about him. Several photographs were taken in quite grand settings, in richly decorated rooms filled with works of art and ceilings glistening with chandeliers. Judging by the occasional glimpse of domes and minarets from the windows, these were thought to have been taken in Constantinople. The rest, including the ferocious-looking Turks with their fez, baggy trousers, embroidered waistcoat, and the wide sash around their waist in which they kept their dagger and knife, remained unidentified.

Of Smyrna, apart from a few commercial postcards of the waterfront, there was very little. One in particular drew Eleni's attention—an elderly woman in a kaftan, sitting on the edge of a fountain in a courtyard dominated by a Judas tree. Eleni thought it to be Dimitra and it was probably one of the last photographs ever taken of her.

'So much of this is as new to me as it is to you,' Chrysoula said, wiping away the tears. 'It's strange isn't it, how you can live with someone for so long and know so little about them?'

The last item to be put away was a beautifully bound book: *The Firebird*. Inside was a dedication written in French.

'What does it say?' Chrysoula asked. 'I can't speak French.'

'To Nina, always in my heart, Nikolai. Constantinople, Jan. 1, 1916.'

'Your mother would still have been a baby then,' Chrysoula remarked.

Eleni pondered the words. It struck her as odd that someone would write such a dedication to a child—so tender and so intimate. But then so much of all this was strange. If she tried to make sense of it all she would go crazy.

'I managed to find this' said Chrysoula. 'It's a photo of your mother and aunt taken in the agora. It was taken shortly before your mother left for Cairo.'

Eleni brought it close to her eyes. She was struck by the difference in their looks—her mother, with her dark, refined, classical features; Maria, the striking Hollywood glamour girl.

'They look so happy, it's hard to imagine what was about to take place.'

Chrysoula agreed. 'If you look closely, you'll see that she's already carrying you—that's why she looks so radiant.'

'Were they so different, Chrysoula—I mean, in character?'

Chrysoula whistled and waved her hand as if stirring the air. 'Like night and day. Your mother was a quiet, studious type, somewhat retiring, but never shy and with a caring nature. Your aunt, on the other hand—well, she was the belle of the ball. Her spirit was infectious and if she turned her charms on you, woe betide you…she could weave you round her little finger—but she had a jealous and venomous streak when crossed. It was her downfall.'

She left the room returning a few minutes later with a small leather satchel. 'I have no idea what's in it but I found it in your grandmother's bedside drawer and I hid it at the same time as the suitcase.' Chrysoula pushed it towards her. 'Before you open it, I also want to give you this.' Reaching inside her apron pocket, she brought out the sapphire ring. Eleni's face tightened. A wave of emotion swept through her and she felt herself shrink from it.

'Just before she died your aunt asked me to give it to you, saying that it rightfully belonged to you.'

Reluctantly, Eleni took the ring. It was exquisite, but knowing how Maria had come by it made her feel uneasy. 'Did she ever wear it when her mother was alive?' she asked.

'The first time I saw it was when she came back to Athens in 1949. I assumed it was just another gift from one of her fancy men…like all her other jewelry.'

'I wish that was the case,' Eleni sighed. 'I'm sorry to say it, but she stole it from her great-grandmother. That much, I did learn.'

Chrysoula shook her head in despair. '*Aman*…What a woman! So that's why she never wore it. May the saints preserve her soul,' she added, crossing herself twice for good measure.

Eleni's eyes focused on the satchel as if spellbound.

'Aren't you going to open it?' asked Chrysoula.

'Not now. I'll save it until this evening. I think I've had enough surprises for the moment. If it's alright with you, I might take a walk into Athens and clear my head. I'll probably arrange my flight home and, if there's time, visit the Acropolis.'

'Good idea,' agreed Chrysoula. 'I have to admit, all this isn't doing my heart any good at all.'

*

'Markos!' the waiter called out to the man behind the bar. 'There's a young lady outside asking for you.' He gave him a knowing wink. How he wished he was young enough to attract the young tourist girls as Markos did. It used to be one of the perks of the job and he lamented the fact that he was now well past his prime for such adventures.

'I want to apologize for not turning up the other night,' Eleni said. 'It's just that…well, things took a turn for the worse. My aunt died. After that there was the funeral, and things to be sorted out.'

'There's really no need to apologize. I'm sorry to hear of your loss.'

'Well, it's all over now. I've arranged to fly home in two days' time.'

'That's a great pity. What I mean is, you're part Greek and yet you've hardly had time to get to know the place.'

On the contrary, she thought to herself, she felt as if she knew it almost as well as he did.

'What can I get you to drink?' asked Markos. 'Perhaps another ouzo or a beer? It's on the house tonight.'

'No more ouzo for a while,' she laughed. 'I'm afraid you must have thought me quite drunk the other evening.'

'I see too many drunks in this job—and you didn't strike me as one of them. If anything, you struck me as troubled and quite sad.'

'I'm sorry, I didn't mean to burden you with my problems.'

'Oh, you didn't. But you did leave me with a great curiosity to know more. I have an idea,' he said, after a pause. 'It's really my night off. I only called by to help out for a few hours. Why don't we go somewhere quiet and you can tell me the whole story?'

Without thinking, Eleni agreed. There was something about him that made her want to confide in him, something sympathetic and sincere, and she felt that he would not betray her trust.

Markos hailed a taxi. 'Lykavittos,' he said to the driver. Turning to Eleni he told her that this was the highest point in Athens. 'From there you will have a 360 degree view of the city, and at this time of the day I can promise you one of the most unforgettable sights in Athens.'

Twenty minutes later the taxi left them at a small open-air café at the summit of the hill. The sun was fading fast, casting a rosy-colored glow over the white buildings of the city below. Over cocktails, Markos told her that the hill was named after the wolves that once roamed the area.

'Now it's a favorite haunt of Athenians who come here to escape the noise and pollution of the city,' he said with a smile.

From the terrace, Eleni admired the panoramic view below. Surrounded by a ring of hills and a view of the Saronic Gulf in the distance, it gave her a sense of just how much the city had grown since gaining independence from the Ottomans. Seeing an endless vista of concrete apartment blocks, it was hard to imagine that this was once an open plain watered by streams and occupied by goatherds. All too soon the sun disappeared behind the hills, and the view of Athens below turned into a teeming mass of flickering lights. On the hill of the Acropolis, the floodlit Parthenon stood out proud and dignified, a tribute to another age. In such peaceful surroundings, Eleni told Markos much of what she had learned since she had been here. Every now and again her eyes filled with tears, as she relived the events.

'And there you have the story,' she said, after she had finished. 'That's why I told you I'm no longer the same person who came here. How can I be after all this?'

Riveted by her story, Markos had not uttered a word. He shook his head in disbelief. 'My goodness. I've heard some stories in my time, especially about the old country, but this takes the cake.'

He told her that he could identify with what he had just heard, as he had been born in Constantinople. 'I came to Greece in 1955 along with my parents and maternal grandmother at the start of the last exodus of the remaining Greeks in that city. I was about fourteen at the time, and I recall that we too left with very little. My father died soon after we landed in Greece. Fortunately, my grandmother managed to get some of her money out and it did give us something for beginning another life.'

This time it was Eleni's turn to offer sympathy. 'I'm truly sorry. I shouldn't have told you all this. I can see its opened old wounds for you.'

'Not at all; I've learnt to come to terms with the past. In time, so will you. Anyway, it's good to talk about it. Too many people have died of a broken heart by bottling it all up. Life still goes on.'

All too quickly the evening drew to a close. 'It's not far to Kypseli,' said Markos. 'Come on, I'll walk you back.'

Eleni thanked him for listening to her. It was a great relief to talk to someone who understood. For a fleeting moment she understood the bond between her grandmother and Vangelis, and why, as Markos had pointed out earlier, so many refugees chose to intermarry.

'Have a safe trip back to England,' he said, shaking her hand and giving her a farewell peck on the cheek. 'I've enjoyed the short time we spent together and I'm only sorry that I haven't been able to persuade you to stay longer. Perhaps you might think of returning? If you do, you know where to find me.'

Lying in bed that evening Eleni realized just how many lives had been affected by the wars with Turkey, and she wondered how long it would take for those wounds to heal. Turning over to sleep, her eyes fell on the leather satchel still on the table where she had left it. If these were Dimitra's memoirs, then she was going to need Chrysoula's help to translate them for her. Above all else, she desperately hoped that they would solve some of the unanswered questions that niggled away in her mind. Who were the couple in the locket? And was the woman really the same person as the mysterious painting in Jean-Paul's studio? Most important of all, who was the enigma that was her great-great-grandmother?

Too impatient to wait until the morning, Eleni picked up the satchel, untied the thin leather ties and slipped out the contents. To her great horror the interlacing and flourishes of the black calligraphy executed on sheets of saffron-tinted paper were not in Greek, as she had expected, but in the old Ottoman script. She knew this to have been replaced by a modified version of the Latin alphabet on the orders of Ataturk in 1928. Groaning in despair, Eleni realized that hardly anyone understood this script any longer. All the unanswered questions that she had hoped to uncover remained as elusive as ever.

# CHAPTER 38

*Istanbul, 1972, one week later*

It was mid-morning when the tour group assembled underneath the canopy of a tree outside the Topkapi Palace in an area known as the Courtyard of the Janissaries. They were the elite fighting force of the Ottoman Sultans until they were disbanded in the first half of the nineteenth century. The booming voice of their guide, Metin, informed them of this. The group surveyed the vast area. Little remained to tell them just how majestic the ceremonies that marked the commencement of a military campaign would have been. They began to take photographs.

Metin waved his hand, indicating for everyone to follow him into the inner palace through the monumental Middle Gate. This Gate of Salutations dated back to the reign of Suleyman the Magnificent. There he pointed out a small suite of chambers that was once set aside for the chief gardener who doubled as the chief executioner. Several onlookers emitted gasps of disbelief.

Metin scrutinized their faces and congratulated himself once again. This was what most tourists came to see and hear: just how formidable and bloodthirsty the Turks had been; how they took women and locked them up in the confines of one of the most splendid harems in the Muslim world—a cloistered, gilded cage guarded by slaves and black eunuchs. During his fifty years as a guide, Metin had learnt to appraise his groups and work on them accordingly. For that he had garnered enough tips to supplement his meager income and buy himself a small home in one of the outlying suburbs of the city. Today, however, his keen eyes were on the young woman who kept to herself. His experience told him that she was not the usual kind of tourist. She intrigued him.

Eleni studied the detail of the architecture, noting the masterful artistry of the calligraphy; her thoughts drifted back to the package locked away in the hotel safety deposit box. In the next few days, she intended to have Dimitra's memoirs translated, but for now she was content to familiarize herself with this alluring city where her mother was born. This was the place chosen by Constantine the Great as the capital of his New Roman Empire in 330 AD, the site of old Byzantium and of two other great empires that were to follow. All of these epochs were to leave their indomitable marks on the great civilizations of two continents. Metin signaled for her to keep up with the rest of the group.

It had been a hasty decision to change her flight to London and instead come to Turkey. Eleni was not used to making such rash decisions but instinct told her this was what she had to do. Chrysoula admonished her for 'putting her life at risk,' as she liked to phrase it. 'You can't trust the Turks,' she warned her. 'Don't forget that you are a Greek.'

Markos, on the other hand, didn't seem at all surprised; after listening to her story and then later finding out that her great-great-grandmother's memoirs were written in Ottoman Turkish, he too agreed that she had made the right decision.

'Be sure to keep me informed. You've made me anxious to know more now,' he laughed. 'In the meantime, I'll see if I can find out anything here. There is one other thing. Since Turkey became a republic, many of the cities and towns changed their names. Only the Greeks refer to Istanbul as Constantinople, and Smyrna is now called Izmir.'

Eleni sighed. She had enough to learn without adding place names to the list.

Apart from Dimitra's memoirs, there was, however, something else that had prompted her to make the trip to Turkey. After her Aunt Maria's funeral, Eleni had telephoned the director of the Knightsbridge Gallery to let them know about the death. During the conversation, Eleni learnt that the sales from the recent Byzantine Icon Exhibition had far exceeded expectations. Flush with funds, the board had already agreed on the next project—nineteenth and early twentieth century Orientalist paintings. If she were to go to Turkey, the director informed her, she was to keep a lookout for anything that might be of interest to them. After learning that her grandfather and great-great-grandfather were both artists, the idea of doing a little research on the subject excited her tremendously.

Eleni booked herself into the Otel Golden Horn in the old area of Sultanhamet. A sign on the reception desk boasted that its clientele included journalists, academics, and interesting people of all nationalities. 'A good place for single women travelers,' the receptionist informed her. That night she dined alone on the hotel terrace, mapping out her plans for the next few weeks. First on the list was the obligatory tour which would help to acclimatize her to the city. Thus it was that on the advice of Ayse, the matronly hotel owner, that she found herself in the capable hands of Metin, whose knowledge of the city, she was assured, was unsurpassed.

Eleni's eyes rested on a fur-lined ceremonial robe once worn by Selim III. The detail was astonishing.

'It's splendid isn't it?' remarked Metin, standing behind her.

Startled by his close proximity, Eleni jumped back. The rest of the group had disappeared outside and were busily taking photographs of each other standing in front of the Apartment of Felicity, which contained the relics of the Prophet Mohammed.

'I was admiring its beauty,' she said.

'It's ermine, I believe,' Metin continued. 'The Sultans had a taste for luxurious furs.'

Eleni thought of Esther. Was it possible that one of her ancestors supplied the pelt?

'I couldn't help noticing that you seem to take more than a passing interest in the designs,' Metin said, 'especially the textiles. Are you a weaver of some sort? If you are, perhaps I can take you to see other such fine works in the city?'

Eleni smiled. 'I'm an historian, but I do have a particular interest in your textiles—especially the embroidery.'

'Ahh,' Metin replied, waving a finger in the air. 'Then I can be of some assistance to you. After we have finished our tour of the Topkapi, the next place on the agenda is the Grand Bazaar—'

Eleni cut him short. 'No. I'm not interested in souvenirs.'

Metin looked offended. 'I am not talking about tourist shops. There are merchants there who can trace their stores back a few hundred years. If you know where to look, there are still wonderful things to be had, some of them quite rare and valuable.'

An hour later, Eleni and the rest of the group stood inside the heart of the Grand Bazaar listening to Metin's account of its early beginnings, from shortly after the conquest of the city in 1453 until the devastating fire of 1954 and the subsequent renovations. Afterwards, he handed each person a small map detailing the various areas and told everyone to meet him in the same place in two hours' time. 'And remember,' he cautioned them. 'Don't take the first price offered to you. Bartering is a way of life here.' The group dispersed into the bewildering maze of arcades.

Metin handed her a separate map and pointed to a few areas circled in ballpoint pen. 'I've marked all of the shops that might be of interest to you,' he said. 'This area has the largest range of textiles, including a few specialist embroidery shops. If you need me, I will be at Hamdi's café next to the *lokum* stalls. Good luck.'

It was the third shop on Metin's map that drew Eleni's attention. At first glance, the shop itself looked rather dingy and unattractive. She was just about to walk away when she spotted a piece of embroidery in the window that reminded her of one of those in the suitcase. The sign over the doorway, partially hidden by a maroon curtain edged with heavy fringing said:

*Selim Efendi*
*Handmade Textile Arts*

Next to it hung a larger sign in bold gold calligraphy. A third sign read simply:

*Private Customers Welcome.*

Eleni entered the shop and found herself in a tiny room surrounded from floor to ceiling with shelves of neatly folded textiles and embroideries. Three glass lamps hung from the domed ceiling, casting a glittering light on several silver and gold embroideries strewn across a glass-topped display cabinet. A gray-haired man with a sallow complexion was carefully wrapping an embroidered cloth in tissue paper for a customer who sipped a glass of Turkish tea from small tulip-shaped glass. The man looked over his half-moon spectacles and smiled a warm welcome in Eleni's direction.

'*Merhaba*,' he said softly.

'*Merhaba*,' repeated the customer, to Eleni.

'What can I do for you?' the man asked, after his customer had left.

'You have a piece of embroidery in the window. I'd like to look at it,' Eleni replied.

With so many fabrics crammed into the small window, Eleni took him outside and pointed to it. 'That one,' she said, 'with the gold and silver thread.'

The man went back inside, unlocked the window, and reached inside. 'It's been so long since anyone looked at that piece that I'd almost forgotten about it,' he said, laying it out on the glass cabinet and smoothing away the creases.

'It's a sash isn't it?' Eleni said.

The man nodded. 'One of the finest; you don't come across these too often nowadays, especially in such good condition as this one. You have a good eye to pick this one. Do you have a particular interest in Ottoman embroideries?'

Eleni went on to tell him she had only recently been made aware of them and wanted to learn more. The man introduced himself as Selim, the owner of the shop, and if she wasn't in a hurry he would be only too happy to show her some of his collections and enlighten her on the subject. Eleni checked the time. She had just over an hour and agreed to accept his offer.

Selim went outside and called out to a young boy to bring his guest a glass of Turkish tea. Throughout the next hour, Selim generously explained the various styles of this textile art and, as an historian, Eleni was astounded by his knowledge and of his passion for the subject.

'So you see,' he said, after they had compared a relatively modern napkin with one of a similar design embroidered almost a hundred years earlier, 'very few women have this skill anymore. There will always be people willing to weave fine carpets, but this sort of thing…never. Life has changed for women. What you are looking at is a lost art.'

Eleni picked up the sash and looked at it again. 'You said you were often able to tell where a piece came from; which workshop, and in some cases who the embroiderer was. Can you tell me where this particular piece came from?'

Selim took out his magnifying glass and examined it again. 'It's a rare, high-quality piece from a workshop in the area of Tepebaşı. Most of their work was produced for the Imperial Court.'

'Have you any work by a Greek lady called Dimitra?' Eleni asked.

Selim smiled. 'Dear lady, that is like looking for a needle in a haystack. Dimitra is a common Greek name, and almost all of them would have been able to embroider. You will have to be more specific than that. What was her surname?'

'Dimitra Lamartine—from Izmir.'

Selim shook his head. 'Lamartine,' he pondered. 'I don't recall anyone of that name. 'Izmir, or Smyrna as it was known before the Great Fire, was predominantly a Greek city. Hardly anything from those days remains.'

'Well just in case you do recall anyone by that name, please give me a call. You can reach me at the Otel Golden Horn.'

Eleni arrived at the rendezvous point just as the rest of the tour group were eagerly showing each other their purchases.

'Well? How did you get on?' Metin asked, as they piled back into the *otobus*. She told him about Selim, and that she had promised to return on another day.

'His shop has been in the family for several generations and was one of only a handful in the Grand Bazaar to bear the tugra, or the signature of the Sultan over his shop. Perhaps you noticed it?' he said. 'It's written in gold and is displayed over the doorway.'

At the end of the tour, Metin gave Eleni his card and offered his services to her should the need arise. She was still puzzled as to why Selim had never heard of Dimitra. If, as Aunt Maria had claimed, she was renowned as one of the finest embroiderers in the land, then why had he never heard of her?

She didn't have to wait long for an explanation. The next day, Selim telephoned her and asked her to call by his shop again. He had something to tell her.

'I'm afraid I wasn't quite telling you the truth yesterday,' he said uncomfortably. 'When I said I'd never heard of Dimitra Lamartine, that wasn't quite right. She did indeed live in Smyrna but was known as Dimitra Hanim Efendi, and she once ran the most successful embroidery atelier in Smyrna. As a painter signs his work with his signature, she always signed hers with a tiny red tulip—often so small you had to look carefully to find it. It was my mother who first told me about her. By all accounts, she rose to prominence after pleasing the women of the court with her work. I was told that she was one of the few outsiders ever to visit the inner sanctum of the Imperial Harem. That would have been during the reign of our great Sultan, Abdulmejid—an enlightened man with a European education. His mother, the Valide Sultan Bezmialem was a Georgian slave and the two became quite close. For her beautiful work, she was rewarded handsomely with the Sultan's official tugra and allowed to set up her atelier in the street of the embroiderers. My mother also told me that she wore a ring set with a rare Burmese sapphire, also rumored to have been a gift from the Valide Sultan herself.'

At the mention of the ring, Eleni winced.

'I took over the business after my mother died a few years ago. Until the Greek army invaded Smyrna in 1919 she was friendly with many Greeks here, but the situation deteriorated rapidly and no one trusted them anymore. As a consequence, she stopped selling their wares.' Selim looked downcast. 'My father was killed fighting the Greeks. After that, it was as if her Greek friends ceased to exist.'

Eleni opened her bag and took out two photographs. 'I believe this may be Dimitra. She must have died in the Great Fire of 1922.'

Selim didn't recognize her. Eleni showed him another photograph. 'And this is my grandmother, Sophia. She was a very successful couturier here. Her atelier was La Maison du l'Orient—perhaps you've heard of it?'

Selim nodded. 'Yes, that name is also familiar—I seem to recall that my mother knew her, but I was a small boy back then. She left after a fire destroyed her business, didn't she? What happened to her?'

'She died in Greece in 1944,' replied Eleni. Metin shifted uncomfortably in his seat again.

Eleni brought up the subject of Dimitra's memoirs and asked if he could read Ottoman Turkish.

'Unfortunately, no. After the establishment of the Turkish Republic, the language was reformed and a new alphabet created. I was ten at the time.' He looked puzzled. 'Why did she write her memoirs in this language and not in Greek?'

'That's something I've asked myself,' Eleni replied. 'And I still don't have the answer.'

'I do know someone else who can help you. His name is Professor Orhan Gunes, head of Classical Ottoman studies at Istanbul University. I'll give him a call.'

Eleni thanked him for his help.

'There's something else. Seeing that photograph of your grandmother reminded me that someone came into my shop a few years ago. She was also looking for Dimitra Hanim Efendi's work. She said she used to work at La Maison du l'Orient.'

'Do you recall her name?' Eleni asked.

'It was quite a while ago but I think she said her name was Munire.'

Eleni's heart skipped a beat. 'Munire was my grandmother's vendeuse. She must be about the same age, perhaps a few years younger. That would make her around eighty. Surely it's too much to hope that she's still alive?'

She tried to remember what it was that her aunt had said about Munire marrying Ismail Bey. She seemed to recall that it was around the time when the Greeks landed in Smyrna in 1919, and that she became pregnant shortly after.

'Do you have any idea where she went to live?'

'Somewhere near Uşak—I can't be sure.'

Selim promised to look into it.

Eleni was sitting in the hotel garden jotting down a few notes when Dr. Gunes arrived with his wife.

'Welcome to Istanbul,' he smiled. 'Selim has told me that you have something of importance in your possession and that I may be able to assist you.'

'I have what I believe are my great-great-grandmother's memoirs and they are written in Ottoman Turkish. Are you familiar with the language?'

Dr. Gunes informed her that in his capacity as head of the department, he could not only speak, read, and write Ottoman Turkish, but he was also fluent in Arabic and Persian. He also added that besides being guest speaker at the faculties of Oriental Studies at the esteemed universities of Oxford and Harvard, he was a translator of many rare manuscripts into modern Turkish. Eleni could hardly contain her excitement.

'But for the moment,' Dr. Gunes continued, 'we will forget about all this as my wife and I would like to extend a little of the famous Turkish hospitality and take you to dinner. Surreya has booked a table at one of our favorite restaurants, overlooking the old city. Then you can tell us all about your family, which by all accounts, Selim tells me, is a very interesting one.'

Less than a month ago, the thought of dining by moonlight on a rooftop garden between the Blue Mosque and the Aya Sophia would have been unthinkable. To her left, silhouetted high above the Golden Horn, stood the magnificent Suleymaniye Mosque built in the days of Suleyman the Magnificent. And to the right, stretching out across the Bosphorus with its hundreds of fishing vessels, ferries, tankers, and ships, were the twinkling lights of the Asian shoreline.

'Over there,' said Surreya, pointing to the farthest part of the shoreline, 'is Uskudar. It was once better known by the English as Scutari, the major hospital where Florence Nightingale worked during the Crimean War. And there, almost directly opposite, is Haydarpaşa, the gateway of the Baghdad railway built by the Germans as a gift to the empire from Kaiser Wilhelm.'

'It was completed in 1908,' said Dr Gunes, taking over from his wife. 'But by then the empire was already doomed. That same year the Young Turks began their revolution and four years later we were at war. By the time those wars ended, the empire lay in ruins.'

Eleni asked about Pera and was told that it was now known as Beyoğlu.

'Almost everything European changed after Turkey became a Republic,' Surreya told her. 'The famous Grande Rue de Pera is now known as Istiklal Caddesi, or Independence Avenue. After independence, many of the Europeans left and the area fell into decline. I'm afraid to say that the decline accelerated after the 1955 riots when most of the remaining Europeans, especially the Greeks, left the country.'

Eleni recalled Markos telling her that this was when his family left for Greece. She asked if they thought that there would ever be peace between Greeks and Turks.

'We have more in common than either of us would care to admit,' replied Dr. Gunes's wife, casting her eyes over the menu. 'A shared history of hundreds of years—it wasn't all bad. Anyway, our countries are still young. It's normal that every now and again we roar at each other like lions trying to exert their dominance.'

Eleni smiled at her analogy.

Jazz music and white-coated waiters juggling plates of delicacies on silver trays above the crowd gave the establishment a Parisian air. Dr. Gunes recommended a *meze* of fried anchovies, minced-meat boreks, and dressed chard stalks with a walnut tarator sauce. During the meal he talked about his work at the university, and of his recent translation of a book of Sufi poetry which was to be released at the end of the year.'

'It was my father who nurtured my love of languages,' he told Eleni proudly. 'He was a diplomat and spent many years in the Middle East. He met Surreya when she was studying at the London School of Economics. Her family were admirers of Ataturk and sent her there with the express wish that she should be a woman of learning.'

'It wasn't an easy decision,' said Surreya. 'Not everyone agreed.'

Eleni couldn't help thinking how apprehensive she'd been about coming to Istanbul. Despite Chrysoula's stern warnings about Turks ringing in her ears, she hadn't experienced any animosity. Indeed, so far it had been the opposite. Back at the Otel Golden Horn she handed Dr. Gunes the leather satchel and asked him to check the contents to see if it was indeed Dimitra's memoirs. Opening it with the utmost care, he was struck by the beauty of the handwriting.

'Astonishing!' he said, with a look of surprise. 'Simply astonishing!'

For a moment, Eleni thought she had made a grave mistake and that the contents were nothing to do with Dimitra. 'What is it?' she asked.

Dr. Gunes shook his head. 'You say your great-great-grandmother was an embroiderer. Then she must also have been a calligrapher. This writing is equal to anything that I have seen before. It is perfection itself. You were certainly correct in your assumption. They are indeed her memoirs.' He carefully put them back in the satchel and patting them with affection, told Eleni it would be an honor to translate them for her.

# CHAPTER 39

*Istanbul, October 1972*

After a few days, Selim telephoned to say that his efforts to find Munire had reached a dead end. Even his contacts in Uşak had no knowledge of her. He assured her that he would keep trying but warned her not to raise her hopes. With time on her hands, Eleni set about researching Orientalist paintings for the gallery in London, discovering amongst others the works of Osman Hamdi Bey. With their attention to fine detail, Eleni poured over them for hours allowing her a glimpse into the life her family once lived—a life that no longer existed.

After almost a week, Surreya telephoned to say that her husband had been called away on business for a few days. Quick to sense Eleni's melancholic mood, she suggested that she take a trip to Izmir.

'You might even find out something about Dimitra and I think it will help you to come to terms with your family's origins. What's more, with Orhan away I might consider going with you. I could do with a holiday.'

Surreya was right: the trip would take her mind off waiting for the translation. Besides, she enjoyed Surreya's company and since learning that she had studied in London, the pair had discovered that they had much in common.

'Splendid,' smiled Surreya, pleased with herself at the idea. 'I will pick you up tomorrow after breakfast.'

It had been Surreya's idea to stay in a hotel on the waterfront, saying it boasted a spectacular view of the Bay of Izmir.

'Besides,' she added, 'the fish restaurants along the seafront are excellent —a legacy of the Greeks.'

Yet as Eleni sat on the balcony of her hotel room watching the ships and tankers anchored in the choppy waters, she couldn't help thinking that the modern city of Izmir bore none of the seductive atmosphere portrayed in the sepia postcards in Sophia's suitcase. To her way of thinking, Izmir was as far away from the old Smyrna as you could be. With its apparent sense of orderliness and wide boulevards, it could have been one of many Mediterranean cities that rose from the ashes of war in the first half of the twentieth century. Many of its boulevards were named after heroes of Mustafa Kemal's army that had wrenched the city from the infidels in 1922. Watching the people going about their business along the waterfront, something else struck her as being different to the images on the postcards. There was not a single fez in sight. Condemning it as decadent Ottoman dress, Ataturk had banned the wearing of it in 1925 as part of his modernizing reforms.

They had been in Smyrna for three days and despite Surreya's relentless questioning, no one could shed any more light on Dimitra. In some cases their questioning was greeted with a certain amount of hostility. 'Let the past sleep, they were troublesome times,' many of them said. One old man even shook his fists at them saying that it was the Greeks who had caused God to seek his revenge by burning down the city. Eleni felt intimidated. Surreya merely shrugged it off.

The sun began to sink over the horizon, turning the bay into a breathtakingly beautiful sea of rich red lava. In less than a few minutes it disappeared, and in its place rose a silver crescent moon. Eleni returned to her room, picked up the letter from her bedside table, and read it once more. It was from Markos and it had arrived the day before she left Istanbul. He was anxious to know if she had found anyone to translate the memoirs. He also wanted to tell her that he had received a letter from his mother. She was in Boston visiting his sister who had recently become engaged to a Greek American. His grandmother had gone with her. After she left Athens, Markos wrote to his mother telling her briefly about Eleni and the death of her aunt. According to his mother, when she read the letter to his grandmother, the old lady had shown a great interest in the story.

> On receiving your letter about the English girl, I read it to your grandmother, her eyesight being extremely poor these days. When I mentioned Maria Laskaris—the opera singer—she sat bolt upright and listened with more than a passing interest. 'What did you say her name was?' she asked. When I repeated the name, she closed her eyes and put a hand to her forehead. She had difficulty breathing, and for a moment I thought she was about to have another turn. I asked if she knew her but she didn't answer. Instead, she asked me what else was in the letter.
>
> As a lover of classical music, she must have been well acquainted with the work of Maria Laskaris, but it wasn't that which seemed to upset her. I got the distinct impression that she knew the family—in particular the grandmother. If so, I am puzzled as to how that can be. We came

to Greece in 1955; your friend's mother and grandmother had already been dead for eleven years. Just lately your grandmother's thoughts have become jumbled. I fear that this is just another example of that sad fact.

Eleni thought no more about Markos's mother's comments and put the letter away. The telephone rang and thinking it was Surreya asking if she was ready to go out for dinner, she picked up the receiver and was about to say that she was on her way when she recognized the voice on the other end of the phone as that of Selim.

'I have some good news,' he said, unable to contain his excitement. 'We have found Munire.'

Before Eleni could respond, he went on to say that she was living with her son and his family in Foca, a resort town which used to be known as Phocaea, about forty-three miles north of Izmir. They could reach it in a few hours. After giving her the address and telephone number, he told her that he had taken the liberty of telephoning her already. Eleni felt a lump rise in her throat.

'Her son answered the phone,' he continued. 'And after a brief discussion with his mother, he said that they would be only too happy to welcome you to their home.'

Eleni sat on the edge of the bed unable to comprehend what she had just heard. Grabbing her shawl, she ran downstairs to the lobby where the patient Surreya sat sipping a cocktail at the bar.

'Guess what?' she smiled. 'We've found her. We've found Munire.'

News that an Englishwoman—the granddaughter of the woman Munire Hanim had held in the highest regard—was traveling from Izmir to see her spread like wildfire through the neighborhood of Eski Foca. By the time Eleni and Surreya arrived, the street was filled with onlookers, all eager to catch a glimpse of her.

'Ingeliz kadin burada,' someone shouted. 'The English lady is here.'

A stocky, middle-aged man appeared in the doorway of what appeared to be the largest of the stone dwellings in the street and waved his hand airily at the crowd in an effort to quieten them. He introduced himself as Hasan, Munire's son, and he welcomed them to his home. Eleni and Surreya followed him into the house and up a steep flight of stone stairs to the living quarters. Sitting on a sofa surrounded by several women and children sat Munire. Although her once-dark hair was now silver-gray, her face still possessed a certain youthfulness and Eleni recognized her immediately from the photographs. Helped by her daughter-in-law, Munire stood to welcome her.

'I give praise to God that I have lived long enough to see this day,' she said, with outstretched arms.

Instinctively, Eleni walked over and embraced her. Whether her feelings were magnified by the revelations of the past few weeks she could not say, but she did know that Munire's embrace was the embrace of a woman who welcomed her as if she were her own child.

'Let me look at you,' Munire said, running her hand over the contours of Eleni's face. 'Your mother was only a child when I last saw her, but already I see a resemblance.' Munire's eyes rested on the locket that Eleni had taken to wearing. She touched it momentarily with the tips of her fingers and smiled.

One by one, Eleni was introduced to the rest of the women in the room. Except for Hasan and his wife Latifa, their two children and a grandchild, all of the others were the children, grandchildren and great-grandchildren of Ismail Bey with his first wife. A maid entered the room carrying a tray of gold-rimmed glasses filled with apple tea and placed it on a table next to an assortment of cakes. Urged on by Latifa, her young daughter shyly offered Eleni and Surreya sweetmeats that were prepared that morning for their special guest.

'You cannot imagine how much this means to me,' said Eleni.

'Your grandmother was like a sister to me. I am honored to welcome you into our family.'

Turning to her daughter-in-law, Munire asked that they be left alone. The women all rose and left the room, including Surreya. Eleni had no need of a translator; Munire's English was excellent. Munire already knew from Selim that Sophia and Nina were no longer alive and she had prepared herself for what Eleni would have to say. Sparing Munire the distressing details, Eleni told her about the family's last days in Smyrna and that only three of them reached the safety of Greece—she didn't reveal the facts leading up to Sophia and Nina's execution by the Germans.

With a weariness of one accustomed to hearing such news, Munire listened in silence. Every now and again, her eyes glistening with tears, she shook her head and sighed.

'I give praise to God that your grandmother carved out a successful life for herself again,' said Munire, 'but that she died fighting for her country does not surprise me. And by what you have just told me, your mother inherited those same characteristics. Life is cruel. Only God knows what lies in store for us.

'I lost contact with your grandmother when the Greeks invaded,' she told Eleni. 'After my husband was killed, we all left for a village near Uşak. They were terrible years for us; even worse than the earlier Balkan wars.

Almost every family lost a loved one and in some cases entire generations were lost. Sometime later I heard that your grandmother had moved back to Smyrna after the loss of her atelier and I tried desperately to find her. But after the great fire, it was impossible. With three-quarters of the city gone, I resigned myself to the fact that the family must have perished in the fire.

'For many years I tried to put it all behind me. No one wanted to be reminded of the Greeks, especially my father. When he finally returned home, he told me that your grandmother's family was wanted for subversive activities against the state. It seems that for some time, Soterios had been a marked man by the Secret Organization. He was known to have been actively involved in covert operations on behalf of the Greeks—the Megali Idea, as they called it. It was the fight for a greater Greece, as it had been before the Ottoman Conquest of Constantinople.'

'Do you really believe that?' Eleni asked.

'Unfortunately, yes,' Munire sighed. 'I was aware of his activities from the time I worked at La Maison du l'Orient. Sophia tried her best to conceal it from me but occasionally I saw and heard things that I kept to myself. My father told me that several of her friends in Constantinople were also on that list. I always wondered what became of them.'

'Did your father say whether Sophia was on that list?' Eleni asked.

'No, but she was a clever woman and she played her cards close to her chest. I am quite sure she would have used the business and her connections to further their cause.'

'What about Andreas?'

Munire laughed. 'Andreas was a sensitive man; he was not cut out for war, but unfortunately he came under the influence of his father-in-law. He disappeared for a while, supposedly on a painting excursion, but when he returned he was never the same. Some said that he had lost his mind. After his last exhibition he spiraled into depression, then there was a terrible accident—your Aunt Maria shot him. I always believed it was an accident. Maria was a troubled child and your mother never really forgave her...and neither did Dimitra. It was a great pity.'

'It saddens me to think that my grandfather died that way.'

Munire stared at her for a moment. 'But your grandfather was buried in a Greek village along with Ali Agha—at least that's the story I heard. They had gone to visit several Greek villages when an accident took place and the car rolled down the mountainside, killing them. Some said one of them got away, but I don't know for sure.'

The look of confusion on Eleni's face told her she had unwittingly opened a Pandora's Box. 'My child,' she said. 'Don't you know?'

Eleni braced herself for what she was about to hear. 'Know what, Munire?'

'Andreas was not your grandfather.'

Eleni's heart hammered in her breast. 'But...that can't be so. That's the name on my mother's wedding certificate: Nina Laskaris, daughter of Sophia and Andreas Laskaris.'

'In the name of God,' said Munire, shaking her head in disbelief. 'Then she took her secret to her grave.'

'Who?' asked Eleni, still reeling from shock.

Munire looked at her with great pity. 'Why, your grandmother of course. The truth is that Leonidas and Maria were his children, but Nina, well...she came along when intimate relations with Andreas had ceased and they no longer shared the marital bed.' Munire reached for Eleni's hand and squeezed it tenderly. 'Nikolai, Grand Duke Orlovsky: he was your grandfather.'

Eleni felt numb.

'If the truth be known, it was love at first sight for both of them,' Munire continued, 'and I believe that Sophia loved him even more deeply than she loved Andreas. Of course they tried hard to conceal it, but such a love cannot be hidden. When she became pregnant with Nina, no one said a word. Nevertheless, we all knew the child was Nikolai's.'

'And Andreas, did he know my mother was not his?'

'He must have done. But he loved your grandmother too much to make a scene. It would have brought disgrace to the family and destroyed them all.'

Munire apologized for the unintentional hurt she had caused. For Eleni, it was just another surprise in a long list of surprises. Eleni asked if she could show her the photographs from the suitcase. Munire was more than delighted. She put on her reading glasses, looked at them, and smiled.

'Seeing these makes me feel young again,' she said.

The first photograph was of Leonidas when he was a child; it was the same one that Eleni had looked at over and over again during the past few weeks. He was standing next to a dresser looking straight into the camera. There was something melancholic about him, something 'other-worldly,' as Chrysoula had pointed out.

'This boy was the apple of his mother's eye. She loved him more than life itself. She would have been inconsolable when he was torn away from her in Smyrna. Many mothers went mad or killed themselves. We Turkish mothers experienced the same thing. War tears us apart, yet in many ways it unites us.'

Munire picked out another photograph, this time of Sophia and Nikolai on a summer excursion to the Sweetwaters of Asia. They were sitting on a rug enjoying a picnic. With them were Leonidas and Maria, and in the background, standing to attention next to his beloved car Mestinigar, was Ali Agha. Eleni commented on how happy they all looked. After what she had just learned, she understood why.

'Your grandmother was one of the most elegant and beautiful women in Constantinople,' said Munire. 'In that way she took after her grandmother Dimitra, who was also reputed to have been the beauty in her time. There was one great difference though. Sophia had the most unusual eyes, a deep amethyst color; they were curiously magnetic. I never knew anyone else with eyes like that. It's hard to see in these photographs,' she laughed. 'You'll have to take my word for it.'

Eleni wanted to show Munire the later photographs taken in Athens that were given to her by Chrysoula. Munire held them close to her eyes and studied every detail. In particular, she commented on the ones of Nina.

'She doesn't have any of her father's features,' she said, referring to Nikolai.

'What was he like?' asked Eleni.

Munire smiled. She sensed Eleni's renewed interest in him.

'As you can see, he was tall and ruggedly built, with a dark complexion; very handsome, with film-star looks and the aristocratic bearing of a man born into the upper levels of Russian society. Unlike Andreas, who was a retiring and studious type, Nikolai was outgoing and enthusiastic. He reveled in life and had an uplifting effect on all those who came into contact with him. Everyone admired his boundless energy and all the women fell under his charms, especially Sophia's good friend Anna, who I believe wanted to marry him at one time. He was a risk-taker at a time when few dared to take risks. The soirées and the dance studio adjacent to La Maison du l'Orient were both his ideas.'

Munire asked about the swarthy gentleman who appeared on several occasions with Sophia.

'That's Vangelis,' replied Eleni, 'a friend of Markos. He took Ali Agha's place after he was killed. When La Maison du l'Orient burned down, he moved to Smyrna with her. He was a gifted musician and played with a band there on the quayside—the Café Aphrodite. Perhaps you've heard of it? Apparently it was very famous. He was with my grandmother when they tried to flee the city, but they became separated and it was years before they finally met again in Athens. Later on, he became quite a successful musician and a bandleader in his own right. From what I gather, he was a loyal and true friend to my grandmother. He was the only one whom she could talk to about her past. They worked together in the Resistance. He was executed at the same time as my mother and grandmother.'

'Your grandmother was fortunate to have had such a friend,' replied

Munire. 'It is testament to the woman she was.'

Munire looked at a photograph of Maria taken at the time of her debut as an opera singer. 'She looks like a film star.'

'What was she like as a child?' Eleni asked.

'As I said, she was not an easy child, if that's what you mean.'

'My impression was that she was shunned because of some sort of prophecy. Is that true?'

'I heard something of the sort,' Munire replied.

'Do you really believe in such things?'

Munire looked offended. 'We cannot escape our fate, Eleni. It is written on our brow.' She paused. 'I have the feeling that you have been quite selective in what you've told me—particularly about Maria. I haven't the slightest doubt that it's because you wished to protect me from things you thought might upset me. But given the wisdom that I have after such a long life, I can only imagine what it was. That she survived those tragic events to live out her days in peace doesn't surprise me in the slightest. Feed a crow and it will pluck out your eyes.'

Once more, Eleni's questions were answered with a proverb which she was left to work out for herself.

At that point the door opened, and Hasan announced that lunch was ready to be served. Munire looped her arm through Eleni's and they followed him into the garden where under a cascade of the last of the summer vines, a row of trestle tables had been laid out for the guests. Hasan seated his mother at the head of the table and went back to supervise a freshly killed goat roasting over the coals. The mouth-watering aromas of baked vegetables, salads, and freshly baked bread filled the garden, as one by one the women brought out trays of food and filled the table. When all were seated, Latifa brought out the largest brass platter of pilav Eleni had ever seen and placed it in the center of the long table. Everyone clapped. Munire leaned over to Eleni and told her that the family was honoring her with Sevkiye's famous pilav.

'I spent hours watching your grandmother's cook Sevkiye make this special dish,' Munire said, with a smile. 'Eventually, I perfected it. Now I have passed on the recipe to Latifa.'

Latifa scooped a large spoonful onto two plates and handed them to Eleni and Surreya. An expectant silence fell over the group as they waited for Eleni's approval. It was one of the tastiest dishes she had ever eaten. Even Surreya, who had tasted many pilavs in Istanbul's best restaurants, was impressed. Eleni congratulated Latifa who clasped her hands together and bowed in a gesture of appreciation.

Before Eleni left, Munire asked what had brought her back to Turkey.

She told her about Dimitra's memoirs, written for Sophia in the last few days before the fire and that Surreya's husband was in the process of translating it.

'Do you have any idea why she wrote it in the Ottoman script?' Eleni asked.

Munire thought about it. She was as surprised as everyone else to hear that it was not in Greek.

'Dimitra was a dark horse,' Munire said. 'She was always different to the other Greek women I knew and I can't put my finger on the reason. I know little about her except for her fine work and that her husband was a French painter. She was also reputed to be a fine horsewoman. That was something that puzzled me greatly, as under the Ottomans, non-Muslims, especially Greeks, were forbidden to ride until much later when the government modernized the laws in an attempt to give equality to all subjects.'

'Do you think that had something to do with her being married to a Frenchman?' asked Eleni. 'Perhaps that lifted her from the constraints of society.'

'I can't see why that should have made any difference. After all, she was a woman of good standing and still a Greek.'

'What do you think happened to her? My aunt said she refused to leave Smyrna.'

'When I visited the city after the fire there was nothing left of the Greek quarter. The fire raged all the way to the Konak and the Muslim quarter, and then the wind changed course. Her atelier in the street of the embroiderers was completely destroyed and her old house had been pulled down. From what I gathered, Dimitra did not approve of the Greek invasion and I think she may have chosen to stay as a matter of principle. Besides, she was much too old to leave and would have been a burden on her family.'

It had been a great privilege to meet Munire, but her health was failing and Eleni knew she would probably never see her again. It would be the end of an era and she felt an overwhelming sense of sadness. She promised to write to her when the memoirs had been translated.

The car turned out of the street and headed towards Izmir.

'What a wonderful day,' said Surreya. 'It's a long time since I experienced such warm hospitality. I enjoyed myself immensely. Do you know something,' she added, 'one of the sons was a history teacher and he told me that all the houses in that street once belonged to Greeks.'

Eleni turned away, staring at the vast gray-green olive groves that lined the highway. It had been too good a day to hear that sort of news.

The following day, Eleni and Surreya flew back to Istanbul. A few days later, Dr. Gunes arrived back from his trip and returned the memoirs to Eleni, along with the much anticipated translation.

# CHAPTER 40

*Istanbul, October 1972, The Memoirs*
For my cherished granddaughter, Sophia.
That she may bear witness to my life as I know it.

Dimitra Lamartine
August 5, 1922, Smyrna

My cherished granddaughter,

For a while now, I have had the idea of telling you things about my past that until now have remained a closed chapter of my life, a life too painful and at times too beautiful to recall. I had always intended to take these memories to my grave and much of this change of heart is due in part to your sweet-natured daughter Nina, and the inquisitive and sensitive Leonidas, for it is through them that I have slowly unlocked the door to my past and have begun to relive my youth. Sitting here in my dear husband's studio, bathed in the warmth of his presence, I ponder where to begin. The present becomes blurred and slowly the mist lifts, taking me back to a time and place I tried so hard to forget. I have little time on this Earth, and I now know that I would have done you a great injustice by taking my secrets to the grave. In you, my life blood flows, just as in me flows the blood of my beloved parents, and I can no longer deprive you of knowing what I should have told you earlier.

My cherished one, the woman you have known all your life as Dimitra was not born with that name. It is without ill-will on my part that I have deceived you, and for this I ask your forgiveness.

I was born in 1822, not far from here on the island of Chios. In those days, the island was part of the vast Ottoman Empire. Prior to the Ottoman Conquest by Suleyman the Magnificent on Easter Day 1566, Chios was ruled for a while by the Venetians and later by the Genoese, whose legacy could still be seen in the fact that some of the people were of Catholic origin and still kept their faith.

Though the island is small, being approximately thirty-two miles long and twelve miles wide, for centuries its merchants and ship owners have exploited its position on the ancient trade routes from the Mediterranean to the Black Sea, Constantinople, and Smyrna. Being well known as the birthplace of Homer, the island boasted several institutions of learning, and hospitals and asylums. It has a most pleasant climate which enabled it to prosper in the cultivation of vines, olives, mulberry trees for the production of silk, fruit, and above all, the lentisk tree, from which is harvested the highly prized gum, once worth its weight in gold, which grows in the south part of the island. Because of all these things, Chios was the most prosperous of the islands in the Aegean and was accorded great privileges by the Sultans. I tell you this so that you may glean a little of the beauty and prosperity of that beautiful isle.

As I have said, I was not born with the name Dimitra. The name bestowed on me and the one by which I would be known for the first thirteen years of my life was Durrusehvar. Yes, my cherished one, it is a Turkish name and one that I am proud of. You may ask how I came by this name and why I never continued to use it. The story is a long and painful one.

My earliest recollections of childhood are of sitting under a carob tree learning to embroider, while listening to stories told to me by the woman who had nurtured me from birth, and who I called Aunt Kuzel. She was the mistress of a fine mansion outside Chora. Two storeys high, the house was built on a hill surrounded by orchards and a large garden. On the upper floor was a spacious, carpeted reception room with a gilt ceiling inscribed with passages from the Koran. The elaborately painted wooden walls were filled with closets for textiles and in small niches were displayed ornaments, vases of fresh flowers, and a Koran. Underneath the large, low windows was a raised platform with long soft cushions. From here, one could spend hours watching the ships come and go in the harbor below and on a clear day, it was possible to see the undulating hills of the Turkish coastline.

In this splendid room, Rifat Bey—Aunt Kuzel's husband—entertained a constant stream of guests. Aunt Kuzel was the third and favorite wife of Rifat Bey and as such, he lavished a great deal of affection on her, bestowing her gifts and jewels whenever he returned from one of his many journeys to Constantinople, the Balkans, and North Africa. He was much older than Aunt Kuzel, who was barely twenty when they married, yet she adored him as much as he did her. Their love was further cemented when she gave birth to their boy Osman, soon after they were married. Osman was two years younger than me and I loved him like a brother. I might add here that Rifat Bey's other wives lived in Chora and he saw to it that they were well cared for. Neither had been able to give him a child, yet on hearing of the birth of Osman, both wives came to the house to pay their respects. Apart from that, we met them on several occasions when we visited the hammam. Being gentlewomen, they were always respectful to Aunt Kuzel and took a great interest in Osman's well-being, just as they did my own.

Aunt Kuzel was the daughter of a pasha and as a result of an enlightened upbringing she excelled in the illustrious arts of calligraphy, music—of which she played both the oud and the kanun—a kind of zither—and her favorite pastime of all, embroidery.

The household had many servants; some were bought as slaves and each one performed a singular duty. When Aunt Kuzel married, she had the good fortune to bring her own maid with her, a Circassian called Emine. Emine had irreproachable manners and always addressed Aunt Kuzel as 'my dearest lady.' When I was three years old, I was given my own maid—a Greek girl called Polyxeni who had been my wet nurse. I later found out that she had given birth to a boy just before I was born and that after the slaughter of her child by the Turks, she and her sister were taken to the slave market in Smyrna where she was bought by Rifat Bey. We never found out what happened to her sister. At first, Polyxeni was forbidden to speak her own language but sometime after she became my maid, Aunt Kuzel allowed her to speak to me in Greek, but only in the privacy of my room. Until then, I only spoke Orta Türkçe—Turkish of the higher classes. Later on I familiarized myself with the Turkish of the lower classes.

Each day after lunch, Aunt Kuzel was in the habit of retiring to her room to rest for a while. A few hours later and fully refreshed, she would call for me and we would spend a little time together. In the warm summer months, this usually meant taking short walks in the garden or going for a picnic in the nearby hills. In the wintertime, when Rifat Bey was not entertaining guests, we spent time together in the reception room which was always kept heated by a brazier. These afternoons always ended with Aunt Kuzel reading a story while I practiced my embroidery. After the storytelling, we were brought sherbets freshly made from the fruits of our orchards. As Osman grew older, he joined us, but I confess that the afternoons spent alone with Aunt Kuzel were the sweetest days of all.

On my fifth birthday, Aunt Kuzel and Rifat Bey bought me a portable writing case with an inkpot and a receptacle for pens. From that moment, a teacher came to the house and taught me how to write Ottoman Turkish and later, Greek. Because of these lessons, the blissful afternoons of storytelling became less frequent. Although young, I was considered a good student and both Aunt Kuzel and Rifat Bey took great delight in my advancement.

As I have said, in those days there were many visitors to the house. One of them was Aunt Kuzel's brother, Yasim-Ali. Uncle Yasim-Ali visited us every week and always showed a great interest in my well-being. Each time he saw me, he gave me a gift of some sort: one day a small hand mirror, another time an embroidered handkerchief, and my favorite of all, a songbird in a beautifully carved cage which Polyxeni hung outside my window. I can never recall him visiting empty-handed. If he had nothing, then he would pick a flower from the garden or a ripe fruit from the orchard. Once, he brought me a delicately striped shell that he had picked up on the beach. It didn't matter what he brought, I accepted them all with a good heart and put them all away in my room until the petals withered and the fruit turned and Polyxeni told me it was better to throw them away.

After presenting me with his gift, Uncle Yasim-Ali would always ask, 'What have you learned today, little one?' to which I would have to think of something to say. If I had nothing to say, then I would think hard and say something like, 'Today the vegetables will be cut.' One day, I replied, 'Today I learnt that if I turn my face to the rain, I need not create my own tears: God will do it for me,' to which he roared with laughter.

Uncle Yasim-Ali never stayed long and he always left with the words, 'In the name of God, the all compassionate, the most merciful, protect this child from the vicissitudes of this world. May she be free of vanity and sin and bring joy to those around her. This is my wish and if that wish be granted, then I can die in peace.' The first few times he said this, I cried myself to sleep thinking that he really was going to die and that I would never see him again. He was a very handsome man with dark expressive eyes that lit up when he was happy. On a good day, he was lively and funny, but it saddens me greatly to say that there were days when he became melancholic, occasionally bursting into tears for no apparent reason. Only Aunt Kuzel could bring him out of these moods.

He had a wife who was a viper and who disliked Aunt Kuzel and me intensely. Aunt Kuzel said she had a jealous heart because she had no children of her own and that I must forgive her. That was not an easy thing to do, as on one occasion when I saw her in the hammam and when no one was looking, she threw hot water at me and hissed under her breath that I was the daughter of a giour. For both Aunt Kuzel and Uncle Yasim-Ali's sake, I bore the pain in silence, avoiding her as much as possible after that. But it was her words that pained me the most. I had heard the word giour before and knew that it meant infidel—a non-believer. As I had been brought up a good Muslim, I couldn't understand why she insulted me in this way. Some days later, I asked Aunt Kuzel if I was an infidel. She looked at me with great sadness and took me in her arms. 'Of course not, little one,' she said. 'What on earth made you think that?'

Uncle Yasim-Ali was well known throughout the island as a fine horseman and he always arrived at the house on his favorite horse, Malik—a blood-bay Karaman from a noble blood line which was given to him by his father. Malik was a magnificent animal with large coal-black eyes and a glistening muscular body that rippled with tension. But he was a brute to handle and whenever anyone other than Uncle Yasim-Ali tried to mount him, he lashed his tail and thrashed his hind legs wildly in the air. Aunt Kuzel told me that her brother loved him more than anything in the world. On the days when he came to the house, I used to watch from my window as he tethered the horse alongside those of Rifat Bey's, always taking the time to see that there were enough oats for him. Noticing my interest, he took me to see him and on hot days when the air rang with the sound of cicadas, we sat on the stump of a tree and without uttering a word, we watched the horse graze. Any sudden movement and he would lift his head, flare his nostrils, and flash his eyes and listen, checking that everything around him was in order. Then he would lower his head again and continue grazing.

Uncle Yasim-Ali took great delight in telling me that his family was descended from a long line of Sipahi warriors. The Sipahi were legendary horsemen and fearless in battle. 'The horse is sacred,' he once told me. 'It is a man's spirit and should be revered.'

Malik became accustomed to me, and one day Uncle Yasim-Ali brought him over to me. Despite his enormous size, I wasn't afraid of him in the slightest. In fact, I truly believed I saw his soul in those huge eyes. At first, he nuzzled his head in my hair, snorted, and backed away. When he realized I meant him no harm, he stood his ground and let me stroke his mane with the blue bead that was carefully plaited in his hair to ward off the evil spirits. He sensed every move I made. Uncle Yasim-Ali thought I had a special way with him and that was a good omen.

One day he put me onto the saddle with him, and secure in knowing that I was in safe hands, we began our ascent into the hills. The sensation of Malik's hooves thudding on the soft earth and the warm breeze on my cheeks was exhilarating. Almost a year later, Uncle Yasim-Ali presented me with my very own horse, a foal sired by Malik. I named her Nillufer—the Persian word for water lily. I was about seven years old when I first rode Nillufer. She was an intelligent horse with a gentle temperament. When Uncle Yasim-Ali thought that I had mastered handling her, he proposed to take me for a ride to the Byzantine monastery of Nea Moni in the center of the island. Until then, we had never ventured far from the house.

I remember that it was a beautiful spring day and I felt a sense of elation as we made our way along a well-trodden pathway until we halted at the top of a rocky outcrop. From there I saw for the very first time the famous monastery that I had heard people say once belonged to the Christians. Uncle Yasim-Ali told me that at one time it was possible to see wonderful mosaics of such splendor equaled only by those of the Haghia Sophia. I was saddened to see that much of it now lay in ruins. We proceeded to the far side of the monastery, eventually dismounting next to a wild fig tree where we lay for a while, soaking up the beauty of the afternoon. The air was filled with the sweetness of blossom and wild herbs and all around me, as far as the eye could see, was a profusion of dark red tulips. Uncle Yasim-Ali told me that it was only in spring that one could experience such a wonderful spectacle. He said that they were the very same tulips that the Turkomen tribes had brought with them from the East all those centuries ago; and that they first flourished in the valleys of the Tien Shan Mountains in Central Asia. For that reason, they had always been considered an important symbol for the Turks, as their appearance in spring represented life and fertility, and the blood-red color was meant to signal eternity. In such peaceful surroundings, I fell asleep.

When I woke, Nillufer was standing nearby, flicking her tail angrily at the iridescent-blue horseflies that pestered her. The breeze had dropped and in the stifling heat the sound of cicadas was deafening. Sitting up, I saw that I was alone. At first I thought nothing of it, thinking that Uncle Yasim-Ali had taken Malik for a ride and didn't want to wake me, but when he failed to return, I became worried, frantically running around and calling his name. In the distance I saw Malik standing next to a collapsed section of the monastery wall. He struck the earth violently with his feet and snorted loudly. The creature's eyes were filled with terror. On the ground next to him lay the body of Uncle Yasim-Ali. A pool of blood was seeping from his abdomen into the earth, mingling with the petals of dark red tulips. In his hand was a dagger, its mottled pale jade hilt covered in blood. Overcome with grief, I fainted.

I remember little of the following few weeks. Uncle Yasim-Ali's death plunged the house into darkness. Polyxeni said that he had been buried near the monastery. I couldn't understand why, as other members of the family were buried in the Muslim cemetery outside Chora. She shrugged her shoulders and said that Aunt Kuzel told them that it was his wish to be buried there. She also told me that it took Rifat Bey's men two days to catch Malik and bring him back to the house. Allowing no one to get near him, and tethered to a post in the stable, he refused to eat. Gradually, his life blood ebbed away and they found him dead in his stall a week later. They say he died of a broken heart.

Throughout the summer, I saw little of Aunt Kuzel and my only true companion was Nillufer. No one stopped me from riding her but I never ventured as far as the monastery. Gradually, the shadow of darkness lifted once more. Aunt Kuzel began to take walks through the garden again and often asked me to join her. She also took a renewed interest in my studies and was delighted to hear that I had not neglected them. Not long after, she and Rifat Bey announced that the pigeons were bringing us another baby and a few months later, she gave birth to a girl, Leyla. We were all delighted.

In the spring of the following year, Aunt Kuzel and Rifat Bey received word that an old friend would be paying them a visit. Aunt Kuzel was beside herself with joy and went to a great deal of trouble to ensure he received the warmest of welcomes. During the following few days, a multitude of provisions arrived from Chora and the kitchen was a constant flurry of activity. As usual, Emine meticulously supervised the household chores, seeing to it that all the carpets were taken outside and thoroughly beaten, the rooms swept, and swept again for good measure, the silverware polished until it gleamed, and that all the rooms were filled with fresh flowers from the garden. On the day of the guest's arrival, Polyxeni was told to dress me in my best clothes—a voluminous emerald-green salvar dotted with clusters of embroidered flowers, a white cotton blouse, and an embroidered waistcoat in delicate shades of peach and pink. Polyxeni was to bring me to the reception room where, with Aunt Kuzel and Osman, we sat on the soft cushions and looked out of the windows hoping to catch a glimpse of his ship as it dropped anchor in the harbor. A few hours later, the guest arrived at the house with two pack horses laden with enormous trunks and crates.

Aunt Kuzel received him in a gold brocade kaftan and embroidered white slippers. I had never seen her look so lovely. While Rifat Bey's men moved the trunks into the house, I was pushed forward and introduced to him. The man bowed, offered me his hand and said a few words in a language I had never heard before. At first his words frightened me and, thinking that it might be a curse, I backed away. Everyone laughed. Aunt Kuzel told me it was French and as I had progressed well in Turkish and Greek, this is the language I was expected to learn next. Realizing that the man meant me no harm, I tried hard to hide my shame.

The Frenchman's name was Jean–Michel Lamartine and he was a painter. I learned that he was once the envoy to the French Ambassador in Constantinople before becoming a full-time painter and that was how she came to know him. In those days he was a bachelor, but after returning to

France he married a Mme. Antonia de Montaubin who died a few months after giving birth to their son.

Jean-Michel stayed with us for three weeks. He was a bright and cheerful man, and I soon became accustomed to his presence. In the evenings, he and Rifat Bey liked to play cards or backgammon on the balcony until the early hours of the morning. Lying in my bed at night, I could hear their low voices deep in conversation. Polyxeni thought they might be discussing politics and the war against the Greeks. I had no idea what she was talking about. When I pressed her further, she said it was better to let sleeping dogs lie and that it was best not to mention this to Aunt Kuzel, as it would result in her being dismissed. I had grown to love Polyxeni and for her sake, I promised to keep quiet.

Jean-Michel was in the habit of rising early and after strapping his portmanteau and easel onto a pack horse, he disappeared for hours at a time on painting excursions. Each time he returned, I was anxious to see what he had done. At such moments, I was always astounded by the fact that when he left the house, his canvases and sketchbooks were blank, yet when he returned, they were full of images that more often than not, I remembered seeing myself. Sometimes the scenes were of Chora itself—the domes of the hammam, the sunny courtyards of the mosques, or the overhanging wooden balconies inside the castle walls. At other times, they were portraits of well-known personalities in Chora: Khalid-Ali, the Egyptian seller of budgerigars and songbirds, or Fatma, the blind orange-seller.

Polyxeni thought his work was a gift from God but I wanted to know more. When I thought no one was looking, I stole out onto the balcony and watched him work in his room through a narrow slit in the latticed window. Then one day, he spotted me and said that as I had shown an interest in his work, he was prepared to give me a few lessons. And so, accompanied by Aunt Kuzel herself, who sat nearby to watch and to translate, he set about teaching me the basics of his work.

At first, I thought his brushstrokes spontaneous, but the more I looked, the more I realized how considered the work was. He showed me how pigments were mixed with various gums and oils to bind them together, and how colors are applied to create the desired effect; the softness and transparency of watercolors, and the intensity of oils. I was fascinated.

'To produce a picture is a science and an art in itself,' he told me. 'We can acquire these skills, but if there is no emotion—no feeling—then the work is nothing.' He drew a comparison with Aunt Kuzel's embroidery. 'You see how cleverly she blends these skills to produce a petal so beautiful that we want to pluck it from the cloth.' I felt as a blind man must feel after receiving the gift of sight. Suddenly it was as if I saw everything around me for the first time.

When the time came for him to depart, I thanked him for his kindness and presented him with a gift; it was a small handkerchief that I had embroidered especially for him. Aunt Kuzel put her arm around my shoulders and I noticed that her eyes were filled with tears. Jean-Michel shook my hand and thanked me. He also had tears in his eyes.

'Elle est comme sa mere, elle apporte la joie a tous ceux qui la connaissent. L'encourager. Un jour. Elle sera son egal,' he said softly.

When I asked Aunt Kuzel what he said, she hesitated for a moment and whispered in my ear. 'He says that you are just like your mother; you bring joy to all who know you, and that I should encourage you, for one day, you will be her equal.' I was confused. It was the first time I had ever heard anyone mention my mother and I felt a strong urge to run away, but with Aunt Kuzel's arm holding me firmly, that was impossible.

The trunks loaded onto the horses, we stood and watched him head down the dusty road into Chora with Rifat Bey. The moment they rounded the corner out of sight, I broke away from Aunt Kuzel's grip, ran back to the house and shut myself in my room. This time I had no desire to join the others and watch his ship sail away. Nothing anyone could do could coax me out of my misery. I had always looked upon Aunt Kuzel as my mother. Now all I thought about was my real mother and I asked myself over and over again, who was she? And if I had a mother, then I also had a father. Who were my parents and why had no one told me about them?

Several days after Jean-Michel's departure, I woke one morning to find Aunt Kuzel sitting next to my bed. She said she had something important to say to me. 'From the day I first held you in my arms, I loved you as if you were my own and you have brought us nothing but happiness. Since then, the time has flown and soon you will be a young woman with a family of your own. What I am about to tell you, I could never say before. You were far too young to understand. You must believe me when I say that both Rifat Bey and I wanted nothing more than to give you a happy childhood surrounded by love. I believe we succeeded. I always knew the day would come when I would have to tell you who you really are. The last words said to you by Jean-Michel, and the deep sadness that clouds your eyes, tell me that time has come.

'Your mother was my one and only true friend and I loved her like a sister. When we first met, I was not much older than you are now and our friendship remained close until the day she died. She was a Greek from a distinguished family. Her name was Artemis and the family name, Florades.

340

The family had lived in Chios for generations. At that time, there were many Greeks living on the island and some of them were among the wealthiest of the Sultan's subjects. The Florades were one such family. They kept several homes—a townhouse in Chora, a country estate in the Kampos where they cultivated their gardens and orchards, and a house in Constantinople, where Michael Florades, Artemis's father, conducted most of his business affairs.

'Like most girls, it was incumbent upon me to learn the art of embroidery and I began my training at the age of four or five, as you yourself did. Your mother was a young woman when we heard of her skills. They said she was born with a needle and silk thread in her fingers and when I saw her work for the first time, I believed it. Not only were her stitches perfect, but her colors equaled those of any painter; her floral motifs were so real that you thought they would wither on the cloth, and her fruit so ripe you could almost taste it. As a result of her reputation, my mother sent me to her for lessons.

'Artemis had an elder brother, Pandely, whom I remember well. He was extremely studious and attended the university. He was the same age as my brother, Yasim-Ali, and they knew each other from childhood. While Pandely studied the intellectual arts of philosophy and law, my father sent Yasim-Ali to Constantinople to study at the Sublime Porte, as it was expected that he would take up a career in the military or the civil service. In the summer of 1820, Yasim-Ali returned to Chios and met up with his old friend Pandely. It was at this time that he saw Artemis. In the years that he had been away, she had blossomed into a beautiful woman and he fell in love with her from the moment he laid eyes on her. Indeed, there were few who could resist her beauty. With skin the color of alabaster and cheeks the blush of a ripe peach, she had the most unusual eyes, shades of amethyst that seemed to draw you in and keep you spellbound. My mother used to say that in a family of starlings, there is only one nightingale, and she was it.

'With Pandely's help, the pair finally met. In that moment, she blushed and Yasim-Ali knew that she had also fallen in love with him. Having exposed her face to him there followed playful games and secretive meetings which both of them concocted to let them catch a glimpse of each other. In my own way I tried to help them and I confess that I was just as guilty as Pandely.

'Around this time, it was my father's wish that Yasim-Ali marry. Several respectable women were chosen from the Turkish community by my mother, but none were deemed suitable. Each time he showed a lack of interest. Now he had lost his heart to a Greek girl. At this point I must tell you that many Greek women were chosen to be the wives or concubines of Turkish men; indeed, some of our greatest Sultans fell in love with Greek women. Some were even allowed to keep their own religion although any children were brought up as Muslims. The misery of these two lovers was that the Florades family would never agree to such a marriage and Artemis knew this. For generations, the Greek nobility of Chios had intermarried and Michael Florades saw no reason to abandon this tradition. Their love was doomed from the start. Soon, her family began to suspect Yasim-Ali's intentions and fearing a rift between the families, hurriedly sought a suitable match for her from the Greek Orthodox community.

'I remember the anguish that this love brought them and in my own way tried to help them. Each time I went for my lessons, Yasim-Ali would give me a note for her which I stole away in my entari and gave her when we were alone. In turn, she always gave me something for him. Sometimes it was a small piece of embroidery.

'It was at this time that a group of French officials visited the island as guests of Michael Florades. One of the men was Jean-Michel and we soon discovered that he was an accomplished portrait painter. Knowing that he had a painter as his guest, Michael Florades commissioned him to paint a portrait of Artemis, with the intention that he might use it to find her a suitable husband. When Yasim-Ali heard of this, he commissioned his own painting of her and at the same time one of himself, only this time they were to be miniatures painted on ivory which he intended to have made into a locket to give her as a token of his love. He asked Jean-Michel not to mention this to anyone. Jean-Michel and Yasim-Ali struck up a close friendship. Being somewhat of a romantic himself, he was sympathetic to my brother's plight. After the French left, the portrait of Artemis hung in the salon in the house in Chora for all to see and the ivory miniatures were given to Yasim-Ali, who sent them to Constantinople and had them set in a gold locket edged with diamonds. He couldn't wait to show it to me. It was exquisite. He told me that when the time was right, he would present it to her. Until then, he would gaze upon her loveliness and be reminded of her.

'With Artemis's family keeping a close eye on her, the pair had no other option but to meet in secret, but to do this they had to win the confidence of her maid, Euphrosyne. This was not an easy task as Euphrosyne was duty-bound to report on Artemis's whereabouts at all times to Kyria Florades. But in the end, she agreed. "I fear that it will lead you into a wilderness from which you will never return," she told her, sadly. "But if that is your wish, then it is my duty to make you happy."

'The lovers made a plan to meet near the Monastery of Nea Moni. Artemis and Euphrosyne would make regular visits there on certain saint's days and Yasim-Ali would take his horse for a ride into the mountains. At a planned time, the pair would meet. It was a great risk for them all but one which they were prepared to take. Thus it was that with the air thick with incense and the congregation deep in prayer, Artemis slipped away unnoticed through a small doorway behind the monks' dwellings at the far side of the monastery to be with her lover. At all times, Euphrosyne watched out for her. When the service ended, Artemis took up her position in the congregation once more. The lovers met in this way several times and then fate intervened in a way that changed all our lives forever.

'In 1821, the Greek Revolution broke out. It began in the Danubian provinces of the empire and quickly spread to the rest of Greece. Immediately, the islands of Spetsai, Hydra, and Psara declared independence and sent their fleets of warships into battle. In August, my father and Yasim-Ali were called to join the Sultan's forces. Before their ship set sail, the lovers arranged to meet at the monastery. It was during this rendezvous that Yasim-Ali gave the locket to Artemis. Not knowing how long he would be away, and fearing the Turks would take their vengeance out on the Greeks, he gave her his precious jade dagger which had once belonged to our grandfather; he told her that in the event that she found herself in trouble, she was not to hesitate to use it. That evening my mother and I stood on the quayside and watched our loved ones sail away. Before he left, my brother made me promise to take care of Artemis and I gave him my word.

'The Chians had already seen the Turks' fury. On hearing news of the war and the slaughter of twenty thousand Turkish men, women, and children by the Greeks, the Grand Seignior, Sultan Mahmud II, hanged the Patriarch of Constantinople along with three of his bishops, and several clerics and prominent Greeks in the service of the Porte. Fearing the worst, the clergy and members of Chios's most distinguished families pleaded with Admiral Tombazes to leave the island alone and they pledged their loyalty to the Sultan.

'Trusting no one, especially the Christians, he demanded hostages from the island's highest-ranking families, along with Metropolitan Plato and his deacon, Makarios. They were all jailed within the castle walls. Michael Florades, who had been away on business at the time, was sent to Bostangi Bashi jail in Constantinople. As time went by I saw less and less of Artemis. Her family was now under the care of her uncle Georgos Florades, an austere and deeply religious man, and they spent most of their time in the Kampos. She told me he was planning to get them away from the island, but neither she nor her mother would hear of it.

'For almost a year, the war raged throughout Greece. In Chios, Turks and Greeks alike were tormented by fear. Skillful fortunetellers profited greatly and everywhere the omens of doom foretold a great catastrophe. In March 1822, a small fleet led by the Samian revolutionary Logothetis headed for Chios and dropped anchor in Karfas Bay, not far from Chora. In fear of our lives, my family was forced to retreat into the castle with our fellow Muslims. Widespread destruction of the island took place and much to our great sadness, we heard that Pandely had joined the revolutionaries and was exerting a great fervor amongst the Greeks, parading through the town and shouting "Long live Greece."

'Day and night we prayed that the Sultan would send help. As dawn broke on April 11, 1822, my mother woke me with the news that the Ottoman Armada was in sight. Masallah. We knew then that God had answered our call. We all rushed onto the battlements to behold the glorious sight for ourselves. Approaching the harbor was the elite of the Sultan's navy led by Admiral Kapitan Kara-Ali in his flagship, Maizural Livo—Victory. It was accompanied by a multitude of frigates, corvettes, and numerous other craft.

'While we wept for joy, the Greeks began to flee. Thousands joined the exodus from the island; others fled into the hills. Almost immediately, the bombing commenced. The earth shook, fires raged, and acrid smoke filled the air. At the same time, four thousand Turkish troops landed from the mainland. Each day at the call of the muezzin, our warriors knelt towards the East, kissed the soil of Chios, and after asking for the protection of God, drew their scimitars in readiness for another day of bloodshed. At the end of the day, they arrived back with their spoils. Heads were deposited in front of a scribe and a bounty paid for each transaction. In the concourse outside the castle walls, where once our peoples mingled in a most cordial manner, public executions took place daily.

'Throughout this, all I could think about was Artemis. I was the only one who could help her but it was impossible to leave the safety of the castle. At this point, the hostages in the castle were still safe but I feared for Michael Florades in Constantinople. Then I heard that many Greeks had taken refuge in the foreign consulates. In desperation, I turned to my cousin Suleyman Bey, an army officer who was close to my brother, and begged him to help. At first he refused, citing Pandely's treachery, but in the end he agreed because of Yasim-Ali.

'After finding the Florades house in Chora ransacked and now occupied by Turkish soldiers, Suleyman headed south to their country estate. On reaching the Kampos, a scene of desolation lay before him. The once-beautiful homes had been looted and destroyed. He picked his way through the ruins of the Florades home, but there was no sign of Artemis or her family. He came across a group of mercenaries dividing the spoils of the day and asked if anyone had survived. They laughed at him. One of them said that those who managed to escape were probably trying to make their way to the coast.

'In haste, Suleyman left in the direction of the mastic villages and the port of Pasha Limani. This tiny port, the place from where the mastic left for the saray was now teeming with terror-stricken Greeks, pushing and shoving in a desperate attempt to board the rescue boats. Everywhere, the Turks took their revenge. After a long search, Suleyman eventually spotted Pandely wading through the water towards a small boat. Georgos Florades and his wife were already heading away to safety in another boat, but there was no sign of Artemis. Suleyman ordered his men to catch Pandely and bring him back alive. Weak and exhausted, Pandely was no match for Suleyman's men and was soon brought back to shore. Suleyman promised to spare Pandely's life if he told him the whereabouts of Artemis. Pandely was in no doubt as to what would happen to him but thinking that by some miracle his sister might survive, he told Suleyman that she and Euphrosyne had refused to leave and were hiding in the well next to the orange grove in the Kampos. Suleyman drew his scimitar and as Pandely prayed for his soul and his sister's safety, the scimitar fell on the traitor's neck.

'Suleyman immediately returned to the Kampos to find the well. He called out. There was no answer. At the bottom of the well lay a heap of bodies and the stench of rotting flesh in the afternoon sun caught his breath. Two Turks sat nearby haggling over the price of a young Greek boy. Suleyman called to them and offered them each a gold sovereign to bring the bodies out of the well. Artemis and Euphrosyne were not among them.

'At that point, Suleyman called off the search. Not wanting to return to Chora and bring me bad news, he decided to join a large band of soldiers heading for the hills to finish their work. Their destination was the monastery of Nea Moni. During this time, I began a spiritual struggle through fasting and prayer. I prayed for my father, for Yasim-Ali, for Suleyman, for my mother, who wept constantly, for Artemis, for Michael Florades and the hostages rotting away in jail, for Pandely and the misguided Greeks, and for all my Muslim brothers and sisters. I prayed until my knees were sore and my body weak and when I thought I could pray no more, I looked up and there stood my dear brother. Yasim-Ali had returned. It was a miracle.

'When I told him that I had not seen or heard from Artemis in several months and had sent Suleyman Bey out to search for her, he held his head in his hands in despair. There was still no news from Suleyman. We feared the worst. I clung onto the hope that she was hiding out somewhere safe. "She is not strong enough to live like a hunted animal," Yasim-Ali lamented. "But...

if she went to the monastery...' All of a sudden, he jumped up. "That's it!" he cried. "Nea Moni. That's the only place she would have gone; the only place she would know where I would find her." Without a second to spare, he mounted his horse and headed for the hills. All I could do was wait and pray, which was something that I was accustomed to by this time.

'Yasim-Ali had only been gone a short while when we saw black smoke billowing into the sky in the distance. "The monastery!" someone screamed. "Nea Moni is on fire!" I knew then that it would take more than a miracle to find Artemis alive.

'Throughout the following day, I sat on the battlements and watched in horror as the never-ending procession of thousands of miserable souls, destined for the slave markets, were brought into Chora—all of them from Nea Moni. There were so many; it was impossible to comprehend it all. In the throng, I spotted Suleyman. Over his horse was draped the body of a young woman. It was Artemis. At that point, I fell to the floor in a swoon. My mother ordered the body to be taken to our quarters, promising to give her a proper burial. Suleyman told us that he found her lying in the church under the majestic golden dome of the Christ Pantocrator. He had recognized her immediately by her extraordinary beauty and by Yasim-Ali's jade dagger which he brought back to give to the family. He added that she died at her own hand. We all grieved for her and in that moment, no one cared whether she was a Greek or a Turk. To us, she was simply Artemis, Yasim-Ali's beloved and my friend.

'Later that evening, Yasim-Ali returned. The look in his eyes will be with me until I die. In his arms, he cradled a tiny baby. That baby was you.'

I listened to Aunt Kuzel's story with tears streaming down my cheeks. She had loved me as her own. I could not have asked for more. More importantly, when I learned that Uncle Yasim-Ali was indeed my father, I now understood the depth of his torment and why he loved me so much. I even found it in me to forgive his wife for trying to scald me in the hammam, for surely she must have suffered never to have won the affections of her husband. No one could replace his love for my mother, and I was a constant reminder of that love.

So you will surely understand, my cherished Sophia, when I tell you from that day on, my life changed forever. The terrible strain of the Greek war left its scars on everyone. I bore no animosity towards Aunt Kuzel and Rifat Bey. Indeed, I felt grateful to have been cushioned from it all. It took me a while to come to terms with who my parents really were. Aunt Kuzel said that my birth was kismet. 'You were conceived in the richness of love and born under the watchful eye of the Almighty.'

On my fourteenth birthday, Aunt Kuzel sent for me and told me that she had decided to send me away. 'There comes a time,' she said, 'when a bird must fly away from the nest. That time has come for you. Rifat Bey and I have given you your childhood and brought you up in the ways of a good and true Muslim, but now it is time for you to live with your mother's people.' As you can imagine, this news came as a great shock and I beseeched her to reconsider. Aunt Kuzel put her hand up to silence me.

'Do you remember that during the troubles I told you your mother had been in the care of her uncle, Georgos Florades, after Michael Florades was imprisoned?' she asked. I nodded miserably. How could I forget? She had also told me that Michael Florades, my grandfather, had been executed several days after my birth. 'Well, I discovered that both he and his wife survived and are living on the island of Syros and I took the liberty of writing to him about you. Naturally, at first he was surprised, but later, after an exchange of letters, it was decided that you should now live with them and learn their ways and their religion. I owe this to your mother. You will not be alone. I am sending Polyxeni with you. She has been a loyal servant and the time has come to give her back her freedom. In a few years, if you choose to adopt their way of life, I will understand. That will be your decision.'

I implored her again to let me stay but nothing would make her change her mind. The day the ship was due to sail Aunt Kuzel called me into the reception room. She had prepared a large box which she said was intended for my dowry, and a sum of money which I was to keep for myself should I ever need it. 'Before you go, there's something I have to give you,' she said. 'This is the locket that your father had made for your mother. You were wearing it when he found you and he kept it with him until the day he died.' She held out her hand to show me. It was the first time I had ever seen a picture of my mother. Her beauty took my breath away. Aunt Kuzel put it around my neck. 'See how well it suits you,' she smiled, handing me a mirror. 'Just perfect!' I stared at myself in the mirror. It was exquisite. 'Now, take it off and put it away safely in this box. We don't want to lose it, do we?' she said firmly. She wrapped it in a towel and placed it in the box amongst the other cloths.

'There's one more thing,' she said, rising slowly and going over to a cupboard at the far side of the room. She brought out a large package wrapped in cloth and carefully untied it. It was the portrait of my mother painted by Jean-Michel. I couldn't believe my eyes—the painting was so real, so alive that I felt her presence. 'But I thought you told me the painting hung in the salon in their house in Chora and that the house had been ransacked!' I exclaimed.

'That is also what I thought,' she replied, 'but during Jean-Michel's visit, he told us what happened. It seems that when Michael Florades commissioned the portrait, he was so taken with your mother's beauty that he painted two of them; one was painted in the privacy of his room. This one, he regarded to be the better of the two as not only was the painting more accomplished, but he considered it to have caught the real soul of your mother and the sadness in her eyes. And so he kept it for himself, intending to exhibit it in France. The other one he gave to Michael Florades. That was the one that was lost. In 1824, this painting was exhibited at the prestigious Salon in Paris alongside the works of other famous painters. Despite many requests to purchase it, he kept it for himself. A year or so later, he received word of your birth from Yasim-Ali and vowed that one day, in honor of your mother, you would possess it yourself. That was the reason for his visit, but as you knew nothing about your mother at that time, we resolved to keep it safely locked away until the time came when we could rightfully give it to you.'

My beloved Sophia, that painting was the same one you saw in my dear husband's studio and when I saw her for the first time, I was spellbound just as you were.

All too soon, the time came to say goodbye. Aunt Kuzel, Rifat Bey, and Osman escorted us to the port. Amid the bustling noise and shouts of the hammals, we embraced for the last time. 'Be brave,' Aunt Kuzel said. 'Do not fear. Nothing will take away our feelings for you.' As the sun set, casting a golden glow across the water, the ship sailed out of the harbor southwards past the Kampos, hugging the coastline where the mastic villages lay hidden beyond the hills, and into the Aegean towards Syros. I would never see Chios or Aunt Kuzel again.

After a violent night on the open seas, we arrived at the island of Syros the next day. Georgos Florades and his wife were there to meet us. I introduced myself and he fixed his eyes on me. It took him a while before he could speak. When he did, my stomach fell. 'Durrusehvar! What sort of a name is that?' he thundered. 'There will be no Turkish names under my roof. From now on you will be known as Dimitra.' He turned his attention to Polyxeni, who stood trembling in fear. 'And who is this?' When I told him she was my maid, he seemed bemused.

Ermoupoli, the bustling business heart of Syros, was now the center of the transit trade of the entire Mediterranean. Georgos Florades, like other refugees, had taken advantage of this. His prosperity had not diminished since fleeing Chios. In fact his wealth had almost doubled through trading in cotton goods, leather, and hardware. He also owned a small Turkish Delight factory exporting to the English, who had acquired a taste for this sweet confection. His home was an imposing two-storey mansion behind the waterfront and within walking distance of his warehouses. The house was tastefully decorated in the European style and, as such, I had expected to be provided with a well-appointed room. So imagine my horror when Kyria Florades showed me to a room at the back of the house next to the servants' quarters. My luggage had already been left in the room and took up most of the space. It was here in this small, cramped room with the most basic furniture and only the light of a tallow candle that I was expected to live. My heart sank at the thought of what I had left behind.

Kyria Florades eyed the box greedily wanting to know its contents. 'My dowry,' I told her meekly. She said that it might be better to keep it elsewhere for the time-being and would send someone up to remove it. I didn't trust her motives. 'And that?' she said, pointing to the painting.

'It's a portrait of my mother. I thought I might hang it on the wall.'

'Dimitra, I don't know what sort of life you had in Chios, but I'm sure it couldn't have been an easy one,' she said coldly. 'You have a new life ahead of you now and very soon you'll forget the old one.'

After she left, I lay on my bed and sobbed my heart out. Shortly after, Georgos Florades knocked on the door. He had brought a man with him to take the box away. Fearing that I might not see the contents again, I had the foresight to remove the locket, which I hid in an earthenware jar on the window ledge and I put the sovereigns under my mattress. Georgos Florades stared at the portrait of my mother on the wall over my bed. To put it there I had taken down an icon of the Virgin, which at that moment lay on the floor until I decided what to do with it. On seeing my mother, he flew into a rage, telling me to remove it at once. 'She has shamed this family,' he said cruelly. 'It is enough that you are here to remind us of her.' When I refused, he cursed me, saying that I was as stubborn as she had been. 'I will not have our good name disgraced again.' He picked up the icon, kissed it and hung it on a nail in the wall over the table. Without another word, he left the room slamming the door behind him. I knew then that he had deceived Aunt Kuzel and Rifat Bey but I could never tell them; to tell them would cause them untold hurt and I loved them too much for that. Conceive then, my beloved Sophia, of my apprehension; I was unable to go back and I had no choice but to make the best of my new life.

So began my life in Syros. I was now Dimitra Florades and it took me a while to get used to my new name and even longer for Polyxeni. She was no longer my maid but a servant doing menial tasks for Kyria Florades. We were forbidden to speak Turkish and whenever Polyxeni accidently addressed me as Durrusehvar, she was reprimanded severely.

As a member of the Florades family, my life was not any easier. My studies came to an abrupt end and Georgos Florades put me to work in the Turkish Delight factory where I was expected to do every menial job imaginable, from cleaning the machines and sweeping the floors to packing the boxes ready for shipment to England. Except for Sunday, which was a day of rest and which I spent with the family, my evenings were spent alone in my room. With my mother's gaze my only comfort, I took strength from her and set about perfecting my embroidery. But first, I needed to buy fabric and silk threads. When I looked under the mattress, my sovereigns had gone. I had no doubt that Kyria Florades had stolen them, but it was impossible to confront her. This placed me in a difficult position, as being a member of the family I did not receive a wage. Having no option, I was forced to borrow money from Polyxeni. When I had completed my first pieces, I took them to the market and sold them and was able to repay her the loan in the first week, but Polyxeni refused to take the money and so I made her a blouse which I embroidered with small flowers and I bought her a hand mirror in order that she could see how fine she looked.

It wasn't long before Kyria Florades found out about my weekly trips to the market. When she heard that my embroidery was well received, she promised to allow me to continue selling my pieces as long as I made things for her. From then on, I was forced to show her all my work for her to choose something. She never paid me for my work, but I did accumulate a tidy sum of money from the market which I hid in the earthenware jar, together with my locket.

My life of drudgery continued in this way for nine years. Then one day when I was at the market, I heard two men conversing in French. To my great surprise, I recognized the older of the two. It was none other than Jean-Michel himself. He had gained a little weight since the last time I saw him and his hair was graying around the temples, but he maintained his cheerful manner. A feeling of shame came over me and I hurriedly tried to bundle up my things and get away before he spotted me. It was too late. The men walked towards me and as they passed by, Jean-Michel stopped for a moment and looked at me. 'Durrusehvar,' he said in a soft voice. 'Is it really you?' I avoided his eyes and continued packing my embroideries together. It was the first time I had heard someone speak my name in years. 'Durrusehvar,' he said again. Curious to know what was going on, the nearby stall owners began to look my way. Jean-Michel would not be put off. 'Look at me,' he said, trying hard to catch my attention. When this failed, he picked up an embroidered handkerchief. 'I'll have this,' he said. 'How much is it?' With the stall owners' eyes fixed on me, I answered in French. 'Ten drachmas—but my name is Dimitra, not Durrusehvar.' Jean-Michel bought the handkerchief and walked away.

'Where did you learn to speak French?' one of the stall owners asked. I told them I'd just picked it up. How could I say that after Jean-Michel left Chios, Aunt Kuzel kept her promise and appointed a French tutor for me?

I tried to put the incident behind me but it was impossible. Then a few days later, Jean-Michel returned. This time he would not be budged. 'Durrusehvar,' he said once more. 'Don't you recognize me?'

'My name is Dimitra,' I replied, trying to conceal my emotions. 'You must have me mixed up with someone else.'

Jean-Michel smiled. 'I would know that face anywhere. You were a young girl when I last saw you and in that time you have grown into a beautiful young woman. You have your mother's looks.' At this point I thought my heart would burst. 'Look at me and tell me you are not the daughter of Artemis and I will go away,' he said.

Unable to speak, I stared at the ground in case he should see my tears. He began to walk away and when he had almost disappeared from sight, I jumped up and ran after him. 'Wait,' I called out. 'You're right. I can't hide anymore.' With that I burst into tears and he held me as a father holds his daughter. My whole body shook from years of pent-up emotion and it was a while before I was able to talk.

'Why don't you tell me what happened,' Jean-Michel said, lifting my chin and wiping away my tears with the handkerchief that I had sold him. 'How did you come to be here?' When I explained about Georgos Florades's deceit in promising Aunt Kuzel that I would be brought up as a gentlewoman, his face reddened with anger. 'The wretch,' he thundered. 'It is he who has brought shame on the family.' He asked to meet him and I agreed…on the condition that he didn't mention our conversation.

Needless to say when Georgos Florades was confronted with his brother's good friend, the miser's face paled in shame. Later that day, I found myself transferred to a well-appointed room overlooking the plateia. More importantly, the portrait of my mother was placed in a prominent position over my dressing table. Even Kyria Florades became more congenial and told me that from now on, I would no longer be required to work at the Turkish Delight factory. Neither of them thought to apologize for the way I had been treated. Having shown their true faces to the world, I could no longer trust them and intended to escape from them and move away as soon as possible. I had saved enough money to allow me to find accommodation of my own and to take Polyxeni with me.

As is often the case, things didn't go according to plan. The younger man with Jean-Michel was his son Jean-Paul, an accomplished artist in his own right. I learned that they were on their way to the Middle East when they had a change of heart and decided to visit the archaeological sites on the island of Delos. They made Syros their base from which to make daily excursions. Knowing that I had professed an interest in painting, he suggested that I join them.

Accompanied by Polyxeni, we made several day trips to the island. While Jean-Michel and his son found a suitable spot to set up their easels, Polyxeni and I explored the classical remains or entertained ourselves with our embroidery. After the oppressive years spent in the Florades household, I felt free again. It was a glorious feeling. There was also something else happening to me. I knew I was falling in love with Jean-Paul and him with me. It was the first time I had experienced such feelings and felt overwhelmed. Like his father, Jean-Paul was full of energy and enthusiasm and I was fascinated by him. Nothing gave me greater pleasure than to sit next to him as he painted, chatting away. We talked about politics, about his life in France, his ambition to exhibit at the prestigious Salon as his father had done, and I told him about my life with Aunt Kuzel and Rifat Bey in Chios. He thought my French most elegant, saying that I had been taught well. They were bliss-filled days and I dreaded the day when it would end. But as observant as ever, Jean-Michel had not failed to notice what was happening to us. He couldn't have been more delighted, even going as far as telling me that in love, my face had the same glow as my mother's. 'But,' he added, 'without her sadness.'

When the time came for them to leave Syros, Jean-Paul asked me to marry him. We were married in the Greek Orthodox Church of Metamorphosis, built in 1824 by the refugees three years after the outbreak of the Greek War of Independence, and the same year that Jean-Michel entered the portrait of my mother in the exhibition in Paris. To the delight of Jean-Michel, I wore my parents' locket for the first time and with the greatest of pride. I chose to keep the name Dimitra as it was to that name which I had become accustomed. Now that we were married, Jean-Michel intended to travel to the Middle East, while Jean-Paul and I decided to make a fresh start in Smyrna. Knowing that Jean-Paul wished to make a living from painting, Jean-Michel gave him his portmanteau and his prized paints as a farewell present. Much to my dismay, Polyxeni chose to stay in Syros and make a new life for herself with the money that I gave her from my embroidery.

Kyrios Florades gave me back my dowry, with no apologies for the many pieces that were missing, and neither he nor his wife was anywhere to be seen when the ship sailed for Smyrna. I didn't care. I had my locket, the portrait, and a husband whom I loved. The years on Syros had made me stronger and for that, I gave thanks to them.

We arrived in Smyrna in the summer of 1847 and rented rooms in a modest area not far from the Greek quarter. This arrangement didn't bother us in the slightest, as being newlyweds and deeply in love, our lives were filled with a sense of excitement and curiosity. During this time I found out that Aunt Kuzel's daughter Leyla had married and was also living in the city. I cannot begin to tell you what a great joy this was for me. Over the next few years, we saw each other regularly and through her contacts, Jean-Paul received commissions for portraits and I was asked to produce embroidery for her many friends and acquaintances. I have always believed that it was because of her that I came to the attention of the Valide Sultan.

Leyla told me Aunt Kuzel was well, but Rifat Bey had been struck down with an unknown illness and had been bedridden for several months. She said her mother talked about me constantly. When I asked why she had never written, she couldn't answer but she was sure her mother regretted her decision to send me away. How I longed to tell her how wretched my life was and that I would have returned in an instant. Both she and Rifat Bey were delighted to hear that I was now married to the son of their good friend. Aunt Kuzel said that God had looked favorably on me and she could not have wished for a better match. Shortly after, I received word that Rifat Bey had died.

With our fortunes beginning to prosper, we bought our first home—it was this house that you know so well. Towards the end of her life, Aunt Kuzel sent me a gift, a beautiful yearling—a progeny of Nillufer, and a horse with her temperament. Recalling the wonderful days spent with my father, I spent many pleasant days riding in the Nymph Dagh Mountains. Your grandfather and I were blessed with seven children but only your mother survived. By this time Leyla and her family had gone to live in Kayseri, and Aunt Kuzel was no longer alive.

When Photeini was still a child, Mehmet, my manservant, brought a fortuneteller to the house. Her reputation was supposed to be unrivalled. I have always believed in their powers, having witnessed evidence of their foretelling for myself many times during my life. When she foretold a sudden death, somehow I knew it was Jean-Paul. But it was her prophecy about the child with the flaming hair that has stayed with me all these years. Ever since she was born, I have thought Maria was that child. She is unlike all of you and there is something about her character that will come back to haunt us all. I cannot say what it is, but I see a dark cloud over her. That said, she is still our flesh and blood and we can do no other than our best for her. The die has been thrown. We cannot escape our destiny.

My story is almost finished. There is a strong smell of burning in the air. They say it comes from the Armenian quarter. Before I draw these pages to a close, there is something else that you should know. I kept in contact with Leyla until her death in 1913. It was like losing a sister and I grieved for her terribly. After her death, her daughter Hateme kept in touch with me and visited me whenever she was in Smyrna. Hateme is the same age as your mother. Given the tension between the Christians and Muslims, we decided that it was best that we continue to keep our relationship secret. It was she who was with me the day that the Greek troops landed, and given our past, we foresaw the tragedy that would unfold. It was she who brought me news of the Greek defeat a few weeks ago. Your children were here that afternoon and it gave her great joy to meet them. To them she was known as 'the lady with the fawn veil.' While my family has seen fit to fight for the Greek cause, her family fights for the Turks. Both of her sons are generals in the Nationalist army. Her eldest is Nuri Pasha, who now occupies the Konak, along with General Nureddin. Yes, my Sophia, the man that you met with the other day was none other than her son. Because of my relationship with his mother, he knows of you.

In a few minutes, I must put down my pen and say my last goodbye to the children. They will do you great justice, just as you have done me. The time is drawing near for you to leave. I cannot go with you. My life is over. I will die here. Others may not make this long journey, but Nuri Pasha will see to it that you leave safely. You go with my blessing.

Finally, there is one more thing. Upon my death, the painting of my beloved mother will be sent to Nuri Pasha for safekeeping. I have bequeathed it to you but you have a hazardous journey ahead of you; it is one that makes carrying such a painting impossible. One day soon there will be peace. Then you can return and claim what is rightfully yours. Take good care of your mother; she is weak and does not have your strength. I give thanks to God that I have lived a fortuitous life. You have all made me proud.

My cherished Sophia, do not weep for the sorrows in this world; in the end you will have no eyes.

Your loving grandmother,
Durrusehvar

# CHAPTER 41

*London, June 1973*

The forthcoming exhibition to be held at the Knightsbridge Gallery was attracting enormous attention in the art world. With just three weeks left before the official opening, Eleni found herself snowed under with work. With public and private collections around the world making their works available, nothing could be left to chance. Her assistant placed a list of names on her desk—everyone who had expressed an interest in a private viewing. She cast her eyes over the names: the directors of the Louvre, the Musee d'Orsay and the Musee des Beaux-Arts in Paris; representatives of the Smithsonian Institute in Washington and London's Tate and National Galleries; numerous private collectors. The list was impressive. One by one, she ticked them off against her diary. One name in particular caught her eye: Vedat Aksoy, accompanied by the Turkish Ambassador. Eleni circled the name and made a special note against it.

She picked up a copy of the catalogue lying on her desk and although she knew every word, every picture in it by heart, she leaned back in her chair and studied it one more time.

*The Oriental Mirage*
*European Paintings of the Nineteenth Century*

Underneath was a painting entitled *The Fortuneteller, Cairo* by a well-known French artist. In it, a woman makes an impression of her hand in the sand while the fortuneteller prepares to tell her future. A veiled woman watches them discreetly from a nearby doorway. Eleni thought of Durrusehvar and how fortunetellers had been an integral part of her life. Even today, she hadn't failed to notice how seriously people still believed in their powers. 'Kismet,' she had heard over and over again. 'We can't escape our fate.' She heard this so much that she had even begun to wonder herself if there wasn't an element of truth in it all.

She turned the page. In all there were eighty-seven paintings on display—most of them by artists of great renown: Jean Gerome, John Frederick Lewis, Ingres, and even a Delacroix—a rich and exciting body of work. But it was the last ten that had provoked the most interest, as these were the only ones to be auctioned. Her eyes fell on the last one, 'Lot 10: *The Embroiderer (La Brodeuse)*, 1820. Jean-Michel Lamartine. Oil on canvas, 19 by 23 inches.' At the back of the catalogue was the artist's biography. 'French artist (1794 Paris to 1856 Algiers).' It went on to say that he had entered two paintings in the Paris Salon Exhibition of 1824. The first one, *View of Nea Moni, Chios*, 1820 remained in the possession of his wife's family until it was sold to a private collector in 1914. The second one, the one that achieved the greatest acclaim when it was first shown was *The Embroiderer*, 1820. Lamartine later gave it to the family of the woman depicted in the portrait. For a long time there was much speculation as to the identity of the young woman. It is now known to be a portrait of a Greek woman, Artemis Florades, daughter of a Chian merchant. It was painted during the same period as *View of Nea Moni, Chios*, one year before the outbreak of the Greek War of Independence. Until now *The Embroiderer* was thought to have been lost. It remains one of his most important works. Lamartine died of typhoid in Algiers at the age of 62.

The painting was estimated to fetch somewhere between sixty and eighty thousand pounds. Eleni wondered if she was doing the right thing by selling it. There was no doubt that it was now hers to do with as she pleased, but she couldn't help feeling a pang of guilt. It had been a wrenching and heartbreaking decision to put it up for auction but she had to do it, as she was in desperate need of the money. The two months away in Greece and Turkey had cost her a great deal; the house in Bayswater was badly in need of repair; and as much as she enjoyed her work, it didn't pay well. In the end, she had no option but to sell.

In her will, her Aunt Maria left the house in Kypseli to Chrysoula. Not that Eleni minded in the slightest. In fact, she was glad to see that for once Maria had done the right thing. After all those years of loyalty, Chrysoula deserved to be looked after well. Anyway, she still had the locket and the sapphire ring which she had had altered to fit her and which she wore constantly...and lastly, there were the memoirs which she intended to publish in due course.

Eleni put the catalogue in her bag, took out a small compact and checked her make-up in the mirror. The dark circles under her eyes showed no signs of diminishing. She dabbed a little concealing powder over them.

'Still not sleeping?' asked her assistant.

Eleni nodded. Since her visits to Greece and Turkey, she had found it hard to let go of the past. After immersing herself in another time and place, coming back to London and carrying on as if nothing happened was virtually impossible. Once a week she made phone calls to Chrysoula or Markos—especially Markos. She could talk to him; he understood what her family had been through. He understood *her* and his presence in her life was now one of familiarity. She asked after his grandmother, who took ill while she was in Turkey, and was told that she was still not well enough to come back to Greece. Nothing more had been said that shed more light on how she knew Maria and Markos concluded that his grandmother must have known who she was because she was an opera fan. During their last conversation, he told Eleni that he was trying to get leave from the university and fly over to see the exhibition. She was thrilled at the thought of it.

Eleni snapped the compact shut and put it in her bag. 'Can I give you a lift?' she asked her assistant. 'I'm going to The Dorchester.'

'The Dorchester!' Her assistant raised her eyebrows. 'My, that will set you back a week's wages. On our pay, we're lucky to be able to afford a night out at the Duke of Wellington.'

'I'm meeting a friend. He's staying there.'

The assistant whistled. 'He must be pretty well-heeled to be staying there,' she exclaimed.

'You could say that I suppose,' replied Eleni with a smile.

Vedat Aksoy was waiting in the bar sipping a vodka on the rocks when Eleni arrived. 'Just in time,' he said, giving her a peck on the cheek. 'I've booked a table, I do hope you're hungry; I believe they do a wonderful pheasant en croute here. But first, please join me in a drink. What will you have?' He called to the bartender and ordered her a gin and tonic. 'It's so good to see you again. I've thought about you a lot since the last time we met. How long ago was it...?'

'Eight months.'

'Goodness. How time flies.'

'I've brought you a catalogue,' said Eleni. 'I'm very pleased with it; there's been a great amount of interest shown and I think we'll do well.'

Vedat flicked through the pages and paused at the painting of *The Embroiderer*. 'So you are still going to sell it?'

Somewhat embarrassed, Eleni avoided his eyes. She didn't want to burden him with her financial worries.

'You might live to regret it,' he said, showing concern.

'It's for the best. Besides, I still have the locket,' she replied, caressing it with her fingers. 'And it means a great deal to me.'

'It suits you.' His eyes fell on the sapphire ring. 'So that's the famous ring,' he said. 'The one given to Durrusehvar by the Valide Sultan, the one she mentioned in her memoirs.'

'It took me a long time before I could wear it,' replied Eleni. 'Every time I thought of how it came into Aunt Maria's possession, it made me angry.'

Vedat smiled. 'Don't be too harsh on her, Eleni. From what you told me, she was a tormented soul. Let her rest in peace.'

Eleni changed the subject. 'I see that you have requested a private showing with the ambassador. Are you thinking of buying?'

'When I saw that *View of Nea Moni, Chios* was for sale, I thought I might put in a bid. I see the reserve is only fifteen thousand pounds. It would add very nicely to my collection, and there's the emotional tie of course. Being where great-great-grandmother Leyla was from, she used to talk about it all the time. We all longed to visit the place but after all that happened, we weren't welcome any more.'

'You'd be welcome now,' Eleni answered. 'I believe Turkish tourists have started to visit the island again.'

'I'm not so sure about that. There's still tension between the two countries, and the current government in Greece only makes matters worse.'

'Ah yes. I've been hearing all about it. From what I gather, things are not going so well there at the moment.' Eleni was referring to the 'rule of the colonels,' as Markos called the Greek dictatorship.

'And you?' Vedat asked. 'Will you visit Chios one day soon?'

'Perhaps…on my next trip to Greece.'

'If you do, then you can tell me all about it. Anyway, enough of that, let's have dinner and you can tell me what you've been doing.'

Vedat Aksoy was a small man in his mid-sixties. Cultivated and possessing a quick wit, he was deeply romantic, reciting by heart the poems of Schiller and Goethe. Like her family, he was born into privilege and had gone to study architecture, first in Istanbul and then in America. With the death of his father in 1960, he decided to leave his city life and take over the running of the family property near Bursa.

Eleni recalled the first time she met him. It was the week after her meeting with Munire eight months earlier. Vedat was the son of General Nuri Pasha. After the revelations in Durrusehvar's memoirs, she set out to find if he or any of the family were still alive. Finding the family proved to be easier than she imagined. As a loyal and fearless officer fighting alongside Mustafa Kemal, Nuri Pasha's exploits were well documented and he had worked tirelessly in the formation of the new Turkish Republic. In the early thirties, he moved his family from Kayseri to their property near Bursa. Eleni was disappointed to hear that he was no longer alive, but delighted that his son Vedat expressed a great desire to meet her. A few days after their introduction, Eleni took the train to Bursa. From there, she traveled by car along the highway towards the Aegean coast, turning off along a heavily forested road until they came to an imposing gateway with an avenue of trees leading towards a large two-storey Ottoman house. But as Eleni had discovered, this was no ordinary property; it was one of the country's best-known stud farms. Driving through acres of immaculate parkland with its rolling hills and herb-rich meadows, Eleni understood at once the family's long-standing connection to their horses. It was in their blood.

When the car approached the house, Vedat was standing in the driveway waiting to greet her. Next to him stood the largest dog she had ever seen, a Turkish sheepdog which only served to make this small man look even smaller. Putting her at ease, he patted its enormous head and sent it away to be fed by the chauffeur, who doubled as a stableman when his duties as a chauffeur were not in demand. Eleni took an instant liking to this little man. He was a gentleman in every sense of the word.

Vedat showed a great interest in Durrusehvar's memoirs, having heard about her from his grandmother, and later from his father. Like Eleni, he was overjoyed that the two families had come together after all these years.

'What sadness had to take place before this day arrived,' he said, with a heavy heart. 'That our families should have lived so close to each other and yet maintained such tremendous differences.'

Eleni agreed. 'Until my aunt's story and the subsequent translation of Durrusehvar's memoirs, I had no idea how steeped in blood these countries were,' she replied. 'It seems that in the end, everyone lost something. Great ideals led to destruction, betrayals, families torn apart…so much human conflict and sadness. Was it all worth it?'

Vedat shrugged his shoulders. 'History can serve the present as a mirror of the past. We must all learn to be more tolerant.' He studied her a while over the rim of his glasses. 'It interests me that you refer to your great-great-grandmother Dimitra as Durrusehvar,' he said. 'Why is that?'

'I decided to make that change after reading her memoirs. I felt it was time to correct things. She said she was given that name by Kuzel, but if the truth be known, her father Yasim-Ali, probably had something to do with it. They were happy years for her, and by calling her by her birth name I feel we are honoring her past. What did you know her as?' she asked.

Vedat chuckled. 'Why, Durrusehvar, of course. To us she was just as Turkish as she was Greek.'

Eleni smiled. It was in this house that she first saw the portrait of Artemis hanging over a writing bureau that once belonged to Nuri Pasha. As it had done with others before her, it took her breath away. So startling was its effect on her that it was some time before she was able to speak.

'She's beautiful,' she said after a while. 'Even lovelier than I imagined.' Vedat nodded in agreement. 'Jean-Michel has certainly painted her with such breathtaking realism that I feel I want to reach out and touch her. It gives me goosebumps. And her eyes, they're quite hypnotic.' Eleni looked closer. 'Extraordinary. They really are the deepest amethyst.' She turned to Vedat. 'Did Durrusehvar inherit those eyes? It's hard for me to tell from the old photographs.'

'No,' Vedat replied. 'It was your grandmother Sophia who inherited them. From what I know, she was the only one. My father often talked about the first time he met her at the Konak. She would have been almost forty then, but he said she was one of the loveliest women he had ever known. "And those eyes," he used to say. "They would drive a man wild with desire." I think he was a little in love with her. At least I think he always hoped one day she would return to Turkey and he could give her the portrait; but of course, she never did.'

Eleni asked if Vedat was aware that her grandfather was not Andreas.

'I knew nothing about the affair until you told me, but from what I know of Durrusehvar, it's most likely that she would have known. Women's instincts are finely attuned to those sorts of things. If Sophia and Nikolai chose to keep Nina's parentage a secret then it was for the best. There was nothing to be gained and everything to lose. It would have caused a scandal.'

He was silent for a moment, reflecting on the situation. 'When you think about it, in many ways the war between the Greeks and Turks, and Artemis's untimely death, saved her from the terrible fate of being shunned by her own society. For that reason alone, I believe Durrusehvar would have gone along with their secret. Maybe that's why she never mentioned it in her memoirs.'

'Perhaps you're right,' Eleni replied sadly.

It was in that house that Eleni saw the jade dagger. When Kuzel died, she left it to Leyla. Vedat unlocked the glass case and took it out for her to hold. 'It was given to Yasim-Ali and Kuzel's grandfather by Sultan Mustafa III,' he told her. 'One day soon, I will donate it to a museum in Istanbul.'

Eleni held it. It was quite light. The jade hilt was finely carved with a fluted grip divided by a molding, a frieze of leaves and animals around the pommel, and set with bands of rubies and sapphires. The length of the watered-steel curved blade was almost six inches—quite small to inflict such a fatal wound. Even after all those years it was incredibly sharp. Holding it and looking at the portrait, Eleni could not begin to imagine the depth of passion needed to thrust it into one's own body. It didn't bear thinking about.

Just before she was about to depart for Istanbul, Vedat said he had one more thing to tell her, perhaps the last piece of the puzzle. 'You know, Durrusehvar did not die in the Smyrna fire. She died by her own hand—by taking a concoction of poisonous herbs and roots. It was Iskender who notified my father, and it was he who arranged her funeral. She is buried in the old Turkish cemetery on the hill above Izmir. A marble headstone in the shape of a tulip was later placed there by my mother. In the end, we must give thanks to God that in such tumultuous times, she lived a long and fortuitous life.'

Eleni pondered how fate had thrown the dice. Neither she nor Vedat Aksoy had any living relatives, except for each other. After all the bloodshed, here they were, a Greek, albeit an English one, and a Turk. United once more.

One month later, the portrait of Artemis arrived in London. With it was a note from Vedat.

Dear Eleni,

It is written on the gate of heaven: "Nothing in existence is more powerful than destiny. And destiny brought you here, to this page, which is part of your ticket—as all things are—to return to God."
– Hafiz (c. 1320-1389)

# CHAPTER 42

*London, July 1973*

During the first week of the private showings Eleni received a phone call from Markos. His grandmother had taken a turn for the worse and was not expected to live. He apologized, but this sudden turn of events meant that he had to fly to America to be with his mother and sister and he didn't know how long he would be away. As a consequence, he wouldn't be able to make it to London after all.

'I understand,' said Eleni. 'Your family must come first. After all, there will be other exhibitions.'

'Not like this one,' he replied. 'I was hoping to see the portrait of Artemis before it was sold.'

'By the looks of things, it seems as though there will be a bidding war between the museums in Paris. You might have to take a holiday there to see it,' she laughed.

When she put the receiver down, Eleni's assistant couldn't fail to notice the look of disappointment on her face. 'You're fond of him, aren't you?' she said with a smile.

Eleni felt her cheeks flush.

With three days left before the official opening, the whispers going through the gallery were that all the pieces to be auctioned would fetch much more than their reserve. There were more than fifty official registrations for the auction already, and still more to come in. As he said he would do, Vedat Aksoy registered his interest in *View of Nea Moni, Chios*. But much of the interest was for *The Embroiderer*. The gallery's directors were optimistic that it could even fetch as much as one hundred and twenty thousand pounds.

The evening before the official launch, Markos telephoned from America to say that his grandmother had died peacefully in her sleep. He was just about to board a flight in New York and, if there were no delays, he would manage to make the opening after all. The next afternoon he arrived in London. With so much going on, Eleni had little time to spend with him, but she did manage to stay behind after everyone else had departed to show him the portrait. His reaction was like everyone else's.

'My God! What a wonderful portrait—and quite frankly, highly sensual and erotic. It's no wonder Yasim-Ali fell for her. Who could resist such beauty? How extraordinary it must be for you to think that you are related to her.'

'Unfortunately, I didn't inherit those amethyst eyes,' she laughed.

Eleni looked at the picture once more. Tomorrow it would no longer be hers. She wondered if Vedat was right. She might live to regret the day she sold it after all.

'Come on,' she said, trying to snap out of her sadness. 'Let's have a quick bite to eat. Tomorrow's going to be a long day.'

Despite Eleni's joy at having Markos there with her, their first evening together was marred by a cloud of melancholy. Neither said much. She—racked with doubts about the sale of the portrait; and he—saddened by the loss of his beloved grandmother.

At two o'clock in the afternoon, the auction room at the gallery was filled to capacity. All the seats had been taken and those left standing were placing themselves in positions of importance around the room. Seated in the second row from the front was Vedat Aksoy. Behind him, looking through the catalogue, sat Markos. He looked up and, seeing her watching him, smiled. It occurred to her that she had hardly given him a thought all day. Now, seeing him there, she suddenly felt comforted by his presence. Quiet descended over the room, as the director of the gallery welcomed everyone and declared the auction under way.

Learned and loquacious, the auctioneer turned to the first painting. 'Lot 1. *Turkish Woman on the Shore of the Bosphorus*. Oil on canvas. 53 by 33 inches, painted in 1845. This fine piece of work by the Italian artist Giacomo Pietrosanto is one of a series painted in Constantinople during his five-year stay in that city. May I start the bidding with…?'

Raising his hammer he named a starting price and the bidding was underway.

Lot 10, *The Embroiderer*, was the last to be auctioned. Eleni felt a huge heaviness in her chest. Overcome by a sudden rush of dizziness, she gripped the chair beside her and wiped the beads of perspiration from her forehead. She had to get some air. Moments later, she found herself walking aimlessly in the busy high street. In her confusion, she hardly noticed the incessant noise of the traffic or the fumes that mingled with the smell of tarmac on the hot July afternoon. Without thinking, she walked into a coffee shop and ordered a drink. The waitress, humming along to Carly Simon singing 'You're So Vain,' looked concerned.

'You all right, dear?' she asked. 'You're as white as a sheet.'

'Thank you,' Eleni replied, fighting back the tears, 'I'll be alright.'

Eleni sat in the café for almost twenty minutes, pondering the wisdom of her decision to sell. She needed the money, she kept reminding herself—it was the best thing to do. Yet her emotions were telling her something else. She looked at her watch. Suddenly she jumped up and headed back to the auction. She had made a grave mistake. If she hurried, there was still time to stop it going to auction. Almost out of breath, she reached the gallery just as the room was emptying. She was too late. Collapsing on a sofa in the foyer, Eleni held her head in her hands in despair. When she looked up she saw Markos deep in conversation with Vedat Aksoy. She felt as though her head was in a cloud of fog. Was this really happening? Minutes later, Vedat left. Markos spotted her on the sofa and came over to join her. Her cheeks glistened with tears. He put his arm around her tenderly.

'Come on, cheer up. It's not the end of the world. Anyway, I've booked a table for us at a very good restaurant. Your Turkish friend Vedat recommended it. Go home and get changed. I'll meet you there at seven o'clock. There's something I have to do first.'

In the morning Markos would be flying back to Athens. There was so much to say and so little time to say it. Wanting to make their last evening a memorable one, Eleni resolved not to mention the portrait; there was time enough to face that when he was gone. And Markos was only too happy to talk about other things—mostly about the political situation in Greece, which was deteriorating rapidly.

When she woke the next morning, Markos had left. Beside her bed was a note saying that he had left her a small present in the drawing room—a token of their friendship, which he hoped would continue. Reaching for her dressing gown, she went to see what it was. For a brief moment, she thought she was dreaming; a dream from which she never wanted to wake.

Over the mantelpiece hung the portrait of Artemis. Propped up against a photograph of her mother was a letter. With trembling hands she opened it and read its contents.

My dear Eleni,

If you had asked me a week ago if I would have been in a position to give you such a goodbye present as this, I would have said no. But circumstances have a way of presenting themselves beyond anything we can dream.

Just before my grandmother died, she asked if I was still in touch with you. When I told her I was, she said she had something of importance to tell me. She said that when she first heard the name Maria Laskaris it had taken her by surprise. She did indeed know of her, but it was not as I expected—because she was a well-known opera singer. Instead, she confessed that she knew her as a young girl in Constantinople.

'I knew the family very well,' she said. 'Every one of them, including the boy, Leonidas—who, I was sad to hear, never made it away safely.'

My grandmother very rarely talked about the old country. Like your grandmother, the memories were too painful. So you can imagine what a surprise it was to hear her at that moment. This is what she told me.

'When I close my eyes, I see them all as clearly as if it were yesterday. They lived in a fashionable area of the city, in a villa with a glorious view of the Bosphorus. The husband Andreas painted that view on the walls of the Grand Salon in her atelier—La Maison du l'Orient. Your friend's grandmother Sophia was a good friend to me, especially after two disappointing marriages. I confess that sometimes I found myself envious of her. She had a wonderful and caring husband who many said went mad because of the war. He was accidently shot dead in his atelier by his daughter. I never believed that he went mad. I think that he knew her love lay elsewhere, and he chose another life because he loved her enough to give her freedom.

'For a while, Kyria Sophia had a Turkish vendeuse who left to be married. Then the Greeks landed in Smyrna and she never returned. It was at this time that I went to work for her. And then an incident took place and La Maison du l'Orient burned down. After that, she left for Smyrna with the three children and I never saw her again. When we heard of the dire things about to take place in Smyrna, there were many who tried to persuade her to leave, including my father, but she was a strong-willed woman and wouldn't hear of it. After the city was razed to the ground, we never heard from her again.

'About this time, my second marriage failed and I married for the third time to a good man who had lost his wife and already had a son by that marriage. At the time, your mother, born to my second husband, was two years old. As you know, it was a brief but happy marriage and I was devastated when he died ten years later. After that, I would not love like that again. Instead, my life was given over to your mother and my stepson. When God blessed us with your birth, and a year later your sister, my life was complete.

'We had a good life in Constantinople but with the escalation of the troubles between the Turks and the Greeks once again, due to false rumors that Greeks had destroyed Ataturk's house in Thessaloniki in September 1955, we could not live there any longer. The Turks were intent on removing the rest of the Greeks from their land and we left a month later.

'My grandson, I have had the good fortune in life to have put away a tidy amount of money—enough to see that your mother lives out the rest of her life in comfort. If it is as you say, that the English girl is truly the daughter of Nina, the girl I last saw as a young child, then I know she is from a good family. Your mother also tells me that she has a valuable painting of sentimental importance which she intends to sell. If the painting means so much, then do not let her sell it. It is my dying wish that you purchase it for her on my behalf. Do not hesitate with regard to the cost; you have been well provided for. This small gesture to a girl I will never have the good fortune to know will make me very happy. It is the least I can do for the woman I was proud to call my friend.'

Eleni, my grandmother was none other than Anna, whose father tried so desperately to get your grandmother to leave Smyrna on his yacht, the Medusa. And the man who later became her third husband was none other than her closest friend and confidant Markos—after whom I am named. So you see, Eleni, I know more about you than you think.

It was with the greatest of pride that I was able to purchase the painting for you. It must hang where it rightfully belongs—not in a museum, but in your home. Do not worry about the money. The gallery has been directed to deposit the proceeds into your bank account. Prior to the auction, I found out that your friend Vedat Aksoy intended to purchase it. After a brief conversation, he decided to allow me the winning bid. He is indeed as you said, a true gentleman.

Your friend,
Markos

Three months later, the whole of Europe watched in horror as hard-line elements of Greece's dictatorship attempted to quash the student uprising at the Athens Polytechnic by smashing down the gates with tanks, resulting in the deaths of twenty-four civilians. Markos was among the protestors. The uprising was the beginning of the end of the seven-year rule of the junta.

Shortly after, democracy was once more restored to Greece. During this period, Eleni left London for Athens. She and Markos were married in a small ceremony in the Church of the Pantanassa in Monastiraki. A year later, she gave birth to twin girls. One had amethyst eyes; the other had red hair.

# Postscript

Amongst the mementos and faded photographs in Sophia's suitcase was a small, tattered and stained notebook. Inside, in neat handwriting, was an inscription; Sevkiye's Recipes. Sevkiye was descended from a family of celebrated cooks, several of whom worked in the royal kitchens of the Topkapi Palace. On page thirty-three was a recipe for pilaf. This is her recipe:

## Sevkiye's Pilav

*Ingredients*
*3 tablespoon of sheep's tail fat (clarified or ordinary butter can be used if this is not available)*
*8ozs/250g long grain rice*
*Lamb or chicken stock*
*1lb/450g minced lamb*
*6ozs/185g chicken livers or lamb's liver chopped into small pieces*
*2 onions, finely chopped*
*4ozs/125g dried sour cherries or 1 tablespoon barberries*
*1 tablespoon sultanas*
*1 tablespoon pine nuts*
*½ teaspoon caraway or fennel seeds*
*½ teaspoon allspice*
*1 teaspoon cinnamon*
*1 chopped tomato*
*½ cup chopped flat-leaf parsley*
*Salt and freshly ground pepper to taste*

*Garnish: a small handful of tiny freshly picked rose buds or petals, (if not in season, substitute for pomegranate seeds), slivered almonds sautéed in butter, a handful of chopped flat-leaf parsley or mint, a sprinkle of sumac and cinnamon.*

*Method*

Wash the rice until the water runs clear.

Melt 1 tablespoon of fat in a heavy cooking pan. Sauté 1 chopped onion gently until softened. Add the cherries or barberries, sultanas and spices reserving ½ teaspoon of cinnamon for the meat. Season with salt and pepper. Stir for 1 minute. Add rice. Stir for 1 minute to coat with spice mixture. Add enough stock to cover. Bring to the boil. Reduce heat, add lid and simmer until cooked and stock has absorbed.

In the meantime, cook the lamb and liver.

In a heavy based pan, melt the remaining fat. Sauté the remaining onion until softened. Stir through pine-nuts. Add the liver, minced lamb and ½ teaspoon cinnamon and flat-leaf parsley. Season with salt and pepper. Cook until moisture from the lamb has evaporated and the meat is lightly golden, breaking up any clusters. Stir through chopped tomato. Remove from heat.

When rice is cooked, fluff up with fork. Layer a serving platter with rice and meat mixture starting with rice and ending with meat.

Serve garnished with rosebuds, flat-leaf parsley and almonds. Sprinkle lightly with a mixture of sumac and cinnamon. Serve accompanied with fresh bread and creamy yoghurt.

# Author's Note

The seeds of *The Embroiderer* were sown during my years working as a carpet designer in Greece, 1972-78. The company was situated in a suburb of Athens populated by refugees from The Asia Minor Catastrophe, 1922-23. Working amongst these people, many of the older generation of whom still conversed in Turkish, I grew to understand the impact of the disaster and the intense yearning these people still held for Turkey, the land of their forefathers and a land in which they are still unable to reside. Significantly they shared a separate sense of identity, so much so that fifty years after the Catastrophe, many of them still referred to themselves as *Mikrasiates* (Asia Minor people) and still chose to intermarry.

The Asia Minor Catastrophe was a pivotal turning point in Greek/Turkish relations which began a century earlier with the Greek War of Independence. The Ottoman Empire was at a turning point and for both Greeks and Turks, ultimately resulting in a war of attrition on both sides. Millions lost their lives and out of the ashes emerged two new nations – the Turkish Republic under the soldier statesman, Ataturk, and the Hellenic Republic – modern Greece.

Today, most of the white-washed prefabricated homes in the refugee neighborhoods in Athens have been replaced by apartment blocks but the street names still bear testament to their origins: Byzantium Street, Pergamum St, Anatolia St, Bouboulina St, and Misolonghi St. to name just a few. And whilst women no longer spill out of their doorways sitting on rush-bottomed chairs chatting to their neighbours whilst embroidering cloth for their daughter's dowry, and basement shops selling bric-a-brac and musical instruments from the 'old world' are few and far between, if we look closer, the history and the spirit of these people still resonates in their everyday lives; in their music, their food, the plethora of Turkish words and phrases that punctuate the Greek language, and the ancient belief in the evil eye. Most important of all, it is through the time-honoured tradition of storytelling that their memories are kept alive.

*The Embroiderer* is as much their story as it is mine.

# ABOUT THE AUTHOR

Kathryn Gauci was born in Leicestershire, England, and studied textile design at Loughborough College of Art and later at Kidderminster College of Art and Design where she specialised in carpet design and technology. After graduating, Kathryn spent a year in Vienna, Austria before moving to Greece where she worked as a carpet designer in Athens for six years. There followed another brief period in New Zealand before eventually settling in Melbourne, Australia.

Before turning to writing full-time, Kathryn ran her own textile design studio in Melbourne for over fifteen years, work which she enjoyed tremendously as it allowed her the luxury of travelling worldwide, often taking her off the beaten track and exploring other cultures. *The Embroiderer* is her first novel; a culmination of those wonderful years of design and travel, and especially of those glorious years in her youth living and working in Greece – a place that she is proud to call her spiritual home.

For more about Kathryn and her work at www.kathryngauci.com

CPSIA information can be obtained
at www.ICGtesting.com
Printed in the USA
LVHW030817260819
628924LV00001BA/17/P